W9-BTN-215

YOU'RE NOT SAFE

Center Point
Large Print

Also by Mary Burton and available from Center Point Large Print:

Before She Dies
The Seventh Victim
No Escape

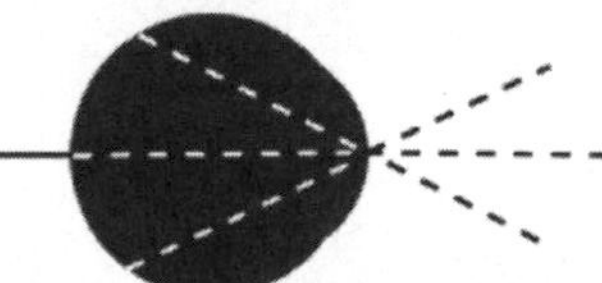

This Large Print Book carries the Seal of Approval of N.A.V.H.

YOU'RE NOT SAFE

Mary Burton

CENTER POINT LARGE PRINT
THORNDIKE, MAINE

This Center Point Large Print edition is
published in the year 2014 by arrangement with
Kensington Publishing Corp.

The text of this Large Print edition is unabridged.
In other aspects, this book may vary
from the original edition.
Printed in the United States of America
on permanent paper.
Set in 16-point Times New Roman type.

ISBN: 978-1-62899-071-3

Library of Congress Cataloging-in-Publication Data

Burton, Mary (Mary T.)
You're not safe / Mary Burton. — Center Point Large Print edition.
pages cm.
ISBN 978-1-62899-071-3 (Library binding : alk. paper)
1. Large type books. I. Title. II. Title: You are not safe.
PS3602.U7699Y68 2014
813′.6—dc23

2014003945

YOU'RE NOT SAFE

Prologue

The Hill Country, Texas
Monday, June 2, 1 A.M.

A hangover punched and pounded Rory Edwards's brain as he woke to discover a hangman's noose coiling around his neck. His hands lashed behind his back, his booted feet were braced on an open truck tailgate. He shifted, tried to wriggle free, but hemp dug painfully deep into an already bloodstained neck and wrists.

What the hell?

He blinked grit and film from his blurred gaze as he glanced up the thick rope meandering over a distant tree branch and snaking down the gnarled bark to a square knot at the trunk.

Shit.

He'd done a lot of stupid things in his life, but what had he done to land here?

Panic rising, he scanned the area, illuminated by the full moon, to find dense shrubs and trees and a patch of dirt too rough to be considered a road. He didn't recognize his surroundings, but a lonely isolated feeling banded around his chest. Wherever he was, it was far from another human. Texas had hundreds of thousands of bleak acres where a man could die and never be found. A coyote howled in the distance.

Dread kicked and scratched his insides. *Shit. Shit. Shit.* He struggled to free his hands, but when they refused to budge, he couldn't silence his fears.

"Help!" He shouted his plea over and over until his throat burned inside and out. No one came.

Breathless, he craned his neck trying to better identify his surroundings, but as he leaned forward his foothold slipped and he nearly skidded off the tailgate's edge. Every muscle in his body tensed as he scrambled and threw his weight back until he was on firm footing. He was hyperventilating now, and minutes passed before he calmed enough to think.

This time his gaze roamed wildly and landed on a picture nailed to the hanging tree. It was an old picture, crumpled, tattered, and faded. Recognition flickered instantly. He'd carried the picture in his wallet for a dozen years, and he'd cherished it. More nights than he could count he'd stared at that picture asking for strength when life shit-kicked him in the gut.

Tears filled his eyes.

The aging image captured a grinning teenage Rory, tall, straight, and broad-shouldered. His thick sun-kissed hair skimmed piercing blue eyes. Tanned skin accentuated a crooked melting grin. His arm wrapped around the shoulders of a petite, young blond girl. She was pretty, not overly stunning like Rory, but her smile could be electric.

At first glance Rory's embrace around the girl appeared casual and playful. Two young teenagers in love. However, closer inspection exposed a wrinkle of tension creasing Rory's forehead and the pointed edge of desperation behind his gaze. The young Rory held the girl a little too close and a little too anxiously.

On that long-ago day, he'd been so worried about himself and his immense burdens. He'd never bothered to look past the girl's forced smiles. Not once had he asked about her feelings. Not once. If he had really noticed her, he'd have seen she hadn't been happy. Yes, she smiled, but her full lips often thinned into a strained line, and her blue eyes reflected the weight of her own demons. She clutched his shirt as if knowing one drowning swimmer couldn't save another.

If he'd been a little less selfish, he would have seen her sadness. Instead of whispering empty compliments in her ear or kissing her when she needed to talk, he could have soothed her wounds. He could have done so much for her. But he didn't.

Twin weights of regret and failure settled on his shoulders as he begged for her help one last time. "I'm sorry, Elizabeth. Save me. Just one more time, please. Don't let me die. Save me."

Laughter crept out of the darkness and rumbled behind him. “How many times is Elizabeth supposed to save you, Rory?” The deep, clear voice made him bristle. “Don’t you think Elizabeth deserves a break from your incessant whining?”

Shocked by the voice, Rory twisted his bound hands against the tight rope. “Who are you?”

Silence.

“Why are you doing this?”

Laughter.

In his peripheral vision, a strike and a flash of flame cut the shadows as the stranger lifted a match to a cigarette’s tip.

Rory craned his neck, trying to see the stranger’s face but the ropes cut and burned until he stilled. The smoke’s acrid scent wandered out from the shadows. “Who are you?”

As if he hadn’t spoken, the voice said, “How many days of sobriety did you wipe out last night? Two hundred and five or six?”

Two hundred and six days of sobriety had bolstered his confidence and plumped up his pride. He believed he’d never go back. And yet he had tossed away those months so easily. He stared at the sparse land as barren as his promises to get clean and sober. Shit. Why had he been so reckless?

The demons, which had stalked him for many, many years, murmured familiar words. *Loser. Stupid. Failure.*

Shit. He thought he'd licked the drinking. Pooling tears spilled down his cheeks.

Loser. Stupid. Failure.

The words beckoned him to step off the tailgate and let the rope end his suffering. Who would notice? Who would care? Likely no one.

And still he clung to life. "I don't want to die. Whatever I've done to you, I'll fix it. I'll make it right."

"How are you going to fix it?"

"I don't know."

The stranger chuckled. "Don't you see? The true fix is death."

Rory swallowed. His throat burned. "It's not too late. It's not. I can make amends and fix what I've done. I've a brother who has money. He'll make it right. Just tell me what you need."

The stranger moved out of the shadows toward the tree, giving Rory a glimpse of a red ball cap and a heavy blue jacket obscuring a lean frame. His tormentor tossed his cigarette on the ground and summer grass dried from drought crackled under his feet as he ground out the embers.

Rory cut his vision to the left toward his tormentor who remained just out of sight. "Come on, *man*." Pure desperation emphasized the words. "I can make it right."

"You can kid yourself, but you can't fool us, Rory. You'll never get it right. It's not in your DNA."

His lean body trembled and he pissed on himself. "What the fuck do you want?"

"We don't want to hurt you, Rory. We want to end your suffering."

"I'm not suffering!" He managed the strained smile of prey facing predator. "I'm living my life as best I can."

"It's a sad miserable life, Rory."

His wrists strained against the unbreakable bindings. "But it's mine, and I've a right to live it. I'll get back on the wagon. Start over."

"I know you're scared." The stranger's voice gentled. "I know you don't have the courage to see this through. Look at that picture, Rory. Even then when your chances were at their best, you clung to young Elizabeth who could barely take care of herself."

"I don't want to die!"

"Do you really think Elizabeth would think your life is worth saving, Rory?"

"Elizabeth was kind and gentle. She'd want me to live."

"Really? You hurt her badly. Disappointed her when she needed you most. And then you proceeded to screw up all the good works your family did for you. You've been in one crap job after another for the last decade, and you managed to piss away two hundred and six days of sobriety in one night. You talk of your brother, but in recent years he's refused all your calls."

Rory had burned the last bridge with his brother last year when he'd missed their mother's funeral. "I've never claimed to be a straight arrow."

"It's as if you feel you don't deserve any bit of happiness."

He'd never wanted to be a suit like his brother or be jailed by the family business. "I like happiness just fine. I have fun all the time."

"Where do you think your trouble began, Rory? When did your life go off the rails?" The stranger's voice was soft but clear. And a little familiar now.

Rory rummaged through his memory trying to isolate the voice. When had they crossed paths? He'd been in that bar in East Austin last night. He'd had a lead on a job and had not wanted to go inside but the promise of work had been too tempting. Who?

"Just because I'm not a choirboy doesn't mean I'm bad."

A click of a lighter and then more smoke from a fresh cigarette. "I think you were done the day you were born, Rory. I think you could never hold a candle to your brother. He's the one your parents loved. He's the one who got all the attention and support."

The stranger's blistering truth rekindled the old anger that had chased him toward reckless choices, gotten him kicked out of a string of private schools, and thrown into too many jails.

"Did my brother send you to do this? I know he's wanted me gone for a long time."

"Face it, it's time you left this world for the next."

Panic extinguished the anger. "That's not true!"

"Of course it's true." The stranger's voice remained soft, steady, and so reasonable. "You were the mistake. The child no one wanted. Sad your own parents wouldn't want their own flesh and blood."

Rory tipped his face up away from the picture and toward the moonlit sky. "Stop."

"It's not good to bury the pain, Rory. Better to face it head-on and deal with it. Admit it. Your parents didn't want you."

Tears stung his eyes. He was thirty-one, could hotwire a car, crack any lock, and hold a gallon of liquor in his belly and still walk straight. He'd grown a thick skin, but the stranger's words stripped away the gristle and left him feeling like the sad, pathetic kid he'd been. "Not true."

"Come on, Rory, it's *Come-to-Jesus* time. The moment of truth. The pain had burrowed deep inside you, and though it does a good job of hiding behind a bottle, it's there."

Rory stared at Elizabeth's face. He fisted his fingers. "Who sent you?"

"We weren't sent, Rory. We were summoned by you."

"What the hell does that mean?"

"You called us. Your pain and suffering beckoned us to find you. I'm only here to take the pain away."

Rory twisted his head toward the stranger and stumbled on the truck's tailgate. Heels skidded up to the edge. Heart racing, he shouted, "I don't want you to take the pain away. I like my life!"

"How long has it been since you've seen Elizabeth?"

"How do you know Elizabeth?"

"I know all about her."

Even now, here, hearing her name and staring into her lackluster blue eyes soothed him. "She told me she loved me."

"And I believe she did. She was willing to go to the mat for you. And you sent all her letters back unread."

More tears spilled. "I didn't want to send them back. I loved her."

"Our deeds define us Rory, not our words."

Rory tensed, shocked a stranger would know deep and intimate details. "How do you know so much about me?"

"I know a lot about you. And Elizabeth. And the others. I know all your deepest desires."

"You don't."

"You once said you'd die a happy man if the last face you saw were Elizabeth's. Isn't that right?"

"Go to hell," Rory spat.

"I'm here to grant that last wish. No one should

go to their grave without getting their last wish granted."

The stranger ground out his cigarette and opened the truck cab door. His body scraped across cloth seats before the cab door slammed closed. He turned on the engine and revved it.

Rory braced.

His gaze bore into Elizabeth's smiling face. In these last moments he ignored her tension and saw only her smile, her smooth skin, and her blond hair, swept recklessly over her right shoulder.

In these last seconds, he transported back to the night by the campfire. She'd raced to the fire laughing, and seconds before the image had been snapped, she'd nestled close. He'd hugged her tighter and attributed her tensing muscles to the evening chill.

Rory gritted his teeth and fisted his hands. He straightened. He'd die like a man for her. "I love you, Elizabeth."

The truck engine roared and the bed moved slowly away from the tree. Even knowing he couldn't escape his bindings, he struggled to free his hands and dig his boots into the rusted tailgate. His bindings clamped hard on raw wrists and his feet slid to the tailgate's edge.

Seconds ticked like hours as the last inches of metal skimmed the bottom of his boots and his body fell with a hard jolt. The noose jerked tight and sliced into his skin. Pain burned through him.

His struggles tightened the rope's grip, crushing his windpipe as his feet dangled inches above the ground. He gasped for air, but his lungs didn't fill. He dangled. Kicked. The rope cut deeper.

He was vaguely aware the truck had stopped. The scent of another cigarette reached him. The driver had stopped to have a smoke and watch him dangle.

Staying to enjoy the show.

And then his brain spun, spittle drooled from his mouth. As the blackness bled in from the corners of his vision, he stared at Elizabeth.

I love you.

His grip on life slipped away.

"Unbind his hands."

Her voice had a shrill quality that made Jackson cringe. Out of spite, he ignored her and continued to stare at Rory's dangling lifeless body. Head tilted to the right. Eyes stared sightless at the sky. Tongue dangled out of his mouth.

"Unbind his hands," she demanded.

He sighed. "Why?"

"Tied hands mean murder and this is supposed to be a suicide."

He hated to admit it, but she was right. Damn her. She was always right. She could be annoying that way. Always so sure in what needed to be done. And so judgmental when he didn't listen.

"Do it!" she ordered.

He stiffened, not sparing her a glance. He couldn't bear to look at her smug, smiling face. One day he'd be rid of her. One day he'd be free.

He pulled the switchblade from his back pocket. He kept his voice steady, choosing to keep the peace for now. "You're always good with the details."

"Which is exactly why you will always need me."

Chapter One

Monday, June 2, 8 A.M.

Fatigue fueled impatience burrowing under Ranger Tec Bragg's skin as he pressed his booted foot against the accelerator of his black SUV barreling along the rocky rural route cutting into the Texas Hill Country. Scrubby trees and low-lying shrubs bordered the road brushed with bone-dry dirt. A handful of plump clouds floated in a blue sky and teased a good soaking rain to ease the yearlong drought.

Bragg could hope and wish the rains didn't destroy his crime scene, but he didn't bother. Life had taught him his wants and needs didn't mean shit to the universe. Whether the rains came or not, he'd deal.

Flashing blue lights of half a dozen police cars

and media vans told him he'd found his crime scene. He drove past them all until he reached the Texas Department of Public Safety officer manning the entrance to the crime scene.

He slowed, unrolled his window as the uniformed officer approached, and touched the brim of his white hat.

"Morning. Ranger Tec Bragg. Heard I'm needed."

The officer touched the brim of his trooper's hat. "Yes, sir, Sergeant Bragg. Follow this dirt road a half a mile, and you'll see the crime scene. No missing it. Sheriff is waiting for you."

"Appreciate it."

"Glad to have you back, Sergeant Bragg," the grinning officer said. "Heard about what you did on the border."

Bragg's mood soured. Fame didn't fit him well. "Right."

The road led him toward a new cluster of cars from the local sheriff's department. He'd received a call just after dawn from the local sheriff requesting a visit on an apparent suicide. The dead man, the sheriff drawled, had an older brother richer than Midas who claimed the governor as a friend. Sheriff wanted a Ranger on site for possible damage control.

Shit. His recent promotion, touted as a reward for his work on the border, required deeds he hated more than the cartels or the coyotes. Hand-holding. Meetings. Press briefings. He'd landed smack in the middle of a politicking world he'd carefully avoided for years.

Since he was sixteen, Bragg had gone his own way and learned it was best to keep to himself. He didn't rely on anyone and was careful to make sure no one relied on him.

His leather boots crunched against the dry earth as he took long impatient strides toward the scene. He wore a starched white shirt that itched, string tie, and creased khakis. His SIG Sauer gun hung on his right hip and on his left side rested his cell and cuffs. He sported a newly polished, albeit well-worn, Texas Ranger star on his chest.

Despite the heat, he resisted the urge to roll up his shirtsleeves as he nodded to more deputies, all curious about the suicide garnering a Texas Ranger the likes of Tec Bragg. He made his way toward the yellow crime-scene tape. Ahead he spotted county sheriff Jake Wheeler.

Tall and broad-shouldered, Wheeler wore his brown uniform, cowboy boots, and a wide-brimmed hat that covered a thick shock of white hair. The sun had etched deep lines in his tanned face. A belly rounded over the edge of a non-regulation thick silver belt buckle engraved with his initials. In his late fifties, Wheeler had been sheriff for twenty years but now faced a tough re-election next year. Though he didn't fit the image of a politician, Wheeler was well practiced at avoiding controversy. Wheeler wanted to pawn off an explosive case.

The morning heat had already darkened Wheeler's shirt with sweat. "Ranger Bragg."

Bragg extended his hand to Sheriff Wheeler. "Morning, Sheriff."

"Thanks for coming, Bragg. I think we might have an issue."

Bragg glanced beyond Wheeler and the ring of officers surrounding the yellow tape to the crime scene. It wasn't hard to miss the body. It hung from a tree.

A couple of hours, let alone a couple of days, in the Texas sun played havoc with the dead. The intense temperature triggered bloating and skin slippage within hours and the decomposition process drew black flies, which already buzzed. "By the looks he's not been out here long."

"I'm guessing not more than six hours. This time tomorrow he'll be one hell of a mess."

"I hear you found his wallet."

"We surely did. It was at the base of the tree. If there'd been no wallet, I'm not sure how easy it would have been to identify him."

Bragg glanced toward the tree and saw the forensic technician's yellow numbered marker by the wallet. "Left it out so there'd be no missing it."

Wheeler hooked his thumbs in his belt buckle. "Someone wanted it found."

Bragg rested his hands on his hips. "I didn't catch the victim's name."

"Didn't want to say it over the radio until we were absolutely sure. Never know. Wallet might not belong to the dead guy."

"Whose name on the wallet?"

"Rory Edwards."

"Edwards? The oil family." David Edwards was indeed a heavy hitter in Texas politics and explained Bragg's summons.

"One and the same. Rory listed his brother's fancy West Austin address on his driver's license."

"Old man was a wildcatter who struck it rich. Family has more money than God. Father died years back as I recall."

"He did. Mother died last year but older brother still owns the family home. Controls the family business and has his eye on the governor's office."

As Bragg moved closer the buzz of black flies mingled with the growing stench of death and decay. "You think this is Rory?"

"Not one hundred percent sure. This guy doesn't look like his picture so much."

"Hell of a way to start the week."

A faint smile lifted the edge of Wheeler's mouth. "Yeah."

"You wouldn't just call me in for a suicide, Jake. I know you've an election coming next spring but a suicide is fairly straightforward."

Wheeler's brow knitted. "Look at the crime scene."

Bragg let his gaze roam the site. First off he noticed there was no discarded chair, stepstool, or ladder near the body. Shifting his focus to the tree, he noted the rope snaked up from the dead man's body, up and over a branch and to the base of the tree where it was securely tied. It wouldn't have been an easy climb up the tree and out onto the branch dragging a rope but a motivated man could do it. Still, if Edwards had jumped from that height, he'd not only have broken his neck but the velocity of the fall combined with the body's weight would have left a deep gash in the neck or, worse, decapitated it.

This wasn't a suicide.

"Who found the body?"

"Surveyors. A vineyard owner recently purchased the land and plans to clear it and plant more vines. The surveyors were out here early just after dawn to beat the heat. They smelled him before they saw him. The buzzing of the flies drew their gazes up. They called it in."

"Surveyors check out?"

"They did. Work for a local firm. I know both of them. They were pretty rattled so I let them go on. If you need them later I'll get you their numbers."

"What vineyard hired them?"

Wheeler cleared his throat. "Didn't catch the name."

"Find out." Bragg rested his hands on his hips, studying the dead man's boots, which were custom-made and would have set him back several thousand dollars. Fancy boots jived with the fancy address on the license.

"Want a closer look?" Wheeler said, offering plastic gloves.

"Sure do." Bragg accepted the gloves and ducked under the crime-scene tape and waited for the tech to log him into the site. He nodded to the forensic technicians as he glanced around the area surrounding the body. Didn't take more than a second to see the tire tracks. He knelt and studied the imprint. Judging by the depth of the tracks, the truck had backed up to the site under the body and then driven straight back out.

Bragg's gaze trailed the tracks down the dirt road cutting through the brush and leading back to the rural route. "Rory might have driven a truck in here, but he didn't drive it out."

"I'm thinking he had a little help."

Bragg rose, stretching his limbs. Too little sleep in the last months had left him stiff. "I'd bet Mr. Edwards stood on the flatbed of the truck when it pulled out."

"And then he dropped and strangled to death." Wheeler nodded. "Forensics also bagged two cigarette butts. DNA will tell us if it belonged to the victim."

They might find Edwards's DNA on one or both

butts but Bragg's gut said no. "I'm guessing it was the second person at the scene. Someone else was here and lingered to watch Mr. Edwards die."

Wheeler rubbed the back of his neck with his hand. "Edwards had a history of trouble. Drugs. Drinking. Had a car accident in my county years back, and the family paid off the guy he hit. Problem went away. Heard similar tales of other such problems. He could have pushed the wrong person too far."

"Maybe." The dead man's hands dangled at his side. Blood, no longer pumped by the heart, had settled in his fingers leaving them dark as if bruised. The nighttime heat, which had reached the low nineties, had also accelerated decomposition, causing the skin on his hands to loosen.

"I've seen murders like this before along the border. Cartels leave their victims out for all to see. Don't see hangings as much as beheadings or shootings. And you sure don't see folks from a family like the Edwardses getting strung up much." Bragg noted the red rope bracelet on Rory's right wrist. It appeared homemade. "Have you called the family?"

"Not yet. Figured I'd run it by you first. Didn't want to stir a hornet's nest if I didn't have to."

And being up for re-election, Wheeler wanted Bragg to do the stirring. "When will they be ready to cut him loose?"

"He's good to go now. We were waiting for you."

Bragg nodded, knowing his day had changed from meetings to fieldwork. He couldn't say he was sorry. "Go ahead and cut him down."

Wheeler nodded to the officer by the tree and both watched as the uniformed officer raised a saw blade to the rope. While two other deputies grabbed hold of the rope, the first officer cut. In a matter of minutes the hemp frayed and then finally gave way. The officers dug their booted feet into the ground, supporting the body's dead weight. While a forensic tech snapped pictures, the officers slowly lowered the body to the ground. Stiff with rigor mortis it stood unbending. As the rope slackened, another gloved tech took the body by the shoulders and eased it to the ground. More pictures were snapped as flies buzzed and swarmed.

Bragg walked over to the body and studied the man's half-open eyes and bloated face. He had grown accustomed to the foul smells of death. The gangs and cartels that moved in and out of the border traded in death as easily as dollars. Whereas the younger cops around him now had paled and taken a step back, he knelt and studied the victim. He'd built a reputation tackling dirty jobs.

Rope burns ringed the victim's wrists. "Why bind his hands and then cut him loose?" he said, more to himself.

"Maybe the killer thought we'd be fooled by the

suicide scenario," Wheeler offered. "If the rains had come as the weather guys had said, those tire tracks would have been washed away. And a few more days out here and those wrist marks would have been gone."

"Maybe." Bragg glanced beyond the scene to the rugged brush and scrub trees around him. "What's around this immediate area?"

"Immediate area? Not much. Brush and scrub. But like I said, on the adjacent land there is a vineyard. It's small and family owned. Been around for twenty-plus years."

Bragg studied the dead man's brown and rotted teeth. He lifted the victim's jean jacket and searched for any signs of trauma, bits of paper, stains—anything to offer clues about the man. He found a receipt in the front shirt pocket for Tate's Bar. In his pants pocket he found two rumpled dollar bills, a room key, a couple of wrapped peppermints, and a half dozen sobriety chips. "Guy has nothing on him worth taking."

"He sure pissed off someone."

"That he did."

Bragg rose and glanced back at the tree. Immediately he spotted the photo flapping in the slight breeze. He moved toward the picture featuring a young teenage couple. Both kids had the look of money. She wore pearl earrings and a gold chain around her neck. And he wore a white-collared shirt flipped up. His hair was thick and blond as if he spent a lot of time in the sun. Bragg leaned in and studied the boy's smooth, hairless face. If he wasn't mistaken, the boy was his victim. "Did you see this?"

Wheeler frowned and moved toward the tree. "Yeah, looks like the victim in the picture. But the image is old."

"Who is the girl?"

"Don't recognize her. A teen crush, maybe?"

Bragg pulled out his cell phone, snapped a picture of the image, and then leaned in to study the young girl's face. She smiled but it wasn't joyful. Wherever she'd been when the picture was taken, she didn't want to be there. Rory, on the other hand, appeared happy. His posture was relaxed and his smile full and genuine.

"The picture's here for a reason." He lingered on the girl's image a beat longer, and then slid the phone back in its belt cradle. "We need to identify that girl."

"It's about a decade old judging by the victim's appearance."

"We need to find out what he was doing ten years ago. We know he didn't kill himself, so whoever strung him up put this picture here for a reason."

Wheeler nodded. "You think she killed him?"

He studied the girl's strained smile. "She'd not be the first woman to track someone from her past and kill 'em." Bragg glanced toward the ground at the wallet lying beside the evidence marker. He knelt, pulled a pen from his pocket, and opened the wallet to find a couple of dollars, no credit cards, and an expired Texas driver's license.

"Ranger Bragg." The summons came from the forensic technician. Melinda Ashburn, if he remembered correctly, was in her late twenties and wore her red hair back in a tight ponytail. Freckles sprinkled her nose.

He moved toward her. "Yes, ma'am?"

"The medical examiner can move the body anytime now. I've shot all the pictures I need, and I've made detailed sketches of the scene. Given the heat it's better if we get the victim out of the sun."

Behind her the medical examiner's technicians stood ready with a stretcher and black body bag. "Go on ahead and take him. I've seen what I need. Though I'd like a set of those photos you took sent to me."

"Sure. Will do."

Often after the confusion of the day he'd sit in his home study and go over crime-scene prints. The camera lens frequently captured what the eye missed during the chaos.

Bragg arrived at the medical examiner's office an hour after the body. He'd been delayed at the scene by the media who'd wanted a statement. While Wheeler spoke, he'd stood quietly off to the side.

Now, the building's cool air greeted him and offered welcome relief from the heat radiating from the asphalt parking lot. The temperature gauge in his car had hit 105 degrees, and he bet it would rise higher by midafternoon.

Waiting for him at the end of the hallway was a tall, long-legged Ranger who now leaned casually against the wall as he checked his phone for texts. On the way in, Bragg had called in Ranger Brody Winchester. The two had worked together years ago in Houston. Bragg had transferred from El Paso two months ago and seeing as he'd dealt with enough changes in his life recently, he liked the idea of working with someone familiar.

Winchester had recently married Dr. Jo Granger, a psychologist who worked from time to time with the Rangers. Rumor had it the two had been married in college, but it wasn't Bragg's style to poke into another man's personal business. Lord knows he had his share of personal crap he didn't discuss.

Winchester pushed away from the wall and tucked his phone in its hip cradle. "Once I heard from you, I called ahead and let the medical examiner know we were coming." He extended his hand. "Told them to clear the decks."

Bragg's iron grip matched Winchester's. "Good. I want answers before I visit with the family."

Bragg and Winchester showed their badges to

the officer at the front desk and then headed to the bank of elevators.

"I pulled the victim's rap sheet, like you requested. Sheriff Wheeler was right. Rory Edwards has been in trouble since he could drive. Family's been cleaning up his messes for years."

Bragg hit the DOWN button, thinking his own old man had never eased his trouble, but had been the source of his burdens. The old bastard had been a worthless drunk who'd used Bragg and his older sister Sue as punching bags. Sue had left home at seventeen. He'd been fourteen and figured she'd send for him when she settled. But she'd found herself a man within months and married. *Sorry, Tec, I just can't take you with me. I got a chance to be happy and need to take it. You'll find your chance one day.*

Sue had sent him a Christmas card the next year and told him she'd had a son, Mitch, but that had been the last he'd received word from her until three years ago when an officer in Houston had notified him she'd died of an overdose. The husband, who'd never legally married Sue, had been long gone and the boy, Mitch, pissed as hell, had enlisted in the Marines.

Mitch had returned to Austin two months ago, recovering from wounds both visible and invisible from his tour in Iraq. Bragg would later learn the Humvee Mitch had been driving had been hit by a roadside bomb, which had all but obliterated the vehicle. There'd been four soldiers inside. Everyone but Mitch had died.

When the boy's commanding officer had contacted Bragg, he'd informed him the boy was in a bad way. Seeing as Bragg was all the family Mitch had, he'd accepted the promotion and transfer back to Austin. His family might be a fractured mess, but it was *his* family.

Bragg didn't hold illusions of a Hallmark family reunion, but he had figured he'd get the boy on his feet before he returned to fieldwork on the border. However, he'd quickly learned nurturing a troubled kid fit him as well as politicking.

Mitch's wounds from shell fragments had been easy enough to fix but it was the post-traumatic stress disorder that had left invisible scars. The kid had nightmares constantly and most were loud and violent. Mitch wasn't eating, and his drinking was becoming a real problem. Last night Mitch hadn't come in the door until four A.M., and he'd been drunk. Bragg and Mitch had one hell of a fight, and Mitch would have left if Bragg hadn't taken his keys. *You're not my father!* The situation had to change soon for both their sakes.

Bragg could track a killer to hell and back, but he couldn't find the words to soothe his nephew's grief.

He shoved aside the unease and focused on the

job. “They won’t be able to help him out of this mess.”

“No amount of money is gonna fix this.”

Bragg checked his phone half hoping he’d gotten a message or call from Mitch. He’d received several calls from the office, but none from his nephew.

After the predawn blowup, the boy had staggered to his room and fallen into bed. Bragg had left him but now questioned that decision. Bragg feared the boy wouldn’t make it to September at the rate he was withdrawing.

“How’s Mitch doing?” Winchester, a former marine, punched the elevator button.

Bragg never talked about his personal life. Ever. But this problem, like the weather, didn’t give a shit about what Bragg wanted. “He’s quiet. Doesn’t talk much.”

Winchester didn’t speak for a moment. “You know my wife is a psychologist.”

“Yeah.”

“Jo would be glad to talk to him. She’s good with people.”

A muscle twitched in his jaw. “Getting Mitch to talk is like pulling teeth.”

“He needs to talk and get engaged. Being alone is the worst. Is he drinking excessively?”

He flexed his fingers. “Yeah.”

Mitch was Bragg’s only family. His problem. His to fix. But he didn’t have any ideas. “The VA hooked him up with a support group at the local crisis center. It's run by volunteers and a guy named Stewart."

Winchester kept his stance casual, his gaze ahead. "Is it helping?"

They stepped onto the elevator. "I don't know. It's hard to get the boy to string more than two words together."

Winchester grunted disapproval. "I can ask Jo about the group. If she doesn't know about it, she'll find out."

Bragg rubbed the back of his neck and punched LL for lower level. Getting outside help went against Bragg's nature. "I'd appreciate that."

Winchester texted the details to his wife. He hit send. Another text came back in seconds. He read it and nodded. "She says they're a good group. Dr. Stewart's well respected and good, she says. She's off to a meeting but will dig up more information."

"Great."

The elevator doors opened. They stepped off and moved down the hallway toward a set of double doors and into the exam room. A foul odor greeted them and drew their attention to a stainless-steel gurney holding a sheet-clad body. Another smaller table held a collection of instruments. A medical assistant, dressed in scrubs, pulled the sheet back.

Next to the gurney stood Dr. Hank Watterson. In

his mid-thirties, Watterson stood tall, thin like a young poplar, in his green scrubs. A thick dark mustache added interest to an average face.

"Dr. Watterson," Bragg said.

The doctor glanced up from a sink where he lathered his hands with soap. Intelligent, sharp green eyes stared at them through horn-rimmed glasses. "So, you two are the reason I was called in on my day off?"

Winchester grinned. "Sorry, doc. No rest for the wicked."

Dr. Watterson grunted. "Body arrived about a half hour ago, and I was just about to start the autopsy."

Bragg didn't care much for the medical examiner's office. Cold and sterile, the buzz of fluorescent lights, it reminded him of the hospital where his mother died when he was six. "Appreciate you getting right on this."

"Sooner it's done, the sooner I can get out of here." Dr. Watterson nodded toward the surgical gowns. "This one is not going to be easy. Might as well suit up."

Bragg and Winchester donned hospital gowns, and stood back. The victim's clothes had been stripped and tagged, and his hands remained wrapped in paper bags, as they had been at the crime scene. Dr. Watterson studied the body's bloated belly.

Rory Edwards's hands and feet were black with

settled blood and his head tilted to the left as it had when he dangled from the rope. His arms and chest were covered with tattoos. A skull on fire. Barbed wire through a heart on his arm. Crosses. The letter E. Stripped he looked leaner and malnourished. Fading track marks peppered the veins of his left and right arms.

The doctor started with an external examination, noted the rope burns around the neck, and confirmed the victim also had ligature marks on his wrists. He went on to catalogue rope marks, tattoos, and the absence of any other trauma.

As he pressed a scalpel to make a Y incision in the victim's chest, Dr. Watterson said, "I hear the victim's brother's pretty rich and has a lot of connections."

"He is." Bragg nodded. "Which is why we wanted to be absolutely sure we've identified the right man before we made the death notification."

Dr. Watterson kept his gaze on the body as he spoke. "No sense churning up a hornet's nest unless you have to."

"About right."

The technician removed the bags from the victim's hands, and Dr. Watterson, after a thorough inspection, scraped under the fingernails. If Rory had fought with his killer, the possibility existed that DNA remained under his fingernails.

"I'll run a toxicology screen but won't have

results back for a day or two. But judging by his teeth, he was malnourished and had one hell of a tooth infection. Left untreated the tooth infection alone would have done him serious damage soon. My guess is he turned to meth in recent years."

Dr. Watterson turned to a light box illuminating dental X-rays. "The bridge work and fillings belonging to Rory Edwards's dental records matches your victim."

"This guy is Rory Edwards."

"Yes. And I can confirm he did die of strangulation."

"He was dangling from a tree," Winchester said.

"You never can tell for sure until the exam." The doctor moved to the head of the table and pulled lighted magnifying lenses toward the dead man's neck. He studied the rope burns. "There is old scarring on his neck."

Bragg frowned. "What kind?"

The doctor was quiet for a moment. "Looks like an old rope burn. The current burn covers most of it up. Could have been easily missed. But it's there." He pointed to a small faint white area ringing the victim's throat. "He hanged by his neck before."

"Suicide attempt?" Winchester said.

"Maybe. Asphyxiation games aren't uncommon in high-risk individuals. And this fellow is definitely high-risk."

Bragg leaned in and studied the faint white scar.

"The crime scene didn't have the look of an erotic game. But who knows. How old are the scars?"

Dr. Watterson shrugged. "Can't say, Bragg. But it's been years."

Bragg thought about the image of the teenage couple nailed to the tree. It appeared Rory had been a happy kid. In fact, conjuring the picture, Bragg would have figured the girl with the moody, edgy glint in her eye was the troublemaker.

Chapter Two

Monday, June 2, 3 P.M.

Temperatures continued to rise in the triple digits when Bragg and Winchester arrived at the sleek glass tower located in the heart of Austin. A centerpiece in the city, the glass building glistened, but despite the heat, had a chilling effect.

They moved through the revolving door and to the main reception desk. Bragg showed his Texas Ranger star to the heavyset, gray-haired rent-a-cop behind the desk. "Texas Rangers for David Edwards."

The request prompted confusion, but the guard picked up the sleek black phone and pressed a button from the dozens on his console. He passed on Bragg's request, listened, and then replaced the phone in the receiver.

The guard stood and tucked in his shirt. "His office is on the twentieth floor. The receptionist said you could come up, but she didn't promise access to Mr. Edwards."

"Then I guess we'll have to take that up with her when we arrive."

"Yes, sir."

The Rangers made their way to the bank of elevators and punched the UP arrow. The doors opened immediately and the ride to the twentieth floor was quick and as smooth as the building's glass exterior.

When the door opened, there were more sets of glass doors and beyond that a receptionist. Etched in the doors was a large letter E.

"Rory had an E tattooed on his body," Winchester said.

"Odd a guy who spent his life avoiding the family would tattoo a memento of it on his chest." Bragg shook his head. "But then dealing with family doesn't go hand in hand with logic."

Winchester pulled open the glass door and let Bragg walk in ahead of him. Bragg pushed back his coat so the thin blonde saw his star. "We need to see Mr. David Edwards."

A cool thin smile added brittleness to her otherwise flawless face. "He's in meetings."

"This is about his brother."

"Rory?" She arched a brow. "What has he done this time?"

"That's between Mr. Edwards and me, ma'am." He smiled but a razor's edge sharpened the words. "I suggest you go ahead and let him know we're here because he's gonna be mighty mad later if he finds out through the media."

Lips pursed, she rose and walked down the carpeted hallway and spoke to another administrative assistant positioned outside another office.

"You've made a friend," Winchester said.

"I've a talent."

Winchester studied the modern reception area filled with lots of chrome and reflective surfaces. "Guy's a thing for the ice."

"So I noticed."

The receptionist returned. "He will see you."

A smile quirked the edge of Bragg's mouth. "Good."

The receptionist passed them off to the administrative assistant, another cool blonde, who opened Edwards's door. The office, like the building, was all glass. The view of Austin was impressive, showcasing Congress Avenue all the way to the white dome of the state capitol.

Edwards, a midsize lean man, had short dark hair, an olive complexion, and square jaw. He was dressed in a hand-tailored suit, white shirt, and a red tie. Gold cuff links winked from his wrists. The family resemblance to the victim was evident. They shared the eye color and skin tone, but this man had a lean sharp stare contrasting the heavy-lidded gaze of Rory Edwards in his Texas Department of Motor Vehicles photo.

Edwards came around his desk, moving with the confidence of a man in his domain. He didn't extend his hand. "I'm David Edwards."

"Ranger Tec Bragg and Sergeant Brody Winchester. Texas Rangers," Bragg said. "We've got some bad news regarding your brother."

"Rory's gotten himself into enough trouble but never enough to attract the Texas Rangers." His tone lacked worry or excitement as if he'd spoken to law enforcement about his brother many times before.

"He has our attention now."

A muscle pulsed in Edwards's jaw. "What's he done this time? And what do I need to do to make the problem go away?"

Rory's rap sheet detailed dozens of petty crimes. Clearly a guy like David wouldn't appreciate a brother like Rory. Bragg had gotten calls in the last months on Mitch. He'd smoothed out the minor messes, growing more frustrated with each new debacle.

"He was murdered," Bragg said.

David raised a brow. Again no surprise registered but perhaps a bit of resignation. Relief even. "How?"

Bragg had never figured Mitch would get himself into enough of a scrape to get himself murdered. But he'd feared car accidents and a half dozen other tragedies when he'd been up late waiting on the boy.

"He was hanged."

Interest sparked brighter than shock. "Hanged? You're sure?"

"We are," Bragg said. "I watched them cut him down this morning."

Edwards rubbed the back of his neck with his hand. "It was a suicide?"

"That's what the responding officer thought at first. But it appears he wasn't alone when he died."

Edwards shook his head. "Rory ran with a bad crowd. Bunch of degenerates interested in their next score. I can imagine one of those clowns watching Rory hang himself and be too messed up or too apathetic to help."

"His hands had been bound behind his back."

Edwards frowned. "He probably didn't have the stones to go through with it so he got help."

"Why would you think Rory would try to kill himself?" Bragg said.

"Rory liked attention. He's pulled more than a couple of stupid stunts to get my attention."

"Hell of a way to get it."

"He was angry I cut him off." He sighed. "He called here about a week ago. Said he was clean and sober and said he wanted to make amends. Nothing I hadn't heard before. I'd tolerated him when our mother was alive, but after she died, I told him to clean up or go to hell."

Winchester rested his hands on his hips. "And you think he staged this hanging to get your attention?"

Anger deepened the lines on his brow. "Yes. He knows I want to run for public office. He wanted to embarrass me. But like every other scheme he hatched, he fucked it up. Like I said, he hooked up with a few clowns and they didn't have the sense to free him."

"He was found in a fairly remote area," Bragg said. "A real bid for attention would be more public."

"I stopped trying to understand Rory a long, long time ago. Like I said, he didn't think through events and consequences too well."

"Do you know some of the guys he hung out with?" Winchester said.

Edwards squared his shoulders and turned from the Rangers to stare out the large glass windows. For a moment he didn't speak but then turned and faced them. "Dan and Spike are two names that come to mind because Rory was arrested with those two idiots about a year ago. I'd start with them."

"When is the last time you saw your brother?" Bragg said.

"A year. The night the Austin cops arrested him with Spike. When he called me from jail begging for help, he threatened to call the media and tell the world what kind of family we came from. I went to see him. Told him our mother was dying. He was more worried about getting out of jail and getting his hands on a few bucks than he was her. So I called his bluff. Told him to contact the media. He never did. And he didn't come to our mother's funeral."

"What was your family like?" Bragg asked.

"Not perfect. I will admit that. My father was driven and my mother, well she had trouble standing up to him. Not perfect, but also not the worst by far. But Rory would have found a way to make us sound like a terrible mess if he could make a buck." David flexed the fingers of his left hand. "I haven't seen Rory since that night in jail. After his first phone call last week, I told my secretary not to put any more calls through."

"Anybody have a strong enough grudge against Rory to kill him?"

"The person who hated Rory the most was Rory. He was never comfortable in his own skin. Believe me, he thought he could stage a stunt, and he managed to screw it up."

Bragg pulled his cell from his belt and located the picture he'd snapped of the image nailed to the tree. "This picture was found near your brother's body. Do you have an idea who the girl might be? The picture appears to have been taken at least a decade ago."

David glanced at the picture and immediately his gaze narrowed. “You said that picture was found near my brother’s body?”

“That’s right. You know her?”

“Yeah.” He straightened as if he wanted to put distance between himself and the image. “Her name was Elizabeth Templeton.”

“Was?”

“Might still be. That picture was taken twelve years ago. She dropped off the radar about that time and I have no idea where she is nor do I want to know.”

“So why would the picture be nailed to your brother’s hanging tree?”

David sighed. “Rory and Elizabeth met when he was nineteen and she was sixteen. He fancied himself in love with her and she in love with him. He wanted to marry her, and when my father laughed, he threatened to run away. But that didn’t happen, of course. My father put an end to their plans.”

The E on Rory’s chest didn’t signify Edwards but Elizabeth. “How did Rory meet Elizabeth Templeton?”

David frowned. “Is this really necessary? Rory hasn’t seen Elizabeth in twelve years. No doubt he put the picture up to create drama.”

“How do you know?”

“Because several years ago I heard he’d been asking about her. He was trying to find her. I kept my cool for Mom's sake, but I wasn't happy. Rory stood to inherit a lot of money when he turned thirty-two."

"Really?"

"Dad would never have left him a dime, but Mom had a soft spot for her baby. I was able to convince her to put a time limit on the inheritance, hoping he'd grow up."

"Or die?" Winchester said.

Edwards's frown deepened. He didn't answer. And though Bragg could have pushed he didn't want Edwards getting an attorney and throwing them out before his questions were answered.

"Why kill himself knowing he had money waiting for him in a year?" Bragg said.

"A year was a lifetime to Rory. He could barely wait week to week."

"And you don't know where Elizabeth Templeton is today?" *Templeton.* The name teased at a deep memory.

"No. And I don't care. As far as I was concerned she was real trouble for Rory. It was her idea to run away. Rory wouldn't have had the spine to stand up to my father if it hadn't been for her."

Bragg glanced at the image of the young girl's strained smile. He'd read her as troubled, but a manipulator? No. Hesitant, afraid, wounded, yes. But if he'd learned any lesson in his ten years as a Ranger, it was people had secrets.

"Where did the two meet?" Bragg had doubled

back to the question. This time he'd get an answer.

"This is ancient history for my family. It's painful history, and I'd really rather not get into it."

"I'm not making polite conversation, Mr. Edwards." Steel now edged the words. "How did the two meet?"

Edwards rested his hands on his hips and straightened his shoulders. He clearly chafed at orders. "I'd like you to keep this confidential. I've done my best to keep Rory's issues out of the press. It's not good for business."

The guy was used to power plays and winning. So was Bragg. "I'm not making any promises."

A moment's silence followed and then David said, "They met at Shady Grove Estates. It's a facility for troubled teens who need to recover from personal problems. Away from prying eyes."

Winchester nodded. "I've heard of the place. It's for high-risk kids who've attempted suicide. Very expensive. Not for your average kid."

"Cost an arm and a leg to send him there for the summer, but my parents did because they thought he really would get better."

"Better from what?" Bragg's patience grew paper-thin. He was tired of playing games.

"Rory fell into drugs when he was about sixteen. We tried a lot of different therapies to get him on the right path, but no treatment worked. His habit grew worse and worse. And then he took a combination of drugs that really messed him up, and he tried to kill himself. That's when my parents put him in Shady Grove."

"Where is it?"

"Northwest of Austin."

Bragg rested his hands on his hips. "How did he try to kill himself?"

Edwards shook his head. "He hanged himself from the rafters in our horse barn. He apparently dangled for several seconds, but the rope broke and he fell to the ground. Our farm manager found him unconscious."

That explained the scar the medical examiner had found.

"As Ranger Winchester just said, many of the kids at Shady Grove attempted suicide," Edwards said.

"Did Elizabeth Templeton make an attempt?" Bragg asked.

"She did. She took sleeping pills and then cut her wrists."

Bragg studied the image on his phone, wondering what drove this girl, his sister, anyone to give up instead of fighting. Given a choice he'd always come out swinging. He shut off the phone and replaced it on the cradle on his belt. "What can you tell me about Elizabeth Templeton?" Again the name tugged at him.

"She was a mess," David said. "Terrible girl."

Tumblers fell into place and then a memory

clicked. “Wasn’t Elizabeth Templeton involved in a car accident?”

Edwards nodded. “Yes. Horrific accident. She was driving late at night. She swerved off the road and hit a tree. Her older brother and the brother’s girlfriend were killed instantly.”

“Elizabeth Templeton tried to kill herself after the accident?” Bragg asked.

“The day she was released from the hospital she took an overdose and cut her wrists. The family kept it quiet. They had enough grief, and she managed to heap on more.” He drummed his fingers on his desk, his impatience and anger telegraphed with the strike of each finger. “Highway patrol figured she dozed at the wheel, swerved, and hit the tree. Brother and girlfriend were piss drunk, but they didn’t test Elizabeth’s blood alcohol until later at the hospital.”

“She was cleared of charges?”

“Cops cleared her, but she didn’t clear herself. Couldn’t shake the guilt. That’s why my parents didn’t like her. A lot of baggage.”

“You know a lot about her.”

A smile tweaked the edge of his lips. “Good to know the threats to your family.”

“You considered her a threat?”

“I did then.”

“And now?”

“I haven’t thought about her in over a dozen years.”

Winchester studied Edwards. "But you said Rory was asking about her a while back."

"He was asking. I couldn't have cared less about her as long as she kept her hooks out of Rory."

"Elizabeth and Rory dated at Shady Grove."

"Yes. We weren't allowed any contact with him for the first thirty days he was in treatment. And then after that we could only exchange letters. His first letter to us was dedicated to Elizabeth. He went on and on about how beautiful she was and how the accident wasn't her fault."

"Is that what she told him?"

"She insisted another car ran her off the road. The cops didn't agree." He tugged at his cuff. "I don't know. The girl killed her brother and another girl, so it stood to reason she was messed up. We didn't have a grievance against her, just didn't want her kind around."

"Her kind?"

"Damaged goods."

A muscle ticked in Bragg's jaw. Edwards could have been talking about Mitch. He didn't trust himself to speak.

Winchester moved toward a wall of awards and photos. He studied them closely when he said, "Sounds like you did a good bit of digging after that letter."

"Like I said, it pays to know your enemies. Dad and I wanted Rory to get well, not get entangled with a very injured girl like Elizabeth."

"Rory had his share of troubles."

"I don't deny it. But he'd never have gotten better hanging around other damaged kids." He shook his head. "If it had been one letter, we'd not have worried. But Rory kept talking about her, and then he sent the letter saying he and Elizabeth wanted to run away together."

"That's when you pulled him out," Bragg said.

"Yes. Dad and Mom told him it was time to leave Shady Grove. Rory was furious and refused to go. He said he was close to his friends and had promised never to leave them. But in the end he had no choice."

"Any more contact with Elizabeth?"

"She kept writing him letters. I intercepted them and told Rory she hadn't written. A couple of weeks after Rory came home Elizabeth showed up on our doorstep. She asked him to run away with her. Rory wanted to go. Dad ordered him back to his room, and though Rory hesitated, he obeyed. Elizabeth fell off the radar right after."

"And what did Rory do after that?"

"A month later he ran away. He was nineteen and there wasn't much any of us could do. We heard he tried to find Elizabeth, but she was gone by then. He begged Dad to hire detectives, but Dad refused. I can tell you her mother is still in Austin. She might know how to find her."

"Do you know how Elizabeth reacted to Rory's rejection?" Winchester said. He'd picked up a round crystal award and handled it like it was a baseball.

Edwards frowned. “Don’t know and don’t care. She left, which was good enough for me.”

“I’ll ask her mother,” Bragg said. “She should know where her daughter is.”

“My mother knew the Templeton family. After the accident Mrs. Templeton would talk about Jeff, the son she lost, but she never mentioned Elizabeth.”

Elizabeth had made a terrible mistake as a teenager. She’d killed two people. And then tried to kill herself. As much as he disapproved of the girl’s choice a part of him pitied her. Some people, like his sister, were simply weak by nature.

What he needed to figure out was if her past losses drove her to now kill.

Edwards rested his hands on his hips. “Do you really think Elizabeth could be involved in this? It’s been twelve years since the two saw each other.”

“It’s been twelve years as far as you know,” Winchester offered as he set down the crystal award. “You said you’d not seen Rory for a year.”

Edwards nodded. “True.”

“We’ll be in touch in a day or two about your brother’s remains. The medical examiner will likely release the body by the end of the week.”

David shook his head. “There’s no rush at this point. It’s over for Rory.”

• • •

Neon lights blinked orange and red in the window of Mulligan's Bar. Greer Templeton pushed through the front door, stopping as her eyes adjusted from the bright afternoon sun to the dim light of the bar. Music played from an old-style jukebox in the corner. There was a long pine bar to her left, backed by a mirrored wall and shelves full of liquor bottles. Every wooden stool around the bar was full of someone with a drink. She searched the faces of the men, her scrutiny catching the attention of several. One grinned and, taking his half-filled beer mug with him, pushed off the stool and walked toward her. He was a tall, burly, jean-clad guy with weathered features and shoulder-length gray hair.

"You searching for me, little lady?" His gruff voice held a hint of humor. "I might be just what you need."

Greer scanned the room, barely acknowledging the man. "Nope."

"How do you know?" He didn't shy away from openly studying her. "I might be just right for you."

Greer met his gaze. "You're not."

The man's smile faded. "I could make you want me."

"Doubtful." With a sharp glance, she dismissed him and the suggestive tone underlying his words. The man muttered an oath, but she didn't bother to turn around as she moved away. She didn't come into Austin during the day often and wasn't accustomed to the crowds, noise, or congestion. Each time she did venture into town the pop-ulation seemed to have doubled.

She made her way through the dim pub toward the back. The guy she wanted was young, tall, and wide-shouldered with posture like a soldier. And if she didn't miss her guess, he had chosen the darkest, most secluded booth because it's what she would have chosen.

She found him in the last booth, slumped over a half-eaten sandwich and staring into his soda. He was young. Barely over twenty, he had dark hair, tanned skin, and a square jaw. He wore a dark T-shirt, jeans, and a thick watch on his left wrist. His face retained a boyish quality contradicting coiled tautness reminiscent of a spring ready to pop.

Drawing in a breath, she questioned the sanity of her decision. She should leave well enough alone. Just walk away. Take care of number one. But a promise was a promise, and the sooner it was met the faster she could retreat.

Gritting her teeth, she slid into the opposite side of his booth. He glanced up, studied her, his gaze narrowing.

"My name is Greer."

Dark circles under his eyes told her he wasn't sleeping. And if she didn't miss her guess, eating was a chore, and he'd pulled away from everyone who tried to help. He amounted to a lot of work and trouble.

Annoyed, he eased back against the back of the booth. He didn't want her here, likely wanted to tell her to shove off, but something in him kept him from being overtly rude.

"You're Mitch."

He swirled the straw a bit faster in the soda as a subtle anxiety rippled through him. "Maybe."

She really did not want to do this. She did not want to reach out, connect, or have contact with this kid and the pain he carried. But she had a debt. And she paid her debts.

She laid her palms on the table and stared at her deeply tanned hands before raising her gaze to him. "Mitch Bragg, right?"

"If my uncle has sent you to talk to me, I'm not buying. I want to be left alone." Fatigue coated each word.

She understood that kind of fatigue. It ran bone deep and demanded he crawl into bed and pull the blankets over his head. That had been her once. And it had taken her a year to shake the exhaustion. "I've never met your uncle. And I honestly don't care to."

He arched a brow. "Who are you?"

"Greer."

"I don't know you."

"I don't know you, either."

"Go away."

"Believe me, I'd love to. In fact, nothing would make me happier right now."

His scowl deepened. "Then go."

She flatted her hands on the table. "I don't come into town much, and I'm not a fan of crowds. They make me irritable. I'm hoping to get out of here before it gets too busy."

A hint of knowing flickered in his gaze as he studied her, taking in her long braided brown hair, weathered blue T-shirt, jeans, and the three silver bracelets hugging her left wrist. "Get to the point."

Several loud patrons burst through the front of the pub. Their loud laughter echoed off the dark walls covered with hundreds of photographs. Soon the place would be filling up, and she already itched to be in her truck driving out of town.

"A friend asked me to talk to you."

"I don't like to talk."

"Thank God." She didn't hide her relief. "I don't like to talk. So we will keep this short."

He studied her, confusion seeping through annoyance. "You aren't making sense."

"I heard you needed a job. I need help. I run a vineyard outside of town."

Amusement flickered behind the annoyance. "I don't know a single fact about wine."

"I need a strong man who can work the land. I don't need experts. I've plenty of those. You'd be doing manual labor. You'll start with picking weeds."

"Why me?"

"Heard from a friend of a friend you could use a job and seeing Memorial Day just passed it makes sense to hire a vet."

A bitter smile twisted the edge of his lips. "I'm your patriotic duty?"

"Maybe. Does it matter?"

"I don't know."

She pulled a card from her back pocket. "This is my place. About thirty miles outside of Austin in the Hill Country. We're really not easy to find so you'll have to be on the lookout for our sign. It's small. If you want the work, then come. If you want to sit in the dark and drink warm soda and eat shitty food, have at it. Makes no difference to me. I promised I'd offer you work, and I've kept my promise." In truth, she hoped he'd refuse. She didn't want the weight of his grief when she had enough of her own.

"Who'd you promise?"

"Dr. Stewart."

"The doc that runs the group?"

"Yeah."

"How do you know him?"

"We're on the board of the Crisis Center together. He was a good friend after my aunt died."

He leaned back against the booth. "Why do you volunteer at the center?"

"I thought you didn't like to talk?"

He shrugged.

"My personal history is boring, and why I volunteer is even less interesting. You need a job, and I'm here. That's all that matters."

Eyes narrowed as he studied her.

"The job is yours if you want it. But you'll have to be at my place tomorrow at nine sharp."

He flicked the edge of the card with his index finger. "I'm getting disability benefits. I don't need money."

"I've had a lot of money, and I've had none. There is more to life."

He shook his head, his T-shirt shifted, and the top edge of a fresh tattoo peeked out from under his shirtsleeve. "Who are you?"

"I told you, I'm Greer and I own a vineyard."

He shook his head. "No way. You can't be more than thirty."

"Twenty-eight to be exact and I inherited it." She rubbed her hand over the silver bracelets on her wrist. "You want the job or not?"

"I don't know you."

"I don't know you, and I'm taking the bigger risk. But Dr. Stewart vouched for you. That's enough."

"Why take a risk on me?"

She tipped her head back, trying to quell her frustration. She wasn't so annoyed with him as herself. She had a million chores to do other than coaxing a wounded bird to safety. "Like I said, I owe a favor."

"What kind of favor?"

"None of your business."

"Do you always find strangers and offer them work?"

That made her smile. "Do you always ask so many questions?"

"Yeah."

The crowd in the bar grew louder and without turning she knew more people had come into the place. The more people came in here the greater the chance she'd be recognized. And she wasn't ready to answer questions about the past. "As much as I'd love to chat, like I said I don't care for crowds or places like this. If you want the job, be at the vineyard tomorrow by nine."

"This makes no sense."

She shook her head as she rose. "No, I guess not."

"Don't hold your breath."

"I won't. You'd be doing me a favor by not coming."

The uncensored honesty caught him off guard. "You always mean?"

For a long tense moment she did not speak. Old feelings kicked and scratched her insides. "You remind me of myself."

He shook his head. "We are nothing alike, lady. You can't pretend to know me."

"But I do," she said, her voice barely a whisper. "I know what it's like to see loved ones die. I know what it's like to have others tell you the accident wasn't your fault and to know deep in your heart it was. I know how to second-guess and to wonder. If I'd been faster. Quicker. Or sharper. If it hadn't been dark or so late at night. I've lived with the *ifs* every day for the last twelve years."

He paled as if he'd been punched in the gut, but he remained silent.

"I know what it feels like to carry pain so heavy my knees wanted to buckle."

Dropping his gaze, he cleared his throat before he met her steady stare. "You plan to fix me?"

Greer shook her head. "I'm no savior. And I can't say for sure if I'm fixed. But I can offer you a job that will work you so hard you'll collapse into bed at night. The job isn't glamorous, but it has purpose. A reason to get up in the morning and put one foot in front of the other."

He tapped his thumb against the table, studying her. He didn't respond.

Without asking she could read his thoughts. *Why would anyone want me? I'm worse than damaged goods. I'm a failure. A killer.*

In the darkest part of the night when her brain wouldn't stop spinning despite an exhausted body, Greer still harbored those same thoughts about herself. A dozen years, and the demons refused to leave her in peace.

"Take it or leave it. You're not doing me any favors either way."

Her heart racing, she turned, dodged a couple of laughing guys, and moved toward the door. A bone-deep cold made her hands tremble, but certain Mitch was watching, she kept putting one foot in front of the other.

"Damn," she muttered as she pushed into the bright sunlight. She walked the half block to her truck and slid behind the wheel. Her chilled body soaked up the warmth and for a moment she merely sat. Finally she dug her purse out from under the front seat and from it fished out her cell phone. She dialed and the phone rang three times.

"Did you do it?"

"I did it." She glanced at the three silver bracelets on her wrist.

"I'm proud of you."

Greer leaned into the seat, letting the hot leather burn into her skin. Physical pain was a tried and true distraction. "Don't be, Dr. Stewart. I didn't issue the most welcoming invitation."

He laughed. "If you'd been nice, it probably wouldn't have worked. He's had his fill of nice."

"Well, then I'm the one for him because I don't have a drop left to give."

"It's going to be fine, Greer. This will work out for both of you."

"I'm not so sure."

"Why?"

Her voice hitched. "He reminds me of my brother."

Silence snaked through the line. "Maybe that's a good thing."

"How?"

"Wait and see."

Greer fished out her keys and started the truck's engine. "I'm pretty damn sure this is the dumbest thing I've ever done."

A spotlight shone on the picture hanging above the desk. It was a happy picture. Five teens, two boys and three girls, arms clasped, smiles bright. They were fresh-faced kids dressed casually. The clothes were carelessly wrinkled, splashed with water from the nearby lake, and smudged with dirt from the game of touch football finished mere moments before the picture was taken. A look beyond the wrinkles and the dirt revealed name-brand clothes costing hundreds and hundreds of dollars. One boy wore a family signet ring and all the girls wore jewelry, not the department store knockoffs but real gold and diamonds. But then only the most affluent families could afford Shady Grove Estates nestled thirty miles northwest of Austin.

"You are always studying that picture," she said.

He kept his gaze on the image. Behind each of the smiling faces lurked wrenching pain. The boy with the signet ring had threatened to shoot himself. The girl with blond hair and the peaches-and-cream complexion had taken an overdose. Another had tried to freeze herself. Another cut her wrists.

So much agony. So many lost souls.

"They were a good group of kids."

"I never understood why you liked them so much."

"Because I understood them. Their pain."

Her laughter rumbled in his head. "If anyone should know pain, it's me."

He winced. "Just stop talking."

"Why?"

"I'm sick of your voice."

More laughter. "Tough."

He traced the images of the young blond girl. Elizabeth.

"You've been fixated on her from the beginning."

"Shut up."

"It's because she reminds you of me."

"Bullshit. She doesn't favor you."

"No, we didn't look alike. But she has my spirit. She's a fighter. Won't let go."

He could deny her assessment but he'd be lying. "Maybe."

"They all have such pretty smiles." Shady Grove taught them to smile. Extra desserts, extra time in the craft center, extra phone calls home if they smiled. Shady Grove taught them all how to hide behind a smile.

"What are you thinking?" she said.

He didn't raise his gaze from the photo. "It breaks my heart to know they're still so sad."

"That last night together when that picture was snapped . . . it was a perfect time."

"Yes."

"Not everyone is fooled by smiles," she said. "Not everyone believes life is preferable to death."

"I don't."

"And they don't, either. You see. I see. Now it's your job to take away their pain for good."

"They don't have to go on pretending any longer."

"No."

Chapter Three

Monday, June 2, 5 P.M.

A background check revealed Spike had been released from prison last year but remained on parole for another three months. It took less than fifteen minutes of calls to locate Spike's parole officer and get the address of the car wash where Spike worked as a buffer.

Bragg pulled up at Chicken's Car Wash located off Exit 6 on Interstate 35. He pulled up in his SUV, paid twenty bucks for a basic clean, and drove down into the washer. Water splashed on his windshield and then soap spattered. He sat back in his seat staring past the machines to the crew of men who waited with buffing rags to dry the car and wash the windows. He glanced at Spike's Texas state prison system photo and then to the trio of waiting men. Black hair, short, a dragon tattoo on his right arm made it easy to spot Spike, who stood apart from the other two. Spike tapped his foot and glanced around as if wishing away the time so he could get on with his life.

Spike had done time for forgery and embezzlement. There'd also been a drug charge, but the prosecutor had dropped it in exchange for the plea bargain on the other two crimes. No violent offenses, but he was the kind of guy you kept away from the till.

The machines hummed and whirred and finally rinsed the last of the dirt from this morning's crime scene. He pulled up close to Spike who spit once to his right and then tugged the drying rag from his back pocket.

Bragg watched as the guy dried the windshield. He studied his hands and face, searching for signs he'd been in a fight. The medical examiner had called minutes ago and said he had found skin under Rory's nails. Rory had scratched someone, likely his killer.

Spike didn't appear to pay much attention to Bragg until he saw Bragg's white hat resting on the front seat. Worry flowed through Spike, but he kept drying. When Spike finished, Bragg got out of his car and pulled a five from his pocket. He held it out to Spike who, eyes downcast, reached for the money.

"Spike Anders?" Bragg said.

Spike chewed his bottom lip as he quickly tucked the money in his pocket. "Tell my parole officer I'm working hard, and I ain't been in any trouble."

"How do you know your parole officer sent me?"

"You're a Ranger. Last I checked Rangers don't make social calls to ex-cons."

"Point taken. I do have a couple of questions for you."

Spike glanced over his shoulder as if assessing his exit strategy.

Smiling, Bragg slid his hand to the gun resting on his hip. "You're not in trouble, Spike, but if you run we are gonna have a real issue. And I don't want trouble. I want to get home to supper."

Spike sniffed as he twisted the drying rag between his hands. "I'm not going anywhere."

"Good." The car behind Bragg beeped, and he waved it toward another dryer.

Spike sighed. "You're costing me tip money, Ranger."

"Tell me about Rory Edwards," he said in no particular rush.

The sound of the familiar name eased the stiffness in Spike's shoulders. "I ain't seen Rory in about a week."

"Where's the last place you saw him?"

"Here at the drive-through. He came by to show me how good he was doing. Said he'd been sober for two hundred days."

"Did you believe him?"

"He looked good, for Rory, I mean. Clear-eyed and his hands didn't shake. He wanted to show his brother he had cleaned up his act. Said there was a woman too who he needed to make amends with."

"He say who the woman was?"

"No. Never gave a name."

"Rory ever visit his brother?"

"I don't know. Rory's kind of afraid of his brother. His brother was good about bailing him out until about a year ago, and then all the help stopped."

"Why'd it stop?"

"Their mom died. David told Rory he only helped him to keep the old lady happy. It troubled her Rory had turned out badly. To her dying breath, she prayed Rory would straighten out." He reached in his back pocket and pulled a crumbled cigarette packet and a book of matches. He lit a cigarette and puffed. "Rory used his Mom's guilt."

"Used it?"

"He'd lean on his mother, who would go to David and make him cut Rory a check. This went on for years. Rory knew which buttons to push when it came to his mother. Rory wanted to find his brother and apologize."

"Where's Rory been the last year?"

Spike puffed on the cigarette. "Up in Houston. A halfway house or something similar."

Dr. Watterson had told Bragg Rory's body tested positive for high levels of alcohol and coke.

"I'd bet my last dollar Rory couldn't stay sober long. It was still a struggle. Rory liked being hammered too much." Spike glanced past Bragg and raised a hand. "Be right back to work, boss. I'm talking to a Texas Ranger."

Bragg turned and saw a thin guy with a clipboard scowling at them. He held up a hand as if to say he recognized he was interrupting and then turned back to Spike. "And you have no information on the woman he wanted to see?"

"No idea. He wouldn't say. But he kept looking at an old picture."

Bragg pulled out his cell phone and showed Spike the image nailed to the tree. "That it?"

Spiked leaned in. "Kind of like it."

Bragg replaced the phone. "Back to the last time you saw Rory."

"He just said he weren't gonna drink no more, and he'd gotten a line on a job. Seemed excited about it."

"What kind of job?"

"He didn't know exactly. Said it was farm work. Said he looked forward to working with his hands."

"Where was the job?"

"If he told me, I don't remember. I reminded him he owed me one hundred bucks, and he said not to worry. He'd pay me back when he got his first paycheck."

"He didn't look sad or upset?"

"No. The son of a bitch was on top of the world." Smoke trailed out of Spike's mouth and nose as he exhaled. "What's he gotten himself into this time? Job turn out to be bogus? He get arrested for doing something he shouldn't? I told him good jobs didn't fall into the laps of guys like him."

Bragg rested his hands on his hips. "Rory died."

Spike paused, cigarette at his lips. "Rory's dead?"

"He is."

Spike took a deep drag. "Dumb son of a bitch. Someone knife him or shoot him?"

"He was hanging from a tree when I saw him this morning."

Spike's eyes widened. "Hanging? Like he was lynched?"

"Someone strung him up. Tried to make it look like suicide."

"Shit."

"He piss anyone off lately?"

"Rory pissed everyone off. He owed money to lots of people. Always made promises he couldn't keep. He was a taker."

"You ever hear anyone threaten him?"

"No more than usual. Like I said he could piss people off."

"I heard he also runs with a guy named Dan."

"Yeah, I met Dan. He's okay. Saw him a month ago. He was driving to Seattle for a job. He's a carpenter who does a lot of custom work. Said some computer bigwig was having shelves installed. Contractor needed extra help so he called Dan. I think they went to school together."

"You've not seen Dan since?"

"Not for weeks."

Bragg pulled in a breath. "Where was Rory living lately?"

"Rented a room in East Austin. Fifth Street. Don't remember the address but there's a taco place on the first floor with a blue chili in the window. One of the last things I told Rory was he smelled like tacos."

"Anything else you can tell me that would help?"

"Naw." He drew in a lungful of smoke. "Is there going to be a funeral?" Spike said.

"I don't have any details. His brother would know."

"Oh, I ain't going. Not worth the hassle. Figure Rory wouldn't have broken a sweat trying to make it to my funeral so I isn't worried about his. 'Sides, I have to work."

A horn honked behind them. The manager now flicked a pencil hard against his clipboard as if warning all he was losing patience.

Spike tossed the cigarette on the ground and stubbed it out with his booted foot. "Speaking of work, if I don't get back, the boss is gonna blow a gasket. And if I don't keep this job, I'll lose my room at the halfway house."

Bragg pulled a card from his pocket and handed it to Spike. "Keep me in mind if you think of something. Especially if you remember who might have hired Rory."

Spike held the white card in callused dirty fingers before cramming it in his pocket. "Sure, Ranger, sure."

Bragg got in his car and pulled out of the parking lot and wound his way back to I-35. The hood of his car glistened, but smudges streaked his front windshield. He checked his phone for messages and seeing none from Mitch decided to swing by the house just in case. After he checked on Mitch, he'd find Rory's rented room.

Fifteen minutes later when he pulled into the drive way and saw Mitch's black truck, relief washed away the lingering concern. He worried more and more for the kid with each new day.

He found Mitch sitting on the couch watching ESPN Classic. The game on television was from a decade ago. Detroit Lions versus the Dallas Cowboys. No doubt the boy had watched it with his mother. Sue had loved football.

Bragg tossed his hat on the entryway table. Guilt tugged at him. He and Mitch hadn't had much time together. Memorial Day should have been a day they'd celebrated, but Mitch barely spoke all day and refused food. No grilled hamburgers. No fried chicken. No fanfare to celebrate the day honoring soldiers like Mitch.

Mitch had made terrible sacrifices he still couldn't voice. And Bragg didn't know how to coax the words from him.

"What say we go out and get a steak? There's a great place a few blocks from here. T-bones an inch thick." He could call Winchester and have him cover the search of Rory's room. But as he figured a way to free himself, he braced for a no. Mitch didn't do much lately.

Mitch's gaze lingered on the television a beat. "Sure. I'm hungry."

Well, damn. He was pretty sure he'd witnessed a miracle.

Bragg thought about changing into comfortable jeans and a T-shirt but didn't want to risk Mitch's changing his mind in the interim. "Let's go."

Mitch didn't have a word to say while they drove the mile and a half to the restaurant, but Bragg didn't mind. The kid had finally said yes, and they were going to share a meal.

He pulled into the parking lot of the steakhouse. It was jam-packed, no doubt full of other families not up for cooking on a hot evening. Most nights Bragg ate alone and accepted the waits as par for the course, but with Mitch with him he wanted the line to move quickly. He wanted them seated, breaking bread and maybe even talking.

They moved into the crowded restaurant lobby. The place was packed with families. Not the kind of hangout most single men frequented, but he liked being around the chatting kids, harried mothers and fathers. It gave him a glimpse into normal family life, an experience he and Sue had never had growing up.

Bragg walked up to the hostess. He'd seen her before. Sandy. A pretty little blonde, she wasn't much older than Mitch. Last month, she'd seated him one night when Mitch had refused dinner. Seeing his badge, she had asked him about a boyfriend who was giving her trouble. She'd wanted advice. She struck him as a good kid, and he'd figured he'd help. He'd scribbled the guy's name, made several calls, and found out he'd violated his parole. Long story short, the boyfriend was back in jail for another decade.

"Sandy," Bragg said.

"Ranger Bragg." A broad smile brightened tired eyes. "Good to see you."

"You too. My nephew's with me, and we're looking to eat. What's the wait?"

She picked up two menus. Her smile turned sly. "Your reservation was for six-thirty, and I've your table right over here."

He grinned. "Thanks."

She led them to a table in the back, seated them, and handed them menus. "Your waitress will be right up."

"Appreciate it, Sandy."

She tossed an admiring glance at Mitch and then smiled at Bragg. "No problem."

Mitch met her gaze. "Thanks."

Her grin broadened, and she returned back to her station crowded with waiting families.

Bragg scanned the menu. "The T-bone is good. Bread is great. It's all good. Order whatever you want."

He nodded. "T-bone sounds good."

"Sure there isn't something else you might want? Don't order it on my account." He wanted to fix the pain the kid carried, but didn't know how. Best he could do now was offer him a great meal.

"T-bone is fine."

Bragg resisted the urge to challenge and when the waitress came to the table he ordered two steaks with all the fixings plus bread. He waited until she returned with their soda order before asking, "How'd your day go?"

Mitch sipped on his soda straw. "Good."

"What's good mean?" he asked, not really expecting an answer.

After a moment's silence, he said, "Got offered a job today."

That tiny bit of news had him sitting straighter and leaning forward. However, he did his best to curb his enthusiasm and the rapid-fire questions begging to be asked. "That so? What's the job?"

Before he could answer the waitress appeared with hot rolls and butter. More hungry for information than the bread, he waited as the boy tore into his bread and took a couple of bites.

Finally, Mitch said, "I'm not really sure. Farmhand, I think."

"Farmhand." It was a hard road to hoe working the land. He wanted his nephew to get an education and have the world open up to him. But that was the big picture. Right now he simply wanted the kid to talk, engage in life. Farmhand would suit fine.

"You know about farms. Mom said Grandpa had you riding a tractor at eight."

"Yeah. I know farms and ranches. Tough work but there's a sense of satisfaction at the end of the day."

Mitch grunted.

"You'll be working the fields, managing a barn, what?"

"Don't know. She just said to show up tomorrow at nine, and she'd put me to work."

He wanted to know who was hiring Mitch and what plans this woman had for him. But he reminded himself Mitch wasn't a kid, and if he babied him it likely would ruin what little they'd gained tonight. "How'd she hear about you?"

"Remember that support group I tried a couple of times?"

"Yeah."

"She knows the guy that runs it. Said she owed him a favor."

"And you're the favor?" The lack of details fueled his frustration, but he kept it to himself.

"I guess." Mitch tore more bread and ate it.

"You know where the farm is?"

He pulled a card from his pocket and tossed it on the table. "She said it's about thirty miles west of Austin. Some kind of vineyard."

Bragg picked up the card. "Vineyard?"

He glanced at the vineyard's name: BONNEVILLE VINEYARDS. Rory Edwards's crime scene had been located on the edge of a vineyard. His gaze slid to the name of the woman who'd contacted Mitch: GREER TEMPLETON.

For a moment the sounds of the restaurant faded away, and there was only the thump, thump of his heart in his ears. His first thought was for Elizabeth Templeton, the woman in the picture. Templeton wasn't a common name, but not so uncommon that he didn't suspect a connection. The hair on the back of his neck rose.

Bragg kept his voice steady. "You know any facts about Greer Templeton?"

“Pretty, dark hair, kind of skinny. Not friendly.”

Dark hair not blond. He flicked the edge of the card with his index finger. “What else do you know about her?”

“She drives a truck. And she cuts to the chase.”

Habit sent the follow-up question back rapid-fire. “And she offered you the job as a favor?”

“That’s what she said.”

Bragg summoned another question but held back, as if Sue had laid a hand on his shoulder. The boy had said more in the last few minutes than in the last month. Go easy. He wanted to go easy. He did.

But he’d been a Ranger too long not to toy with his suspicions. The Templeton name had been attached to a murder investigation this morning. Though the girl in the picture did not match Mitch’s description it had been a dozen years and people changed a lot. He’d not had much time today to dig into Elizabeth Templeton’s accident, but it would be first on his agenda after dinner. Rory’s apartment would keep until morning.

Their waitress brought two more sodas and another basket stacked high with warm rolls. She told them that dinner would be right up before hurrying to another table.

Bragg drank his second soda. He didn’t want to discourage the boy but at the same time wanted him to understand the lay of the land.

Bragg eased back in his chair. "You thinking about taking the job?"

Mitch grabbed a roll, tore it, and watched the steam rise. "Don't know."

As frustrating as pulling teeth. "Did she talk about pay?"

"No."

He reached for bread. "Had a murder investigation this morning. Don't need to get into a lot of details, but an Elizabeth Templeton's name came up."

Mitch glanced up from his soda, his gaze showing a spark of interest. "She kill someone?"

"No. At least I don't think so." He wanted to tell him about the picture but hesitated. It was a detail in an active murder investigation. "Wanted you to know, seeing as a Templeton offered you a job."

"Kind of a stretch, don't you think?"

"Maybe. But it's my job to connect dots no one else notices."

Mitch nodded as if mulling what Bragg had told him. "Maybe I'll ride out there tomorrow. See what she has to offer."

Their waitress brought two large steaming plates, each sporting a T-bone and a baked potato with generous sides of butter and sour cream. No green vegetables because it was a shame to serve what neither would eat.

Bragg was about to ask him to wait on the job until he could poke around in the woman's background when the boy glanced at his steak, picked up his fork and knife, and cut a large bite. He ate the piece and then another and then another. Strain banding Bragg's lower back eased a notch. Whoever the hell Greer Templeton was, she had made an impact on this kid, which for now, appeared to be for the better. As much as he wanted to tell Mitch to stay clear, he held back.

Later he'd do a little digging.

Dinner ended with slices of apple pie with heaping scoops of vanilla ice cream. Mitch hadn't said much more during dinner, but he'd eaten his entire meal and the pie. Some might view eating a meal as a baby step but as far as Bragg was concerned it was the first sign of life he'd seen in the boy since he'd returned home.

They arrived home right at nine. Mitch thanked him for the meal, another first, and headed straight to his room.

While a pot of coffee brewed, Bragg changed into jeans and a faded Texas A&M T-shirt. Then, coffee in hand, he settled in front of his laptop and clicked it on. He searched Bonneville Vineyards.

Immediately the vineyard's Web site popped up. It featured rolling land and rows and rows of thick grapevines stretching toward the setting sun on the horizon. Another picture showcased a group of smiling people, wineglasses in hand around a table. An older woman with long graying hair smiled and laughed with them. The caption underneath read:

> Bonneville Vineyard owner, Lydia Bonneville, greets guests at spring tasting.

Bragg clicked through more images, read some of the site's blog entries, and on the events page news of an upcoming fund-raiser for the Crisis Center. Though he dug through the entire site he found no telling tidbit about the woman who'd offered his nephew a job today.

Sipping his coffee he searched Greer Templeton. No hits came up. On the Crisis Center site there was a mention of her six months ago when she'd joined the board. The blurb also mentioned she'd been volunteering at the center for the last decade. There was also a piece about a fund-raiser this Wednesday at the vineyard, but no picture of Greer Templeton.

None of this set well in his gut. None of it. The Templeton name was associated with a murder investigation and a Templeton meets Mitch. And Rory Edwards's body had been found at a vineyard near Bonneville.

Coincidence did happen but not often by his way of thinking.

Shit.

Yeah, he'd be driving out to Bonneville Vineyards first thing in the morning.

Bragg glanced at the clock. It wasn't ten yet and he had time to get by Rory's room. Refilling his mug, he changed, retrieved his gun, badge, and hat. A quick check into Mitch's room found him sleeping. He left as quickly as he could.

The drive to Rory's took fifteen minutes, long enough to finish the coffee and summon a second bolt of energy. He was accustomed to going long stretches without sleep and tonight he'd get little. It didn't take much time to spot the Mexican restaurant with the blue chili in the window.

Inside, he was greeted by a dimly lit interior and the blend of recorded guitar and trumpet music. Small round tables with patrons filled the room, and in the back a bartender poured shots of tequila. Colored lights draped the walls alongside pictures of Mexico.

Bragg stopped at the register where a short stocky man with thick black hair and mocha skin stared up at him. The man wore a brightly colored shirt and a silver chain around his neck.

"You here for dinner?"

"I'm with the Texas Rangers. I'm here to search Rory Edwards's room." He showed the man his badge. "I've been told he's renting a room upstairs."

The man glanced at the badge and back up at Bragg. "I don't want trouble."

"I don't want any. Just want to have a look at his room."

"Second door on the right." He fumbled in his pocket for a ring of keys, slid one free, and handed it to Bragg. "I don't want trouble."

"Appreciate it." Bragg took the key. "Rory get many visitors to his room?"

"I don't know. I don't ask. Long as they pay, I don't ask."

"No commotion. No trouble."

"He paid his first week in cash and the second week wasn't due until Wednesday. Good enough for me."

Bragg followed the stairs behind the register up to a hallway lit by a single flickering bulb. There were four doors on the hallway. He unlocked the second on the right and flipped on the light.

The room was small, not more than eight by eight, and it was filthy. Soiled rumpled sheets covered the bed, and dozens of empty food cartons littered the floor. A mouse scurried under the bed.

A pile of dirty clothes was mounded at the foot of the bed beside a pair of expensive cowboy boots. The boots were nice but not as nice as the ones found on Rory's body. Wherever Rory had thought he was going, he'd dressed up for the occasion.

In a small closet he found a couple of jackets and a muddy pair of boots. He was on the verge of closing the door when he spotted the box on the floor. He picked it up and opened it. Inside were dozens of pictures of a woman. At first glance he didn't recognize her, but closer inspection identified her. Elizabeth Templeton.

All the photographs appeared to have been taken not twelve years ago but recently. Elizabeth standing on the front porch of a ranch house. Elizabeth surrounded by long rows of grapevines. Driving a red pickup truck. Leaving a store.

Rory had been keeping close tabs on Elizabeth.

Her face had leaned out in the last twelve years, and her hair had gone from blond to dark brown. But her figure was still slight. In most of the images she was frowning and he remembered what Mitch had said about the woman who'd hired him. *Dark hair. Not nice.*

Frowning, Bragg retrieved his phone and snapped pictures of the images before setting them aside to continue his search. He found a small careworn Bible and a stack of note cards with handwritten affirmations. *Do it! One step at a time! Believe!*

However, no strings to connect Rory to Elizabeth.

Bragg descended the stairs and found the manager. He showed the man his phone sporting an image of Elizabeth. "You ever seen her here?"

"I don't ask questions."

"Yeah, I know, as long as they pay. Look real

close, partner. Look real close because if I find out you've seen her you're going to get some real trouble from me."

The man glanced at the picture and shook his head. "Never seen her."

"You sure?"

"Never seen her. 'Sides, she's too pretty for Rory. He thought he was sober for good and better than everybody, but he hadn't changed. No good. Barely had enough for a week's rent. I was figuring he'd not show tomorrow with the rent, and I'd have to toss him out."

"He have any visitors?"

"No. Kept to himself. Heard him on his cell phone once or twice, but I never made out what he was saying."

There'd been no cell in Rory's belongings. Bragg pulled a card from his front shirt pocket. "You call me if you hear anyone talking about Rory."

"Where is he? Is he coming back?"

"No, sir, he is not coming back."

The man muttered an oath in Spanish. "What about his room?"

"I'm calling a forensic team now to dust it for prints."

The man smoothed agitated fingers over oiled black hair. "Are you gonna stay here and wait for them?"

"Yes, sir, I am. That a problem?"

The man's frown deepened. "You are bad for business."

Bragg grinned. "I've been called worse."

He returned to Rory's room and called in a team. As he waited he sifted through each picture of Elizabeth. Beautiful. Striking. But stern and solemn. He sensed life hadn't much eased the burden of her tragedy.

"What the hell was going on between you and Rory?"

Chapter Four

Tuesday, June 3, 6:30 A.M.

Bragg left Austin before the morning tangles on I-35 south. He also wanted to arrive early at Bonneville Vineyards not only to meet with the woman who'd offered Mitch a job, but the woman who owned the land near his crime scene. Even if she didn't have a connection to the case he wanted to meet her and find out how she'd found Mitch.

Remembering yesterday's route to the crime scene, he took the rural route exit off of the interstate and followed it another twenty miles before his GPS directed him over more back roads familiar to him. There were no directional signs to guide people to the vineyard, suggesting visitors weren't welcome.

An unpaved gravel ribbon of road wandered alongside a barbed-wire fence corralling row after row of vines bursting with a thick canopy of green leaves sheltering plump grapes clinging to well-maintained trellises. In the distance, the sun rose above the horizon casting a warm glow over the hills.

The entire area was lush and green and all he could think about was what it cost the family in water bills. Drought had been a problem in central Texas the last couple of years and signs were the hard times weren't letting up anytime soon.

Hard to believe Rory Edwards had been strung up right over the hill to his left.

Around the bend, a ranch house came into view. Complete with a wide front porch, its original windows and tin roof hinted of nineteenth-century cowboys. However, the ranch's porch now sported potted lavender, rocking chairs, and a sign on the front porch read PRIVATE and directed visitors to a larger stone building where the road dead-ended. Near the house stood a small barn painted with fading chipped red paint and a small corral.

The larger one-story main building just beyond was made of stone and glass, and though it had the air of new construction was styled like a medieval European keep. But unlike a fortress, it didn't dominate the land but hugged it as if the designer wanted a seamless connection between structure and terrain.

Small succulents floated in beds filled with earth-toned landscaping stones to add interest. However, it was the yellow and white wildflowers in brightly colored clay pots and a turquoise front door that rescued the place from being bland. To the right a stone patio outfitted with wrought-iron furniture overlooked vineyards that would catch the setting sun. Beyond the main building the land had been cleared for more construction.

Again, he gave credit to the site manager. He wasn't a wine drinker but the place might have lured him in for a look if there'd been signs along the road to coax and welcome.

He pulled up behind an older dark truck with a bed filled with tables and chairs. Grabbing his white Stetson from the passenger seat, he settled it on his head and eased out of the Bronco. In the distance a dog barked. Resting his hand on the hip close to his gun, he surveyed the area.

As he approached the building, a woman pushed through the glass doors of the main entrance. She wasn't tall, barely standing over five feet, but she held her shoulders back and her clear blue eyes cut. Not more than thirty, she had gently tanned smooth skin that accentuated a high slash of cheekbones. She wore her light brown hair in a braid that brushed slender shoulders, a white BONNEVILLE VINEYARDS T-shirt billowing over full breasts and tucked into faded work jeans hugging gently rounded hips. Her boots were dusty, well worn. “Can I help you?”

Her voice had a rusty, whiskey quality giving this wholesome farm girl a seductiveness enjoyed by older more sophisticated women.

Elizabeth Templeton.

She was a far cry from the girl in the old image or the pictures Rory had taken. The last dozen years had thinned her frame and face, adding maturity and an appealing naturalness. But Rory’s images had gotten her all wrong. What he’d taken for anger and bitterness in the photos, in person, appeared to be a fascinating intensity. He suspected this woman did no job halfway.

“I’m with the Texas Rangers.”

Elizabeth cocked her head, studying him closely, as if sensing this place wasn’t his kind of place. However, even as her gaze catalogued his large frame and the scar on his face she showed no fear. “How can I help you?”

He managed a smile. “You Elizabeth Templeton?”

Mention of her name triggered waves of tension that straightened her spine and narrowed her eyes. Hesitation flickered as if she seemed to toy with a lie. “That’s right. But I go by my middle name now. Greer.”

Elizabeth Greer Templeton. Greer. The woman who’d offered his boy a job. “Sergeant Tec Bragg.”

She took an involuntary step back before stopping. “Bragg. You’re kin to Mitch Bragg?”

He nodded. “He’s my nephew.”

She drew in a breath as if bracing. “What can I do for you?”

“I hear you’ve offered Mitch a job.”

“I have.”

“Doing what?”

She held his gaze and took a step toward him. “General farmhand.”

“He doesn’t have experience as a farmhand.”

Her lips flattened. “He already told me.”

“Then why hire him?”

A line furrowed her brow. “Did he send you up here? Is he not coming today?”

“As of last night he was planning to be here.”

She nodded, as if understanding flickered. “And you’ve come to check the place out.”

“Not the place. You.”

Her eyes sharpened. “You did a search on the vineyard, my name popped up, and you did a search on me and the alarm bells went off.”

“Why would they?”

Her sigh sounded weary. “You came looking for Elizabeth. I’ve not used that name in twelve years, so let’s not pretend. I’ve a full day ahead of me and don’t have time for games. Ask direct questions, then I’ll answer them. You don’t want your nephew working for me then have a conversation with him. But from where I stand,

Mitch is twenty-one, a man who can take care of himself, and doesn't need his uncle running interference."

Temper scraped along his insides. "How did you find Mitch?"

"I found him. If you want more details, talk to him."

"Not good enough."

Fire sparked in her blue gaze. "Well, it's going to have to be because I don't have to share my reasons with you or anyone. I offered him a job, he took it, end of story."

"Dr. Stewart arrange this?" He tossed out the doctor's name searching for a reaction.

Mention of the man's name triggered flickers of recognition in her gaze. "Ask him your questions. Again, my reasons are my own and none of your business. Now, if you will excuse me, Ranger Bragg, I'm expecting a delivery any minute."

He tapped an impatient finger against his gun belt as he struggled with his words. His temper prowled inside him like a mountain lion anxious to be unleashed. "Mitch has had it rough."

Taut muscles in her jaw softened a fraction. "I know."

"Watch your step with my boy." He wrapped the words in threat and menace.

Her shoulders stiffened as if he'd insulted her. "If that's all you got, I've work waiting."

Her annoyance didn't deter him. In fact, it drew

him. "Got one more question for you, Ms. Templeton."

She glared at him now, a brow arched and a hand on her hip. "Shoot."

He studied her expression closely. "I investigated a murder bordering your land yesterday."

A hint of remorse darkened her gaze. "I heard about that. Some fellow hanged himself." And then as if to head off his next question, "A cruiser came by yesterday and spoke to my farm manager while I was in town. I'm supposed to call him back but haven't gotten to it."

"You hear anything else?"

"No. I don't have time for gossip and news. So if you're here to ask me about the dead person, I'm afraid I can't do much for you. I spend most of my days here working. I don't venture out much."

And yet you'd made your way into town yesterday to talk to my boy. "I think you might know the victim."

"Could be, but I only know a handful of people in the area."

He studied her face closely. "The victim's name was Rory Edwards."

Irritation gave way to surprise. Pursing her lips she drew in a deep breath, letting it out so slowly he barely saw her move. "Is this some kind of trick? Are you trying to prod information out of me because I hired your nephew?"

"No trick. The medical examiner confirmed the identity of the body yesterday."

She folded her arms over her chest. "I've not seen Rory in a long time. At least twelve years."

"You've had no contact with him in this time?"

Her lips pursed. "I had a message on my voice mail a week ago. The caller said he was coming to see me. He was an old friend. I did not return the call."

"Why not?"

Blue eyes clouded before sharpening. "Some matters are better left in the past."

"I get the impression he still cared about you after all this time."

She shook her head. "I have no idea."

"I searched his room last night. He had a box full of recent pictures of you."

Her face paled. "I don't know about that."

"Can I ask how you two met?"

The grip on her biceps tightened. "I get the sense you already know."

Apprehension rolled off her and all but slammed into Bragg. Rory Edwards and her past were sore subjects. "Answer the question."

She glanced around as if making sure no one was around. "We met when we were teenagers. We were both in a clinic for troubled teens."

"You both tried to kill yourself."

The lines in her forehead deepened. "I'm not proud of that time, but what does it have to do with Rory's death? Like I said, I haven't seen him in a dozen years." Bragg unclipped his phone and scrolled to the picture he'd taken of the photo found at the crime scene. He held out the phone, coaxing her closer toward him. "You remember this picture?"

She didn't approach right away but then moved closer. The soft scent of soap rose up around her. No flowery perfumes or exotic scents but simply clean soap. His body tightened, unmindful of logic or reason.

For a long moment she didn't say a word and then she cleared her voice. "It was taken the last night we were both at the camp. Rory left the next morning."

"How'd he end up with the picture if he left?"

"I sent him a copy from camp. I didn't want him to forget me."

"His brother said you wrote to him several times a week but Rory's father threw out the letters."

Her jaw tensed, and he suspected an old wound opened. "I guess one letter made it through."

"Rory never forgot you."

She stepped back. "I wish he had."

"Why's that?"

"Really, do you have to ask? It was a painful time, and I've done my best over the last twelve years to forget about it."

He locked his phone and tucked it back in its cradle. "Were you really able to forget?"

She cleared her throat. “Rory’s family did us a favor by keeping us apart. But the rest? No, I have not forgotten that I wrecked a car and killed my brother and his girlfriend. I ruined so many lives. I carry that with me every day.”

“That why you tried to kill yourself?”

A darkening in her gaze told him his words struck their mark. “The months after the accident were a painful time. My parents’ marriage fell apart and my mother ate tranquilizers like candy. I saw it as my fault. When you’re sixteen life is black and white. I thought it was better for everyone if I left.”

She raised her hand to brush back her hair. The silver bracelets jangled and for a faint second he saw the pale lines marking where she’d cut into her wrists.

“Were you drunk the night of the accident?”

She swallowed. “I’ll give you credit, Ranger. You ask the questions most people think or talk about behind my back.”

“Had you been drinking?”

“The police cleared me.”

He’d been fishing for a yes or a no. And he suspected she evaded an answer to annoy him. “And your family had a really damn good lawyer. Were you drunk?”

“No, I didn’t have one drink that night. That’s why my brother asked me to drive. My crime was that I’d had my learner’s permit a matter of days, had no experience, and didn't have the sense to tell Jeff no."

"When did you see the other car had switched into your lane?"

Her head cocked. "The cops didn't believe there was a second car."

"Humor me. When did you see it?"

She hesitated as if weighing each word. "I don't know. Not soon enough."

"Radio blaring, brother and girlfriend laughing?"

"I think so," she whispered.

"Lots of distractions."

Greer closed her eyes and nodded. For an instant, she grew still and calm as if drawn back to another place and time. For a moment she didn't speak. He watched her closely, and to his surprise pity mingled with his suspicions.

When she met his gaze again anger had sharpened her blue irises into sapphire shards. "I'm sorry Rory killed himself. I am. No one deserves to carry that kind of pain. No one. But I won't stand here and rehash the past. I won't."

"And when did you say you saw Rory last?" He repeated questions often. Questioning someone involved in a murder investigation was like a fishing expedition. Sometimes tossing the same bait in the water garnered better results the second time. Police work and fishing were often about patience.

"I haven't seen him in a long time, and I really can't help you."

Elizabeth Greer Templeton was a hard one to read. She said all the right words and hadn't triggered any alarm bells. But the best liars spun the best tales.

Bragg realized pushing Greer could ruin the job for Mitch. But he had to push, not just for Rory's sake but especially for Mitch's. If she was unstable in any way, he needed to know it.

He studied her face closely. "I don't believe Rory killed himself."

Her head cocked. "He wasn't the man hanging from the tree?"

"Oh, he was strung up from the tree all right. Hell, he was a sight to see. Hell of a mess." Graphic details shocked, tossed people off balance and triggered unexpected reactions.

Her lips flattened but she kept silent.

"I don't think there is a way a man could have secured the rope, shimmied up the tree, and then hung himself. If he'd jumped with the rope around his neck, it would have just about snapped his head off. The rope did slice into his neck, but the marks cut like a man dangling versus falling."

"And the purpose of that graphic description was meant to do what?" No missing the pop of annoyance.

He wasn't ready to talk about the cigarette butts or the tire tracks. Though he did note the flatbed truck behind her.

Shifting gears he said, "What have you been

doing all these years, Ms. Templeton? You sure haven't been in the news at all."

"I lived here. I earned several certificates in viticulture in summer courses in California. When my aunt died last winter I took over the place."

"You've changed your name, and you keep a low profile. What are you hiding from?"

"I'm not hiding. I needed a fresh start after the accident. I didn't want to be with people who suffered loss and pain because of me. I have no intention of reconnecting with my past or the people I'd known a dozen years ago."

"Then why not leave? Your aunt is dead." He nodded toward the new construction. "Looks like you're putting down roots."

"It was my aunt's dream to make wine, and so we cleared ground for a winery and tasting room this past winter. She'd been suffering from cancer, but we thought she had it licked, and clearing the land was our way of celebrating." Her voice hitched. "And then she suffered an unexpected heart attack at the hospital during routine tests and died."

"Again, why stay here?"

"This is my home. Bonneville is as much a part of me as I am of it."

"What do you do here?"

She arched a brow. "You want a rundown?"

"I'd also like a tour of the place."

"You'll have to come back another time for the

tour, Ranger Bragg. I've a horse farrier arriving in about five minutes."

With or without an excuse, he'd return to Bonneville. "That's five minutes for a quick overview."

She shook her head. "Tell me what you're looking for, and I'll show it to you. You want to listen to my phone messages in case Rory called me more than I admitted? Want to check my boots for dirt or look in the barn for rope?"

He smiled. "We'll keep it simple today. Tell me about Bonneville."

Her lips flattened. "The new tasting room is behind me, but it's not furnished yet and there's little to see. The winery won't be finished until December."

"Show me all your trucks."

She cocked a brow but didn't miss a beat. "You see the one there. It's ten years old. I use it for general transportation. I've three other trucks, but they're out with the morning crew who are weeding. They break at lunch. If you come back at noon, I can arrange a viewing."

Pushy and hard-edged, she didn't resemble the kid in the photograph. Hard not to have sympathy for that kid; however, the woman was a ballbuster.

In no rush, he walked over to the dark pickup and using his phone he photographed each tire. "What if I want the trucks brought in earlier."

Her gaze narrowed, and he sensed she was

gauging if this was worth a fight. "It'll cost me money to bring in the crew and have them sit while you do whatever it is you do. The crew will be in at noon. I run on a tight budget, Ranger Bragg."

He didn't care about her bottom line or her crew. But before he could rebut, a truck pulling a large horse trailer rolled up the hill toward them. Dust billowed around the wheels and coated the already grimy truck with more grime.

Greer shot him a glance. "Give me a minute."

"Sure."

She tossed him a wary gaze and headed for the truck.

There was no middle ground for Greer Templeton. Hot or cold. Sad or angry. She acted stunned by the news of Rory's death, but then she could be one hell of a guilty-as-sin actress.

Chapter Five

Tuesday, June 3, 7 A.M.

Greer could barely breathe as she put one foot in front of the other and walked toward the truck hauling the horse trailer. The Ranger had remained behind but his gaze trailed her like a hungry wolf. Those eyes. Gray. Hard. Penetrating. In those eyes, she'd seen that he'd tried and convicted her like all the others had done over the years.

Her aunt had told her time after time she'd needed to forgive herself. Live your life. Find a man. Have sex. Smile more.

Doubtful a smile would have swayed Bragg. His six-foot-three-inch height and broad shoulders radiated substantial power and a total absence of tenderness. His warrior energy didn't threaten danger but promised it.

Smile. Don't let him see you sweat.

Right.

She'd tried smiling after the accident, hoping to soothe her parents' grief, neighbors' questioning stares, and finally the judge's final opinion. But smiling hadn't worked. No matter how nice she was or how much she tried to atone for her sins, no one ever looked at her the same again.

And so she'd stopped smiling, choosing instead to come out swinging. Might as well cut to the chase, air the suspicions, and accept the inevitable rejection.

She nodded to the farrier. "Mac, thanks for driving up here today. I know we're a bit out of your way."

White hair and a handlebar mustache accentuated the farrier's tanned, deeply wrinkled skin weathered by sixty-plus years of harsh Texas sun. He wore a long-sleeved cotton shirt, jeans, and a battered cowboy hat. "For the life of me I don't know why you want to get into the horse business, Ms. Templeton. You'll be tossing good money after bad feeding these old nags. I don't want to think about the vet bill."

"Oh, so that's why they were free?" She might not smile, but she could still tease.

Muttering, he climbed out of the truck. "The fella that gave you these horses is doing a jig right now. You've saved him the cost of burying these old gals in the next year or so."

Mac unlatched the back door and standing in the trailer were two old mares, both swaybacked with knobby knees. One was a brown-and-white dapple and the other black except for a patch of white on her nose. The dapple was still and quiet, but the black horse swished her tail, as if to tell Greer she didn't appreciate the change in routine or the journey.

"I've a temporary corral set up for them next to the main house. Got a man coming today to work on expanding it so these gals should be sitting pretty by the end of the week."

He pulled out the ramp, opened the door, and led the dapple out. Her ears twitched as she glared at Greer. Whereas Greer didn't have much interest in people, her heart always went out to animals. They were all about the here and now, and if you were good to them, they loved you with no reservations.

"Hey, old lady. How you doing?" She rubbed the horse's snout. The other horse stomped its foot. “Your friend has a bit of attitude.”

“A bad attitude,” Mac said as he led the black horse out. “She’ll kick and bite if you don’t keep an eye on her.”

Kind of like me. “Did the farmer send feed like he promised?”

“In the back of the truck.” He handed the reins of the second horse to Greer.

The black horse snorted.

Greer couldn’t resist a smile. “Don’t worry, old lady, we’re gonna do just fine. I bet before summer’s end the vineyard guests will be spoiling you rotten.”

Like any vineyard, Bonneville’s survival depended on many factors beyond growing grapes. One of the reasons she’d built the tasting room was to earn income from hosting weddings, festivals, and tastings. It was about marketing. It would be a year or two before she held actual Bonneville wine tastings, but the facility itself was already booked for several events this fall. Perhaps the horse rescue would also add a hook that would draw customers.

She met Mac’s gaze as he came around toward her. “Do I owe you any money?”

“Nope, the seller paid all as agreed. But if you change your mind right now, I’d run these two back to where they came from, and you can just forget all this foolishness.”

The dapple horse nudged her shoulder and

snorted. The black horse ignored her. "No, the girls are staying with me."

Laughing, he shook his head. "Well, don't say I didn't warn you."

She rubbed the dapple on the snout. "I've been duly warned."

"Well, I always did like your aunt Lydia. She was good to me, always treated me with respect. Was real sorry to hear she passed this winter. Always good and fair." He cleared his throat as if emotion got the better of him.

Lydia had literally saved Greer's life. As her release date from Shady Grove had approached, her parents had made it clear they couldn't have her around as they worked through their grief for Jeff. She'd tried to reach out to Rory because he'd been such a good friend to her at the clinic. But he'd not answered her letters and then his brother had driven out to Shady Grove and told her to leave Rory alone. *He's a good kid. He doesn't need your kind of trouble.*

As she'd left the facility, she really did not know where to go and questioned again if she was meant to live. And then she'd spotted the old red truck with the rusted bumper sporting a faded tie-dyed peace sign sticker. Behind the wheel sat her aunt Lydia, her riot of gray curls framing her smiling face. She'd been waving as she climbed out of the truck.

Greer had stood and stared at the woman as she

had approached. Lydia had wrapped Greer in a warm embrace, hugging her tight. Her aunt had smelled of grapes, earth, and sunshine. Greer had been stiff and fearful, but instead of letting go, Lydia had squeezed harder until Greer had wept and melted into her arms. Her aunt had offered her a home, a job, and a sanctuary she'd accepted gratefully.

"Lydia was real special," Greer said softly.

"Well, you let me know if there's something I can do for you and those nags. Name it and I'm your man."

"Thanks, Mac. I appreciate it. Oh, what are their names?" As she reached out to shake his hand she caught a glimpse of Bragg in her side vision. For an instant, the horses had made her forget him. An achievement, she thought. He wasn't someone easily forgotten.

Mac took her hand and clasped it firmly before he released it. "The horses? I don't rightly know. I should have asked."

"I'll give the former owner a call."

"Just give 'em a new name. It don't matter so much."

"Names do matter. But perhaps new names are a good idea. Signals their fresh start." She had dropped her first name after leaving Shady Grove, opting to become Greer. In many ways, Elizabeth had died on that stretch of road with Jeff and Sydney.

Mac glanced at Bragg, touched the brim of his hat, and moved to the truck's tailgate. "Where should I unload the feed?"

"See that storage shed over there?" She pointed to a small wood building that held all the extra tables, chairs, and props she would use for receptions. "Leave it by the door, and I'll put it inside."

"Okay."

As she stood next to the horses and watched the farrier drive off toward the shed, the crunch of the Ranger's boots against gravel had her back straightening and her breath slowing. She wanted to absorb more positive energy from the horses to ward off Bragg but suspected there wasn't enough energy in the universe to fend him off.

"You going into the horse trading business?" He came up beside the black horse and petted her on the side of her neck. She jerked and nipped at him.

Greer already liked the horse. "No. Just offering a home to a couple of old horses."

Bragg, not put off by the black mare, scratched her behind the ear. The horse shook her head as if to say, *no*. "You take in stray horses?"

When the black mare jerked her snout away from his hand, she swallowed a smile. "Not before today."

Bragg eyed the mare but dropped his hand as if conceding this round. "You know how to handle a horse?"

"Not a lot. Some." The dapple nudged her again and she wondered if the mare was trying to send her a message. Maybe she was hungry?

As if reading her mind, the Ranger rubbed the dapple horse's neck. "Don't feed them right away. Water's okay, but feed right now will unsettle their stomachs."

The old mare leaned into his strong fingers, clearly reveling in the attention. The black mare, not to be ignored, snorted. However, Bragg ignored the horse, letting her know right away he'd not tolerate any bad behavior. The Ranger expected to be met on his own terms or not at all.

Not at all suited her just fine.

He took the reins of the horses and led them to the corral. When they were both settled inside the gate, he met her gaze. "Ready for that tour."

"Sure. Is there anything in particular you'd like to see?"

"A general tour will do for now."

For now. As if he'd return. Great.

She nodded toward a house made of rough brick and stone. "That is the original ranch house. It belonged to my aunt and now is my home."

He studied the wide front porch, the twin rockers, and the half wine barrels filled with dirt and wildflowers. "How old is the house?"

"At least a hundred years old. The family originally settling the land raised cattle. Lydia bought the house and land from the original settler's great-grandson twenty years ago."

He listened with a keen interest, not missing a word.

Unsettled, she nodded toward the dirt path leading to the tasting room. Without asking she started toward it. "The new building here will be the tasting room when we have wine, but for now we'll be renting it out for parties. Steady income is always welcome. That clear plot of land behind it will be the new winery. It should be finished by spring."

"Looks like Italy."

"My aunt spent a good bit of her early twenties in Italy. When she returned to Texas and saw this land it reminded her of Italy." She pushed through the front door of the tasting room and strolled toward the large bar made of gray granite, so polished light reflected back. Behind the counter stood ceiling-high shelves waiting to be stocked with wines. The floor was clay tile and the walls a stucco. Brick-lined arches hung above the tasting counter, windows, and doorways. Throughout the large room were round tables made from wine casks. "We own a total of five hundred acres and right now have vines planted on most of it."

Her mind flashed to the new one thousand acres she'd once hoped to clear and cultivate. Rory had been found on that land.

He walked to the French doors opening out onto a brick patio that offered a stunning view of the rolling green landscape and the vineyards. "Impressive operation."

Judgment and a hint of approval rolled off the statement. But she wasn't swayed, too accustomed to being judged and found lacking. "Do you know much about wines?"

"Not a bit."

She appreciated the honesty. Too many folks tried to pretend they understood wines, and it always led to confusion. "We grow grapes for Zinfandel, Chablis, and Viognier wines. They thrive best in the Hill Country heat. My aunt preferred the taste and so do I. I'll likely produce a thousand cases of wine next year and then it will depend."

He faced her. "You have much competition?"

"So much I try not to think about it."

He studied her as if trying to peel back the layers. "Opening this tasting room and the winery is going to put you out front. I also saw you're hosting a fund-raiser."

"Time to rejoin the world, I suppose." She'd learned a steady tone made most statements sound true.

"Why jump back into the fray now? You've been tucked away here for a dozen years."

A sigh trickled from her lungs. "My aunt asked me to."

"So you're just going to put yourself out there?"

How could she explain to him what she didn't fully understand herself? "I owe her."

"You'll get a lot of questions about your accident."

Every muscle in her body constricted. "I'm expecting some questions, but people have enough in their lives to worry about. I will quickly become yesterday's news."

"But you said you've been in hiding for going on a dozen years."

"Hiding isn't the right word."

"How would you describe it?"

"Self-preservation."

He arched a brow but kept quiet.

She was accustomed to silence and didn't mind it, but silence took on an edgy meaning when Bragg stared at her. "After the accident, folks wanted details. They pretended to care, but they only wanted a bit of juicy gossip to share. It was easier to retreat. I also had to physically recover from the accident. I was pretty banged up. It took six months before I could walk without a limp."

"And now you're stepping up on center stage."

She wasn't sure why she'd been so candid about her past. Walls slid back into place. "Nothing so dramatic. I'm working at my vineyard and building my winery. That's all. And I'm hoping the past stays buried."

"Rory's death might stir up the past."

His words zinged like arrows. “I hope you’re wrong.” She flexed her fingers.

He checked his watch. “Your horses are gonna need watering. And I need to get back to Austin.”

Waves of relief washed through her, but she couldn’t resist poking the bear. “I thought you wanted a tour of the fields and the vehicles.”

“I’ll get to it another day.”

Had earlier demands for an extensive tour and vehicle inspection been a threat? Doubtful. He’d be back when it suited him.

Greer should have bid him a good day and left it, but again directness wouldn’t allow questions to remain unvoiced. “Why would the Rangers care about Rory’s death? It should be a matter for the local sheriff.”

“His brother has friends in high places, let’s just say.”

She’d not seen David Edwards in a dozen years but lingering memories were of a young man driven hard to succeed like his father. The one time they’d stood face to face, his gaze had been sharp and cold. “David can be a force.”

“You remember him?”

“Very clearly.”

“You don’t resent David?”

“I did then. But not now.” She managed a smile. “Time heals all wounds, right?”

His gaze remained on her a beat longer. “If I

have more questions, Ms. Templeton, I can give you a call."

A statement not a question. "Sure."

"And you are still going to hire Mitch?"

For the first time she sensed disquiet in Bragg, perhaps even a flicker of vulnerability. His job was at odds with his family. "Why wouldn't I?"

He studied her carefully. "As you might have guessed, with Mitch here I'll be stopping by a lot until I know he's doing better."

"That just makes my day, Ranger Bragg."

Her sarcasm gave him pause. "As long as we understand each other."

"Loud and clear."

He moved to the door, opened it, and held it for her while she passed. Gravel crunched under his boots as he followed her into the courtyard where the heat already beat on the earth.

Despite his stony expression, he cared about the boy and perhaps had come face to face with a problem that confounded him.

"This is a good place for Mitch," Greer said. "It brought me back to life, and it might do the same for him."

Questions clearly stirred behind his dark eyes, but he kept them to himself. "If there is a problem with Mitch, I want to know about it."

She shook her head. "Short of it being a nine-one-one emergency kind of a problem, if you have something to say to him then say it. I'm not getting between you two."

A smile tugged at the edge of his lips. "You already are."

"No, I offered him a job. That's between him and me. You showed up on my land and insinuated yourself into the mix."

"Just doing my job."

"As a Ranger or an uncle?"

"Both." He touched the brim of his hat and turned to leave.

She didn't wish him well or ask him to come again like she would have most. Instead she stood silent, afraid to turn her back, as he climbed into the front seat of his SUV. As the engine turned and roared, she remained in the same spot for a long time, watching the SUV move along the dirt drive, chased by a cloud of dry Texas dust. Only when his vehicle vanished around the last bend did she let her shoulders slump a fraction.

"What did you get yourself into, Rory?" she said.

An hour later the sound of another approaching vehicle had her lifting her gaze from a collection of chairs she was assembling for the reception room. Another vehicle, but not Bragg's SUV. Instead, it was a dark pickup, with a back rusted wheel well, gun rack hanging inside the cab, and a *Semper Fi* sticker on the back bumper. She recognized the driver. Mitch Bragg.

She'd thought yesterday she'd seen the last of him. He'd shown next to no interest in her offer and in truth she'd wished he'd decline. That would eliminate a good bit of emotional turmoil and Ranger Bragg.

But she'd promised to extend the invitation and she kept her word. By her way of thinking, when Mitch was back up on his feet, she was off the hook.

Consider yourself paid in full, Aunt Lydia.

She waited and watched as the kid parked his truck and reached for the hat on the passenger seat. He nestled it on his head as if he worried more about delaying their meeting than the sun. Finally, he eased out as if his body were stiff and when he walked toward her, his posture was erect despite a limp. Once a marine, always a marine.

Her heart clenched as she watched him. He so reminded her of Jeff. The broad shoulders. The swagger. The hint of uncertainty lingering behind the direct gaze.

She cleared her throat. "I didn't think you'd show," she said. She wouldn't mention Bragg's visit. She'd meant what she'd said about staying out of the middle.

His gaze roamed the land as if assessing the terrain and possible threats. "Almost didn't."

"Why'd you come, then?"

"Can't rightly say. Maybe because I don't really belong anywhere else and here is as good a place as any."

Now he reminded her not of Jeff but of herself when she'd first ventured on this land. Lost. Desperate. Afraid. "Fair enough. Ready to get to work?"

He dug his hands into his jeans pockets. "What kind of work do you have in mind?"

The same work her aunt had given her all those years ago. "I've a couple of old horses. They need tending. They'll need to be fed and their corral extended. After that, the vineyards always need work. It takes four of us to run the place. It's me, my manager, José, and his two sons. The sons return to college mid-August and come fall I'll be shorthanded. If you work out, you can have a full-time job in the field."

He didn't balk at the job description as his gaze trailed hers to the horses. "Hope you didn't pay a lot for them. They've one foot in the grave."

"Had it in my head to rescue these old gals. They're not good for much, but they've worked hard all their lives. They should enjoy the years they have left."

She walked toward the corral hoping he'd follow. He did. When they reached the smooth fence the dark horse glared at them but made no move to approach. "They're just the start. Like I said, we have harvest in a few weeks and come fall I can use the help." She'd purposely left the fall open-ended. One moment, one hour, one day at a time.

He held out his hand to the horses. The black one snorted and turned her head away while the brown one ambled forward to nudge his fingers with her snout. He scratched the brown one under the chin, not smiling but not frowning so hard either. “Do they have names?”

“They didn’t come with names but they need ’em.”

Silent, he waited for her to handle the official naming.

Before she thought too hard, she said, “Beauty is the black one and Buttercup is the brown one.”

The black horse snorted and not to be ignored moved toward them. “Beauty has an attitude.”

“She’s had a rough go of it, I suspect. I imagine she’s loved and lost one too many people. Losing leaves a scar.”

Mitch didn’t respond, but his hand stilled for a moment on Buttercup’s snout. “You have feed for them?”

“Over by the utility shed.” She’d not thought about what she’d have done with the old horses if Mitch hadn’t shown. Last thing she needed was the added work let alone the expense of a couple of horses. But when she’d committed to take them she’d known one way or the other she’d have made it work.

“So what are they supposed to do?” he said.

“Not much they can do. When folks come out to tour, they can enjoy the picnic area and visit the horses. Maybe we'll have carrots or feed for them to give the animals. Most folks like animals."

"I had a dog growing up. Sergeant. Other than my mother he's about the one thing I miss about my life before the Marines."

She rubbed Buttercup on the nose, letting silence persuade Mitch to speak more.

"Spent my summers on a ranch. My mom sent me there to get away from the city. I liked the work but haven't been to that place since I enlisted. Three years."

As tempted as she was to ask about what had happened to him while he was serving, she didn't. Her aunt had never asked her a single question about her accident. She'd left Greer be until one day she'd been ready to talk.

She was doing this her aunt's way. Might not be the best way and she was pretty sure this method wasn't written up in any textbook. But it had worked for her and would have to do. "I pay minimum wage, and I cut paychecks on the first and the fifteenth. If I send you into town on errands, mark your miles, and I'll reimburse you for the gas. Does that suit?"

For a moment he rubbed Buttercup's nose while Beauty watched. "Can't promise how long I'll stay."

She'd never figured she'd stay at Bonneville, either. She'd seen it as a life raft, not a destination. "I'd appreciate three days' notice if you decide it doesn't work for you. I'll need to rearrange my schedule to care for the horses."

He nodded. "You know much about horses?"

"Not a darn thing other than they're tall and more animal than I know what to do with. The farrier said the feed load he dropped was about a week's worth."

Mitch glanced at the hay bales. "Barely a week. Explains why they're too thin."

"You can tell me what kind of feed to buy?"

"Yeah."

"So you've got them? You can do whatever it is they need."

Beauty moved closer but remained out of Mitch's reach. "Have they been watered?"

"I put water in the trough."

"Where can I find a water hose and a bucket? Don't want to overdo the water, but I imagine they'd appreciate a splash on a hot day."

She showed him around the storage shed, which she said he could rearrange to suit himself. She gave him a rough idea of where she wanted to expand the field for the horses and showed him the pile of lumber she'd had delivered yesterday. He nodded and listened but didn't say much.

She left him, retreating into the main tasting room to the chairs still needing assembly. A large picture window framed the west wall and a view of the horses and Mitch. He didn't move quickly but with a halting, uneasy pace as if his body was relearning how to move again.

Grief and sorrow could rob you of will and energy so that all you wanted to do was crawl under the covers and let life pass you by. Giving up was a little too easy unless there was someone waiting on you to get out of bed each day. It was one thing to disappoint yourself. But it was another to let a loved one or an animal down.

She picked up the phone and dialed. Next came a calm and steady, “Dr. Stewart.”

“Dr. Stewart, this is Greer.”

“Greer.” His chair squeaked as he leaned back. She imagined his desk piled high with papers and the shelves behind him crammed full of books, papers, and pictures of his family. “Mitch arrive?”

“He’s with the animals now.”

“Greer, this is great.”

“I don’t know, Dr. Stewart. I didn’t expect paying off my aunt’s favor meant babysitting a soldier with PTSD.”

“You’ve been in his shoes. You get him. You’ll be good for each other, Greer. You’ll see.”

“I don’t know what I’m doing. I ended up buying a couple of old nags and told him his job was to take care of them.”

“That’s a great idea!” His rich voice was ripe with approval.

She cleared her throat. “What if Mitch wants to quit?”

"Think back to what it was like for you, Greer. Mitch is no different. He lost his buddies in a roadside bombing."

"He shouldn't blame himself."

"But he does. And you know logic and emotion don't go hand in hand."

"What if this doesn't work?"

Dr. Stewart laughed. "Don't you worry, Greer. I've all kinds of tricks up my sleeve."

Chapter Six

Tuesday, June 3, 11 A.M.

Why did Greer Templeton need Mitch? Growing up on the ranch, Bragg had worked the land long enough as a kid to know when a farm was efficient and Bonneville Vineyards was a well-run farm. His boy was smart. Quick on his feet. But he knew less about wine than Bragg.

And as much as he wanted to let go of the reins and trust this was good, he couldn't. It wasn't his nature to avoid trouble. Last night's Internet searches didn't come close to satisfying what he wanted to know about Greer.

He dialed his phone and after several calls he was connected to Hays County Deputy Eric Howell, who'd been the chief investigator on the Templeton accident. Bragg identified himself, explained what he needed. Howell promised to pull the files within the hour.

Bragg drove straight to Howell's office located in San Marcos, halfway between Austin and San Antonio. He found the tall, slim officer with thick graying hair in a small back office waiting for him. The man rose and extended his hand.

"Ranger Bragg?"

They clasped hands. "Deputy Howell. Appreciate you seeing me on such short notice."

Deputy Howell extended his hand toward a chair. "Got to admit I was surprised. I haven't heard the Templeton name in a while. Can I ask why the interest?"

"Her name came up in a murder investigation yesterday."

Thick brows rose. "Elizabeth Templeton's name came up?"

"She goes by her middle name, Greer, now. We found a picture of her and our victim nailed to a tree by the body. The picture was taken about twelve years ago."

"That would have been right around the time of the accident."

"Correct. The picture was taken at Shady Grove Estates. A camp for troubled teens."

He opened a thick, dog-eared file. "I heard Elizabeth had been sent away after she tried to kill herself. Hell of a burden to know you drove the car that killed your brother and his girlfriend."

"Tell me about the accident. The Internet articles gave bare facts."

He reached for a pair of wire-rimmed glasses in his coat pocket. "Her family spent a lot of money keeping the story as quiet as possible. Of course when you've a couple of fatalities, it's impossible to keep it completely silent no matter how much money you spend."

"Can you give me a recap of the accident?"

He slipped on his glasses and glanced at the file. "When you called I had the file sent up from archives. I'd forgotten more details than I thought. It was a horrific accident." He flipped through a couple of pages. "It was Jeffrey Templeton's twenty-first birthday and the family was celebrating at the Austin Country Club. According to friends it was a big party, and the liquor had flowed. Elizabeth, rather, Greer, was fifteen."

"How'd those three end up leaving?"

"Witnesses said the brother had been drinking heavily and was sick. He had an early morning appointment, so Greer had offered to take him home away from prying eyes. The girlfriend was also drunk but insisted on riding shotgun in the car because Greer was so young. According to Greer while she was driving a dark stretch of road, a car appeared out of nowhere. She said the car switched into her lane and was headed straight toward her. She said she beeped the horn, but the other driver didn't budge. At the last second,

Greer veered, went off the road, and hit a tree. Jeff and Sydney were thrown from the car. Greer had on her seat belt."

"Was Greer drinking?"

"At the scene the responding officer could not run a Breathalyzer on Greer because she was so badly injured. He did report her saying she'd not been drinking. Her blood tested negative at the hospital. I saw her several days after the accident. She was recovering from surgery to repair a badly broken leg. By then, the family had lawyered up and a representative from her attorney's firm was with her. Her parents were not at the hospital. They were at their son's funeral. Elizabeth was still so injured she couldn't leave the hospital for the funeral."

"They wouldn't delay it for her?"

"They refused."

"You ever talk to the parents?"

"Sure. A couple of times. Their focus was on losing Jeffrey not Elizabeth." He leaned back in his chair. "Jeffrey was the favored son. Smart, athletic, and handsome. He had the world on a string. Family had high hopes for him. And then in an instant he was gone. Her mother could barely speak Elizabeth's name."

Bragg was silent for a moment, wondering how he'd have handled the weight of such grief. He hoped like hell he wouldn't have condemned the surviving child. "She goes by Greer now."

"Right."

He leaned back in his chair. "Greer was torn up about the accident. Knowing she killed her brother had broken her. I think she wanted to talk to me about Jeff because her parents refused. But with the lawyer there it was hard for her to finish a sentence without being cautioned."

"How badly was she hurt? You mentioned her leg."

"Her left femur was broken and her left wrist. Shattering glass cut her arms, she was pinned in the wreckage for several hours before rescue crews could cut her free."

"Greer said there was another driver."

He flipped through more pages. "No evidence of another driver. There were no skid marks on either side of the road so if there had been a second driver we found no evidence of it."

"And the other family sued?"

"They did. The Templetons' insurance company settled out of court for millions."

Bragg studied more pictures detailing the tangled metal of the black BMW convertible. It was a miracle she'd escaped the mangled metal alive.

He came to an image featuring Greer being pulled from the car. Blood splashed her white blouse and caked her hair. Her left arm was in a splint and the EMTs were securing her leg. Her gaze was wide-eyed and vacant. Shock, he supposed.

Howell's chair squeaked as he leaned back.

"You said Elizabeth . . . Greer's name came up in another investigation. Who was killed?"

Bragg closed the file. "Rory Edwards. He was at Shady Grove Estates with Greer. He was hung from a tree not five miles from her place."

"Where's she been all this time? She vanished after the trial and her suicide attempt."

"Working at Bonneville Vineyards since. Her aunt took her in after the accident."

"Thirty miles west of Austin?" He shook his head. "I always figured she's moved as far away from Austin as she could get. My wife was out there for a tour. An older woman ran the place."

"Her aunt. She passed about six months ago."

He pulled off his glasses and cleaned the lenses. "I'm glad someone looked after the kid. She was damn near like the walking dead when I saw her last. What's she like these days?"

"Attractive. Hair's not blond anymore but natural brown. She's guarded and not fond of law enforcement."

"She associates cops with the accident." Howell shook his head. "Nobody should have allowed Greer behind the wheel of that car. She was fifteen and too young to be driving the back roads unsupervised."

"You mean the trio didn't just slip away?"

"Nope. Mother told Greer to drive Jeffrey home, but after the accident Mom put all the blame on her fifteen-year-old."

• • •

Greer's accident file in hand, Bragg arrived at the Rangers' Austin office minutes after two. He'd grabbed a burger on the fly and ate it in his car on the drive across town. Once he hit the office it would be nonstop. In addition to the Edwards murder, he had a bank robbery weeks from trial, a request for evidence for a kidnapping case, and subpoena requests to write in a drug case.

He dropped Greer's file on his desk and instead of sitting, headed straight to Winchester's office. He found the Ranger leaning back in his chair, the phone pressed to his ear. Winchester beckoned Bragg inside. Bragg took the seat in front of the desk and sat back, balancing his hat on his finger.

"That's right, the name is Edwards. Keep your ear to the ground. Any word comes up about him, I want to know about it." He nodded. "Good. Talk to you soon."

"What did you find out?"

Winchester hung up. "Rory Edwards's been busy the last decade."

Bragg sat back. "Was it like his brother said?"

Winchester's seat creaked as he leaned forward. "And then some. The guy's record is as clean as it was because his brother was always intervening. And like big brother said, he stopped intervening when their mother died last year. If Rory had lived, he'd have been facing serious jail time for fraud and breaking and entering. There's also a possession charge out there."

"A drug addict stealing to feed his habit."

"From all I've read that's exactly what he is. No amount of help was enough to keep this guy out of trouble until last year. He landed in a state rehab program and cleaned up. By all accounts he stayed out of trouble."

Bragg shook his head. "Can't say I feel sorry for the guy. The world was at his feet, and he found a way to screw up his life."

"He isn't the first to be controlled by addiction and won't be the last. You talk to Greer Templeton?"

The muscles circling the back of his neck tightened. "I did. She admits Edwards called her days ago but she did not return the call. She's a hard one to read. But I know she's holding back. The question is why."

"I did a little reading up on her accident."

Bragg nodded. "I did, too. She had one hell of an accident."

"Kid screwed up. Doesn't mean she was evil or bad, only young and stupid."

"I know. She paid one hell of a price for seconds of carelessness." He worried about the residual marks influencing Greer and ultimately Mitch.

"What motive would she have for killing Edwards? The accident is a matter of public record. And it sure was big headlines for a long time. And if you're going to kill a guy, why leave the body on your property?"

"Maybe she didn't like the idea of him digging up the past? Maybe she figured hiding the body in plain sight would deflect attention in the long run. Every time I think I've figured out the bad guys they throw me a new curve ball."

His gut didn't whisper a warning about Greer but without all the facts he couldn't make a call on her yet. "What about his cell phone records?"

"Put in the request for the warrant. We should have it by tomorrow."

Bragg checked his phone. No word from Mitch. "What about the truck imprints? Greer Templeton has one truck I saw but she could have many, and this is Texas, home of the pickup truck."

Winchester nodded. "Here's hoping the tire has a distinctive trait. Also forensics pulled DNA from the cigarette butts found at the scene. When we get that back I'll run it through CODIS."

"Be our lucky day if the killer was in the FBI's DNA database."

Winchester grinned. "Sometimes it's better to be lucky than smart."

Luck had abandoned him years back so he wasn't counting on her. "Right."

"David Edwards will want an answer. He might not have liked his brother, but he'll want this case closed so it can be forgotten."

"Rory gets my best just like any other victim."

He straightened. “Did you hear Mitch took a job?”

“No. That’s good, correct?”

Bragg brushed a bit of dust from his cuff. “The offer came from none other than Greer Templeton.”

Winchester didn’t hide his surprise. “You’re shitting me.”

“No, I am not.”

“Hell of a coincidence.”

“Hell of a time for a coincidence.”

“They do happen. Sometimes.”

Winchester shoved out a breath. “You going to pull the plug on the job?”

He thought about Mitch gobbling his meal last night and of Greer’s willingness to keep the boy even after his grilling. “No. Not for now. But as I told Greer, I will be watching.”

Jackson sat straight behind the wheel of his car, parked on the grimy side street in East Austin. “It won’t be easy to fool this woman.”

“Did you send her the package?”

“Yes. She should have gotten it yesterday.” His hands trembled a little when he thought about leaving the neatly wrapped box on her doorstep. “You are always so calm?”

“My cool head is why you keep me around.” He heard the smile in her voice.

“Is that the reason?” His anger leached out in his tone.

"Now. Now."

The woman, Sara Wentworth, slid out of the Lexus and her designer heels clicked with each crisp step. A sleek blue blouse draped her slim shoulders and was tucked into a white pencil skirt that showed off a narrow waist and hips. She carried a briefcase that was as expensive as her diamond earrings and pearl necklace. A French manicure and a neat haircut finished the look of a woman used to the finer things.

"She looks nice. Perfect."

"Fine clothes and a smile hide so much. We both know that."

Annoyance snapped. "You always do that."

"Do what?" She sounded amused.

He gritted his teeth, his gaze on Sara as she moved toward the old warehouse. "Bring up the past."

"The past never goes away. It is with us forever."

"Some people leave the past behind."

"Maybe. But not you. And certainly not me."

"I want to."

"You never will as long as I'm around." Her laughter rumbled in his ears.

For a long moment he was silent and sullen. He hated it when she taunted him. She could be such a bitch.

"Now you are mad," she teased.

"I am."

"Was it something I said?" She laughed.

He would not be baited. Not today. "We have a job to do. Today. In the here and now. We can quibble about the past another time."

"You are no fun."

"Focus on the woman. Sara Wentworth."

After a brief silence she said, "Vice president of commercial sales. She'd moved up the ladder quickly and managed to make a sizeable fortune beyond what her family has given her."

"By everyone's standards she is the model of success. Perfect. Had a tight hold on the brass ring."

"She's not what she seems," she said.

"I know." But he didn't need her pointing out Sara had mastered the art of elaborate disguise to hide bitter sadness. Once Sara had wanted to leave this life and go on to a better existence. Though she'd failed the first time, he wouldn't fail this time.

"Can you do this alone?"

"Yes."

"We'll see." Her smart-ass undertone jabbed at his temper, teasing it as if it were a bear in a cage, but he didn't have time for another argument. He had a job to do.

Irritated, he drove into the parking lot and got out of his car. He adjusted his jacket and moved toward her, careful not to startle her. Rory's weakness had been booze. Sara's was making money. She was as addicted to it as Rory had been to the bottle.

"Ms. Wentworth?" His voice was clear and direct.

She started, turned abruptly, and then faced him. She studied him a beat, clearly assessing threat, and then, finding none, her painted red lips widened into a smile of white teeth. "Mr. Corwin, good to see you again."

He grinned and extended his hand as he approached. He kept his gaze indirect, his posture slack, nonthreatening. "Sorry I had to miss our meeting yesterday. I had to fly back to D.C."

"No problem."

This close he could smell the subtle rich scent of her perfume. "I'm excited about the property."

She appraised his expensive sports jacket, the rich tan accentuating a white starched shirt and his heavily creased khakis. Appreciation flared and she smiled. "I am, too. How many restaurants did you say you wanted to open in Austin?"

"I'm starting with the one. I've a chain back East but want to take the Texas expansion slow. I'm conservative about growth."

"Texas loves business."

He grinned, knowing his smile melted hearts. "That's what I hear."

She reached for a ring of keys and unlocked the padlock on the property's front door. "The property is fifteen thousand square feet, three levels, and has lots of freezer space as you requested."

"Excellent. Let's look at the freezers first. They need to be large."

She grinned, bright, her eyes all but flashing dollar signs at the possible sale. "Right this way."

He thought about the other woman in the car waiting and watching. He couldn't disappoint her. "Great."

One down, four to go.

Chapter Seven

Tuesday, June 3, 12 P.M.

The site selection for Bonneville Vineyards had not been scientific. Greer's aunt had said many times she'd chosen the land because it had felt right, whole and spiritual. Twenty years ago when the thousand-acre site had beckoned Lydia away from the social circles of Austin, she'd known little about growing grapes or *terroir*, the juxtaposition of soils, climate, and topography. She'd only understood the land rolled and swayed like a beckoning hand and the old ranch house had been in need of a new occupant.

And so on a cold January day two decades ago, Lydia had moved into the nineteenth-century ranch house made of board-and-batten walls and encircled by a wide porch. She'd spent those first months restoring the house and making it habitable and then in the spring had planted her first vines.

What Lydia lacked in science she made up for in luck. She'd inadvertently chosen the perfect site to grow grapes. Though Texas was a land of extremes—cold, heat, hail, and drought—Bonneville enjoyed the right blend of moisture-laden soil, hot Texas sunshine to nourish the vines, and gentle steady breezes to chase away pests.

And as Bonneville had welcomed Lydia, so it had greeted Greer with meandering hillsides, orange-yellow sunsets, and temperate breezes. She'd been too battered to appreciate the beauty initially, but soon the land had eased her sour moods and guided her away from grief. Now she couldn't imagine living anywhere else.

"Good morning, Miss Templeton," José West said.

She smiled. "Good morning, José."

José West was a midsize man with thick arms and deeply colored skin from years in the sun. There'd been a time when he could heft one-hundred-pound sacks of fertilizer without a thought, but in the last year much of that boundless strength had waned. The graying at his temples had deepened and his eyes no longer sparked with challenge.

He had been managing Bonneville Vineyards for twenty years, and he'd not been pleased when Lydia had brought Greer to Bonneville. He'd made it clear he did not have time to babysit. Greer had made it clear she did not want to work in the dirt with a gruff man. But Lydia had insisted in a not-too-friendly tone that the two get along. "The grapes do not care about your problems," she had shouted to them both.

Neither liked the other but both respected Lydia enough to try. And so Greer had followed José to his truck that first morning at sunrise. She'd had a terrible headache, still limped from her accident, and had wanted only to return to her bed and pull the covers over her head. José, mumbling in Spanish, had grumbled about moody teenage girls. When she'd glanced back at Lydia hoping for a reprieve, she'd found her aunt smiling.

By noon of that first day, Greer had been covered in sweat. Her hands had ached and her legs were covered with scratches from the vines. To say her mood had lightened would have been a lie. José had explained how to prune the dead vines and leaves and watched as she'd practiced. Midday, he'd ordered her to return to the main house to rest her injured leg. Though she'd never have admitted it then, she would confess now there'd been a flicker of accomplishment when she'd limped to the waiting truck.

José had come again for her the next day and

again on the next. She'd followed him, sullen and silent, into the fields. That first harvest season, neither had spoken more than six words to the other. But she'd learned how invasive weeds could be to the Texas Hill Country vines and how to curse them in both Spanish and English. She'd grown adept at jiggling the truck's spark plug so it would fire and the engine would start. At harvest time, she'd learned to sharpen the blade of her pruning knife and how to cut, twist, and toss a cluster of grapes quickly and gently.

The vineyard allowed no time for self-pity or much reflection. It required her full and immediate attention all day, every day. No weekends off. No vacations and abbreviated holidays. The vineyard wanted her body and soul, and she was grateful to give herself over to it.

Over the next two seasons, José had taught her about soil, sun, rainfall, and drainage. He'd taught Greer about the life cycle of a grape and how to tell when the grapes were the sweetest. Without a lot of words spoken, they'd become friends.

By the end of her third season, her mother had started talking of college back East. But by then the land and the grapes had infected Greer's blood and filled her mind with dreams of expansion and winemaking. To her mother's disappointment, she'd forgone an Eastern school and earned a viticulture certificate from Texas Tech.

Now, accomplishment burned as she studied

her land. This was her last season as a grower. This time next year she'd be making wine. She didn't yearn to mass-produce wines but to create wines conveying quality.

"Your aunt would be proud," José said.

"Yes." It still saddened her Lydia would never taste the first Bonneville wine. "We'll drink a toast to her with the first bottle."

He cleared his throat but didn't speak.

José had been hit as hard by Lydia's death as Greer. Though they'd not made their relationship public, Greer knew José and Lydia had been lovers for years. For Lydia, he'd always grieve.

"How is the new boy working out?" she said.

He squinted against the sun as he watched Mitch watering the horses. "He's done well with the horses." He frowned. "We're not a horse farm and we cannot afford to feed the horses or the man who feeds them."

"We can afford a couple of old horses, and Mitch knows he'll work in the fields."

"When?"

"You can have him today. After he feeds the horses he's all yours."

Lines around José's mouth deepened as he studied the animals. "Lydia gave you a dog. Why didn't you give him a dog?"

She thought back to the mutt Lydia had given her after the first harvest. The Golden Shepherd mix had been six weeks old. Like the grapes, the dog had not cared about her past. There was simply now. Sadie had lived eight years and been there to greet her each morning, barking when she'd left for Texas Tech and when she'd returned.

"I spotted the FOR SALE sign at the horse farm while I was driving home. Buying the horses made sense."

José snorted and kicked the dirt with his boot. "You can't save the world."

"No, not the world."

José flexed his hands, now bent and swollen by arthritis. "But you hope to do for him what Lydia did for you?"

"I promised Lydia I would help one person. Just one."

"And he is your one?"

"I asked Dr. Stewart to give me someone to help. He gave me Mitch. So yes, he is the one."

"Why was there a Texas Ranger here yesterday? Was it about the hanging?"

"Yes." She shoved out a breath. José didn't trust the law. "And he's Mitch's uncle."

A string of Spanish curse words rumbled out with his next breath. "Was he here for the hanging or the boy?"

"Both."

"Why would he ask you about the dead man?"

She rubbed the back of her neck with her hands. "Because I knew him."

"How?"

"From before Bonneville. From Shady Grove."

José frowned. They'd never talked about that time but Lydia had told him. "That is not good."

"No."

"What are you going to do?"

"I don't know."

She'd thought a lot about Shady Grove in the last twenty-four hours. She'd not kept up with any of the kids from her pod, not even Betty, whom she'd had a chance meeting with a couple of years ago at a wine festival. Greer had been taken back. Their conversation had been awkward, each anxious to gain distance from the other.

Shady Grove and the accident had been a distant dull pain until yesterday.

Why did you do this to me, Rory? Why now?

With Rory's death, Mitch, and now Bragg's watching, she feared she'd bitten off too much. "How do the grapes look today?"

"They're plump and ripe. The spring was good to us, and if these next two or three weeks are hot and dry, we will be ready for harvest by early July."

"How many tons do you think this year?"

"The new vines you planted five years ago will be ready. With them, I think we'll have twenty-thousand tons."

"A sizeable load."

"The wineries will be pleased. We could turn a nice profit this year."

"Next year we will be making our own wine, just as Lydia dreamed."

Frowning, José pulled a bandana from his back pocket and glanced back toward land cleared for the winery. He disapproved. They were farmers in his mind. They grew the finest grapes in Texas and were no winemakers.

A smile teased the edge of her lips. "Go ahead and say it, José."

For a moment he was silent. "I fear you've extended yourself too far, Greer."

There were days when she thought she teetered on the edge of the cliff. "I've taken a risk."

José again wiped the sweat from the back of his neck. "You've always done the work of three, but you are only one person."

I'm living for me, as well as Jeff and Sydney. "Maybe I'm tired of playing it safe."

Bragg arrived at the forensic technician's lab at a quarter before five. Melinda Ashburn leaned over her microscope, analyzing a section of rope. "That the rope that hanged Edwards?"

She didn't lift her gaze as she adjusted the focus. "It is."

"That unusual?"

"It's a natural synthetic, heavy duty, and could be purchased at any number of hardware stores."

"How much do you have there?"

"A couple of hundred feet. It couldn't hurt to

check area stores for anyone who bought this kind of rope."

"That's something. What about the cigarette butts?"

"Did get some DNA and have sent it off. It'll take weeks or months unless your victim's brother puts a little heat on the system."

"I'm sure he wouldn't mind. I'll give him a call."

"Good. Because I'm a little curious myself."

"Tire tracks?"

"Got a clear print. I'm now checking databases to find the make and model. Shouldn't be long."

Bragg dug out a slip of paper from his pocket. "Let me know if it matches this brand."

She glanced at the paper. "Who does the tire belong to?"

"Vineyard near the crime scene."

"You'll be the first I call."

"Any other evidence from the crime scene?"

"Footprints. Size eleven. Athletic shoe. Hard to tell if it's a man or a woman. The wearer's left foot pronates out. Note how the back heel is worn."

Bragg studied the print. "Another piece to the puzzle. What about fingerprints?"

"Only the victim's on the photograph. Whoever else was out there was careful not to leave prints."

He thought about the roads leading to the area where they'd found the body. Back rural country roads had little traffic at night. “The closest gas station to the site is five miles away.”

“And there are no cameras there. I checked on the way out.”

Bragg had barely stepped through the front door of his home when he heard Mitch’s keys in the door. He stood at the small kitchen table, his hat tossed casually in the center, and was reaching to unsnap his gun from the holster.

He straightened, doing his best not to look like a Ranger. He’d perfected this stone-faced expression during his years with DPS and the Rangers. He could slide on the expression as easily as a worn pair of boots. But with Mitch, he’d worked hard knocking down barriers. Life had done a good bit to build walls between them, and he didn’t want to add more bricks.

But the more he showed concern for Mitch the more the boy retreated into himself and so he was training himself to hold back. A little.

His boy’s face and hands were covered in dirt and his hair was askew as if he’d run his fingers through it. His jeans and T-shirt were soaked in sweat and his boots covered in mud. Rode hard and put up wet.

“How’d the job go?” Bragg couldn’t help a smile.

Mitch glanced up and met his gaze. “Good.”

“They drag you through the mud?”

A slight grin tugged the edge of his mouth. "I'm working with a couple of horses. Nags, really. One has a bad attitude."

The black one. "That's your job?"

His muscles didn't constrict with customary strain. "For starters. Today I was in the field. Dude name José showed me how to weed."

Not she. Not Greer. "You like the boss?"

"Hard to read. Kind of edgy but shoots straight."

"José?"

"No. Greer." As tempted as he was to press for details about Greer, he held back.

Mitch sat on the hearth and tugged off his boots. Bragg had wondered why any Central Texas builder would put a fireplace in a house. The temperatures rarely dipped below fifty even in the dead of winter, and he'd never built a fire in the damn thing. They both used it as Mitch was now: a way station to pull off or stow dirty boots.

"Judging by your clothes I'd say it's been a good day's work."

"Not bad."

"Get yourself washed up, and I'll make us a couple of burgers."

"Sounds good."

Bragg watched his nephew vanish down the hallway toward the bathroom. There was a small spring in his step he'd never seen before. Mitch might not ever recapture the naïve youth he'd had before Iraq, but a bit of the darkness had lifted.

Greer had bought those nags for Mitch. She'd said the boy's hiring had been a favor, a promise to her late aunt. He supposed he should be grateful she'd reached out to Mitch.

But why Mitch? Why now? The Ranger would not let the man enjoy this good fortune and simply let go of the gnawing suspicion tugging at his gut.

Most nights Greer crawled into bed by eleven, her body too tired to function. Often her aunt had said she was pushing herself too hard but Greer hadn't agreed. The way she figured it, the more she crammed into her life the more she believed she'd make up the time Jeff and Sydney had lost.

Earlier in the evening she'd been working on the books and fatigue had struck with such force, she'd broken a rule and made a strong pot of coffee after two in the afternoon. The caffeine kick would throw her off but she'd needed to crunch numbers.

That burst of energy now exacted a price of worry and restless energy.

Hoping to relax, she'd showered and donned an oversize T-shirt that skimmed her thighs. Damp hair hung around her shoulders, and she'd traded contacts for glasses. But relaxation escaped her.

So here she sat, wired, her mind tripping back through the day analyzing every detail. A sample tasting had revealed the grapes were sweetening on schedule. Science helped determine peak flavor, but much of the process remained up to educated guess. A wrong guess—too sweet or too sour—meant a less-than-successful harvest and loss of much-needed profits.

Her mind skipped from grapes to the new hand. Mitch. He'd done well today. Quiet, he'd remained to himself but he'd kept a close eye on the horses, and he'd worked to complete the corral expansion. There'd been times during the day when he hammered so hard, she wondered if he pounded nails or nightmares. He'd worked to exhaustion far past the five o'clock quitting time.

Too early to tell if she'd made the right choice with Mitch, but, as with the grapes, all the analysis and thought simply translated into a gut feeling and hope.

The last time she'd reached out to really help another boy, she'd chosen Rory. She'd been filled with youthful optimism and a deeply rooted need to atone. She'd thought then if she could save him, she could somehow make up for the loss of Jeff and Sydney. And so she'd poured her heart and soul and love into him, and he'd lapped it up like a starving man. For weeks she'd thought perhaps she'd found a savior in Rory. Together they would heal.

Though Rory said all the right words about change and a brighter future, his actions told a different story. He was such a beautiful boy, and he caught everyone's attention. The girls wanted him. The men resented him. At first she'd convinced herself the attention wasn't important to him because he only had eyes for her.

But in the coming weeks, she realized he craved attention as much as he had drugs. He often stopped to speak to the girls and savored their flirting. Several times she'd spotted him lurking around the medical center, his expression lean and hungry. She'd known if not for her, he'd have stolen whatever could be sold or traded for a high. Never enough attention. Never enough drugs.

And then he'd left camp, and his promises to stay in touch had been forgotten.

Greer drew in a tight breath. She'd thought the years had softened the old wounds but seeing Mitch today had brought so much back. His eyes glistened with the same dullness she'd seen in Rory's. The urge to rescue had risen up strong.

Mitch, like Rory, came with a family that did not trust or particularly like her. Whereas David Edwards had intimidated her twelve years ago, now she could handle him. Tec Bragg was another matter. He had a distinctive energy about him. Caged and prowling, it moved under the stony façade like an animal.

"Bragg," she muttered as she pushed her hair off her face and sat back against the pillows.

If Ranger Tec Bragg was a likeable man, then he did a great job of hiding it. He wore the Ranger's traditional attire but she sensed he'd chafed at the uniform. A tall, powerful man, he didn't suffer fools gladly. Though she'd dealt with enough men like him in the fields and on the construction crews, she doubted any she'd ever encountered matched him in tenacity.

She reached for her laptop and searched Ranger Tec Bragg's name, really not sure what would pop up. To her surprise there was an eight-month-old article about Bragg's working on the border. A cartel had crossed into Texas and killed a half dozen Mexican nationals and two border agents. Bragg and a couple of other Rangers tracked the shooters to a small town miles inside the Texas border. The article had said there'd been fierce fighting. A standoff in a warehouse. The survivors would have been overrun if not for Bragg, who positioned himself on top of a vehicle with a rifle equipped with a night scope, and had fired. He'd received tremendous return fire, but he'd not flinched. He'd held his position until help had arrived.

It wasn't what the article said that caught her attention but the image of Bragg leading a man away in cuffs. Bragg's cheek was bleeding as if it had been slashed with a knife and his T-shirt was covered in dirt and blood. His expression was fierce to the point of feral.

Greer stared at the computer image of Bragg. His dark eyes projected an anger contacting like a bare-knuckled fist.

Had she made a mistake tangling with Bragg? No matter, she'd set out on a course and would not stop now. She could only hope he stayed clear of the vineyard. But with Mitch she'd be seeing him again.

She slid under the covers, hoping if she closed her eyes the caffeine would take pity and let her sleep. "Just a few hours," she muttered. "Not much time. Barely a little."

Breathing deeply, in and out, as she'd been taught so many years ago, her body did relax. She focused on breath and let the day go.

Soon she was asleep.

But slumber did not bring relief. Instead of blissful oblivion she found herself back behind the wheel of her brother's new red sports car.

Her manicured hands clutched the wheel and the wind blew her blond hair. She felt free. Grown up. Her brother was in the back. And beside Elizabeth, Sydney lay with her head against the headrest.

Elizabeth had not begrudged them this night. It had been a great night. The party perfect. And Jeff had been the son any parent revered. She had been anxious to please her mother and quietly spirited away the overzealous brother who'd had a bit too much.

Elizabeth reached for the radio, switched stations, and turned up the volume. The moon was full and the stars bright.

She considered herself more grown up than most fifteen-year-old girls. A step ahead of the rest. She cranked the radio.

And when she'd first spotted the headlights on the horizon, she gave them little thought. She let the music wash over her. She approached a small two-lane bridge, knowing she was less than fifteen minutes from home.

However, as the two cars approached the bridge, the other car switched into her lane. For a moment she thought she'd imagined the move but quickly realized the other car was headed right toward her.

She laid on the horn, startling Jeff.

"What the hell, Elizabeth?" he shouted as he wiped the drool from his lip.

Elizabeth gripped the wheel, her gaze now darting wildly to the left and the right for an escape route. If they made it to the bridge, they'd collide.

She laid on the horn again.

"Shit!" Jeff shouted.

She had seconds to decide but those seconds dragged like minutes. Closer and closer. Fifty feet from the bridge.

Left was a stream, right trees.

The other car barreled toward her, gaining speed.

Jump or dive.

Her heart thundering in her chest, she jerked

the wheel to the right and the sports car rumbled over the rutted ground and crashed head-on into a tree.

The next moments blurred in a barrage of pain, crunching metal, and blood.

Greer started awake, shoving a trembling hand through her hair as she swung her legs over the side of the bed.

Her palms were sweating and her head throbbing. “Dammit.”

In the weeks after the accident she’d been haunted by the dream. It had been the same every time. The oncoming headlights. Jeff’s panicked expletive. And the crash.

Her next memory had been at the hospital. Later she learned from EMTs she’d talked about the other car. She was certain the other car had stopped. That the driver had spoken to her.

But she had no memory to offer more specifics.

In the end the police had determined she’d fallen asleep at the wheel. She’d been young. Inexperienced. No fault. Just a terrible accident.

Greer shook her head.

It hadn’t been an accident.

She’d known for a dozen years.

But that didn’t change the fact that two people were dead. And the burden of their deaths would always weigh on her.

Chapter Eight

Wednesday, June 4, 1 A.M.

David Edwards sat on the leather sofa in his study, surrounded by his richly bound first edition books, paintings of Texas landscapes, and a collection of knickknacks he'd paid a designer a fortune to choose.

On the mahogany table was a bundle of ten letters. Written twelve years ago, the writer's handwriting was precise for a teen and the words surprisingly articulate. The letters had been written by Elizabeth Greer Templeton and sent to his brother, Rory. On orders from his father he'd confiscated the letters and had promised to destroy them. But when he'd opened them, he'd been curious about anyone who saw redeeming qualities in his brother.

> Dear Rory,
>
> Camp is not the same without you. We all miss the way you could make us laugh. I miss the way you hugged me and the way your eyes lit up when you told me I was pretty.

David sat back on the sofa staring at the letter as he sipped whiskey. After he'd read Elizabeth's first letter he'd done some research on her. It hadn't been easy because her family guarded their secrets as closely as the Edwards family guarded theirs. But enough money opened the right doors at Shady Grove, and he'd gotten a copy of her file.

The instant he'd read her dossier he knew she was trouble. Nothing good would come of Rory's dalliance with her or anyone else.

David continued to confiscate her letters to Rory and Rory's to her. David had expected Elizabeth to give up on Rory, but she'd kept writing until finally he'd been moved to drive out to Shady Grove and speak to her. She'd been defiant, determined and insistent about visiting Rory. No threats had swayed her. She'd sworn she'd find a way. And she had tried. In the end, Rory, being Rory, had failed Elizabeth.

Over the last dozen years, he'd kept tabs on Elizabeth. He'd known all along she lived at Bonneville and had invested her trust fund in the vineyard. Financially, she was stretched thin and having Rory's fortune would have been handy. He'd gone out of his way to ensure Rory never found her.

David had lied to the Rangers. He had not only spoken to Rory last week on the phone but had also seen him. His brother had been clear-eyed, clean, and lucid. He'd said he'd joined AA and NA and had been substance-free for eight months. His little brother had been proud of his accomplishment and showed him his sobriety chips. Rory had returned to make amends with his family and Elizabeth. When he came into his inheritance, he planned to do good things with it.

Good things. That idiot didn't have a clue how to handle that kind of money. And he'd feared Elizabeth would soon gain control of the fortune.

David had been furious. He'd told Rory to leave her be because she wanted his money and not him. But Rory had been unusually stubborn and sworn he'd drive out to Bonneville in the morning.

A soft knock on his study door had him straightening. "Enter."

His wife, Deidra, was a tall, slim blonde. She wore a silk nightgown and though she wasn't wearing makeup her skin looked like porcelain. "David. It's late."

"I know. I'll be there soon."

"I miss you." They'd been married two years now and she'd gotten in the habit of pressing. He didn't like it.

"Soon," he said sharply.

Deidra pouted but said no more as she eased out of the room and closed the door behind her.

David swirled his drink, watching as the light caught the cut edges. A smile played on his lips. But ol' Rory had never made it. And he'd ensure none of those fuck-ups from Shady Grove poisoned his future.

• • •

Bragg pushed away from Rory Edwards's murder-scene photos, rose, and stretched. He'd been studying the pictures for hours and had not made any new discoveries. Winchester had visited Tate's Bar and had shown Rory's picture around. The place had been crowded and loud and the bartender hadn't seen Rory. If the killer had met him there, no one had noticed.

Wheeler had gotten more calls from the media. Instead of answering them, he'd forwarded them to Bragg. He'd fielded what he could, said as little as he could get away with, but interest over the death of an Edwards was growing.

He moved into the kitchen and poured coffee from the pot. It was cold so he put the mug in the microwave. As the seconds ticked off, he shrugged his shoulders, trying to work the kinks free. When the microwave dinged, he took his cup and sipped. Bitter.

Sipping his coffee, he sat on the couch, considered clicking on the television, but decided against it. He reached for his cell and scrolled to the picture he'd snapped of Greer. Not the old photo but one taken recently by Rory. Of all the ones taken of her he'd liked this one the best. She stood on the porch of her house staring out over her vineyard. The sun was setting and orange-yellow light illuminated her face. He'd chosen the picture because it was the only one that hadn't caught her frowning. In this image she looked almost at peace. Bragg traced his finger over the line of her jaw. Looking at her made him hard, hungry, and wanting more than he could put into words.

He frowned when he thought of Rory taking the picture. He didn't like the idea of the guy watching her, stalking her.

No way he could have gotten close and she'd not seen him. So where had he been? He conjured the image of the terrain around her ranch house. There'd been a hill at three o'clock. He'd had to have been there. And the photo had to have been taken with a telephoto lens.

There'd been no camera in Rory's room. Where was the camera? Where had he gotten it? He shifted his attention from Greer to the background. Thunderclouds formed in the distance. Monday's rain clouds hadn't materialized and there'd been no dark clouds in the sky. The last hard rain that area had seen had been three weeks ago. Everyone had reported Rory had been in town only a week. Had they been wrong? Had he been here longer? Or had someone else taken the photos?

"Get the fuck out of there!"

Mitch's strangled cry shot down the hallway like a bullet.

Bragg jumped off the couch and ran down the hallway to the kid's room. Mitch lay on his back, shirtless, a sheet twisted around his midsection as he thrashed back and forth. "Get the fuck out of there!"

Bragg crossed the room in three strides and reached for the boy's shoulder.

"Mitch! Wake up!" he commanded.

As quick as a rattler, Mitch balled up his fist, drew it back, and swung. It hit Bragg square in the jaw.

The Ranger wasn't prepared for the blow, and the pain cut through him, making him ball his own fists as he staggered back. Anger rose up in him like an animal and his first instinct was to strike back hard. Heart racing in his chest, he took a step back until he could corral the fury.

"Mitch," he shouted. "Wake up!"

The kid started awake and sat up in bed. Sweat beaded on his forehead and his breathing was labored and quick. His wild gaze slowly cleared.

"Mitch." The calmness in Bragg's voice surprised him.

"Yeah." He shoved his fingers over his short hair.

"Bad dream?"

"Yeah."

He rubbed his knuckle over the tender skin on his jaw. "Want to talk about it?"

Mitch shook his head and lay back down. "No."

"Want a glass of water or a soda?"

He rolled on his side away from Bragg. "No. Thanks."

A heavy silence hung between them as Bragg

searched for the right words. He couldn't find one so he backed out of the room. He closed the door partway, leaving it cracked so that light from the hallway could seep inside.

Bragg hadn't planned on attending Greer's fund-raiser but knew now he would. And though he could tell himself his interests were for Mitch or the case, he'd be lying. He wanted her for himself.

"When is she going to wake up?"

"I don't know," Jackson said.

He stared through the small window at Sara lying on the floor of the freezer. He'd turned the temperature down low, but not so low that it would kill her before she woke.

"Can't you wake her?"

"I want her to wake up on her own."

"Why?" she challenged.

"Why are you so impatient?"

"We don't have a lot of time. If you're going to keep to the schedule, we have only five more days."

Jackson traced Sara's image on the glass. "She'll wake up soon, and we'll meet our schedule."

"How can you be sure?"

He smiled. "Because I am."

"What about the one after her? Have you laid the groundwork?"

He frowned. "Yes. I've prepped all the rest. And I will deal with each in their own time."

Chapter Nine

Wednesday, June 4, 8 A.M.

Greer sat in her office going over the details for the fund-raiser she was hosting for the Crisis Center. She'd started at the center years ago answering phones during the late-night hours. She'd planned to simply answer phone calls. Stay on the fringe. But somewhere along the way she'd caught the attention of Dr. Stewart, who became chairman of the nonprofit's board last year. Dr. Stewart had liked Greer and invited her to join the committee.

Greer had said no at first but Dr. Stewart wasn't an easy man to refuse so she'd promised to help a little. Give Dr. Stewart an inch, and he'd charm you out of a mile.

Greer had found herself on the marketing committee and somehow had agreed to host a fund-raiser at Bonneville.

No sense worrying how she'd gotten sucked into this event. She was here and all she could do was make the best of it.

Tables. Chairs. Signs. Food. Wine, of course. Her checklist was complete. She was good at logistics. Ask her to arrange the field workers for harvest. Done. Coordinate Bonneville's booth at the growers' association meeting. Easy. Handle a truck, broken irrigation lines, or bug infestation. No sweat. But ask her to deal directly with people, and she was damn near a mess.

She'd not always been like this. Before the accident she could walk up to anyone and start a conversation. Her parents had held many business cocktail parties, and they expected Greer and Jeff to make an appearance. Ironically, it was Jeffrey who didn't like the limelight and Greer who filled the conversation lulls with lively chatter and laughter.

The crunch of gravel under tires had her looking out her office window toward the main entrance. No one came or left the vineyard's main entrance without her seeing. She didn't like surprises. Too many lawyers and reporters had surprised her at her parents' Austin home after the accident. Twelve years had softened the leeriness but not broken it.

A white four-door sedan drove up in a cloud of dust, parking in front of the main tasting room. She didn't recognize the car and found herself tensing as she rose. She still hated surprises.

The driver's-side door opened and a tall, slender woman dressed in soft pinks appeared. Dark sunglasses hid her face but Greer would have recognized the stiff-backed posture anywhere. Her mother.

Smoothing her fingers over her hair drawn back

into a tight ponytail, she moved toward the front door. Though the urge to hide was strong, she refused. She'd made a promise to stop hiding from the world, and though she had her faults, she never broke a promise.

Greer pushed open the front door and found her mother studying the building with a critical eye. Mom had not been to the vineyard in well over a decade and the times they'd met had been at the family home in Austin or at Jeff's grave. The vineyard had changed a good bit since then. Greer took pride that she'd been so much a part of the vineyard's transformation.

"Mom," Greer said. "This is a surprise."

Glancing from side to side, Sylvia Templeton approached her daughter. Those who didn't know Sylvia would describe her smile as bright, but Greer saw the frost. "How are you doing, Greer?"

She allowed her mother to wrap a stiff arm around her. "I'm fine. What brings you out here?"

Sylvia released her daughter and stepped back as if she didn't like the physical contact. "Can't I come and see my daughter?"

"Of course." Already formality had hardened Greer's tone. Before the accident her mother had not been the most approachable person, but after she'd all but ignored her second child. Hard disappointments had enabled Greer to build the wall between them brick by brick. "You've not been out here in over ten years, Mom."

"Maybe it's time, Elizabeth."

The sound of her first name grated. "What do you want, Mom?"

Sylvia and Lydia had been sisters. Lydia was the younger of the two and from what little Greer had gathered Lydia had been the vivacious one. The outgoing one. The sisters had had a falling out long before Greer was born and had barely spoken over the next three decades. Family lore hinted Sylvia had stolen Lydia's fiancé. Greer had always discounted the idea. She could never picture her father with her aunt. Once she'd asked her aunt, who'd not laughed at the absurd question. Instead, Lydia's expression turned sad. Greer had never received a real answer.

Manicured fingers carefully brushed a stray hair from Sylvia's eyes. "I can't visit?"

"Of course you can." She noticed the nail on her mother's right index finger was chipped. Mom never chipped a nail. Ever. A small insignificant detail but it mattered. "Why now?"

Sylvia took a step back and surveyed the new tasting room. "You've made so many improvements out here."

Avoidance. It was classic Sylvia. But Greer was curious enough about the visit to play along. "We completed the tasting room last fall. With Aunt Lydia so sick it was important to me it be finished before she died."

"Our financial advisor called me when you

cashed out your trust fund to invest in these buildings. I considered calling you then but decided you are old enough to make such decisions."

"What's the point of having the money if it's not working for me?"

"You have no safety net now."

"No." She'd come to believe safety nets were an illusion. She'd had money and family behind her before the accident but neither had cushioned her fall. Money was nice, but it couldn't protect you completely.

"You aren't worried."

"I'm not." For a moment neither spoke as memories of the accident and Jeff danced between them like specters.

Sylvia's lips flattened and she turned as if the distant horizon held great interest.

Greer didn't push. Her mother was a hard woman but not unfeeling. Losing Jeff and then several years later her husband had devastated the woman. She couldn't fully love Greer anymore but that didn't mean she couldn't love.

"I hear you are having a fund-raiser for the Crisis Center tonight."

"You hear? From who?"

"David Edwards. He also told me about Rory and what happened."

She straightened. "What did he tell you?"

"That Rory was dead." She shook her head. "We

don't need to rehash the details." She fingered her long pearl strand. "I'd think you'd avoid the public eye, especially now."

"I did nothing wrong. I didn't have any contact with Rory." And still a tiny hint of guilt poked and prodded, asking, *Could you have done more for him?*

"That has little to do with public perception."

It shouldn't hurt that others judged her still. But it did. "I can't control what people think, nor will I worry about it."

"You should worry."

"I stopped wondering what the David Edwardses of the world thought about me a long time ago."

"Men like that can make your life hard, Elizabeth."

"Greer. My name is Greer."

Sylvia stood silent, the chipped manicured index finger wrapping and unwrapping around her strand of pearls. "Why are you doing this? Why must you bring up the past?"

Lydia's dream would not survive if Greer couldn't learn to deal with her fears of a more public life. "The Crisis Center is in real need of funds. I want to help."

Her mother studied her. "If you hadn't given all your money away, you could have written them a check."

"I didn't give it away. I invested it in the vineyard. And the Crisis Center needs the publicity as much as it does the money. It's a way I can help and I am."

Her mother shook her head. "You realize by helping a crisis center you will be raising questions about the past. I think you chose them on purpose. You want people to remember."

Ah, here was the crux of the visit. Though a flip response begged to be spoken, she saw the truth in her mother's words. She'd not only stopped running from the past but was running toward it head on. "I'm helping the Crisis Center with a need. I cannot help what people choose to think."

"Of course you can, Elizabeth. You could have chosen a different charity. Animals. The environment. Cancer, for God's sake. But you chose a center that helps people in crisis. People who have . . ."

The silence hurt more than an oath. After all this time, her mother couldn't acknowledge the pain that drove Greer to such a desperate place. "People who have tried to kill themselves."

Sylvia grimaced. "I don't think it's necessary to say it."

"Why not? It's the truth." She couldn't summon anger or outrage. Her voice remained quiet and calm. "I tried to kill myself after the accident. I'm not proud of it, and I'm forever grateful you found me in time."

Her mother raised her chin, which trembled just a little. "Don't."

Vague memories of her mother screaming for help echoed in her mind. "Thank you for saving me."

Sylvia drew in a deep breath. "You're being dramatic."

Frustration welled inside her and she found herself getting irritated despite years of telling herself her mother's opinion didn't matter. "If I can help someone who is in a bad place and keep them from making the choice I did, then I guess it's worth the risk of people dredging up the past."

"You don't care if the past gets unearthed? I would think you of all people would want to bury it deep."

"It's there regardless. Pretending it didn't happen doesn't change anything."

Sylvia's lips flattened. "When you dredge up the past, you fuel the gossips."

Greer struggled with temper and a deep disappointment. "Are you worried about me or yourself?"

Sylvia raised her chin. "Both of us."

"You have no reason to feel ashamed, Mom. You didn't do anything wrong."

"Didn't I?" For the first time in a long time raw pain flashed in her gaze. Tears glistened. "I am your mother. It is not easy for me to relive the past."

"I'm not trying to relive it, Mom. I'm trying to learn from it."

"What is there to be learned?"

"Forgiveness," she whispered.

Green eyes flashed. "Mine or yours?"

"Maybe we both need to forgive each other."

Her mother hesitated and then shook her head as if clamping her armor back in place. "Your actions are a direct reflection of me."

Bitterness settled in the pit of Greer's stomach. "So what you're saying is forgiveness is impossible?"

She huffed her exasperation. "I didn't say that."

"You didn't have to."

Sylvia shrugged her shoulders as if trying to fend off unwanted weight. "I don't need more gossip at the club."

"You don't want me to hold the fund-raiser because it could make some of your friends at the country club talk?"

"Is that so terrible? They're all I have left."

"You have me."

Sylvia moistened dry lips. For a moment she didn't speak and then she cleared her throat. "I plan to come to your fund-raiser."

"Really?"

"I'm invited, aren't I?"

Greer wrestled with the lump settling in her chest. As saddened as she was by this conversation a part of her wanted her mother to recognize what she'd accomplished. "Of course. I don't control the invitation list. The board of directors does. It never occurred to me you'd want to support me."

Sylvia arched a brow. "Don't be smart."

"I'm not being smart. I'm stating facts. You've not wanted any communication with me since the accident. Did we exchange five words at Aunt Lydia's funeral?"

"I don't do well at funerals." She shook her head. "You are so much like Lydia. She was never happy with her life. Always wanted to strike out and make her own path. I cringe when I think of the mistakes she made."

"What mistakes did she make?"

"I don't want to discuss it."

"Was loving Dad her mistake?"

Sylvia's gaze turned icy. "Did she tell you that?"

This moment confirmed the stories about Lydia, her father, and mother were true. "No. She never said a word. All I know is she took me in after I left Shady Grove. She gave me a home and a purpose."

"I often thought all this was to spite me. She could be willful and devious."

Greer flexed her fingers. She'd done her best to keep her emotions in check but if they continued on this same path she'd regret what she was going to say. "You can trash me all you want, Mom, but don't say a word against Lydia. Ever." The sharp edge to her words had her mother straightening.

"Lydia was my sister."

"I know. And you loved her. Like you loved me." In the distance the black nag whinnied and swished her tail, drawing Greer's attention away from her anger. "Thank you for coming, Mom, but I've a full day ahead of me. I have heard and understood your message. You are not happy with me. Again. But there is nothing I can do about it." She smiled as well as any Austin debutante. "We'd love to have you at the event. You can get the tickets at the center. They cost a hundred dollars each but that includes a lovely afternoon here and all the wine you can drink."

Her mother looked as if she'd say more but then thought better of it. She walked to her car, lowered herself into it, and drove away, leaving Greer standing there alone, fists clenched and more determined than ever to force herself back into the public eye.

An hour later, Greer was at her desk, trying to concentrate on a column of numbers that refused to add up. Her thoughts had been distracted by her mother's visit and, of course, Rory. Mitch. Bragg. The list grew.

A white van drove up the driveway toward the tasting room. She pulled off her glasses, rubbed her eyes, and shut off the computer screen, grateful to leave the accounts receivable behind for today. She stretched out the stiffness in her lower back and moved outside, grateful for the day's warmth after so many hours inside. She wouldn't love the heat in twenty minutes but for now it warmed her bones.

She walked up to the driver, smiling. Reggie was a stocky man with short dark hair shaded by a UT ball cap. They'd never worked together before but he'd come highly recommended by her neighbor, Philip Louis.

She held out her hand. "Reggie. Right on time."

"I hear you're hosting a party." His handshake was strong.

She cupped her hand over her eyes, shielding them from the bright sun. Another man climbed out of the front of the cab. He was younger, Hispanic and short. Like Reggie he wore the REGGIE'S CATERING shirt and khakis though his tennis shoes looked far more careworn. "We are. We're hosting a fund-raiser for the Crisis Center."

Reggie glanced around the building, his gaze appreciative. "I heard you were building out here."

"You heard?"

"From your neighbor, Mr. Louis." He jabbed his thumb up toward the house on the hill. "He keeps a close eye on all the changes at Bonneville."

Louis had been an attorney by trade but ten years ago had entered the world of winemaking. He owned a large winery in Fredericksburg and bought most of her grapes at harvest time. He'd purchased the adjacent land hoping to grow grapes as succulent and sweet as Bonneville's.

"When he has a band playing at one of his parties, the music drifts my way."

"The man knows how to throw a party and thinks he can grow grapes like you."

She smiled. "The more, the merrier."

He laughed. "So what have you built here?"

She explained about the tasting room and the winery she planned to build.

"Well, that's just great. Be sure to keep ol' Reggie in mind when you host that grand opening party."

"I will."

"According to my order you're hosting one hundred people."

"That's right."

"Will be good publicity for the vineyard." He handed her a clipboard with an inventory. "If it's those fancy folks from Austin, then this will be a good event for you. I hear they're a wine-drinking bunch."

She signed her signature on the bottom of the form, refusing to feel nervous about facing folks connected to her past. "Let's hope."

"So where do you want the food tables and chairs set up?"

"In the main tasting room. I've installed the wine shelves but not furnished it yet so you have a blank canvas." Greer had worried her wine racks would be empty but finally had to let the worry go. Next year she'd have wine and for now settled with small battery-operated votive candles in the bottle spaces, which created a glittering effect.

"Great. Shouldn't take Manny and me long. The food truck is about an hour behind us."

"In this heat you're right not to bring it all at the same time."

"One big melted mess."

She spent the next half hour helping the two unload and setting up the tables in the tasting room. She covered each table with linens and in lieu of flowers decorated each table with a cluster of wine bottles and candles. As promised the food truck arrived right as they were putting the final details on the food table.

Reggie unloaded the food, which meant Greer had about a half hour to shower and dress for the event. As she headed out of the tasting room, she spotted Reggie and his assistant unloading a dove ice sculpture. She'd not seen an ice sculpture since the night of Jeff's party—the night he died.

Despite the afternoon heat a chill ran down her spine as she watched the men wrestle the sculpture onto a pushcart. Years ago, her mother had insisted on the sculpture for her brother's birthday party. "A touch of class," her mother had said. Jeff hadn't cared less about the fancy detail but Greer remembered being jealous of her brother and the dazzling party her mother had created to celebrate his birthday.

Greer cleared her throat. "Reggie, I don't remember ordering an ice sculpture."

He settled the sculpture on the cart. "One of the folks at the center ordered and paid for it. Thought it would be a nice touch for the event."

He pushed the cart toward the air-conditioned room knowing no block of ice would last long in the heat. "Do you know who?"

The cart's wheels rolled heavily in the graveled driveway. "Not off the top of my head, but I can check when I get back to the office. I made it myself this morning. Is there a problem?"

"No. It's beautiful. I was just curious." She summoned a smile. "I need to change. I'll be back in a half hour."

"Will do. We should just about be set up by then."

"Great."

She sprinted to her house, pushing through the main door. The main room had the same polished wood floor her aunt had laid with her own hands and a large wool Indian rug warming it. A leather couch, two chairs, and an ottoman circled a large, round coffee table made of an old wagon wheel now set under glass. There was a fireplace used often on chilly winter nights and paintings of the Texas sunset. Her aunt never would say who had painted the pictures but she'd cherished the pieces.

She ducked into her room furnished with a

simple double bed, a quilt comforter, and a chair by the window for reading. Stripping as she moved, she made her way to the bathroom off her bedroom and turned on the showerhead in the single stall. Soon hot water steamed, and she climbed in under the spray.

The water splashed against her skin, washing away the dirt and the grime from the day's work. She closed her eyes, savoring this last quiet moment before the people from town arrived.

She understood that many coming didn't support the Crisis Center but wanted to see her. Many wanted to know what had happened to her after she'd deliberately dropped off the radar a dozen years ago. She'd barely moved fifty miles from her home, but she'd effectively dropped out of sight.

And now she was about to step back into it. She was about to show Austin that she was alive and well and ready to face the past and all its ugliness.

She shut off the hot tap, toweled quickly, and hurried into her room. When she'd been in town days ago, she'd ducked into a dress shop to find a dress for the evening. There'd been a time when shopping had been her mission in life and her day centered on all the right stores and the best designers. But in Zoe's dress shop she might as well have landed on an alien planet. She'd lost her knack and had wandered through the racks simply lost. Thankfully, the owner had taken pity and chosen a simple blue sheath dress that skimmed her body to her knees, gold sandals, and gold hoop earrings to match. She'd been grateful and not noticed all the items had been on sale until later.

She quickly dried her hair and applied what little make-up she owned: mascara, blush, and lip gloss. Slipping on her sandals she hurried back toward the tasting room so she could do one final inspection and be ready to meet her guests.

Today, full of chaotic activity, had given her barely any time to think or worry about much. She had hustled from one crisis to the next as she did most days at the vineyard.

The room sported three long tables, filled with food supplied by Reggie. In the center of the food stood the dove ice sculpture. Flowing cold lines added elegance to the table but its grace didn't calm her unease.

The reds were open and breathing and the whites chilling at the tasting bar. José's work, no doubt. She'd chosen six wines for tonight. Two whites, a blush, two reds, and an ice wine for interest. None was an adventurous wine but they rested easy on the palate and would be a crowd-pleaser. Other than the facility her donation tonight had been the wines. She could scarcely afford it but pride had had her offering the best. She'd not go stumbling back into her old life dragging bad wine with her.

As she stood alone in the tasting room, the beats

of silence greeting her provided enough space for apprehension to flower. This was her first party since the accident. The first time since she'd seen anyone from her old life. They were bound to judge. To scrutinize. That's what they did. And no doubt she'd be found wanting.

She conjured the image of her aunt standing beside her. *"Do you really give a crap what they have to say, Greer? Really?"*

A smile played at the edges of her lips. "No, I don't. I don't."

"And you shouldn't, kid. Don't give a crap."

Greer was smiling when the door to the tasting room opened, and she turned to find Dr. Stewart in the doorway. He wore a simple white shirt accentuating sandy hair, tanned skin, khakis, and leather loafers. He possessed a casual relaxed air that drew people.

"I expected to find you rattled with nerves, not smiling."

"Don't let the grin fool you," Greer said. "I'm a nervous wreck. In fact, I might scramble behind the bar right now and hide if you say *boo.*"

Dr. Stewart laughed. "Humor is a good sign. I think you are going to do fine."

"Keep saying that. Please. I need to hear it."

"Has Dr. Granger arrived?"

"Not yet. She said she might be a bit late." She'd also met Dr. Granger on the board. The tall redhead was a psychologist and if Greer remembered correctly was married to a Ranger. A Ranger. Great. One in her life was enough.

Dr. Stewart surveyed the room, and his face glowed with appreciation. "This looks wonderful, Greer."

"Thanks." She didn't filter out the pride from her tone.

"You've come a long way since that day we met in the hospital chapel."

They'd met minutes after her aunt had died. She'd been sitting alone in the chapel wondering what she'd do next.

"I'm proud of you." His gaze softened. "Remember when I first suggested the idea of a fund-raiser?"

It had been on the heels of her aunt's funeral when he'd brought up the idea of a signature fund-raiser. She'd summoned her courage and suggested a wine tasting.

"I feel as if you've pushed me into the deep end of the pool."

Dr. Stewart smiled. "And you are swimming just fine. Give it a little more time, and it will even feel comfortable."

"I don't know. I think I'm taking on water now." She moved toward the bar and slid behind it. "Have a drink with me?"

Wrinkles creased the edges of warm eyes. "I'd love one. Long day."

"You look as if you are dressed for court." She

set two sparkling wineglasses on the bar and filled both knowing she'd barely drink from her own. She'd face her demons tonight sober as a judge.

Dr. Stewart sipped his wine. "Lovely. I was in court today. Testifying on behalf of a mother trying to win custody of her son from an abusive father. He's got money. She doesn't. Messy."

"I bet you won them over."

"I think, hope, I did." He sipped the wine. "Really, outstanding wine, Greer."

"Thank you. That was made by a Texas winemaker who uses Bonneville grapes."

"And next year you will be making the wine."

Greer crossed her fingers. "I can't wait."

"With you at the helm, this place will really take a leap forward."

"My aunt had visions of turning the winery into a showplace."

"And now you will realize her dream. I'm proud of you, Greer."

She swirled her glass, inhaled the bouquet, and then sipped. "How about I get through the evening first. It could get ugly fast."

"You will be fine."

Greer shook her head. "Have you heard about the body the cops found on the edge of my property?"

He nodded. "A few details, not much."

She swirled her wine and watched as it coated and then dripped down the inside of her glass.

Winemakers called these drops tears, which was so appropriate now. "I knew him. From a long time ago."

Surprise flashed in his gaze. "Before the accident?"

"Just after." She studied the empty room soon to be full of guests. "I don't think most people know the dead man and I were friends."

"But his death, nonetheless, will cause more gossip."

She sipped her wine and let it coat her mouth. "Gossip is what's pulling people here tonight. I suppose the more the better."

"I promise these people don't have horns or third eyes. They put their pants on exactly like you."

A small smile. "You might be right about the pants, but I'm not so sure about the horns. This is a tough crowd."

"And you will woo them and make lots of money for the Crisis Center."

"What can I say, I'm a multitasker." Greer glanced beyond Dr. Stewart. "Is your wife coming tonight?"

"She's promised to be here but she said she'll be coming straight from work and may be late. Never know what last-minute problems come up in a pediatric practice."

Dr. Stewart spoke often of his wife, clearly taking great pride in her work. More cars arrived and she spotted Dr. Granger getting out of a BMW.

Dr. Stewart smiled as he watched Dr. Granger get out of her car.

Jo had rotated off the board as Dr. Stewart was joining. Though Greer didn't know the psychologist well, she liked her.

Jo's auburn hair, pinned back with a dark clip, accentuated her pale skin and high cheekbones. Jo would never be described as stunning, but she possessed a quality that made her lovely and unforgettable. She wore a dark suit, white blouse, and sensible high heels suggesting she'd come straight from her office.

As the two women chatted, Dr. Stewart got Jo a glass of wine and then excused himself to meet more arrivals.

Jo smiled, not raising her glass to her lips until he'd ventured outside to meet an older woman dressed in blue silk. "Mrs. Vander Hal loves Dr. Stewart. He has a way of sweet-talking her. And from what I hear he's charmed more than one or two donations out of the good citizens of Austin."

Greer watched the old woman's face light up as Dr. Stewart kissed her on the cheek. "Is your husband coming?"

"Yes."

"He's a Texas Ranger."

"That he is."

"I met a Texas Ranger the other day."

"Did you?"

"Tec Bragg."

"Ah. Bragg. A hard man to read or to be ignored."

"You've met him."

"Through my husband. He's quiet. Not fond of crowds."

"Very intense."

Jo laughed. "An understatement. How did you meet Bragg?"

"They found a man dead on the edge of my property."

The lightness in Jo's gaze dimmed. "Really? What happened?"

"The man hanged himself." Greer didn't want to delve into the details.

Jo hesitated as if waiting for details but when Greer didn't offer more, she didn't push. "How awful."

"Yes."

Outside more guests arrived and parked out front. Anxiety crept up Greer's spine. She did not want to face these people. She did not.

"You okay?" Jo said.

Greer summoned a smile. "I'm about to meet a lot of people I've not seen in years."

Jo studied cars parking outside and the people exiting the vehicles. "They don't look so scary to me."

"No?"

Jo leaned forward so only Greer could hear. "Imagine they're all naked."

Greer laughed, despite her anxiety. "Okay."

"Do you want me to hang around?"

"No." Greer appreciated the offer. "Thanks. But this is something I have to do." The first guest to arrive at the front door was Mrs. Mark Johnson. She had been a friend of her parents' and had played doubles tennis with her mother over the years. "Excuse me?"

"Of course."

Greer moistened her lips, and though she shifted her stance, she did not retreat. "Welcome."

Mrs. Johnson's black linen dress set off her tall lean frame, her silver jewelry, and her blond hair. Her ultra-smooth skin was a testimony to her favorite plastic surgeon. "Elizabeth?"

Greer extended her hand. "How are you, Mrs. Johnson?"

Mrs. Johnson studied Greer, boldly absorbing every detail. Cool fingers slipped around Greer's callused palm. "It's been a long time."

"Yes, a long time."

"When I saw your name on the invitation I just about fell over. Your mother led me to believe you'd moved to Europe."

That didn't surprise her. "No. I've been here all the time."

"I called your mother, but she didn't get back to me. She's been traveling."

Avoiding the questions. "No doubt."

"I had to do a little digging to find out you've been here working with your aunt."

"That's right." More guests were arriving out front and judging by the collection of cars the evening would be a crush. She teetered between cringing and celebrating.

Mrs. Johnson didn't notice anyone but Greer. "I have so many questions for you. But let's start with that dead man they found by your property. I heard he was David Edwards's brother."

Greer smiled, determined to be calm. *Breathe.* "So they say. Why don't you come inside and have a glass of wine."

A line of people formed behind Mrs. Johnson but again she didn't noticc. Shc caught thc gazc of her neighbor Louis. He tossed her a warm grin, and she couldn't help but relax a little.

Louis moved toward her, his long lean body accentuated by his dark trousers and dark shirt. "You look like you're holding up well."

"So far so good." Not exactly a lie.

He grinned at several older ladies who were staring at her. They looked away. "Keep up the good work. I'm excited to introduce our wines tonight."

Louis had purchased the property next to Bonneville but also owned other land in the Hill Country where he made the wine using Bonneville grapes. "They should be a huge hit."

He squeezed her hand. “I’m headed in. Holler if you need me.”

Despite nerves chewing at her, she was determined to do this well. “Right.”

She remained at the door greeting guests for at least another hour. With the sound of each new car, she expected her mother, but she never came.

She fielded more questions than she wanted to about herself. *I remember Jeff. Such a handsome man. How old would he be now? And Sydney, such a stunning girl. A perfect couple. You must miss him.*

After a while, she found she could distance herself from the story, as if she were recounting another’s life. The wounds weren’t hers. The losses belonged to someone else. Later she imagined there’d be an emotional price to pay when it was quiet and the emotions rushed back over the barriers. But for now she was getting by and that was good enough.

The tasting room was all but filled by seven, the guests laughing and enjoying themselves. She could tell the wines were a hit, and judging by the caterer’s table, so was the food.

She slipped out the front door, needing to get away from subtle and not-so-subtle stares and whispers. *She looks good. Reminds me of her brother more than ever. She was here the whole time? She must think of Jeffrey. Did you notice the scar on her arm? And those bracelets. I think they're engraved with their names.*

The heat, which still tipped the thermometer at ninety-nine, would allow only a quick respite, but a little break was better than none. The night air was fresh, not heavy, and the sky filled with stars. In the distance a coyote howled.

The crunch of tire against gravel had her turning toward a dusty, black SUV. A tall man with a white Stetson climbed out and she immediately recognized Ranger Winchester, Jo's husband. Not Bragg. Relief rushed over her like a burst of cold air.

The Ranger settled his hat on his head and moved toward the tasting room with a quick impatient stride. She'd noticed the way he watched Jo, lean, hungry, impatient, as if he could barely keep his hands off his wife. He adored her.

She opened the door for him. "Welcome, Ranger Winchester."

He glanced at her and grinned. "Ms. Templeton. Good evening. I'm guessing my better half has paved the way for me."

His easy smile had her relaxing as she extended her hand. "She has sung your praises."

He took her hand. "So I hear you're the one throwing the party tonight."

"I'm one of many players." She glanced inside toward Jo who laughed with a young couple. "Your wife knows everyone."

“That’s my Jo.” He glanced beyond her as if trying to glimpse his wife.

“I’ve seen her glancing toward the door. I think she’s been waiting for you. Glad you could make it.”

He winked. “She’s the only one slippery enough to rope me into one of these parties. No offense.”

“None taken.” He must be aware of Rory’s murder. The Rangers were a small, elite group. For a moment she stood tense, waiting for a question. When none came to breach the growing silence, she was tempted to ask him about Bragg, but quickly decided that could lead to trouble. “The food is worth the crowd.”

“Well, seeing as I never say no to food, I’ll dive into the hornet’s nest. Wish me luck.”

“Luck.” When he vanished into the building, she thought for a moment the evening would end without any great drama. She might walk away in one piece and sane.

The crunch of boots against gravel had her turning and wondering why she’d not heard another car drive up. She saw Bragg making his way up the drive straight toward her.

Chapter Ten

Wednesday, June 4, 8 P.M.

He stood tall, his white Stetson settled squarely on top of his head. He wore dark pants, a white shirt, a string tie, and black snakeskin boots. Whereas Winchester moved with impatience, Bragg's stride radiated caution.

She rubbed suddenly damp palms together and then forced herself to relax. "Ranger Bragg, I wasn't expecting you tonight."

Surprise, and then a hint of appreciation flickered from his gaze as he reconciled her voice with her appearance. She allowed pride and was glad to know she could still garner appreciation. There'd been a time when she'd lived to turn a man's head. She'd spent hours primping and pampering. If this had been twelve years ago, she'd have considered herself severely underdressed.

He moved to within inches of her. Soap mingled with a masculine scent. "Ranger Winchester told me about it. I hear his wife was talking this party up."

"I'm glad you could join us."

He arched a brow. "Are you?"

"Of course." Tempted to take a step back, she

stood her ground. The scar on his face caught her attention before she wrestled it free. "We've a nice Merlot and a Chardonnay at the bar."

If he sensed her nerves, he wasn't inclined to ease them. "Afraid I'm more of a beer man."

His tone was light and easy but the idea of relaxing around him was downright foolish. Even sleeping rattlers were dangerous snakes. "Tell the bartender. We've several local beers behind the bar as well."

"A vineyard owner drinks beer?"

"We can be quite the beer drinkers." She extended her arm toward the tasting room. She wanted to shoo him into the tasting room far away from her. "The food's also delicious."

Instead of leaving, he held his ground, but his gaze moved to the party. "You got a lot of fancy folks in there."

"They dress up well, but they're exactly like the rest of us."

"First time you've seen a lot of these folks in a while?"

He'd been asking around about her. "That's right."

"How's it going?"

"About as well as you could expect. I'm sure my ears will be burning for a week or two and then people will forget about me. I'm the flavor of the week."

"I doubt they'll forget you." An edge sharpened his words.

Her heart beat faster. "You overestimate me."

"Rory Edwards didn't forget you."

The statement hit her square in the chest like a one-two punch. "No, he did not. Have you found out what happened to Rory?"

"Still working on it. His brother didn't have many nice words to say about you."

"No, I don't suppose David did." The last time she'd spoken to David was when she'd shown up at Rory's house. Her aunt had driven her there right after she'd left Shady Grove. David had answered the door. She couldn't remember the entire conversation, but it ended along the lines of: they didn't need her kind of trouble. "I was young and very upset the last time I spoke to him."

"You made a hell of an impression on him."

She refused to attach to the anger and frustration building in her. "If you are here to enjoy the party, then please do so. But if you're here to dig up my past, I'm not going to play tonight. I've made a commitment to raise money for the Crisis Center and I won't be effective if you reduce me to tears."

His eyes sparked with humor. "You don't look like you're about to cry to me."

"Don't believe it."

He shook his head. "You're one tough gal, Ms. Templeton. I bet you do exactly what needs to be done no matter how tough the job."

"That good or bad?"

"Suppose that depends on what job needs to be done." He studied her a beat. And then as if rethinking his line of questioning, he said, "How's Mitch doing?"

"Quiet. But a hard worker. I like the kid."

"Why?"

She shook her head. "He's patient and kind with the animals. Beauty is not an easy horse, but he keeps his cool no matter how difficult she can be."

He rested his hand on his hip inches from his badge. "Tell me why you hired Mitch."

Insistence underscored his words, and she had the sense he'd not take her standard line of making the world a better place. She shoved out a breath and opted for the pure truth. "He reminds me of myself." *And my brother.*

"How so?"

"I know he served in Iraq and he saw some bad stuff. I know he lost friends. I also know the kind of pain that goes with losing someone you love. I thought I could give him a place to heal."

"What makes you an expert?"

"In all honesty, I don't know if what I'm doing is right. But sitting around and isolating himself is not doing him a bit of good. Working with the animals helped me. Spending hours in the vineyard pulling weeds and picking grapes gave me a focus. I thought it might help him."

He glanced toward the empty corral. "My

nephew is not a project to make you feel better about yourself."

"No. No, he is a young man who needs time to heal."

"And when he's better, you'll cut him loose?" Anger edged the words.

"He may cut me loose. He may wake up one morning and feel like his old self and take off. I have no idea what's going to happen. Like I said, I don't have a master plan."

Bragg didn't strike her as the kind of guy who had a family. She couldn't imagine him living in a house with the white picket fence. "You must have been young when Mitch was born."

"He's my older sister's boy. She was nineteen. I was fifteen."

No elaboration. Mitch had said she'd died three years ago. Her death had left a hole in their lives. As much as Greer wanted to ask, she didn't. Tec Bragg's personal life was none of her business, even if it intrigued her. "Mitch is a good kid."

"He is." He settled his hands on his hips. "Keep an eye on him. And keep me posted on his progress. Let me know what he's thinking."

"We've been through this. I already addressed that."

"Not to my satisfaction."

She laughed. "Your way or the highway."

"That's right."

She found herself waiting for a smile to soften

the words and let her know he wasn't that black and white. None came. "I can only do what I think is best for Mitch. If he confides in me, I'm not going to go running to you with the information."

Frown lines deepened. "He's my family."

"He's a man."

"I know that." Annoyance flashed. "He had another dream last night."

"That explains the bruise on your chin."

"Kid's got a punch like a jackhammer."

She shook her head. "The best we can do is give him the opportunity to work through and find his way out of it."

"*We*. Good. Then we're a team."

"I didn't say that."

"Yes, you did."

The door to the tasting room opened and the sounds of conversations and laughter trickled out. "I need to go."

He frowned but simply nodded. Unsure of what else to say to him, she returned to her party, surprised she was happy to reenter the lion's den if it meant getting away from Ranger Bragg.

Bragg watched Greer disappear back into her party. He didn't need a guest list to know the people inside were the Who's Who of Austin society. And though Greer had been born into that world, he recognized she didn't fit there anymore. She smiled. She moved from couple to couple chatting. She filled wineglasses. But she was the outsider. People stared at her oddly when she walked away. They talked about her.

Twelve years had passed since the accident and her suicide attempt, and yet she remained cut off from her old life. Though he sensed the society crowd could be judgmental and hard, he also realized Greer was as much a party to her isolation as anyone. She'd built a wall around herself: always polite, guarded, and distant.

Greer punished herself with her self-imposed isolation. She hadn't rejoined the world, choosing purgatory instead.

She'd maintained a distance with him, but that didn't really surprise him. Most folks didn't cozy up to Rangers right away, and publicity surrounding his work on the border had changed how people viewed him. Leeriness now simmered under the respect. Some folks were flat-out afraid of him.

Mitch wasn't afraid nor were the Rangers, but most everyone else kept their distance. Greer met his gaze directly, no hint of fear. If she'd heard about his past, she gave no sign it bothered her. She noticed the scar as well, but didn't appear put off by it. And he was oddly glad.

Curious, he moved inside and stood in the back of the tasting room. His gaze scanned the room quickly and then settled on Greer. A stunning dark dress hugged her figure just right. Her hair glistened in the soft light. But if he had to choose, he preferred her in her jeans, T-shirt, and hair in a thick braid.

She now stood at the front of the room next to a tall slim man who wore an expensive suit, white shirt, but no tie. Blond hair swept off a face of chiseled features and smooth skin. Appreciation glistened in the man's eyes as he stared at Greer.

Bragg shifted his stance, annoyance snapping at his heels.

Greer rang a bell and soon the hum of conversation in the room faded. She clenched and unclenched her fingers and then offered a big bright smile. To the casual eye, her smile was radiant but there were subtle cues indicating the opposite. A stiff back, raised chin, and a slight quiver in the corner of her mouth told him the smile was a lovely front.

But judging by the attentive expressions around the room, he wondered if anyone peered beyond the smile.

"Welcome to Bonneville Vineyard's first annual fund-raiser for Austin's Crisis Center. Our vineyard has been here for over twenty years and though we don't make our own wine, we hope to by this time next year. Tonight, I want to introduce you to Philip Louis, who is supplying tonight's wine from Sun Valley Vineyard in Fredericksburg." She grinned at Louis. He smiled back at her, his gaze hungry and excited.

"Bonneville supplied the grapes to Mr. Louis who, at his winery in Fredericksburg, turned them into several lovely wines."

"Greer." Louis's voice was smooth, even, and deep. His smile was quick and easy. "Thank you for having Sun Valley Vineyard here tonight. It's a great honor to introduce our wines to such a sophisticated audience."

People in the crowd responded well to the compliment. Louis coaxed people to follow like a damned pied piper.

Bragg shifted his attention to Greer, curious about her reaction to Louis. She didn't shy away from him nor did she lean toward him. Her smile was genuine but not flirty. She liked Louis, but he suspected she saw him as a colleague and not a potential lover. Good.

"The winemaker and the wine grower must have a close relationship," Greer said.

"But great wine begins on the vine," Louis added. "If not for Greer's talent for reading the soil, air, and water, I would not have such stunning grapes to put into my winery. We will be sorry to lose Bonneville grapes next season but anticipate tasting their wine. And now that we are neighbors, we hope to grow grapes as rich and succulent."

An older woman dressed in a sapphire-blue dress raised her hand. "Greer, the soil here looks awful. Why on earth choose such a rocky, hot place as Bonneville?"

Greer relaxed when attention turned to Bonneville. “The vines need to suffer to produce grapes of character. When the roots must burrow into the earth and fight to survive, they develop a wonderful complexity. The struggle is what makes them so flavorful.” She spoke about careful strategizing, of watching the grapes closely, of taste-testing the fruit. “Great art comes from stress and hard work.”

Greer, like her vineyard, was the product of struggle and hardship. If she’d lived a pampered life in Austin, she’d not have been as unique or interesting.

As waiters filled the patrons’ first glasses with a white wine, Greer watched as Louis talked about the first wine, a Viognier. “Tasting is not drinking. You drink with food but you taste the wine naked.” He held the glass high and talked about the color and how it should be admired. He then swirled the wine in the glass and put his nose into the flute.

Louis’s explanation about wines held no interest for Bragg. He found the whole party a foolish dog-and-pony show. You either liked what was in your glass or you didn’t.

However, his interest for Greer remained keen. He watched as she smelled her wine, closed her eyes, and tasted. Her face softened and took on a sensual, seductive quality. Bragg’s body tensed with desire and he imagined peeling the dress from her honeyed skin. Would she show him that same expression as he kissed her?

Unsettled by the veracity of his attraction to Greer, he stepped outside. For a moment he stood with his back to the tasting room, staring at the stars blinking in the black sky.

The door to the tasting room opened and Winchester and his wife, Jo, appeared. Jo's smile suggested the two had slipped away from the crowd for a private moment.

"Party's inside," Bragg said.

Winchester grinned and held his wife close. "I like the one outside better."

Jo jabbed her husband in the ribs. "Brody."

Winchester shrugged as his grin widened. He showed no sign of loosening his hold on his wife.

Bragg watched the two banter for a moment, wondering what it would be like to have a woman at his side. He'd never given it much thought, knowing the life he'd chosen didn't leave room for families. He'd never questioned the decision until Mitch had made him accountable for someone other than himself.

"Well, I for one am ready to leave," Winchester said.

Jo smiled. "I suppose you've done your duty and mingled."

"You leaving?" Winchester said.

Bragg nodded. "In a minute or two."

Winchester glanced past Bragg to Greer, who stood at the front of the room. "There a reason to stick around?"

"No reason. Just enjoying the night air for a minute or two."

"Well, we'll leave you."

Jo smiled. "Night, Bragg."

He touched the brim of his hat. "Ma'am."

Bragg lingered outside watching Greer. She moved with an easy confidence he'd not seen when they'd first met or before this evening. He shouldn't care one way or the other, but he liked seeing her smile.

The door opened, the din of laughter escaping into the night as a tall slim man stepped outside. The door closed and the man glanced up at Bragg. "Good evening."

Bragg touched the brim of his hat. "Evening."

The man cocked his head and extended his hand. "Texas Ranger?"

"Yes, sir."

"Hope it's not trouble bringing you out here tonight."

"No, sir." He wasn't sure really what had brought him out here tonight.

The man extended his hand. "Dr. Andy Stewart."

The name registered immediately. "You speak to a group of veterans?"

"I speak to them regularly."

"My nephew is a marine. Mitch Bragg. He's been in your group."

Dr. Stewart nodded in recognition. "Mitch. Good guy. I thought he didn't have family. Said his mother died and his father ran off."

"He's got me." The words tumbled out with surprising authority. "Is it your doing he's working out here?"

The doctor shrugged. "I connect people who might be of help to each other. Greer needed someone to help with the vineyard. Mitch needed work and purpose. Seemed a good fit."

Bragg managed a smile for the doctor, but couldn't decide if he liked him or not. "I hear it was your idea for the fund-raiser."

"It was."

"And Ms. Templeton jumped at the idea of inviting everyone out here?"

He chuckled. "It took some coaxing," he offered. "She's a bit shy."

Bragg tossed a line in the water, wondering what the good doctor might offer. "I read about the accident. She's had a tough road back."

Dr. Stewart's sympathy for Greer was evident. "That's why she's such an invaluable asset to the center. She understands tough times."

"She's a stubborn gal," Bragg said. "You must have done some real fast talking to get her to do this."

"I did."

“How does she handle herself at the Crisis Center?”

“Very professional. Effective with callers.”

“How so?”

“She’s good with people.”

“I suppose her past left a lasting mark.”

Dr. Stewart smiled. “Ranger Bragg, I coax information out of people for a living. I know when someone’s on a fishing expedition.”

Bragg grinned. “Hazard of the job.”

The door to the tasting room opened and a laughing couple emerged. “Well, it’s been a long day. I need to get going.”

“Nice meeting you, doc.”

“You as well, Ranger Bragg.”

As the doctor walked toward his car, Bragg’s gaze trailed him. When he’d driven off, Bragg’s gaze skimmed the horizon and landed on a glimmer of light up on a distant hill. It was a house. He thought about the pictures of Greer that had been taken with a telephoto lens. The angle would be about right to get some of the shots.

He looked back inside at Greer, who stood near a group of folks made of money. Now that her presentation had ended her smile had faded. When she wasn’t talking about her grapes she wasn’t happy. Doing penance was the sense he got.

She felt guilty. Unworthy. Was it the accident or was there another secret she was hiding from everyone?

• • •

Their group had been tight-knit. Two boys and three girls. None had known each other before camp but now they knew they'd be friends forever.

Forever. Forever had proven to be fragile for the three remaining teenage girls standing around the campfire holding hands, matching red rope bracelets dangling. Fingers clasped tight, they fought tears. Their numbers were dwindling. First Sam had left and then Rory. Elizabeth didn't have Sam's address but Rory had given his freely so she'd written him and told him how much she missed him. Every day when mail arrived she rushed to the counselor's office to see if he'd written. No correspondence from her mother. Not a card or letter from Rory. She'd grown accustomed to her mother's silence since Jeff's death, but Rory's silence stung.

Tomorrow Joan would leave and soon Robin would go. Elizabeth prayed they didn't abandon her like the others.

Tears ran down Robin's face as she shook her downcast head. "I swear I'm going to write and call and visit. I know we've not heard from Rory, but I will be different. I'm not going to forget you guys."

Joan nodded. "Me, too. I'm not like

Rory. I promise I won't forget." She squeezed Elizabeth's hand a little harder. "I'm sorry Rory didn't love you enough to stay connected."

Elizabeth wasn't such a young fool that she didn't realize Rory was weak and needed support or that Joan wanted him. In here she'd been his support. But out in the real world, there was no telling whom he'd turned to. And she didn't want to lose him. She loved him. She'd already lost so much. "Please don't forget me."

Joan frowned. "I will be different. I won't forget."

"Me, either," Robin said. "It will be different with us."

It will be different with us.

The words swirled in Elizabeth's head. But when she turned to hug her friends, they were gone.

She was alone.

She searched the circle frantically for Robin and Joan but couldn't find them.

From the woods an owl hooted. She stared into the dense ring of trees expecting one of her friends. But there was no one.

And when she turned back to the campfire, the embers had died and darkness swooped on her like a net.

• • •

Greer sat up in bed, her heart racing, and sweat matting her hair against her forehead. She dragged shaking fingers through her hair and allowed a sigh to shudder from her.

The other night she'd dreamed of the accident and now Shady Grove. Rory. Tonight's party. Both events had triggered too many past losses.

When she'd come to Bonneville she'd made the choice to put the past behind her. And she had. It had taken time to build herself up but she had. She'd not only learned how to work on the estate but how to run it. She was Bonneville. She was not the frightened teen at Shady Grove.

And still her hands shook. And her heart raced.

Sara woke up in stages. Her head pounded and her mouth was as dry as cotton. She pushed up from the floor, her brain confused. She couldn't figure out where she was now.

Moistening dry lips, she steadied herself as she drew in air. Cold, refreshing air, to the point of bracing. Confused, she searched the gray metal room. Patches of frost clung to the walls. Where was she?

She rubbed her chilled arms as she rose. The cold floor burned into her bare feet and she discovered her shoes were gone.

She drew her designer jacket closed, but its summer-weight fabric was a paltry match against the cold. It had been designed to withstand the Texas summer heat, not a Montana winter.

She studied the windowless room. Not more than ten by ten, it had the look of a large industrial freezer. But no meat hung from hooks, no frozen foods stocked the shelves, no ice blocks flanked the walls.

The room was completely clean save for the bits of ice and frosting clinging to the walls.

"Oh, God!" She ran to the door, silk stockings sticking to the cold floor and ripping as she moved. She pounded on the door. "Let me out! There's been a mistake!"

It couldn't have been the man. He'd been normal. And she'd vetted him completely, calling his contacts back East and doing a complete check on him. He couldn't have done this to her. It made no sense.

The cold burrowed deeper into her bones. She pounded harder on the door. "Let me out! Please!"

After minutes of silence, the chill demanded she generate warmth in her body. Moving around the room, she searched for another way out, slamming her fists against the walls until her hands burned from the cold. There was no escape from this icy prison.

Returning to the door, she beat on it with her fist until she couldn't raise her arm anymore.

"Who is doing this to me?"

Her answer was a blast of cold air into the vault. She shivered, her silk blouse little help against the bone-gnawing cold.

So where was she? How had she gotten here? "Think, Sara. Think."

She struggled to remember the man she'd seen last. He'd wanted retail space for restaurants. He'd not thrown off one signal triggering worry or making her think twice. He'd carried a cooler in the trunk of his car, and it had been stocked with bottles of cold water. She'd gladly accepted the water. Though she'd grown accustomed to the Texas summer heat, she'd drank too much last night, and was thirsty. She'd drained the bottle.

They'd taken a dozen steps toward the warehouse when fatigue settled in her bones. At first she'd blamed it on the heat, but the lethargy had rushed through her, draining all her strength. When her legs had given way, strong arms had caught her.

And then she'd woken up here.

Hot tears burning her eyes, she tilted her head back against the wall. "Why are you doing this? I don't know you."

Her answer was the whoosh of the cold air flowing in the vents.

For a moment she closed her eyes. The cold sapped her energy as the heat had earlier. It drew her inward and coaxed her to shut out the world and draw into herself.

"You like the cold, don't you?" The soft, soothing voice came over a loudspeaker.

Her eyes opened. "Who's there?"

"You've always been drawn to the cold. Remember that winter when the snows were so heavy, and you couldn't resist going out into the drifts?"

She blew on her bluish fingertips. "That was a long time ago. I was wrong to go into the snow."

"You weren't wrong. In fact, it was probably the first time in your life you did something right. It was the first time you followed our true path."

"My true path is not to freeze to death." She flexed fingers and then shook them hoping to keep the blood circulating. That's when she noticed the red rope bracelet around her wrist. With a trembling hand she touched the uneven braided thread.

Immediately, her mind tripped back to the day she'd received a similar bracelet. She'd hated that bracelet as much as she hated this one.

Gripping it in her hand, she ripped it from her wrist and tossed it on the icy floor. "I'm supposed to live my life."

"Do you remember why you went into the cold?"

She thought about the package she'd received on Monday. Sick. Twisted. "I don't know who you are but I don't want to play this sick game. I want you to let me out of here!"

"You don't really want out, do you? Aren't you

tired of struggling each day just to get up in the morning? You work hard at looking like you're happy but you're not."

"I'm fine." Her teeth chattered. "I've made the best of my life. Ask anyone."

Soft laughter rumbled over the speaker. "You can say it as many times as you like, Sara. But we both know the truth. You don't want to live. How could you want to live after what you did?"

A sadness colder than the frigid room twisted around her heart. "I've done nothing wrong."

"Your mother didn't see it that way. What was it that she called you? Slut? Whore?"

Sara shook her head. "Shut up. You don't know my mother."

"I know a lot about your mother and you. She hated you after she found out what you'd done. What did she call you?"

Sara shut her eyes and shook her head. Perhaps her mother didn't say the words, but that didn't mean she didn't feel. How could a mother not love a child? "My mother loves me. My mother loves me."

"That's what you want to believe, isn't it, Sara? You want her to tell you she loves you."

"I don't need to hear it. I know it."

"Sara, you are going to die today."

"I'm not."

"You are." The voice was tender and soft. "That fact is a given and won't change."

"No."

"It's okay. You know what it feels like to let the cold seep into your bones and steal your life. This is how you tried to kill yourself all those years ago. You ran into the snowstorm without shoes and in your pajamas. You huddled under a tree, and you waited for death to take you."

"That was a mistake! I know that!"

"When you lay dying, what did you wish for most?"

"I didn't make a wish!"

That was a lie. She'd wished for several things that night. Most of all she'd wanted to turn back the hands of the clock and erase her meeting Colin Little, the nights of awkward sex, the pregnancy, and the abortion.

Sara, how could you have been such a stupid slut. Your actions are of common trailer trash. You make me sick!

Uncontainable hot tears now spilled over her cold face, burning a path to her chin.

"It's okay to cry," he said. "It's okay to give in to the pain you've carried for so long."

"I've not carried the pain." That was a lie. She had never fully wrestled free of the pain. To this day an icy chill lingered between Sara and her mother. No matter how hard she worked to distance herself from the past it always lurked in the shadows.

"I have a fiancé," she said. "He will miss me."

"He won't miss you. Your mother won't miss you. You are going to fade away, Sara, like you never happened."

More tears fell. "Stop it."

"No. I can't stop."

Sara rubbed her hands together as her teeth chattered. As she did she noticed the slim red bracelet curled on the floor. It had been a symbol of friendship. Of loyalty. Though she'd pledged like the others, she'd never intended to keep her promises. She'd thrown away her bracelet the moment she'd left camp.

And now it was back.

Sara tipped her head back. Tears welled in her eyes. "Is this about that time? Is this about that stupid confession?"

"Tell me your dying wish. No one should die without their last wish being fulfilled."

Her teeth chattered. "I don't have a wish."

"Sara, you do. Tell me."

He spoke to her as if they were great friends. As if she could bare her soul, show him all her warts and he'd never judge or think less of her.

"I want . . ."

"Tell me," he coaxed.

She closed her eyes. "I want to hear my mother say she loves me."

For a moment there was only silence and then she heard her mother's voice. *"I love you, Sara."*

Sara sat straighter and searched the corners of the room half expecting her mother. But she remained alone.

"I love you, Sara."

It was her mother's voice as clear and distinct as it had always been.

"I love you, Sara."

The words sounded sweet and perfect. "That's not my mother's voice. It's a fake."

"Not fake, Sara. You requested to hear her voice and that's what I've given you. It wouldn't be fair of me to rob you of your dying wish."

"I love you, Sara. I love you, Sara."

Sara glanced toward the discarded red rope bracelet and then closed her eyes, listening to the sweet words rolling over her.

She huddled close to the wall, not cold anymore but oddly warm. It was as if the cold had wrapped around her like a big blanket and held her close as her mother had done many years ago.

Sara gave in to the cold and felt oddly grateful.

I love you, Sara. I love you.

Chapter Eleven

Thursday, June 5, 6 A.M.

The sun crested the horizon as Bragg wound up the gravel driveway to the house overlooking Bonneville. A quick check had confirmed Philip Louis owned the property and Rory's body had been found on the border between this tract and Bonneville.

The house at the top of the drive was all new construction. Sleek and modern, it sat on the hill as if it had staked a claim.

He parked and instead of ringing the doorbell, he walked around the property searching for a view of Greer's house. Following a stone path, he wound around the house until he came to a small backyard. From the yard he had a clear view of the valley below, including Greer's ranch house.

Hand on hip, he stood and stared. It would be easy to photograph her from here. As he turned, he saw her emerge from her house. From this distance without a telephoto lens he couldn't tell what she was doing. But he saw her plain as day.

She'd had a late night but had risen early. He gave her credit. She had an iron grip that kept her moving no matter what.

Feeling a bit like a stalker himself, he turned

from the view to find a man hustling across the back lawn.

"Excuse me?" A man's groggy voice drifted over to him. Bragg looked at Philip Louis standing there in shorts, an unbuttoned shirt, and bare feet as if he'd just rolled out of bed. His hair stuck up on end. Hardly the smooth winemaker of last night.

Bragg approached him with several steps. "Ranger Tec Bragg."

"What are you doing here?"

He nodded over his shoulder. "You have a clear view of Bonneville from here."

Louis frowned. "Yeah, so?"

A not-too-friendly smile tweaked the edge of his mouth. "How long have you owned this land?"

"A few years. Bought it from Lydia Bonneville. Why are you asking?"

"We found a body not too far from your house on Monday."

Louis yawned. "Yeah, I heard about that."

"Did you?"

"My surveyors told me. Used it as an excuse to delay their work."

"They can't work in the area of the crime scene until I release it."

Louis sniffed. "And when is that going to be?"

"Can't say." He turned back toward the view of Bonneville and Greer. "Found pictures of Greer in the dead man's rented room. He was taking pictures of her from right about here."

Louis shook his head. "That's impossible. No one has been up here."

"You sure about that?"

"Sure. Why not?"

Bragg shrugged. "That could lead me to believe that you took the pictures."

Louis's eyes narrowed. "Look, if you are insinuating that I had anything to do with that guy you're wrong. I couldn't even tell you his name."

"Rory Edwards. That ring a bell?"

"No."

"How long you known Greer Templeton?"

"Eight years, since I started buying my grapes from Bonneville."

A bite of jealousy jabbed at Bragg simply because the man had known her for years, and he'd just met her days ago. "You own a winery in Fredericksburg, right?"

"Yeah, sure. That's no secret."

"Why buy this land?"

"Because it's great land, and if I can duplicate Greer's success in growing grapes, then it won't hurt so bad when she doesn't sell hers to me anymore."

"Her making her own wine, that a problem for you?"

Annoyance flashed. "Yeah, it is. I like her grapes,

and I don't need any more competition than I already have."

"Make you mad enough to derail her operation?"

He shook his head. "No. Why would you say something like that?"

"Suppose I got a suspicious mind." He grinned. "But then I guess that's why the Rangers pay me the big bucks."

Louis did not laugh, but he tempered his annoyance and tried to relax his stance. "I don't like Greer going toe-to-toe with me, but I'll live with it. I like her. Respect her. I don't want to hurt her."

Hadn't that been what Bragg's daddy had said when he'd been beating the tar out of him? *You make me lose my temper.*

"Sure about that?"

Louis ran long fingers through already ruffled hair. "Yes, damn sure. Look, do I need to get a lawyer?"

Bragg worked the stiffness from his shoulders. "Only if you feel like you need one."

Bragg studied the guy, not liking him for no other reason than he'd stood too close to Greer last night and had spoken words that had made her laugh. He pulled a card from his breast pocket and handed it to the man. "If you see anyone up here, Mr. Louis, best let me know. Someone is spying on Ms. Templeton, and I don't like it one bit. Not one bit."

• • •

Bragg's cell rang as he approached the front doors leading into Ranger headquarters minutes after eight. He unclipped the phone, glanced at the number, and recognized it as dispatch. "Ranger Bragg."

"Sir, this is Officer Paul Smith with DPS. I've been asked to give you a call."

Bragg paused, hand on the front door. "What can I do for you?"

"We have a body. A woman froze to death in a meat locker on the east end of town."

Bragg turned from the air-conditioned lobby sensing he'd not see his desk anytime soon. DPS didn't call the Rangers on a whim. "I'm not sure why you're calling me."

"The responding officer first thought the woman had committed suicide but on closer inspection he believes she was murdered."

Like Rory Edwards. "Have you identified the victim?"

"Her purse was in the room beside her. Her driver's license identifies her as Sara Wentworth."

"I'm not familiar with the name."

"Judging by her clothes and home address she comes from money."

Like Rory. "Where's the body?"

The officer gave Bragg directions, and he was in his car and headed toward East Austin in less than a minute. As he drove, he called Winchester and filled him in on the details.

"I'll be there soon," Winchester said.

The drive took Bragg twenty minutes in morning traffic. When he pulled up in the East Austin parking lot, his mind already ticked through a checklist that might connect this victim to Rory Edwards or Greer Templeton.

Surrounded by cop cars and media, the area had a frenetic quality. Cops, clearly not assigned to the case, had gathered here, curious as anyone about what was happening. Two media vans were set up across the street.

He scanned the perimeter tape to make sure the area was under control. He didn't need anyone, curious cops or media, contaminating the scene.

He got out, settled his white hat on his head, and moved toward the first uniformed officer. He approached a tall slim officer with graying hair and a thick mustache. The nameplate on his chest read SMITH.

Bragg extended his hand. "Officer Smith. You called me?"

Smith's handshake was firm. "Yes, sir. I wasn't sure if this case fell into your jurisdiction, but I remembered the Edwards murder from the morning briefing. Rich. Apparent suicide. Murder. This victim hit all those notes. Plus you don't often see a rich white woman in East Austin frozen to death."

Bragg nodded as he pulled rubber gloves from his pocket. "Appreciate the call. I'll have a look."

He ducked under the yellow crime-scene tape and moved toward the three-story building once housing meat. The paint peeled and the sign that had read SAWYER'S PACKING had faded. A thick, rusted chain, cut in two, and a padlock lay puddled by the front door and several of the windows were busted.

He nodded to several other uniforms and paused as his gaze adjusted to the dimmer light. He glanced around the large space, full of dust and cobwebs. Crossing the cracked tile floors, he moved toward the bank of freezers and the one sectioned off with more crime-scene tape. The forensic tech's camera flashed several times inside the freezer.

He waited outside the freezer door and glanced inside. Rebecca Rio, with DPS forensics, stood over the body, her camera focused on the light blue, frosted face of a young woman. The woman lay on her side, curled in a tight ball as if she could draw deeply into herself and protect her body from the frigid temperatures. The room had been open for a couple of hours but still held a chill, making his skin prickle.

The victim was nude from the waist up. Discarded near her body were a beige, lightweight suit jacket, blue silk blouse, and bra. She still wore her skirt and pantyhose, but no shoes. Her fingers curled into tight fists clutching the folds of her jacket close. Hair was blond, pulled back in a neat ponytail and make-up applied with a skilled hand. However the mascara, frozen and now thawed, streaked over pale cheeks leaving a trail of black tears.

Despite the state of undress, she was no homeless woman or hooker from the streets. This woman did indeed come from money and quality. Women like her did not come to this part of town.

"Officer Rio," Bragg said. "So what are your impressions?"

Rio brushed a springy black curl off her face with the back of her hand. "She froze to death."

He studied her naked torso, curled into a C shape. "Signs of sexual assault?"

"None I saw but the medical examiner will have to check. I think the undressing isn't a case of sexual assault but of paradoxical undressing."

"Explain."

"In about thirty to fifty percent of the cases, the victim suffering from severe hypothermia gets confused and disoriented and actually believes they're getting hotter. They take off their clothes. Of course this just accelerates heat loss, and they die that much faster."

He thought about her peeling off the lightweight jacket, designed for Texas's summer heat, and believing she was hot. He glanced at her discarded clothes and noticed the blouse had been ripped, as if she'd torn it off herself. "Be sure to run a rape kit. I don't want any assumptions at this point."

"Will do."

"Signs of trauma?"

"None I've seen so far. No cuts or scrapes and no bruising. Like she just walked in here and closed the door behind her."

At first glance, Rory had hung himself. Only a closer inspection revealed the hand of another. "Fingerprints?"

"I've not dusted yet. That comes next. But I'm sure I'm going to get a lot of prints. A place like this sees vagrants."

"I'd like a tox screen run. I can't believe she merely walked in here."

Rio glanced toward her purse. "See her purse in the corner?"

He glanced toward the black bag, tossed on its side and the contents spilling out. "Yeah."

"If she were going to kill herself, why bring in her purse? She'd not have needed it where she was headed."

"Habit?"

"Maybe. But it seems she'd have not bothered. And her cell is missing and it's as if someone rifled through her bag, took it, and tossed her purse in here."

"Maybe she lost her nerve. Maybe she was looking for a way out of here."

Rio shrugged. "That option wouldn't get my vote."

Bragg nodded. "What about a driver's license?"

"By the purse."

He moved to the purse and spotted the license lying faceup. He shot a picture with his phone. Straightening, he studied the image. Sara Jane Wentworth. Age thirty-two. No denying the victim was Sara Wentworth.

The old picture of Greer and Rory came to mind. "Find any pictures at the scene. Photographs?"

"No."

"Make sure you bag all the clothes and her belongings. I want to go through them all."

"Sure. And did the officer tell you about the tape?"

"What tape?"

"An audiotape was playing when the officers arrived."

"What was on the tape?"

"A woman's voice. She kept saying, 'I love you, Sara.' "

"What did the voice sound like?"

Rio glanced toward the officer outside the freezer door. "Key up the tape."

The officer nodded and seconds later they all heard, "I love you, Sara."

Bragg listened, almost fearing he'd hear the rusty, whiskey quality of Greer's voice. But this voice was older and the Texas accent deeper.

"Any idea who the voice belongs to?" he said.

"None. That's for you to figure."

He nodded. “How long do you think she’s been in here?”

“The cold will make that a hard one to pin. At least hours.”

He studied the icy walls now dripping with the heat streaming in from the door. “What powered the freezer?”

“A big generator with enough gas to run for another twelve hours.”

“I’ll leave you to the scene. I want to go outside and trace the steps into the building.”

“Will do, Ranger Bragg.”

Bragg threaded his way through the growing number of cops assembling in and outside of the warehouse. This bizarre death scene would soon make the news.

He spotted Winchester as the other Ranger pulled up in his black Bronco. Out of his car, Winchester stopped and surveyed the scene. The Ranger’s scowl deepened as he studied the warehouse.

Bragg shrugged, knowing soon the heat of the day would make getting around tedious. “It’s like DPS said. Female frozen to death in a freezer.”

“It’s going to be one hundred and ten today.”

“Officers tell me the temperature in that freezer dropped below zero.”

“Frozen to death in the Texas heat. Do you think she did it on purpose?”

“No.”

"We need to talk to her family and find out if she had a history of suicide attempts."

"Agreed," Bragg said. He gave him the victim's details.

"And you are sure it's Sara Wentworth?"

"If the victim is not her, then she's her twin." He pulled off his rubber gloves. "Look at the generator used to power that freezer and find out if anyone in the area has bought one recently. Got to be easier to track than the rope."

Winchester's gaze cut through the crowds, searching. "Where's her car? If it's here, it should be roped off."

"Hasn't been found."

"She sure didn't walk here."

"No, she did not." Bragg stared at the dilapidated building, listened to the rush of cars from the interstate as the heat intensified the rotting scents of nearby garbage. "We need to find it."

"Sure."

Bragg shook his head. "Hell of a place to end up."

It wasn't hard to locate Sara Wentworth's parents. They lived ten miles north of Austin in the Hyde Park area, an older upscale area reserved for those with money.

He drove past the neighborhood's stone entrance, over a brick arched bridge spanning Waller Creek's near-dry bed and toward a Spanish-style home built at the turn of the last century. The front yard was green and lush, and stood in stark contrast to the dry brittle grasses surrounding his rented home. The recent water restrictions didn't apply here.

Bragg parked at the top of the driveway and went directly to the front door. He rang the bell and waited barely seconds before the door opened to a petite Hispanic woman dressed in a blue uniform.

"I'm Ranger Bragg with the Texas Rangers. I'm here to see Mr. or Mrs. Wentworth."

The woman's slight frown indicated his visit was unwelcome. However, she nodded politely and stepped aside so he could enter. The entryway was tiled with a light marble and an arched niche across from the door housed an angel statue.

He removed his hat, glancing through a doorway leading into a sitting room with wood floors and light fussy furniture. Above a stone fireplace hung a picture of a young Sara.

The sharp clip of heels and loafers had him turning to face a gray-haired couple. The man wore khakis and a white starched shirt with the letters RW monogrammed on the front pocket and the woman wore dark slacks and a short-sleeved white shirt. Simply dressed, but high quality.

The man stood a good foot taller than his five-foot-two-inch wife. Frowning, he did not extend his hand as he faced Bragg.

"I'm Ridge Wentworth. This is my wife, Mandy. What can I do for you, Ranger?"

"Ranger Bragg, sir, ma'am. Is there somewhere private we could talk?"

Mr. Wentworth's scowl deepened but he ushered Bragg into the sitting room where the portrait hung. "Why the visit?"

Death notices were never easy. And when the notice involved telling a parent about a child it always dug in his craw. "I have bad news about your daughter, Sara. Her body was found in a warehouse in East Austin."

Mrs. Wentworth's hand rose to her mouth. "Sara is dead? I don't believe that. She never goes to that part of town."

"We found her driver's license next to her. It's a clear match."

Mr. Wentworth draped his arm around his wife's slender shoulders and she leaned into him. "What happened?"

Bragg shoved his emotions deep. "We're still trying to figure that out."

Mrs. Wentworth shook her head as if this was all a terrible mistake. "You must be wrong."

"No, ma'am," Bragg said.

Mr. Wentworth's eyes flashed with anger. "You are very, very sure it was our Sara?"

"Yes, sir."

Mrs. Wentworth's eyes welled with tears that quickly spilled. "I don't believe it. I just don't believe it."

The older man cleared his throat. "How did she die?"

Bragg hesitated. "We found her in a freezer. She froze to death."

The couple glanced at each other and then back at him. He'd expected such an odd manner of death to trigger confusion or surprise. But in an unguarded split second the couple showed no surprise.

Mrs. Wentworth moved to one of the over-stuffed couches and sunk into the folds, perfectly at ease in the frill and fluff. "I can't believe this."

Bragg studied her closely. "There are indications she might have killed herself."

Mrs. Wentworth shook her head as her husband snorted. "Sara did not kill herself. She had a wonderful life ahead of her."

Bragg caught a slight hesitation in the woman's voice. "How well did you know your daughter?"

"I knew her well," Mrs. Wentworth said. Watery eyes turned angry and defensive. "She and I were close. We had lunch together two days ago. I called her last night and wondered why she didn't answer but thought she must be out with friends."

"Our daughter was a successful and accomplished woman," Mr. Wentworth said.

"What did she do for a living?"

"She was a commercial real estate broker."

"Did she have properties in East Austin?"

The older man wrinkled his brow, disgust clear. "No. She didn't work in that part of town. Too dangerous."

"That area is known for drug dealers. Did she have a history of drug use?"

Mrs. Wentworth barely stifled a pained cry, and it gave Bragg no pleasure to ask such questions. But he needed to know. Needed to ask while the shock remained because when the shock wore off their guard would rise. Later when the adrenaline ebbed and their thoughts cleared a little, they'd regroup, think about their stories, and maybe hire an attorney. This was his best shot to discover what secrets they hid.

"She did not use drugs," Mrs. Wentworth said, teeth clenched. "Sara was a successful and bright girl. She didn't need to put poison in her system to function."

"Sara was engaged and planning to marry in the spring," her father said. "She'd been to New York weeks ago and picked out her dress. She had no reason to hurt herself. Someone must have done this to her."

"Did she have a history of mental illness?"

Mrs. Wentworth's mouth flattened, hesitated. "No. She has none of those troubles. She is . . . was . . . a *good* girl." She dropped her face into her hands and wept.

"Ever hear of a place called Shady Grove?"

Both Mr. and Mrs. Wentworth shook their heads.

The old man laid his wrinkled, deeply veined hand on his wife's shoulder. "Sara would not have done something like this to herself."

Bragg pulled a small notebook from his back pocket, wondering whom the man wanted to convince. "Can you give me the name of her fiancé?"

"Michael Fenton. He's a recent graduate of law school and months ago began his first job at Fenton and Davis."

"It's a family business."

"That is correct."

Bragg hesitated. "Have you ever heard of or met a Rory Edwards?"

Mr. Wentworth frowned. "I knew Rupert Edwards, his father. But he passed away several years ago. Why do you ask?"

"No concrete reasons. Just had a thought." He glanced at Mrs. Wentworth, who'd paled a fraction. "Does the name ring any bells for you?"

"I know of the family, of course. But we didn't socialize together."

Bragg studied her, noting how her mouth compressed. It was grief and shock and something more. His gaze trained on Mrs. Wentworth. "Did you know Elizabeth Templeton?"

This time there was no missing the narrowing of

her eyes and tightening of her jaw. "I know her mother, Sylvia. But I never met Elizabeth."

"What can you tell me about the family?"

Mrs. Wentworth didn't hide her confusion. "They were a fun couple to be around. Devoted to family and then their son, Jeff, died. Jeff was the family star. The heir. Could do no wrong. When he died that family died."

Greer Templeton was serious and pensive. And if she'd been fun-loving like her parents, death had dimmed lightness to darkness.

"Why would you ask about the Edwardses or the Templetons?" Mr. Wentworth said. "What does either have to do with Sara?" A hitching voice told him emotions held at bay by shock would soon spill.

Bragg didn't manage a smile but he softened his gaze. "Just asking. Their names came up earlier this week."

Mrs. Wentworth lifted her chin. "I can assure you, our Sara had no contact with either of them. Dear Lord, Rory Edwards was a mess."

As much as he wanted to believe them, most parents didn't know as much as they thought about their adult children. "Did anyone give Sara any kind of trouble lately?"

Mrs. Wentworth lowered her face to her hands and wept. "No."

Her husband met Bragg's gaze. "It's time you go. You've delivered your news, and we've told you what we know. We can't keep talking to you."

Mrs. Wentworth shook her head. "Her life was perfect."

Perfect. He'd never seen or experienced it. "I will have questions later."

The old man's lip curled into a sneer. "Later. Sure. Whatever. But you must leave now."

As much as Bragg wanted to keep a foot in the door, he heard it virtually slam shut. Mr. Wentworth called his housekeeper and asked her to show Bragg out. As he left, his thoughts turned to Greer. She had been hiding in plain sight all these years and had only recently resurfaced. And now two people with connections to her family were dead.

Bragg rubbed the back of his neck. He hated coincidences.

Chapter Twelve

Thursday, June 5, 11 A.M.

Greer hadn't planned to visit the cemetery today. In fact it was the last thing she'd have pictured last night when she'd fallen into bed exhausted. The party had been a success. She'd survived the curious looks and some not-so-polite questions. It hadn't been fun but it wasn't as awful as she'd imagined it to be when Dr. Stewart had first floated the idea.

She'd gone to bed feeling hopeful.

And then she'd had the dream. Though it had lasted seconds, it had shadowed her entire morning and left her unable to concentrate.

So after she'd driven into the fields this morning and inspected the vines, she'd told herself she needed to run into town for supplies. The vineyard always needed something, but as she approached the exit for the dry goods store she'd passed it by and kept driving north. Without much thought, she'd found herself driving through the thick iron gates of Longwood Cemetery and up the hill to her brother's plot.

Greer eased out of the car and, keys in hand, walked the ten yards over the grass lawn to the headstone belonging to Jeff.

The iron urn in front of the white marble headstone was filled with fresh white roses. Judging by their freshness and the day's growing heat, the flowers must have been placed here within the last hour or so. Her thoughts shifted immediately to her mother, who loved white roses.

Greer knelt in front of the grave. "I'm sorry it's been so long. Life's been pretty crazy. I'm still at the vineyard and still trying to grow the best grapes in Texas."

She touched a blossom, perfect and delicate. "I

remember how the country club was full of white roses the night of your birthday party. You cringed when you saw all the flowers. Said it looked like a girl party. But you enjoyed the attention." She touched a bloom, adjusting it so it sat a little taller. "I was jealous of you that night. I wanted to be twenty-one, and I wanted to be going back to college like you. You had it all, Jeff."

She sat back on her heels and stared up at the cloudless sky. "I was glad you needed me. I was glad to drive you and Sydney home. I felt grown up."

Tears welled in her eyes. "I really thought I had it under control. I've gone over and over those last minutes before the crash and will always swear there were headlights on the road. No one ever believed me but I know. I'm sorry I didn't react fast enough."

Greer swiped away a tear. "I failed you, Jeff, Mom and Dad . . . so many people hurt because of me."

A shadow cast over her and drew her attention up to an older man wearing a green jumpsuit. He carried a rake in one hand and a shovel in the other. Years in the sun had left his face well lined and deeply tanned. He'd tied his thinning white hair at the nape of his neck and wore a silver chain around his neck. "You all right?"

Greer swiped at her tear and rose. "Yeah. I'm fine. Sorry."

"Don't be sorry. I see folks here all the time that aren't happy. I make a point to stop and say a word."

"Thanks." She studied the flowers. "Do you happen to know who left those flowers?"

He studied the roses. "Don't know. They were here when I arrived about ten to seven."

The hot day's sun burned her skin and had her wishing she'd worn a hat. "I didn't think they'd been here long."

"I do know they get changed out regularly. About once a month new flowers arrive."

"Really?" How could she not have known?

"Yep. Usually before dawn 'cause I'm here by seven. And it's always white roses."

She shielded her eyes with her hand. "How long has this been going on?"

"For as long as I can remember. I can't say exactly when they started."

"I guess my mom has been putting out the flowers." However, the statement didn't ring true. As much as her mother had loved Jeff, she didn't like coming to the cemetery. Sylvia dealt with life's ups and downs by avoiding them. But if her mother would ever make such an exception, it would have been for Jeff.

"Couldn't say. But I'll keep an eye out going forward. I like a mystery to figure out."

She didn't. "Thanks."

The old man nodded to the headstone. "He was young when he died."

"Just twenty-one."

"Real shame."

"Yes."

He adjusted his weight as if his hip bothered him. "Was it cancer? Cancer strikes many these days."

Greer cleared her throat. "It was a car accident."

He shook his head. "Young kids drive like bats out of hell. No sense."

She'd not been driving recklessly. Or at least she'd not thought she had been. Rising, she dusted the dirt from her knees. "Thanks."

"Sure."

In her car, she switched on the engine. The blast of cold air did little to cool the heat of her skin, now flushed and hot. She put the car in drive and glanced toward Jeff's grave. The caretaker stood next to her brother's spot, leaning on his shovel and staring at Greer's truck. She raised a nervous hand in farewell and he nodded.

She drove back toward the entrance and as she pulled out on the main road, she glanced in her rearview mirror. The caretaker was still staring at her.

Bragg had inspected Sara's belongings and had found the red rope bracelet bagged and tagged in the box. His heart sped up when he lifted the bag and studied the red rope bracelet. Made of three braided thin red strips of yarn, the bracelet's craftsmanship was amateurish and reminded him of something a teenager would wear. It hadn't appeared out of place on Edwards but on Wentworth it was a huge red flag. What the hell did the red rope bracelet mean?

It took him a couple of hours, but he put all the details of the two murders into the ViCAP system. The national database contained details of other murders throughout the country, and if his killer had a hit anywhere else in the country maybe this detail would pop a match. ViCAP was not a perfect system. Cops in small localities with limited funding didn't always have time to enter crimes into the database. His inquiry was a crapshoot but better than no shot at all.

He pushed away from the desk, grabbed his hat, and headed to the medical examiner's office. Dr. Watterson would be doing Sara Wentworth's examination this afternoon and he wanted to be present.

The heat hit him hard as he stepped outside. One hell of a hot spell had hit Texas, and now they were knee-deep in summer's brutal temperatures. He'd grown up working outside and had learned to ignore the heat. For some reason, he thought about Greer outside. She'd said harvest time would be soon, which meant she was likely in the fields working in the heat preparing.

It was a hell of a lifestyle switch. Knowing she was raised in the world of country clubs, pools, and fancy trips, he doubted she'd known a bit of manual labor before she'd moved to Bonneville. But he'd felt the scrape of calluses on her hands and seen the depth of her tan when he caught a flash of white flesh just inside the cleavage of her dress.

That little bitty peek shot right through his body. As he'd stood there wondering if she could kill a man or if she was trouble waiting to happen, he'd been rock hard. His voice had been calm, steady, as he'd imagined touching those white breasts.

Bragg shook his head. "Son, you been out of the game too damn long."

He'd dated over the years. Even been serious about one gal about ten years ago. But he'd never been able to bring himself to pull the trigger. He'd had a host of excuses. Work earned the lion's share of reasons. The last gal he'd dated had been just fine. And he couldn't give her a reason why he didn't want to get married. And when it occurred to him not having a reason wasn't reason enough, he'd broken it off.

He parked and strode the short distance inside. He stepped onto the elevator and found the doctor and his assistant preparing the instruments standing by an exam table holding a body clad with a white sheet.

Dr. Watterson pulled on rubber gloves. "Usually I don't have the pleasure of seeing you twice in a week."

"Not that I don't like you, doc, but this isn't my idea of a fun date."

The doctor chuckled. "You weren't the pretty face I was imagining when I started this day."

"Looks like we're stuck with each other."

Dr. Watterson pulled down the microphone, suspended over the table, until it was inches from his mouth. He clicked it on and pulled back the sheet covering the body.

Sara Wentworth's pale bluish body lay on the table still and flaccid. Her head rested on a block and her blond hair was brushed off her face. The tech had removed her make-up. She'd been a pretty woman. And it was clear she'd taken pride in her appearance. Her skin was in excellent shape. Her hair neatly trimmed. Her nails manicured. She'd not scrimped on herself.

"Not often we have someone freeze to death in Texas during such a bitch of a heat wave."

Bragg donned rubber gloves and approached the table. "No, I suppose you don't."

"I've sent her blood off for analysis so we'll know soon if she had drugs in her system. There is no sign of physical trauma on her body. No defensive wounds."

"Like Rory Edwards."

"Yes."

"You think this is a suicide?"

He shook his head. "Can't say right now."

Bragg thought about the red bracelet. She'd

worn one and so had Rory. Could the two have had something going on no one knew about? His death had clearly been assisted, whereas hers showed no signs of a second party.

Winchester was running the numbers on Wentworth's phone and searching for connections to Rory and Greer.

"I did find an interesting fact about her." The doctor walked from the head of the table to the foot. "Look at her left foot."

He glanced at the pale, long, manicured nails and instantly saw what the doctor found odd. "She's missing her two small toes."

"A recent injury?"

Watterson turned the foot so Bragg had a full view. "No. They've been gone a long time."

"Birth defect?"

"No. Look closely, and you'll see suture lines. The toes were removed."

"Why?"

He shrugged. "It could have been an accident, but given her cause of death the first thought that comes to mind would be frostbite."

Bragg leaned in and studied the old injury. "Frostbite?"

Dr. Watterson peered through protective goggles. "Sure, if she'd been exposed to the elements for a long time she could well have lost toes or fingers."

"I asked her parents directly if she'd had any mental instability problems and they said no."

"Might not have been a suicide attempt. Could have been a ski accident. And remember, frostbite is a guess. She could have dropped a rock on her foot or God knows what."

Bragg would have bet a month's paycheck Sara's past included more instability than her parents had conceded. "I'll see if I can find her medical records."

Dr. Watterson reached for his scalpel and made a neat clean Y in the chest's center. "I'd be curious myself."

The doctor continued the exam for several hours while Bragg watched. After he'd sutured her back together and covered her with a sheet, the doctor shook his head. "I can find nothing wrong with her. She was a healthy woman."

"So why'd she end up dead in a freezer in East Austin?"

Willie Nelson's "Georgia on My Mind" played on the radio as Greer studied the stack of invoices on her desk. Several times she'd lost her train of thought and had had to recalculate a column of numbers. When she added a row of numbers and came up with a different answer for the third time, she tossed her pencil on the desk and sat back in her chair.

She glanced out the window and saw Mitch working with the horses. He'd barely spoken since his arrival, but she'd noticed he carried a little less worry in his shoulders. His patience with the horses remained endless even when Beauty nipped or Buttercup lagged. And José had said he listened well in the fields and had caught on quickly with operating the equipment.

At first blush she'd never have put Mitch and Bragg together but the more she'd watched him today the more she'd seen similarities. Mitch's coloring was lighter, but he had a square jaw like his uncle and he carried himself with the same straight-backed posture. Both were over six feet and though Bragg had a broader chest Mitch would fill out more given time.

Bragg.

Why did her thoughts keep circling back to Bragg?

The man didn't trust her. His distrust reflected in his gray eyes. Though he'd kept silent about Mitch's working here, he didn't like it.

She rubbed her hands over her eyes and tried to work away the fatigue. She didn't have time to worry over what was out of her control.

As she pushed away from the books, the afternoon news started. She was half listening when she heard the newscaster say, "Woman found frozen to death in downtown Austin."

The temperatures had been well over a hundred the last few days and the idea of a woman freezing to death struck her as wrong. The reporter gave scant details so she switched to another radio station hoping another report would air. When she found none, she turned to her computer and searched the story. On the newspaper Web site she spotted the small blurb: *The Austin resident, 32, was found dead in an East Austin warehouse freezer.*

She sat back in her chair, thinking back to another girl she'd known who had nearly frozen to death. That girl had gone out into the frigid cold night air with the intent of killing herself. She'd been found in time and saved. Like Rory and like Greer. Her name had been Joan. And she'd not only known Rory but had loved him. It was hard not to love Rory. He was so handsome and beautiful. Most girls noticed him, but Joan had had a deep affection for him and was furious when he'd chosen Greer. One of the last nights they were all in camp together, Greer had been late meeting Rory. She'd been delayed by extra chores in the kitchen. As she'd approached his tent, she'd seen Joan inside with him.

She'd watched as Joan had wrapped her arms around Rory's neck and kissed him hard on the lips. Rory had responded and kissed her back. Greer's heart sank. She'd wanted Rory and had been ready to give him what he'd been begging for.

Finally, Rory eased out of her grip and whispered something only Joan could hear. She'd smiled, kissed him good-bye, and left.

Greer, lingering in the shadows, could have slipped away into the night and written Rory off. But she'd lost so much and to lose him was unbearable. So, she'd summoned her courage and slipped into his tent. Before she thought, she rushed up to him and kissed him on the lips. He'd folded his arms around her and held her so close she could feel the erection Joan's touch had created. But she'd ignored his attraction for another girl and she'd deepened the kiss thinking maybe she could make him forget Joan. He'd kissed her back and then took her by the hand and led her into the woods to a soft grassy patch of land.

As she sat at her desk now, nervous energy churned in her stomach. Silly to think there'd be any kind of connection today between Rory and the woman in the news report. The cops had said Rory ran with a rough crowd and could very well have angered the wrong guy. And this woman who'd frozen to death could be a woman in the wrong place at the wrong time. There could have been any number of odd circumstances why she'd met such an odd ending.

Not her business.

Not her problem.

She had so much work to do.

And after she reminded herself again of the reasons why she should just drop this, she reached for her purse and car keys. She went in search of

José. They had a quick discussion about the daily tasks still to be done, Mitch's assignments, and the target date for harvest. Both agreed they'd be harvesting soon. And with José mumbling in Spanish, she left.

"This is stupid," she muttered as she turned off the route onto the main road. "This is so none of my business." Bracelets jangled on her arm as she ran her fingers through her hair and continued toward town.

She didn't know anyone in the Austin police and likely if she approached them they'd shuffle her to the side and make her wait for hours. It wasn't as if she had real evidence to offer them.

But she did know Ranger Tec Bragg and Rory's case. If there was a slim possibility the two deaths were connected, he'd know.

For the second time that day, she made the thirty-minute drive into Austin. With each new mile she questioned if she'd made the right choice. Once or twice she considered turning the car around. But she somehow stayed the course.

By the time she pulled into the Rangers' parking lot every muscle in her body quivered. Her back ached and her jaw was clenched. Bragg unsettled her in more ways than she could articulate.

As she searched the lot for his car, her breathing grew shallow. Not seeing Bragg's vehicle, she allowed a relieved sigh to shudder through her. He wasn't here. Relief collided with disappointment.

Maybe she'd overreacted. "This is nuts. I need to leave."

She thought back to Joan, who had lain in the snow and wished for death. That girl hadn't been her friend, but she wasn't so different from Greer. She had been just as lost and desperate for love.

"Damn." Greer shut off the truck and cut across the parking lot to the main entrance of Ranger headquarters. Gritting her teeth she moved up to the security window.

An older man dressed in a Department of Public Safety uniform stared up at her with a mixture of mild curiosity and suspicion. It occurred to her she'd not taken the time to change from her shorts, faded Bonneville T-shirt, and work boots. Her long braid fell down her back and a glance at her reflection in the glass revealed a halo of stray curls framing her face. She looked a little crazed.

She tightened her grip on her purse strap. "I'd like to see Ranger Tec Bragg."

The officer raised a bushy gray eyebrow. "Do you have an appointment?"

"No. I wanted to talk to him."

"Is this related to a case?"

"I'm not sure."

The officer shook his head as he reached for a pen. "Give me your name and number, and I'll have him contact you."

Leave her name. She hesitated.

The officer's gaze narrowed. "Go ahead and leave me your name. I'm sure he'll want to know you came by."

His tone added an edge to the words. "Greer Templeton. But it's not an emergency. I'll call him later."

She turned to leave, grateful to put distance between her and Bragg's office. She'd made it ten steps outside the door when a tall man blocked her path. Annoyed, she glanced up to find Bragg, his face shadowed by the Stetson's wide brim. Damn.

"Greer Templeton." His deep rich tone had her squaring her shoulders.

"Ranger Bragg." So much for a clean getaway.

His gaze burrowed into her. "What brings you my way? Mitch all right?"

She cleared her voice, annoyed at the nerves chewing at her. "He's fine. Working with the horses this morning and in the fields in the afternoon. A little ham-fisted with the grapes, but we're working on that."

"The boy never did have a delicate touch."

"No."

"Why the visit?" The unease had melted from his voice. "Did I win a door prize last night?"

Had he made a joke? He didn't strike her as the kind of guy who joked. "No. No. Nothing like that."

He stood silent, letting the quiet burrow under her skin. His height had her stretching her spine, but the extra quarter-inch she eked out was paltry in comparison to his six feet three inches.

"Why have you come, Greer?"

Her name sounded as if it had been roughened with sandpaper when he spoke it. "I heard a news story on the radio about a woman that died."

He stiffened. "What about it?"

"She froze to death?"

His eyes narrowed a fraction. "Yes."

"I knew a girl once who tried to kill herself by running into a snowstorm."

If it were possible, his scowl deepened. He took her elbow in his hand. "It's hot outside. Let's get inside."

A glance at the building had fear shooting through her. An office shouldn't scare her but Bragg's office would be more like a lion's den. "We can talk out here."

He was already walking, tugging her with him. "It's a hundred degrees."

"I'm used to the heat." Sweat soaked the back of her T-shirt.

A half smile tipped the edge of his mouth. "Then you're a better man than I. I want out of the heat."

She kept moving forward toward the building as if caught in a riptide. She could pull and fight, but Bragg, like a riptide, wouldn't yield. And so she let herself be pulled inside. It wasn't like she was in trouble. And she half believed her information wouldn't be of use. She'd say her piece and then leave.

The lobby's cool air chilled her skin and puckered her flesh. She chanced a glance at the guard who stared at her with more interest as Bragg flashed his badge and escorted her to the elevators. Neither spoke as they waited for the elevator. When the doors dinged open he guided her inside. He kept his hand on her elbow as if he expected her to bolt. Smart man. She could easily turn on her heel, slipping through the doors before they closed and scurrying out of here. It wouldn't take much to convince her that her visit had been prompted by an active imagination.

They moved past cubicles, the hum of conversations buzzing around them. Some folks paused to look, as if wondering whom Bragg had snared. Just her luck she'd worn her Bonneville T-shirt. Smart. Imprint her business's name in the minds of a dozen Texas Rangers.

Bragg flipped on his office lights and motioned for her to sit in a wooden chair in front of a large desk as he removed his hat and tossed it on a desk, piled high with neat stacks of papers. The office was filled with shelves, stocked with manuals and a handful of awards. No family pictures. Not even an image of Mitch.

She took her seat and rested her purse in her lap as he moved behind her and closed his door with a soft click. The exit now blocked, the room shrunk. Her feet tapped nervously on the floor.

He paused behind her, and she could feel him staring. Instead of sitting behind his desk as she'd hoped, he took the seat in the chair beside her. He settled back as if he didn't have another worry in the world other than her.

"So you heard a news story?"

She steadied her feet, pretty sure Bragg, like most in law enforcement, could read body language. He'd no doubt guessed she was nervous, but she hoped he'd not read her as just shy of terrified. "I think I might have overreacted."

He threaded his fingers together and rested them on his flat belly. "You've come all this way. Why don't you run it past me and let me decide."

Dark eyes bore into her. Was this what it felt like to stare into a gun barrel? "Like I said I heard the story about a woman who froze to death in East Austin."

The faintest hint of tension tightened his shoulders. "And you said you knew someone who'd nearly died like that before."

"It all made sense earlier, but now it feels like a stretch."

"You ever contacted the police before about a death you read about in the paper?"

"No." She fiddled with the bracelets on her wrist and the action caught his attention, making her stop. If he'd read her file, he'd know about the scars. She wanted to explain about the scars, explain about that regretful moment, as if needing him to understand she was not that person anymore.

Slowly he raised his gaze from her bracelets and wrists. "Then why are you here?"

She folded her hands in her lap. "You know my past pretty well."

He didn't speak, but the certainty in his gaze confirmed what she'd said.

"You know about the accident and my suicide attempt."

The mention of suicide deepened his frown. "Yes."

She'd never spoken to anyone outside of camp about the past except Lydia. "And I went to a camp for kids like me. Kids who'd tried to hurt themselves. It was called Shady Grove."

He watched her closely, not missing a word or microexpression. Her gut tightened. Is this what prey experienced when caught in a hunter's sights?

"Rory was there. There was also a girl there who'd tried to freeze herself to death."

He leaned forward a fraction, and she was aware of a hint of that same soap mingling with his scent.

"We all had to talk about what we'd done as therapy. We were arranged in pods, and Rory and this other girl were in my pod. When she told her story she said she'd been waiting for the temperature to drop while she and her family were on vacation in Colorado. When the temperature dipped below zero, she snuck out in the middle of the night wearing sheer pajamas. No coat or shoes. She wanted to lie down in the snow and let the cold take her."

"Why did she do this?"

"She'd had a boyfriend, and they were in love." She couldn't keep the cynicism from her voice. "Long story short she got pregnant. The boyfriend refused to see her, and the idea of telling her parents terrified her. They'd be furious. So she had an abortion, but she wasn't counting on complications or her mother finding out. Her mother was furious. Called her all kinds of names. She said their relationship was never going to be the same again, and she went into the snow to die."

"Who found her?"

"Ski patrol from what she said. They rushed her to a hospital barely in time to save her. Her parents were mortified. They sent her to Shady Grove to be fixed, in a manner of speaking."

"Did the clinic help her?" The deep timbre of Bragg's voice had her relaxing and lowering her guard.

"I think they did. She'd been at the clinic months when I arrived. She jokingly called herself 'the official greeting committee.' And she was a help to some of the other kids who were having a rough time. Hearing her story gave me courage to tell mine."

"And when did she leave?"

"Days before me."

"Do you remember her name?"

"Not all of the kids used real names. We called her Joan."

"Joan." He frowned. "What did she look like?"

"Tall. Blond. Freckles. Pretty smile."

"That could be half of Austin."

Greer shrugged, knowing he was right. "I do remember when they took her to the hospital she was in bad shape. The doctors salvaged the fingers on her right hand, but I know she lost toes on her left foot. She usually wore shoes, but I saw her coming out of the showers one day and saw the scars. The wound was still raw." Given the same circumstance today, she'd never have done what she did next. "I asked her to show her foot at circle time."

"Circle time?"

"Every night at seven we gathered around a fire and talked about our feelings. It could get pretty emotional sometimes."

"Okay."

"Color rushed Joan's face, and I knew she was embarrassed. But she took off her shoe. I could see the deformity disgusted Rory."

He stared at her, not speaking but not missing one word, or one inflection in her voice.

"I knew I hurt her feelings and even then I felt bad. I'd used our oath of honesty against her." She shrugged. "Kids can be cruel."

His brow knotted and for a moment he was silent. "Why'd you do it?"

She frowned, remembering the slight widening of Joan's eyes and her pooling tears. "I was trying to punish her."

"Why?"

"She was dating Rory, and I wanted him. The night before I'd seen her with him. I'd been jealous and angry. I wanted to make her feel bad. Wanted him to see I was the better choice. Anyway, she told the group she'd lost her toes to frostbite. It was a reminder every day to her how lucky she was."

"Lucky?"

"Toes, she'd said, were a small price for a life."

"Do you think she meant it?"

"She sounded convincing. I felt like a real creep for asking."

"I'm assuming you saw her kissing Rory."

"They were kissing, but Rory never made me any promises. And she'd wanted him before I'd even arrived at camp."

"Did she say anything else?"

"No. We weren't really close. And with me pining for Rory, it didn't make sense we'd end up friends."

"When did Joan leave camp?"

"A couple of days after Rory. After he left she didn't want to stay anymore."

Bragg threaded his fingers together again, studying her.

She curled her fingers into fists and then relaxed them. She'd said her piece. "This information might not have to do with your case, but like I said the news story caught my attention and I needed to mention it. I could have missed the mark altogether but now you know."

In no rush to stand or end this interview, he studied her. She didn't budge or fidget as she waited for him to comment.

Finally, he rose and reached for a file on his desk. "Look at this picture. It's of the woman we found frozen to death. Could she be Joan?"

She moistened her lips. "That was twelve years ago."

"People don't change that much."

Maybe not on the outside. She rose. "Sure."

He held up the color headshot of the woman. Eyes closed and slack-jawed, her blond hair was brushed off a pale face peppered with dark blotches. The woman was indeed older, but there was no mistaking. "That's Joan."

"You're sure?"

"I don't remember the discoloring on her face but the shape of her jaw and the slant of her eyes is Joan's. Yes. I'm sure."

"The discoloration is part of the decomposition process."

"Oh." She lifted her gaze from the image to his face.

He tucked the picture inside the folder and placed it back on his desk. He hitched his hip on the edge of the desk and folded his arms over his chest. "When is the last time you saw her?"

"Twelve years ago."

"You're sure this is Joan?"

"Ranger Bragg, I've not seen a lot of people outside of the vineyard workers in the last decade. I'd have known if I'd seen her."

"Did she and Rory have any contact over the years?"

"I don't know."

"Would she have cared enough to find and kill him?"

Her stomach dropped. "Why do you say that?"

"He couldn't have killed himself alone, but she could have killed herself without help. Murder and suicide happen."

"I can't imagine why she'd care after all this time."

He was silent for a moment. "Her real name wasn't Joan. It was Sara Wentworth."

"I know the name. My mother knows the Wentworths. They made a fortune in real estate."

"You ever have dealings with the family?"

"No. Though my aunt may have when she tried to sell farmland a couple of years ago."

“To Louis?”

“Yes. It’s adjacent to the vineyard. Good land. Drains well, no trees, and lots of sun. Great for growing grapes.”

“Why sell?”

“We’d had a bad summer and the crop didn’t come in well plus Lydia’s medical bills were mounting. We agreed to sell the land to pay bills.”

“How’s Louis doing with his new purchase?”

“He’s built a house that’s stunning but only just shifted his focus to planting vines. I hear he had surveyors out there and plans to break ground in the fall. Still, it will be several years before he has grapes.”

“Were you disappointed to see the land go?”

“What does that land have to do with anything?”

His gaze darkened, and she sensed a veil dropping. This Ranger played his cards close to his vest. “Just asking. Were you disappointed?”

“As a matter of fact, I remember being relieved. We had enough on our plate at the vineyard, especially with Lydia getting sick.”

“How’d you get the money for the tasting room and the winery?”

“When I turned twenty-five, I was able to cash in my trust fund. We invested all of it in the buildings.”

He digested the information. “So now you have everything tied up in Bonneville.”

“That’s exactly right. If it goes under, I lose it

all." She'd said what she'd come to say. "I've overstayed my welcome. If you need anything else, let me know."

He didn't move, again in no rush to end the interview. "Who else were your friends at Shady Grove?"

"I don't remember them all, but in our pod it was Rory, Joan, Sam, and Robin. I don't know who used real names and who didn't."

"You and Rory used your real names."

"At the time I didn't think to make up a new name. My face had been plastered all over the news and everyone knew me at that point." Hands sweating, she rubbed them over her jeans. "After I left I decided to break with the past and take my middle name. I wanted a clean start."

"Understandable."

"Rory used his real name because he wanted to embarrass his family. I think that's why they were freaked out about my letters. The return address was Shady Grove."

He straightened. "What about the other two people in your pod?"

"Sam and Robin."

"Know anything about them?"

She hesitated. "Only what they said about themselves at camp."

"What did they say?"

"We'd all promised we'd never tell on each other."

He shook his head. “This is not the time for secrets, Greer.”

“We *promised* we’d never talk, and until now I’ve kept that secret.”

His gaze burrowed into her. “How did they try to kill themselves?”

On the defensive now, she rose. “Why do you need to know?”

He remained still. “Someone knew about Sara and Rory.”

“You just said you think she might have done it.”

“That’s one theory I’ve yet to prove. There could be someone else out there who wanted all of you dead.”

A crease furrowed her brow. “I can’t say.”

“Why did they try to kill themselves?”

“I can’t say.”

“Can’t or won’t?”

She fisted her fingers. “I won’t. I can’t. Not yet. I swore I’d never tell.”

His gaze grew so fierce it took her breath away. “There could be someone tracking you and the others.”

She shook her head. “And this could be about Sara and Rory. Until you know otherwise, I won’t say.”

Sara was dead, beyond hurt and pain, but the other two had lives and to dredge up the past would be cruel. She had no way of finding Sam, but Robin might be reachable. If she could track her, she could give her a heads-up. A warning. And then she'd send Robin to the Ranger.

A tightening in his jaw questioned her honesty, but after a long moment he said, "Thanks for coming in. You gave me a piece of the puzzle I didn't have."

"Sure."

He walked her to the elevator and when the doors opened stepped inside with her. A long tanned finger pressed the lobby button and she found her gaze drawn to the watch on his wrist. His hands were those of a working man, lean and callused. When she'd been younger she'd never liked calluses. She'd loved the feel of Rory's smooth hands over her skin.

But as she'd begun working in the fields and building emotional and physical strength, she'd come to admire hands like his. They spoke of hard work and dedication.

She thought about Bragg's hands, not Rory's, on her skin now. Touching her fingertips and sliding up her arm, making her forget the past. It had been a long time since a man had touched her, and she wondered how she'd react if Bragg did. Would she pull away or lean into his touch?

Her breathing grew shallow as tightness warmed her belly. If she'd had the courage to ask him to kiss her, she wasn't sure what he'd say about reinitiating a naïve woman into the world of sex.

The doors opened. When she stepped into the lobby and away from him, sadness trailed her.

"You will be at the vineyard?" he said.

An order poised as a question. "I'm a fixture there."

Bragg offered a nod and without another word she left, grateful to venture back into the heat and away from him and the troubling emotions chasing her.

Chapter Thirteen

Thursday, June 5, 4 P.M.

Bragg watched Greer drive away, not turning from the window until her truck vanished around the corner. It wasn't lost on him she'd come to him with this information. She could have gone to the local police and avoided him altogether. But she hadn't. She'd chosen him.

And yet, he had the sense she was holding back. Was she burdened with misplaced loyalty to an old friend or manipulating him? She knew both Rory and Sara had tried to commit suicide and the reasons behind the attempts. She wouldn't be the first killer who'd pretended to help police.

He found his way back upstairs to Winchester's office. On the phone, Winchester nodded for Bragg to enter as he scribbled details on a pad.

Plagued by restlessness, Bragg remained standing and did his best not to pace. His mind returned to his conversation with Greer and began to analyze it as if it had been a crime scene. He hated thinking of her as a killer, not only for Mitch's sake, but his own.

When Winchester hung up, he rose, stretching the tight muscles of his back. "What do you have?"

Bragg never chatted idly and only stopped by to discuss business. "Just had a visit from Greer Templeton."

"Really? Why'd she come into town?"

"She read about the woman that froze to death in the paper. She knew the woman. The victim, Rory, and Greer were all in the same camp for troubled teens."

Winchester set his jaw. "Sara Wentworth's parents said she never had any emotional problems."

A wry smile lifted the edge of Bragg's mouth. "They wouldn't be the first people to lie to a Ranger."

Winchester rested his hands on his hips. "They strike me as folks who put a lot of stock in appearance. A troubled daughter wouldn't have done much for them in their social circles."

Bragg rubbed the back of his neck with his hand. He thought about his own reluctance to take Mitch to counseling because he'd worried for the boy's reputation. If Mitch had killed himself, would he have kept the boy's past hidden out of loyalty? "They'll have lawyered up by now. It'll be tough getting any more information out of them."

"I feel for them, but if they're lying I don't mind squeezing."

"Neither do I. But they've been hiding secrets for over a decade. They're not likely to give 'em up easily."

"Even to catch their daughter's killer?"

"Maybe they're worried that it was suicide. That she killed Rory and then herself."

"So did Greer have anything more to say?" Winchester asked.

He summoned images of Greer's face as she'd met his gaze and told her story. Regardless of her motives, she had backbone. Not many men faced him as she'd done today. "Greer said Sara, who called herself Joan at camp, had a crush on Rory at the camp."

"You believe her?"

He really wanted to believe Greer. And that insight surprised and concerned him. "At this point no reason not to believe her."

Winchester arched a brow. "Mighty convenient Greer connected two dots for us so neatly."

"Could it be as simple as Sara killing Rory and then herself?"

"Sometimes the answer is simple and easy. Sometimes a case comes together. But it's not happened often enough for me to expect it or trust it."

"Meaning?" Bragg challenged.

"Greer's making a play to reenter the world. She's made a big financial bet with her vineyard, and she knows any bad press would endanger that."

Bragg, the man, didn't like Winchester's thinking. Bragg, the Ranger, recognized the logic. "Greer had all her dirt dragged through the media a dozen years ago."

"A dozen years is a long time and folks tend to like second-chance stories. I think the time lapse would be enough for folks to be more accepting. But if there is more dirt . . ."

"Like what?"

"Hell if I know. I want to believe Greer but right now I trust her about as far as I can throw her."

A half smile tugged the edge of Bragg's mouth. "Guess we'll see. In the meantime, I've a warrant to search Sara's house."

"Let's do it."

Minutes later the Rangers were in Bragg's SUV driving toward the west end of town where lush trees lined rich green grass-covered lawns. It took money to keep landscaping alive and connections to get around water restrictions.

As it turned out Sara Wentworth lived about a mile from her parents' place in a small, gated community. The homes weren't as large as the estates in her parents' area, but they were some kind of pricey. He could work a lifetime and not be able to afford this kind of neighborhood.

He'd never aspired to live in this world. There was something to be said for living simple and remaining flexible. He'd never worried or thought about roots. Until now. It could have been Mitch's arrival, but he suspected it had more to do with Greer. She'd stirred feelings in him. He didn't know if those feelings would settle, but he half hoped they'd keep churning.

They walked up to the large front door and found it locked. He glanced next door and spotted an older woman out on her front porch. She held a watering can but was more interested in the Rangers than her plants.

Bragg and Winchester made their way toward the gray-haired woman, who wore a pink sleeveless blouse, long black shorts, and a pink-and-black belt with matching shiny flats.

Touching the brim of his hat, Bragg reached for the star badge clipped to his belt. "My name is Ranger Bragg, ma'am, and this is Ranger Winchester. Was wondering if we could ask you a couple of questions, Mrs. . . . ?"

"Mrs. Vivian Thomas." She set down her watering can and removed pristine gardening gloves. "I heard the news about Sara. Her mother was here this morning clearing out boxes. She was beside herself, poor woman."

Frustration knifed Bragg. If the Wentworths had already been here, then they'd come right after his morning visit. "You know what was in those boxes?"

"She said it was clothes for the funeral. Sara's mother is always controlled and an expert planner so I wasn't surprised by her visit."

"But the visit stuck in your mind for another reason?"

"Some of the boxes didn't have clothes in them but papers. And they also took her laptop computer."

"You know what kind of papers?"

"I asked but she pretended she didn't hear. I wanted to press, but it didn't seem right, considering."

"Don't suppose you have a spare key to Sara's house, do you?" Bragg asked.

"I do. I would water her plants for her when she traveled, and she took care of mine when I was gone. We single girls have to stick together." Her head tilted. "You have a warrant?"

Bragg reached in his back pocket and pulled out the order signed by the judge. "I do, as a matter of fact."

She took the paper and read it carefully before handing it back. "If I don't give you the spare key, how will you get into the house?"

"We'll find a way." Bragg smiled but suspected it didn't look friendly.

"Rangers are resourceful," Winchester added.

She considered the two. "You're not going to break anything or tear things up while you search, are you?"

"We always do our best not to."

Frowning, she considered them before nodding. "Wait a minute while I get the key." She closed her front door and left them to wait on the front porch for a minute before she returned with a key hooked to a key chain with a tennis ball on the end. "This will get you in the front door."

Bragg took the key. "Appreciate the help, Mrs. Thomas."

"Least I can do. I've never known anyone to die like she did. Terrible. She had a lot to live for."

Winchester nodded. "Did she ever give you a reason to suspect she'd want to end her life?"

"She was always smiling when I saw her. And she liked to date around. A lot. Until she met her fiancé a few months ago. A whirlwind relationship, but they were happy."

"Any of those dates ever cause her trouble?" Bragg asked.

"Not that I saw. But it was hard to keep up. Different one or two each week until that Fenton boy. That's her fiancé. He's a lawyer."

"How'd they get along?" Winchester asked.

"He's polite. Helped me move a planter once, and he was always opening the door for Sara."

"See anyone around her house that didn't belong?"

"No. The only one around other than Michael was her contractor. She hired him last week to do the addition on her house. She was going to add a sunroom. He was in the yard the other day taking measurements. He rang my bell because she was supposed to meet him. But she didn't show." The woman frowned. "He wanted a key to the house but I wouldn't give it to him."

"When was this?"

"Three days ago. Monday afternoon. When she came home that night I told her about the contractor, and she was upset she'd forgotten. Said it had been a bad day."

"Did she say why the day was bad?"

"She didn't say. But she was upset. Rattled."

Bragg nodded. "Thank you, ma'am."

"Sure. Let me know if there is more I can do."

"You can count on it."

They strode next door and Bragg slid the key into the lock. It turned easily and the front door slid open. Both Rangers pulled rubber gloves on their hands before Bragg switched on the entry light.

The polished marble entry sparkled in the light and still-fresh flowers filled a gilded vase in an arched alcove. The entryway opened to a large living room carpeted in white. The furniture was covered in white damask and the walls painted a soft blue. A crystal chandelier hung from the center of the living room. This room fed into a dining room showcasing a long antique table surrounded by straight-back chairs custom-fitted with more white fabric.

The kitchen was equally as pristine as the first two rooms. The solitary sign of life was a juice glass, still half full, lipstick marking the glass's rim.

He imagined Sara standing at this sink Tuesday morning, drinking her juice as she stared out the window. No sign of coffee, but if she'd been too rushed to finish her juice she'd likely taken her coffee to go. A woman who liked success and money didn't have time to linger.

"Lot of space for one gal. And she was adding on."

Bragg shrugged. "Never professed to understand the rich."

They moved through the house, finally settling in an office located off her bedroom. A fancy French desk dominated the space. There was a frilly sofa built for style, not comfort, and country landscapes on the walls. All perfect and all so damn sterile.

Bragg eased into a delicate chair behind her desk and opened the desk drawer. The contents were in disarray as if someone had gone through them. "Neighbor said the mother was in the house."

"What kind of papers would she want that badly?"

He searched through a stack of receipts to the right of a white blotter. "Hell if I know. I can tell by these receipts Sara Wentworth liked to buy furniture. Has four pieces on order."

"Likes to shop. Dates lots of men. Adding to a space that does not need it. Jo would have a field day with those symptoms."

"Restless and troubled or just spoiled and bored?"

"Maybe sitting still gave her too much time with her thoughts and she wasn't comfortable in her own head."

"Maybe she just likes nice things."

"Maybe." He didn't sound convinced.

He found a receipt for wine. Sun Valley wine. The only brand he knew because he'd remembered it from Greer's party. The wine Louis made at his winery. "Greer says she'd not talked to Sara in twelve years, but Sara bought a good bit of wine from a winery that uses Bonneville grapes."

"An odd coincidence."

Bragg shook his head. "I'd be willing to bet it wasn't." He studied the vineyard's simple logo. "Greer said Sara called herself Joan at the camp, whereas Greer never tried to hide her identity when she was at Shady Grove. And a motivated searcher could have found Greer because she kept her last name."

"Why find Greer after all these years?"

"Good question." Bragg flipped through more papers on Sara's desk finding no notes, correspondence, or e-mails. All he found were monthly bills. He glanced under the desk and saw the double outlet in the floor. The lamp cord on the desk snaked into one whereas the other was empty. "Mrs. Thomas said Sara's mother took the computer."

"So what do you think Momma is hiding?" Winchester asked.

"Greer said she and Rory were an item at camp and Sara had also dated Rory," Bragg said.

"A love triangle?"

Bragg frowned. He didn't like thinking of Greer and Rory together. "That would be the simple explanation, wouldn't it?"

"When's the last time you stumbled across a simple explanation?"

"Been a while."

"Time to pay Shady Grove a visit."

"That's where all this began."

Outside, Bragg studied the backyard. Neat, manicured. No red flag to catch his attention. And then he spotted the trash cans sitting beside a toolshed. Amazing what people tossed in a backyard bin and considered it gone for good.

He strode toward the cans and raised the first lid. The bin was empty. Replacing it, he lifted the second as Winchester approached. Both Rangers stared in stunned silence into the can. Inside the plastic trash bag was something bloodied and battered.

Bragg removed the bag and carefully opened it.

"Shit," Winchester said.

Bragg's stomach churned. A baby. Covered in blood.

He looked closer, compartmentalizing the horror and focusing on the facts. Not a baby, but a doll covered in a sticky red substance and encased in a brown box. Sara's address was printed clearly on the outside. "What the hell?"

Hours passed before forensics could free up a team to examine the box in Sara's trash can. Despite a thorough search, no note had been found. Forensics had taken the box and would conduct a complete analysis.

"Who the hell would mail that?" Winchester said.

Bragg kept his gaze on the road. "I don't know. But it could explain why Monday had been such a bad day, and why she flaked and missed the contractor." He followed the twisting road into the Hill Country and rechecked his GPS. "Greer said Joan, or rather Sara, had had an abortion."

"Her parents strike me as people good at keeping secrets."

"The kids at camp would have known."

They fell silent as Bragg drove farther and

farther into the country. A wrong turn had him muttering an oath as he slowed and turned the SUV around.

"No one accidentally stumbles upon Shady Grove," Winchester said. "You have to know exactly where you are going."

It was past six when Bragg finally spotted the low-key sign on the side of the rural route. A simply painted black-and-white sign set low to the ground. No flowers or fancy landscaping surrounded the sign. The lettering wasn't gilded or showy. It was a plain marker that whispered to the searcher: *You found us*.

He wound along the dirt road driving another mile before spotting the large building. Though built in the last twenty-five years, it reminded him of a nineteenth-century home, not a modern facility for children.

The two-story building was white with tall columns in the front. A wide porch banded around the house and sported a collection of rockers. Potted flowers decorated the front porch and there wasn't an extra stick or twig out of place. Perfectly swept clean. Stood to reason. If rich folks sent their kids away from prying eyes they wanted their offspring in a fitting place.

Bragg parked at the top of the circular drive and locked his car. He tried to imagine Greer arriving here at age sixteen. She'd still have been recovering from her physical injuries as well as the mental trauma of causing her brother's death. She'd have had bandages on her wrists. And her hair would have been dyed the blond she'd favored as a teen.

Like he'd told Winchester, he took pity on that kid. He'd been thirty-three when his sister had died. It had been years since he and his sister had spoken, but losing her had hurt. And Greer had endured the same pain as a kid. She'd been alone. Cut off from family and friends.

As he tried to imagine this place through her eyes, the crisply painted buildings and the perfectly pruned plants didn't feel welcoming. In fact, their perfection likely mocked a young life in ruins.

In the distance from the surrounding thick woods, he heard the laughter of young adults and thought it strange to hear a joyous sound. Sadness often did mingle with joy. The years he and Sue had lived in his father's house there'd been some good times. His old man had always liked to do it up at Christmas and take pictures. One great day to wipe out the really bad ones.

His boots thudded against the steps as he climbed the stairs to the front door. A tasteful WELCOME sign dangled from a brass hook.

A glance to his left and right revealed surveillance cameras pointing at the front door. Swiveling around, he spotted more cameras in the trees. Behind tasteful elegance lurked the camera's watchful eye.

He tried the front door and discovered it was locked. Noticing the button to the right of the door, he pressed it. The buzz of a bell inside the facility echoed in the hallway and soon he heard the clip of steps as someone approached.

Bragg stood back, his hand on his gun. Of course the chance of trouble out here was remote, but a chance was a chance and he never liked waiting by a closed door without his hand on his gun.

He'd been a rookie cop in El Paso, and he and his partner had approached a house known to hide illegal aliens. Reports of children screaming had brought them to investigate. His partner, Nate, was an older guy, and he'd nudged Bragg to the side of the door before he'd knocked.

"Stand in front of that door, and you might as well have a goddamned target on your chest."

Bragg didn't remember the smart-ass quip on the tip of his tongue as he stepped aside. But he remembered the double blast of a shotgun eating through the front door as the drug dealer inside had opted to take his chances with the gun.

The wood fragments had splayed, one cutting him across the face. His partner had drawn his weapon and Bragg had fumbled to get his at the ready. Seconds later they'd been in a gun battle that had left two coyotes dead and his partner injured.

His partner had taken early retirement, and

Bragg had learned to expect trouble every minute of every day he was on the street.

The front door to Shady Grove opened. No gun blast or drama, just a young woman wearing a simple black dress and a white lab coat.

Her gaze roamed quickly from his Ranger's hat to the star on his belt before meeting his gaze. "Texas Rangers. Is there a problem?"

Behind the cool and composed smile, he noted her jaw's subtle tightening. Shady Grove billed itself as a peaceful place, and a Ranger standing on her front porch was liable to bust that image.

He touched the brim of his hat. "Ma'am. Names are Rangers Tec Bragg and Brody Winchester. We're here for the director. I saw on your Web site that his name is Dr. Marshall Leland."

"Dr. Leland is in a late meeting."

"Tell him I'm here." Now that he'd announced his interest in the place he'd not be leaving until he saw Dr. Leland. That first visit, when everyone was too shocked to be on guard, could be the most productive.

"It's not really good timing."

"Doubt the timing will ever be just right. Would you get Dr. Leland please?" He could be polite when he needed to be, but he could jack up the heat if *please* didn't work.

She stepped aside. "Why don't you come in and have a seat? I'll let him know you're here."

"Appreciate it."

Bragg and Winchester stood in the corridor filled with dozens of plaques regaling Shady Grove. First in Education. Outstanding Work with Children. The list of awards went on and on, and he supposed they were comforting endorsements when a parent wanted to drop off his troubled child.

There were no pictures of the students. No smiling faces. No kids canoeing or making crafts or standing around a campfire. The identity of the guests, as the Web site had said, was closely guarded.

"Place makes me sad," Winchester said.

Bragg nodded. "Yeah."

A door closed and footsteps sounded and grew closer. Bragg turned to discover a tall thin man sporting a dark mustache that matched thinning hair. He wore a lab coat over a suit and his nameplate read DR. LELAND.

The doctor's quick and easy smile said he was practiced at handling difficult surprises. He extended his hand and Bragg took it. The doctor's handshake was firm and sure and his eye contact steady.

Dr. Leland said, "My secretary tells me your name is Ranger Tec Bragg."

"That's right, Dr. Leland," Bragg said. "This is Ranger Winchester. We're from the Austin office of the Texas Rangers."

If their business had rattled the doctor he gave no

sign of it. But then being calm in tough situations would have been part of his job. "Why don't you come back to my office and we can talk."

Bragg and Winchester followed the doctor along the carpeted hallway toward the back corner office. Dr. Leland's office was large and carpeted in a rich burgundy shade and decorated with a mahogany desk, paneled hunter-green walls, and framed degrees that said he should know what he was doing.

The doctor indicated for the Rangers to take a leather-padded seat in front of his desk while he retreated to his chair behind his desk. Threading his fingers the doctor leaned forward, a moderate level of concern on his face. "What can I do for you, Rangers Bragg and Winchester?"

"I'm hoping you can help us," Bragg said.

"I'll do whatever I can." He offered a smooth easy smile.

Bragg relaxed back in his chair, in no rush to get to the punch line. "You handle a lot of kids here every year?"

He steepled his fingers. "About one hundred."

The doctor had no hard edges. His voice, his smooth hands, and his rounded face were all pleasant and invited trust. "That's not a lot."

"We offer specialized care including one-on-one counseling as well as group counseling. It's intensive. The children who come to us are in tough shape."

This guy sounded like a walking-talking marketing video. "Would you say you have a good success rate?"

"We do. We pride ourselves on helping these children." He adjusted his glasses. "Just because a child comes from money doesn't mean they're happy."

"Money doesn't buy happiness," Winchester said.

"No, it does not."

"But it does buy privacy and a really nice place to get well," Bragg countered.

"We pride ourselves on making a nurturing place for the children."

"What's the age range for your patients?"

"We've children as young as ten and as old as twenty."

"That's a sizeable gap. A twenty-year-old might not have much in common with a ten-year-old."

"That's why we divide our children into pods. We try to match the ages of the children who share pods. They live in separate buildings located beyond the woods."

"And all the children here have tried to commit suicide?"

Annoyance flashed in Dr. Leland's eyes as if the hard word were taboo. "Some of our residents also grapple with drug addiction, anorexia, or self-mutilation. We are equipped to handle just about any crisis."

"Basically, you treat messed-up kids." He wanted to sound unfeeling. He wanted to rattle the doctor and find out what he could shake loose.

Dr. Leland frowned, but didn't rise to the bait. "You make it sound harsh."

"Because it is harsh," Winchester said.

Absently he straightened a sheet of paper on his desk. "We try not to judge the children here."

"I wasn't judging. Only trying to get to what you do for the children."

"I've indulged your questions, Ranger Bragg. Now can you tell me why you are here?"

Bragg switched tactics. "How long have you been at Shady Grove?"

"I've worked here for a decade."

"How long have you been the director?"

"I'm not just the director. I own the facility now."

"How long?"

"Barely over a year."

"What happened?"

"Nothing overly dramatic or nefarious. The founder of the camp, Dr. Gary Putman, died. In his sleep. Of a heart attack. He was seventy-six."

"Dr. Putman founded the camp?"

"He did. Twenty years ago. Though he was a leading psychologist, his oldest child, Rebecca, was a troubled girl. She killed herself when she was fifteen. Her death prompted him to create a haven for troubled children."

"You purchased the clinic."

"Yes, from the family."

Bragg hesitated, letting his gaze roam the room as if he had all the time in the world. He met the doctor's gaze. "I've had two of your former clients die recently."

Dr. Leland cocked his head and frowned but kept his thoughts to himself.

Bragg had the sense the doctor was calculating the media fallout from the murders. He didn't speak, using the silence to prompt the doctor to talk.

Dr. Leland cleared his throat. "Can you tell me who?"

"The first was Rory Edwards and the second Sara Wentworth. They were both here at the same time about twelve years ago."

"That was before my time. As I said, I've been here a decade."

"I assume the facility keeps records."

"I'm not allowed to release the names of my current or former clients. I signed several privacy agreements when I bought the camp. Dr. Putman's son was clear about maintaining the camp's reputation. Discretion is key to our work."

"We know doctor-patient privilege is binding," Winchester said.

"But the sole link between the two victims was their stay here," Bragg added.

"Many of our clients run into each other when

they leave. I have no control over what happens then." Dr. Leland clearly favored damage control and not assistance.

"Rory Edwards was here because he hanged himself. And Sara Wentworth, who went by the name Joan while she was here, tried to freeze herself to death. Rory was hanged several days ago and Sara froze to death in an industrial freezer."

Dr. Leland straightened the sheet of paper on his desk again. "We have a high success rate, but we do lose some clients. Mental illness is a tough and complicated issue to tackle. Outside life is stressful and can trigger a relapse."

"I've no doubt. No doubt at all. There was another gal here, Elizabeth Templeton."

His lips compressed into a thin line. "Did she die?"

"No. No, she's doing well for herself now. She speaks well of Shady Grove. But she knew the two victims."

"Why are you calling them victims? I thought you said these two individuals killed themselves."

The doctor was astute, but then to be a success here he'd have to key into the nuances of words. "I know Rory was murdered or at the least was assisted with his suicide. Sara may have been the one who helped or killed him before killing herself. Or someone else killed them both."

Dr. Leland arched a brow. "I would think the

police would know the difference between suicide and murder."

"We do most times. But then we get a killer who tries to cover up. Takes more digging to get at what happened."

"I still don't see how we are connected."

"Odd that two folks from this fine establishment would choose to kill themselves two days apart," Winchester said.

"I don't know what to say."

Bragg leaned forward. "I'm real interested in the group of kids here the same time as the two victims and Elizabeth Templeton."

"I've told you I can't tell you. We keep names a secret for a reason."

"I need to have those names."

"You won't get them from me."

"One way or another I'm going to get a list of those names and figure out if I'm chasing any kind of pattern."

"I can't confirm or deny what you are saying."

Bragg shook his head. "I want to handle this as quietly as I can, Dr. Leland. I don't want to make a fuss. Media can turn a situation sideways. Couldn't be good for your business. But I promise you if I don't get your help, I'll mention both my victims were Shady Grove residents."

The doctor paled. "I would help you if I could, but I can't break doctor-patient confidence."

"Tell you what. Why don't you locate the folks

in that group and find out how they're doing?"

"I don't have that kind of information. People scatter and move away."

"I bet you know more than you realize. Bet their grateful families are generous donors."

"You're putting me in a bad position. Making calls like that could be awkward."

"Not my worry, Dr. Leland. I need to find out what happened to the kids in that group."

"What if there is no connection? What if I find out they're all good and well, and you're stirring trouble for no reason at all?"

"Well, then, I'd say it will be your lucky day. I'd say, you won't have to worry about me anymore." Bragg leaned forward. He grinned, knowing the effect could be menacing. "I'm not the kind of person people like having around on a regular basis. I make them nervous."

A slight widening of the doctor's eyes confirmed he wanted Bragg gone. "And if they're dead? Then what do I do?"

"Then you best let me know. In the meantime, I'm going to get a court order. That might help you with your legal dilemma. But news of court orders has a way of leaking out."

"Don't want that getting around," Winchester said.

Dr. Leland adjusted his tie. "You are backing me into a corner."

Bragg rose, knowing hardball came next. "Nope,

just hoping you'll do your civic duty and help out the Rangers. But if you don't help then you can bet we're going to back you into a corner and make your life miserable."

Winchester stood, as if in no rush. He grinned.

Shoulder to shoulder, the mass of the Rangers' bodies ate a hefty chunk of floor space. They left the stunned doctor in his office and strode out the front door. On the front porch Bragg settled his hat on his head and surveyed the grounds. A flash of metal in light caught his attention. He strode across the gravel driveway and the ground toward a large tree. At the base of the tree he found a plaque. It read:

IN LOVING MEMORY OF REBECCA,
WHOSE GENTLE SPIRIT AND SOUL
INSPIRED THE CREATION OF
SHADY GROVE ESTATES.

Bragg studied the name, and touched the tip of his hat out of respect before leaving the uncomfortable beauty of the camp.

He sat in the sunshine, his eyes closed as he drank up the warmth. He loved the Hill Country. The quiet. The trees. The slower pace. He could stay here all day.

"How much longer are we going to sit here?" she said.

He ignored her, hoping she'd go away.

"I know what you are doing and I'm not going to let you ignore me." She'd ratcheted up her voice, adding the shrill he hated. "Open your eyes and pay attention to me!"

He didn't need to open his eyes to picture her brown hair, peaches-and-cream complexion, and the sprinkle of freckles over her nose. When she was irritated, her eyes blazed blue and her cheeks flushed pink. "Can't you just leave me in peace? Do we always have to be talking?"

"You don't like talking to me?"

He didn't have to open his eyes to know she was pouting. "Not now."

"We need to talk now. We don't have a lot of time."

"We've got twenty-four hours. That's plenty of time."

She huffed. "You were never a good planner. Always putting the important matters off until last."

The nagging raked over his nerves, shattering the day's calm. "Leave me alone."

"You know I can't. You know if not for me you wouldn't have the drive or gumption to take care of the others."

He sat up, his jaw tight, as he stared at the distant horizon. "You need to back off. I've gotten us this far."

"Because I've been poking and prodding you

the whole time. If not for me you'd still be living that boring life in Austin lost in the mindless details of your day."

"Those mindless details have made a lot of money. Someone has to take care of business."

"We've plenty of money. We don't need more. What we need to do is talk about the next one. We need to review the details so we don't make any mistakes."

He sighed. "If I go over the details with you, will you leave me alone?"

"If you go over each and every detail, then yes I will leave you alone."

"For how long?" That's the way it had always been with them. Endless negotiations.

"I'll leave you be. For now. Maybe even a day."

"Swear."

"Don't I always keep my word?"

He laughed. "No."

She giggled. "You love me. Admit it."

He hated her when she bitched at him. Hated himself more when she was nice and he acquiesced.

"Come on admit it," she cooed. "You love me."

"Fine. I love you. Now let's talk about killing Sam so I can get some sleep."

Chapter Fourteen

Friday, June 6, 10 A.M.

Her body still hummed with nervous energy as Greer watched the clerk ring up the feed for the two horses. She still couldn't decide if going to Bragg had been a good idea or not.

"That will be three hundred and two dollars," the clerk said.

She'd known taking the old horses on would be expensive, but she'd not really put pen to paper and calculated the cost. She handed the clerk her charge card and tried not to be bothered by the expense.

She stepped back from the counter looking, but not really looking, at flower seeds as Rory and Sara's images elbowed back into her thoughts.

Beautiful Rory had been interested in her from the start. He'd been sweet and charming, and Greer had been so grateful someone showed any interest in her. She'd never noticed Joan, or rather Sara, resented the relationship. Sara had slept with Rory a couple of times at camp and she'd really liked him. But Rory being Rory had moved on to Greer, and she'd not cared about Sara's loss. Greer thought herself in love. If only she could have seen Sara hurt as much as she had and let her have Rory.

But Greer had literally been starving for love and Rory's paltry offering had been nectar. She'd been naïve enough to believe the youthful, hasty promises Rory and she made. Write. Talk on the phone. Friends forever. Karma had brought them together.

But of course, outside the camp walls Rory's old life swept him away from Sara and Greer.

The clerk handed her a receipt and she signed it, tucking the card back in her wallet. "My truck's out front. Can I get someone to load up the feed?"

"Yes, ma'am. Go ahead and pull around back."

As she moved through the store, the hair on the back of her neck rose. It was a subtle, practically imperceptible feeling but when she thought about it there was no denying her unease.

Stiffening, she reminded herself the sensation wasn't uncommon. When people from her past recognized her, they stared. In their minds, once a sinner always a sinner and there's no event more entertaining than the appearance of a she-devil to brighten an otherwise boring day.

Most times she kept on walking and didn't bother to speak. In fact, there'd been times when she'd slinked back to her truck and raced home. But since she'd met Dr. Stewart, she'd been refusing more and more to run. She had a right to stand her ground. Yes, she'd sure as hell made a lot of mistakes, but the last she checked no one could cast the first stone.

She stopped and turned, her hand gripping the worn leather strap of her purse.

Greer spotted him instantly. He was a tall lean man. Well dressed. He still carried himself with a straight-back posture. Like his sister and his parents, he'd been a rider. The family owned a stable of the finest horses in Texas and a far cry from the nags she now owned.

When she made eye contact his gaze locked on her. His hair remained dark, but gray now lightened the temples. Deeply tanned skin gave him a youthful vigor. He had to be close to forty now.

His eyes narrowed as if he wanted to assure himself she was who he thought she was. "I haven't seen you in town in a long time."

"No, I don't get into town often." He'd been wearing a suit the last time she'd seen him. They'd been in court.

His eyes darkened. "I didn't realize you were still in the area until I heard about your party the other night. I couldn't believe it when they told me you'd never left. Thirty miles outside of Austin the entire time."

"Texas is my home."

He shook his head. "It was my sister's home, too. Until you killed her."

Her memory jumped to Sydney Dowd, Jeff's girlfriend. She'd been in the front seat of her brother's car the night of the accident. When the car had hit the tree, she'd been thrown clear. Her neck had broken instantly.

Sydney's parents had sued her parents because Greer had been driving on a learner's permit and was supposed to be accompanied by an adult driver. Jeff had been passed out drunk, the attorney had argued, so the Templetons had broken the law by allowing Greer to drive unmonitored.

She remembered Mr. and Mrs. Dowd coming to the hospital after the accident. They'd stared at her with such a stony silence she'd wept. She'd wanted to apologize or say words to comfort them, but her mother had been in the room, and she had refused to let her speak. There'd been a heated exchange and the Dowds had left when her mother had called security. Later, Greer's mother had warned her to stay clear of the Dowds. *Don't make any more trouble for us, Elizabeth.*

She'd known Sydney had an older brother, Rick. She saw the resemblance and tried to imagine Sydney if she'd lived.

"What can I do for you, Mr. Dowd?"

Rick Dowd cocked an eyebrow. "What do you suggest, Ms. Templeton?"

The edge in his voice had her bristling. "I've no suggestions. But you clearly have words for me."

He flexed his fingers. "Not sure what either of us could say to the other. You gutted my family. Hard to come back from an obstacle like that."

Her breathing thinned as regret knotted in her belly. "I will always be sorry, Mr. Dowd."

"I doubt you know the meaning of the word, Ms. Templeton."

A rush of anger and shame rose up in her, coloring her face. "That's not true. You've no idea how I felt."

"Well, your feelings pale in comparison to mine and my parents', who lost a child."

A pained sigh escaped her lips. "I lost a brother. I know your pain."

He jabbed a finger at her. "Don't pretend to know how I feel. *Don't*."

This was a losing battle. "What do you want me to say, Mr. Dowd?"

"Like I said, not much." His gaze roamed over her, the anger all but snapping from his eyes.

How could she ask him to forgive when she'd not really forgiven herself? More words wouldn't take away his pain or her guilt. "I wish you the best, Mr. Dowd."

As she turned to leave he hurried to block her path. In a voice loud enough for her alone to hear, he said, "You aren't sorry, but you will be."

A chill twisted along her spine. She met his gaze. "What does that mean?"

He shrugged and smiled. "Doesn't mean a thing."

They both knew it would be his word against hers.

She balled her fingers into fists. "Is that a threat?"

He smelled of sandalwood and leather. "It's whatever you want it to be."

"I heard a threat."

He shrugged. "Oh, well."

The cruelty behind his grin made her want to charge him. She'd spent over a decade sequestered and locked away from the world, and she was tired of carrying this indomitable weight.

Brushing past him she hurried to her truck and slid behind the wheel. Her hands trembled as she shoved the key in the ignition and drove around to the back of the building to collect her feed.

She backed up to the loading dock and for several seconds sat still. Her nerves jumped and snapped and her breath hung in her throat. She'd stayed out of the public limelight all these years to avoid the pain she'd just encountered. Last night's party had gone well. They'd raised thousands for the Crisis Center, and she'd lulled herself into believing people had put the past behind them. But some would never let the past go. And no amount of penance or apologies would change that.

A knock on her window had her turning. A gray-haired man with a face deeply etched grinned at her. "Got your feed."

She blew out a breath. "Great."

Restless, she slid out of the truck, walked

around to the back, and opened the tailgate. As the men on the dock loaded her order, she took several deep breaths as she willed the stress away.

A whimpering sound caught her attention. Turning, she spotted a box on the loading dock tucked to the side. Peeking out of the box was a puppy. Short haired and small, he'd been born without a right eye, she realized even at this distance. He wagged his tail as he looked at her. Clearly the deformity didn't bother him.

Without a thought, she climbed the stairs to the top of the dock, crossed to the box, and picked up the puppy. Excited, he wagged his tail and licked her face. And then he peed on her.

Despite her encounter with Dowd, the puppy melted her worries and allowed her to push him out of her thoughts. "This is the day for people peeing on me."

The puppy kicked his feet and licked her face.

She grinned. "Though I don't mind yours so much."

The one-eyed puppy was a cross between a dachshund and a terrier, which left him with wiry hair and a long back. The patchwork of reds, browns, silvers, and blacks wasn't wholly attractive, and she suspected once he was no longer a puppy, he'd be one homely fellow.

The dock foreman came up behind her. "He's the last of the litter. Spunky little fellow but that eye. Damn, won't be many folks that want him."

“Where’s his mom?”

“She left as soon as the pups were weaned. A stray.”

“Are you gonna keep him?”

“Can’t have a dog running around the dock. Especially one that looks like it was made by a bunch of politicians.”

“He have a name?”

“ ‘Dog’ is all we been calling him.”

She studied Dog’s closed right eye and then the excitement in the left as his wagging crooked tail thumped. And just like that she couldn’t imagine leaving him. “They say there is one born every minute.”

The old man chuckled. “You falling for that ugly face?”

“I don’t need a dog. Especially a puppy. I don’t need it.” And she didn’t need two old horses. And she didn’t need a sullen ex-soldier working her land.

The old man chuckled. “Seen that look in my wife’s eyes. Led to a dozen dogs in our thirty-one years of marriage.”

She tucked the dog under her arm, noticed that he fit well. He hunkered down as if staking a claim. No doubt the dog was smart, saw his ticket out of here, and hoped charm overcame ugly. “She willing to make it a lucky thirteen dogs?”

“Wife passed a year ago. Can’t have no more hounds in my house. But he’s all yours if you want him. I'll even throw in a big bag of puppy chow."

She'd think back on this moment in the near future and truly question her sanity. "I don't suppose he's had shots?"

"Matter of fact he did. Got all his puppy shots and been wormed."

The dog licked her face. "You two drive a hard bargain."

"He's ugly as sin, but he is the smartest of the litter. Listens well."

"Yeah, yeah. You can quit with the sales job. Load up the dog food. Dog's coming with me."

His grin widened. "Good for you."

She shook her head as she stared at the contented pup. "Yeah. Right."

As she settled into the front seat of her truck, Dog settled on her lap, and promptly rested his head and fell asleep. For a moment she sat still, savoring the warmth of his body against hers. He'd accepted her without question. She was kind to him now and that was all that mattered to him. He didn't care about twelve years ago or twelve years in the future. It was about now.

She rubbed him on the head and fired up the engine. As she backed out of the lot, she spotted Rick Dowd. He sat in the front seat of his Lexus staring at her. Pure hate summed up his expression.

Tightening her grip on the wheel she shifted into drive and with her hand on Dog headed back to the vineyard. She glanced in the rearview mirror and saw Dowd's car and to her relief he didn't follow. But she suspected this would not be the last time for them.

Even with Dog nestled close, she couldn't shake the shock of seeing Rick Dowd today. He'd reopened the wound.

She shifted gears as she rounded a corner, moving her left leg slowly so Dog didn't awaken. As she pulled into a straightaway, her mind drifted back to Jeff and Sydney. The two had been the golden couple. Beautiful. Smart. Funny. Greer had often called them Barbie and Ken because they'd been perfect. And then the headlights had appeared in the distance. Horns blared. Jeff cursed. And then pain, death, and an unbearable sadness.

"Possibilities, not the past," she'd said. The slogan embraced by the camp leaders. The words they'd drilled into their young charges. Words she still held on to.

She'd not told Bragg the entire truth today, and it weighed on her mind. She had seen one of the others since she'd left camp. Two years ago, she'd bumped into Robin. Lydia and Greer had been in Fredericksburg, Texas, at a wine tasting. They'd decided to build the winery and had decided to again check out the local competition.

The small quaint town had been jam-packed with outsiders who'd come to taste the wines of local vineyards. It had been her idea to attend. Her aunt had finished her latest round of chemo and was feeling good and hopeful for the future. Greer had been feeling hopeful. Greer had wanted the world to know Bonneville grew the best grapes but also would soon be making the best wine.

There'd been close to fifty vendors that day. Not only were vineyards present, but also cheese makers, local farmers' markets, pig farmers, and bread bakers.

Greer had been sampling a port from a winery near Houston when she'd heard her name. *Elizabeth*. Instantly, she'd tensed. Elizabeth signaled her old life.

She glanced up, surprised and shocked, to see Robin standing there. She had a glass of wine in her hand and judging by her flushed face she was drunk.

Greer adjusted her ball cap. "Hey, Robin."

Robin was a tall brunette with a runner's long lean body. A white tank-top dress set off her tanned body and her full breasts. "I thought that was you. Despite the ball cap, I couldn't miss the set of that jaw. You always struck me as determined."

Greer straightened and set down her glass of port, suddenly losing all taste for it. She turned from the vendor and managed a smile for Robin. "You're looking well."

"Life is good these days." Robin leaned in a

fraction and Greer could smell beer mingling with wine and perfume. "Not like before."

The abrupt mention of her past slammed against Greer's defenses, and she'd instantly gone rigid. "Yeah."

Robin had shared her story at circle only once. According to her, when she'd been seventeen, she and her brother had gone swimming at their parents' lake house. Two children had set out on an adventure on a picture-perfect day. And then Robin's brother had dived into the lake, hit a stump, and broke his neck. Robin had pulled him from the water immediately but the damage had been done. He was paralyzed. He'd lingered for weeks in a coma, hooked up to a ventilator. Finally, his parents had shut off the machine and let him go. Robin had been devastated. She'd been the one who'd goaded her brother to swim that day. He'd not wanted to go, but she'd made him. And then he was dead.

After her brother's death, Robin had spiraled into a deep depression. Finally, she'd taken an overdose of pills and gotten into a full bathtub. She'd barely been breathing, her nose hovering above the waterline, when her mother had found her. She'd spent the entire summer at Shady Grove, but like Greer no matter how much counselors spoke of self-forgiveness neither could manage it.

"I almost didn't recognize you, Elizabeth. You're not blond anymore."

She didn't mention her name change. The name like the hair color was a tie that would remain severed. "Got tired of the upkeep."

Robin glanced at her nails. "You've also given up the manicures, I see."

Greer glanced at her shorn nails. Vineyards and French manicures didn't mix. "I'm kind of back to basics these days."

Robin's grin widened. "Doing the Mother Earth thing. I get it. It's a good fit for you."

"Thanks."

"So do you come here often?" She swayed as she spoke. Dark sunglasses hid eyes Greer guessed were bloodshot.

"Enough."

"I just opened a dress shop in Austin," Robin said. "High end. Very cutting edge. It's called Elegance."

Greer felt frumpy next to Robin. She might have turned her back on the old life, but pride had her wishing she were a little more pulled together at this moment. "You always dressed well."

"Like I always say, you can feel like shit, but you have to look great."

The comment caught Greer off guard. Old protective instincts born in the camp welled. "You doing okay?"

An unexplained emotion crossed Robin's face and then she smiled. "Never better. In fact, you should come visit me sometime in Austin. And my name is Jennifer. Jennifer Bell."

"I go by Greer now. My middle name."

"Call me."

"Sure."

This wasn't the place to pry or dig and honestly Greer hadn't wanted to revisit the past. She'd grinned and accepted the explanation she'd known in her heart wasn't true.

Jennifer lifted the near-empty glass to her lips and grinned. "Great." She hesitated. "Elizabeth . . . Greer. I really do wish you happiness."

Greer had hesitated as if sensing there was more she wanted to say. "You okay?"

Jennifer sipped her wine. "Yeah, fine. I really wish you the best."

"Right."

They'd exchanged more meaningless comments, made plans for a lunch date they'd never keep, and then Jennifer had drifted into the crowd leaving Greer rattled and distracted.

Greer now searched the Web on her phone for the dress shop Elegance. The Web site popped up and Greer learned the shop was located in an exclusive section of Austin. She hit the Web site's ABOUT button and Jennifer's picture popped up. She stood in front of her store, dressed in a richly tailored blue suit, heels, and diamond earrings. Arms folded over her chest, her smile was casual and full of life, as if she had the world by the tail.

And maybe she did. Maybe Jennifer was doing

really well. Maybe it was possible to let the past go and move on to a happy life.

She wondered if Jennifer remembered their chance meeting two years ago. She wondered if she'd heard about Rory or Sara.

Instead of getting on the interstate, Greer tucked the puppy close to her and wove through town toward Jennifer's dress shop.

Greer parked in front of the store and watched as ladies went in empty-handed and came out with bags bulging. She shut off the engine and glanced at Dog. "Too hot to leave you here. How about I tuck you close under my shirt and pay a quick visit?"

The dog licked her hand. Grabbing her purse, she slid out the driver's-side door and hurried into the shop. Greeted by the scents of lavender and expensive perfume, she was aware of her jeans, T-shirt, and dusty boots. A saleslady smiled at her but didn't approach. Hedging her bets, she thought. There was a lot of money in Texas that was covered in dust and this gal didn't want to take the chance of offending money. But she also didn't approach, a clear sign she really didn't want to deal with Greer.

Tough. Greer moved toward the woman, Dog tucked under her arm as if he were the fanciest purebred in Texas. If Greer's mother had taught her any lesson, it was to grab the upper hand. "I'm a friend of Jennifer's."

The saleslady glanced at Dog and then took a step back. “She’s in her office.”

“Tell her Elizabeth Templeton is here. We went to camp together as kids.”

The woman cocked her head.

“We saw each other at the wine festival in Fredericksburg a couple of years ago. I run the Bonneville Vineyards. We promised to get together but, well, life has been crazy and I don’t get to town often. But I’m here now.”

The salesclerk’s eyes narrowed. She wasn’t convinced.

Greer leveled her gaze as her mother had always done with the hired help. She reached for the phone in her back pocket. “I can text her and let her know I’m here.”

The clerk straightened. “I’ll let her know.”

Greer and Dog waited by the front counter aware several ladies stared at her. This might have been her world at one time, but it wasn’t any longer. She’d sensed it at the party the other night, and knew it for certain now. Her world revolved around the earth, the sky, water, and most importantly the grapes. Here she was the fly in the ointment, capable of driving away customers.

Jennifer emerged from the office dressed in a sleek black sleeveless dress grazing her calves. A large silver Concho necklace dipped below her breasts and matched a thick manacle bracelet and dangling earrings. Perfect make-up. Heels for fashion not for function.

She glanced around the store at her customers and smiled as if welcoming an old friend. "Elizabeth. I mean, Greer, right? What a surprise. Please, come back in my office."

Sensing fear behind the smile, she followed Jennifer behind the counter and into the back office. Jennifer closed the door behind her and the friendly drunk from two years ago had transformed into a stone-sober, annoyed, and angry woman.

Jennifer faced her and glanced at Dog. She smiled. "What is that?"

Greer held Dog a little closer. "A puppy."

"A dog?" She laughed. "It's missing some pieces."

"Aren't we all?" Greer glanced at the little guy and smiled so he wouldn't be worried about the chill in Jennifer's tone.

Jennifer drew in a slow, steady breath, as if her nerves had suddenly frayed. "What are you doing here, Elizabeth?"

The sweet scents of lavender and perfume reminded Greer she smelled of dirt, dog, and sweat. "I came to ask you about Shady Grove."

"Shady Grove?" She dropped her voice a notch. "Why would you want to talk about that?"

Her stomach clenched. "Believe me, it wasn't on my wish list this morning when I woke up."

"Then why are you here?" She shook her head, her eyes dark and turbulent. "I don't want to talk about that place. I don't want to think about it."

A bitter smile tweaked the edge of Greer's lips. "Join the club. Did you hear about Rory and Sara? We knew her as Joan."

Jennifer flexed ringed fingers. "I'm all about my shop and my customers. I'm dating a great guy. I have so much now, and I don't want to lose it."

"I'm not here to take. I want to know if you've had any contact with Rory and Sara."

She folded her arms. "God, no."

"Not any?"

"No."

The dog nestled closer to Greer. "Anyone else from camp?"

"No." She shook her head.

"You and Sara work in the same town."

She shoved out a breath. "Okay, I saw Sara at a business-to-business function last year. I'm not sure if she saw me, but I didn't approach her. In fact, I left shortly after I spotted her." Her voice sharpened. "And I heard Rory was a mess. Drugs. Again."

"Did you know Rory died?"

Anxiety moved through her body, straightening her back. "Like I said, I don't keep up."

Greer couldn't let this go. Two of the five kids in the pod were dead. "He hung himself. The cops think it's murder."

Jennifer's face paled. She shook her head and took a step back as if she needed distance. "I've not seen Rory since camp. Heard rumors about the drugs. He never got his act together. Why are we doing this? Can't we let the past go? I know we both made terrible mistakes but when do we stop suffering and move on?"

"I work at it every day."

"I do, too."

Greer sighed. She'd liked Jennifer when they'd been in camp. The girl had been frightened and skittish but she'd been nice to Greer. "Sara is also dead, Jennifer. She froze to death."

Her mouth dropped before she snapped it closed. "She committed suicide?"

"Cops don't know for sure."

"You think she and Rory are somehow connected? I know she really had a crush on him at camp."

"Who knows? He might have remembered she liked him and hit her up for money. That would be classic Rory. He could have made promises he couldn't keep. She had a bad temper."

"You think she could have killed him and then herself?"

"I don't know. I'm trying to understand what happened."

Jennifer raked her hand through her hair. "Leave it up to the cops. Just leave it alone."

"I can't. Rory's body was found near my vineyard and he had a picture of us taken at camp on him when he died."

She paled. "A picture of all of us?"

"Just Rory and me."

Relieved, Jennifer shook her head. "I don't know about them, and honestly I don't want to know. I want all that past junk to stay buried. I don't want to lose what I have. I met a guy who is so great there are days I wonder how I got lucky."

A heavy silence hung between them and clearly Jennifer wanted her to leave. But Greer couldn't let it go yet. "You never think about that time?" She'd not meant to ask the question but it had been a long time since she'd spoken to someone who'd been in as bad a place as she.

Jennifer shook her head. "No, I don't. I don't. I have forgiven myself."

Greer leaned toward her a fraction, genuine curiosity pulsing through her body. "How did you manage forgiveness?"

She frowned and took the question as a challenge. "What do you mean how? I just did."

Greer shook her head. "I still struggle with it."

Jennifer shrugged. "I can't help you. I just know I manage it. The past is the past. End of story. Please."

Greer searched Jennifer's eyes for a flicker or a waver that signaled a lie or doubt. But there was none and she was both glad for her friend and a little jealous. "Maybe one day I will find peace as well."

For a moment Jennifer's face softened as if she wanted to say more. "Greer . . ."

And then beyond the office door the voices of customers drifted toward them. The front shop door opened and closed.

Jennifer straightened and the emotional guards slipped into place. "I don't want to talk about this anymore. I've work. My customers expect personal attention."

The moment, the near connection they'd shared closed with the shop door. "Yeah, I have to get back to the vineyard." The next moments were awkward. A dozen years ago they'd have hugged. Now it didn't feel right, whereas walking away bordered on cold. She managed a smile and then turned toward the door.

"Elizabeth," Jennifer said.

"Yes?" She turned, a little hopeful.

"Please don't come by here again. I'd fix both our pasts if I could. I'd wish it all back, if possible. But I can't. Now, I've a good thing going and I'm going to be married in eight months. My fiancé and his family don't know about Shady Grove, and I want to keep it that way. Let the dead bury the dead."

Greer hugged Dog a little closer. "Sure."

Mitch didn't much like the black horse, Beauty. Turn your back on her for a second, and she'd find a way to nip at your shoulder. He had a couple of healthy bruises on his shoulder and a couple of times she made him yelp. But not anymore. He might not know all the rules yet, but he was a fast learner. She kept him on his toes. If his mind wandered back to the darkness, she was there to bite and remind she would not be ignored.

As he tossed the hay in her feed bin, he kept one eye on the job and one on her.

The day was hotter than hell, but not as blistering as Iraq. The air in Texas was clean and clear and in the Hill Country free of the Middle East sand lurking in the air ready to clog his throat and nose or burrow under his clothes and irritate his skin.

The first time he'd gotten off the plane the air had been so hot he'd thought the heat had come from the jet's engines. Sweat-soaked clothes became a matter of course and a good night's sleep was impossible in the oppressive heat.

Yeah, Texas could get hotter than hell, but it was home and would always beat Iraq.

If only Iraq would stay on the other side of the world. But it had followed him here. Stalked him. If he closed his eyes he could hear the grinding noise of vehicles, the shouts of soldiers, the drone of low-flying planes and gunfire.

He'd remembered when he'd first arrived back in Austin and dumped his bag on the spare bed in his uncle's rented house. The cool air, quiet, and soft bed had been distracting and for several weeks he'd put a sleeping bag on the floor. He hoped the hard floor would offer a familiarity that might ease the transition home. But when he'd closed his eyes and fallen asleep the dreams began. They'd all been the same, not varying a little.

He'd been behind the wheel of the Humvee. He'd been in the country for a year and grown accustomed to the coiling heat and the weight of his body armor. A battery-operated radio that dangled from the ceiling had been blaring Bruce Springsteen. His buddy Max had cracked a joke about a girl's breasts. He and his buddies had been laughing.

The mission had been routine. And though they said they were on their toes at all times, familiarity with the job had made them a little cocky. As the driver, it had been his job to avoid the IEDs, to keep the vehicle on the road, and to keep his friends alive.

And then he'd been distracted for a moment by the flicker of a light in the distance, and he'd edged too close to the edge of the road. The next moment a loud explosion ripped through the music and the laughter, shredded his eardrums and battered him about like a piece of meat. Next, he'd been crawling through hot twisted metal, clawing at the dirt as he pulled himself free. He'd called out to his buddies, searched the blackening smoke, but pain and a blow to the head had made the world spin, and then he'd blacked out.

Later he'd awoken in the hospital. Burned on the left side of his body. His first question had been for his men, and when he'd found out they'd all been killed he'd retreated into himself as far as he could go. He didn't want to be around people. Talk again. Care again. Live again.

He'd thought about ending it all, after the third military funeral. It would be easy enough to let the final darkness take him and make the pain go away.

But as much as he'd thought about it he couldn't manage it. He was too scared to die and too undeserving to live.

Tec had given him a roof and a bed. But it was clear his uncle didn't know what to do with him. Hell, Tec was a goddamned legend in the Rangers. He'd pursued outlaws, faced human traffickers, and been in a couple of gun battles. He'd walked away from it all unscathed with no lingering regrets.

Maybe Mitch was too much like his own mother. Well-meaning but simply weak.

A sharp pain dug into his shoulder and he whirled around at Beauty's braying. He rubbed his shoulder, annoyed at her but angrier at himself. "Damn it, girl. Can't you lay off for a minute? Shit, there won't be a bit of my flesh left at the rate you are going."

The horse neighed.

"Yeah, you are the smart one. You got all the damn answers. Just like my uncle. You think you know."

The horse did not move or look away.

"You think because you outweigh me that I can't take you? Think I won't haul off and deck you if you bite me again?"

The horse cocked her head as if bored.

Mitch sighed. "Shit, I'm out in a damn corral having a conversation with a stupid horse." And again for the fifth time today he wondered why he'd taken this job. He had his Marine pay to tide him over. A buddy of his had told him he could get a job on the oil rigs in a matter of hours. But here he was with a bitch of a horse, making crap wages and sweating his ass off in the afternoon heat.

The rumble of an old engine had him turning toward the cloud of dust kicked up by Greer's old black truck. She'd said she'd go into town today for feed, and he was glad she'd returned. Beauty was cranky on a full stomach but when she thought she was going to miss a meal she was hell on wheels. Not that he blamed her. It was clear she'd not been fed too well the last year. She was pushy for her food because she was a survivor.

Buttercup's tail twitched as she too spotted Greer's truck. She was more laid back than

Beauty, but she stuck close to her when she pushed for the next meal. Buttercup knew enough to know she'd get her fed.

The old nags had been at Bonneville merely days and already the animals knew Greer would somehow make their lives right.

And somehow he'd had the same sense when she'd walked into that bar and offered him this job. He'd been suspicious and wary of all other forms of help, but in Greer he'd sensed a survivor and a fighter. He'd seen it in her eyes when she'd sat across from him. And she hadn't begged or pleaded with him. In fact, he had the sense she didn't want to do him the favor. But she'd offered, and he'd realized she was his lifeline.

Greer's truck came to a stop by the storage shed and she got out, cradling a small creature close to her belly. She was also talking real soft and slow. Beauty and Buttercup's ears perked as Greer approached.

Mitch didn't say a word as she approached, her ball cap covering her hair and her dark mirrored sunglasses tossing back his reflection. When she was several feet from him a small head popped up from under her arm and barked at him.

He shook his head. "If that's a dog, it's the ugliest dog I've ever seen."

Greer covered the pup's ears. "He's smart, and he knows when you are making fun of him."

He couldn't help a smile. "He does?"

"I kidded with him about his mug on the ride home and that annoyed him."

"Really?" He waited for the punch line.

Her expression remained serious. "Honest. He's smart."

The dog opened his eyes, well, eye, and yawned. He sniffed the air and glared up at Mitch as if he were some kind of squatter. "What's his name?"

"Right now it's Dog. That's what they called him at the feed store."

"That's not a name. It's a noun." Shit, the animal deserved a name.

"I know. I've been trying out names all the way here but none fit. A cute name really doesn't work with that face."

"He was born without the eye?"

She stroked the dog between the ears. "From what I hear."

"He's lucky his mamma nursed him. Most will nudge out the offspring that ain't right." The boss had found herself another outcast.

"Guess if he wasn't so smart he'd not have survived."

He scratched his head. "You have an attraction for the broken. Me, the horses, this dog. What's it with you?"

She scratched Dog between the ears. "Takes one to know one, I suppose. Someone helped me once. Now I'm paying it back or forward, I guess."

"I read about you on the Internet." When Tec had tossed a couple of warnings his way about Greer he'd done some digging. Tec was a man of few words and when he spoke, Mitch listened. "You've been through it."

Her fingers stilled. "So have you. So have the horses and so has this little guy. None of us has a corner on pain and suffering."

The counselors had tried to talk to him over the last month or two, but he'd never wanted to talk to them. They were good, well-intentioned people but their questions made him mad. Greer never asked questions. As long as he was working, she left him alone. If she saw him sitting, she found a task for him to do.

"So how did you do it?" he asked.

She tilted her head back and his reflection caught in her mirrored sunglasses. "Do what?"

Emotion threatened to break his voice and he paused until he had his voice under control. "Pull yourself up?"

She sighed. "I don't know. I came out here to live with my aunt and she told me to put one foot in front of the other. But those first days, the idea of one or two steps exhausted me. But she kept giving me chores, forcing me to keep moving."

"You do that to me."

"I know."

"So when did you turn the corner?"

"Honestly, Mitch, I think I'm still searching for

that corner. I still don't think beyond one step at a time."

"But you plan ahead for the vineyard. I heard you talking about the harvest. You are going to build that winery. You are living."

"I still believe I'm living for Jeff and Sydney. To squander my life would be an insult to them." She drew in a breath. "And I've fallen for the vineyard. I didn't expect to but I did. The grapes are like Beauty. They don't care about my sob story. My emotions. All that matters is to keep working so that the vineyard doesn't turn on me."

The pain in his shoulder had been Beauty's reminder for attention. He was silent for a moment watching as she scratched the pup between its ears. "So the pain never goes away?"

"Not totally. But it lessens a little bit every day. At first it feels like a boulder on your shoulders. And then one day it feels like a handful of rocks. And then pebbles. Always there, but it becomes manageable."

She wasn't feeding him rainbows and happy endings. Just honesty. "I'm not sure I want it to go away completely."

"Me, either. I never want to forget the people I loved."

A heavy silence settled and for a moment neither spoke. Then he studied Dog. "Shit, that's an ugly dog."

She covered the dog's ears and nodded. "Shh."

The one-eyed dog stared at him as if challenging his right to be here. “It wouldn’t have lasted a day in the shelter. People want cute and easy.”

“I know.”

“Folks were kind of like that with me when I came home from Iraq. Everyone wanted the war stories. They wanted the glory. But when I tried to tell them it was dirty and ugly and painful, folks just walked away.”

She was silent for a moment. “I have a knack for scaring people off, too. No one knows what to say to me. Hell, I don’t know what I want to say to me.”

Greer wasn’t afraid of scars. Maybe because she was brave or maybe she had so many of her own she didn’t notice them too much anymore.

But he did know she hadn’t walked away from him, those damn horses, or the ugliest dog in Texas. And that counted for something.

“I don’t know why you don’t kill her now. I’m so tired of waiting.”

Jackson hated her voice’s constant buzzing in his ear.

Kill her. Kill her. Buzz. Buzz.

With eyes still pressed to the binoculars’ eyecups, he watched as she handed a mangy dog to her new farmhand. “I just took care of one.”

“But she wasn’t her.”

“It’s not time for her.”

"How do you know it's not time? My God, all you've done is talk about Greer. Elizabeth. Greer. I get sick of hearing about her."

Buzz. Buzz. Buzz.

It was getting harder and harder to ignore her. With an effort, he kept his focus on Greer.

He knew a lot about Greer Templeton.

And not simply the information anyone could read about on the Internet. He knew her current daily routine as if it were his own, and he also knew her hopes, fears, and dreams.

He'd come to learn Greer rose at five every morning. She rarely varied her wardrobe, choosing a Bonneville T-shirt, jeans, and the same scuffed boots. He liked the jeans and the way they showed off her narrow waist and hips that rounded just right.

Meticulous watching had taught him her daily order of business was to dress and then to take her first coffee onto the small stone patio adjacent to her house. Overlooking her vineyards, the patio caught the morning sun. Rarely, did she miss a sunrise or raise her cup to it before she took her first sip.

After her coffee, she headed out into the fields to check on her vines and to meet with the farm manager, José. Together the two rode up and down the rows, inspecting branches, the leaf canopy, or sampling grapes. No detail was too small for Greer. She clearly loved Bonneville.

Once her grapes were inspected she returned to the small ranch house she'd shared with her aunt for over a decade and enjoyed a small breakfast. Her tastes were simple, usually toast and an egg. And then it was off for more meetings or trips into the fields. Afternoons were spent working on the books. Last year she'd overseen the building of the new tasting room with the dedication she gave to her vineyards. And now that laser attention would shift to her new winery.

Her days often didn't end until eight or nine when she'd drag herself back to her home and eat a small dinner. She ate lots of salad, always a side of bread with a little butter and a glass of wine. Merlot was her favorite.

Her routines followed the seasons and this season, summer, was her busiest. Soon the grapes would peak and the harvest would commence. She'd harvest with care, only taking the grapes that were ready, and always patient enough to leave the others behind until they'd ripened.

He was very much like Greer. He understood the best harvester was patient. Like her he understood the best grapes were those that had suffered some hardship, for it was the hardship that truly formed great taste and character. Greer and her grapes weren't sickly sweet because they'd been tested and tried.

"So when are you going to kill her?"

He lowered the binoculars from his eyes.

"Greer, like her grapes, is nearly ready for harvest."

"What difference does a day or two make?"

"It makes all the difference. It's the difference between perfection and swill."

Soon Greer would be ready. Soon he'd harvest her like the others.

Chapter Fifteen

Saturday, June 7, 7 A.M.

An Austin police patrol car spotted Sara Wentworth's car parked in an industrial lot along the river in East Austin, five miles from where her body had been discovered. He'd called the find in at seven, the very end of his shift.

Bragg had been at his desk when the call had been received. He'd grabbed his jacket and hat and headed out.

As he drove, he realized this had been the first "normal" morning he'd had in months. Mitch had been up early and eager to get to Bonneville, and so Bragg had left with him right after dawn. Before Mitch, he'd worked long, sometimes crushing hours, but since Mitch's arrival, he'd lingered in the mornings or gotten home earlier. For the first time, his personal life had elbowed ahead of his professional life.

But today, he had his old schedule back. And to his surprise, it didn't fit as well as it once had. A bit tight and restrictive. Since he'd arrived this morning, he'd not only wondered how Mitch was managing, but Greer as well. Several times, he'd had to resist the temptation to drive out and check on them both.

Bragg spotted flashing police lights. Out of his SUV, he settled his white hat on his head and strode toward the police car lights and the yellow crime-scene tape surrounding the white Lexus.

The car's hubcaps had been stripped and the front driver's-side window had been smashed and the air bag and radio stolen. It was doubtful the thefts were related to Sara's death. An unattended Lexus in East Austin attracted thieves like flowers attracted bees. He was amazed any portion of the car remained.

The warehouse by the car was a two-story brick building with rows of broken windows. Faded paint on the building's top floor read MCGREGOR'S. The building had once been a dry goods store and later a restaurant that had closed three years ago. The place was up for sale, but Sara Wentworth did not have the listing.

The forensic tech was a short woman with an olive complexion and dark hair pulled back into a ponytail and tucked under an APD ball cap. She wore a blue regulation T-shirt that read AUSTIN POLICE and rumpled khakis in need of hemming.

Standing back from the scene, inches inside the yellow tape with a clipboard in hand, the technician sketched the scene.

As Bragg moved closer to the tape she turned and nodded. “Ranger Bragg?”

He touched the brim of his hat. “Yes, ma’am.”

“I’m Carla Sellers. I’m with Austin PD.”

“Yes, ma’am. Can you tell me what you’ve found?”

“We had a BOLO on your victim’s car. The uniform who spotted it realized the car was out of place. This isn’t the kind of place most leave a Lexus unattended. My guess is the damage done to the vehicle was done by vandals and thieves.”

He rested his hands on his hips and searched for a security camera. He spotted two on the building across the street and hoped they were operational. Many businesses put up cameras but many also didn’t bother to connect them hoping the camera alone would be a deterrent. “Has anyone contacted those businesses about their cameras?”

“Had a couple of uniforms knocking on doors and trying to find out about them.”

“Good. I want to see that footage.”

Carla stuck her pencil in her ponytail. “Where was your victim found?”

“Five point two miles from here. I just clocked the distance.”

“And she was a suicide?”

The doubt in her voice echoed his concerns. "Remains undetermined."

Sara Wentworth certainly could have assisted Rory in his suicide. And she could have parked her car here and walked five miles in high heels in the Texas heat to the warehouse. Yeah, he'd seen all kinds of things. But unless she'd totally lost it, the scenario didn't hold water. There'd been the matter of the bloody doll in her trash can, her heels found by her body had been pristine, and the medical examiner had found no traces of blistering on her feet.

"I'm going to need the footage from those cameras ASAP. I'd bet good money she didn't walk away but was taken away."

"Sure."

"Mind if I have a look in the car?"

"I've dusted for prints. Found a lot of them, by the way. But seeing as the car was torn apart no telling whose we'll find. Also photographed the interior. The GPS, radio, and air bag were gone. Another day, it would have been stripped clean. It's all yours." She pulled a set of rubber gloves from her back pocket and handed them to him.

"Appreciate it." He pulled on the gloves and then ducked under the tape, moving to the driver's-side door first to study the light tan interior. There was a coffee cup from one of those high-end shops in Austin with red lipstick smudging the top's spout. The glove box was open and inside he found area maps. GPS could be wrong and a savvy Realtor needed to get around efficiently to make a living. The car looked as if it once had been showroom clean. He imagined no trash, vacuumed carpets, and polished windows. Between the seats was a collection of CDs. Classical music, self-help and motivational tapes. *The Million-Dollar Deal. Ten Steps to Record-Breaking Sales*. Not fodder for thieves.

He popped the trunk and walked around to the back of the car. In the trunk there was a bin with one remaining sandal but he suspected they'd been full of shoes. Sara would have been prepared for any kind of terrain or trip. A five-mile walk was feasible, but remembering the pristine shape of her heels, he doubted it. There was also a cooler filled with water bottles and a collection of signs sporting the MANLY AND DOBBS real estate logo and Sara's smiling photo-shopped face.

By all appearances, Sara Wentworth was an ambitious woman with her sights set on the future. She had no apparent reason to track a drug-addicted man from her past, kill him, and then herself. Sure, it could have happened. Rory could have sent her the doll and triggered a deadly chain reaction.

It could have been a murder-suicide scenario; however, if he had to bet money, he'd wager someone else had murdered them both.

• • •

Bragg arrived at the real estate office of Manly and Dobbs a half hour later. Located in the center of Austin blocks from the white dome of the state capitol, the building had lots of glass, a sleek sign out front, and manicured planters with lush green plants.

He pushed through the office door and a young, blond receptionist glanced up at him with a bright smile on her face. The instant she saw his white hat and star badge the smile vanished. He wasn't a customer. And he was here about Sara.

She rose. "Ranger. You've come about Sara?"

"Yes, ma'am."

She flipped her hair out of her eyes. "We are all in shock about it. No one can believe Sara would kill herself. Her life was perfect."

"She didn't give you any indication that she wasn't doing well?"

"Nothing. She was a happy woman."

Smiles could hide a lot of pain and everyone had secrets. "There someone here that kept up with her appointments?"

"All our agents are independent. They use the office primarily for mail and the occasional meeting. Often, I'd not see Sara for days or weeks. She was in her car most of the time. But I can buzz Rita Herbert. She's our office manager, and if Sara had been in touch with anyone it would have been Rita."

"Appreciate it."

When she vanished down the hallway, he waited in the lobby studying the glossy pictures of high-end properties in the Austin area. Manly and Dobbs handled the best clients, which fit with Sara's profile.

Greer and Sara had come from the same privileged world and ended up at Shady Grove. But Shady Grove had been a fork in the road. Sara had returned to her old, sheltered world, whereas Greer had upended herself and built a life the opposite of her roots. She'd traded beauty salons, manicures, and high-end clothes for jeans, hard work, and a vineyard that likely took as much as it gave. This reinvented Greer fascinated him to no end.

"Ranger Bragg?"

He turned to find a tall brunette studying him. She wore conservative dark pants, a white long-sleeved shirt, and a matching jacket that skimmed full hips. Horn-rimmed glasses accentuated large blue eyes heavily made up. Gold hoop earrings matched a gold rope necklace that dangled below full breasts.

He extended his hand, and she moved to meet it easily as if she'd shaken millions of hands in this office. "Ms. Herbert?"

"Yes. I'm Rita Herbert, the office manager." Her thick brows drew together. "I hear you've questions about Sara."

“I’m trying to piece together her last day or two. I was hoping you might have an idea about some of the clients she met with that last day.”

With manicured fingers, she combed away a strand of hair from her face. “I don’t understand. Why do you need her client list? I thought Sara killed herself.”

No sense triggering alarm bells. For now he wanted answers. “It’s standard to examine the deceased’s last days.”

She sighed. “I still can’t believe it. Sara was our best agent. She had just sealed the deal and made a six-figure commission. She was at the top of her game.”

“What kinds of property did she sell?”

“Some high-end residential but for the most part she handled the corporate sales. Her family has been in Austin for fifty years, and they had all kinds of connections. She used those connections to get her start. But she quickly proved to everyone she was more than just a rich girl. She was talented in sales and worked harder than anybody.”

“Did you keep track of her appointments?”

“No. She kept her own book. She did call in on Tuesday asking about a missing business card. She sounded rattled and upset.”

He thought about the trash-can discovery. “She say what was bothering her?”

“I asked but she laughed it off. Said she was a

little forgetful these days." She dug a card from her pocket. "This is the card she wanted. I still had it on my desk."

He accepted it. "She have anything to say about the client?"

"Only that he owned restaurants back East and had his eye on Austin."

He glanced at the card. Howard Corwin. From Washington, D.C. His chain was called Legends. "Have you contacted him since Sara's death?"

"No. We've all been a mess since we heard the news. Sara really was the backbone of corporate sales."

He glanced at the number. "Where'd they have coffee last week?"

"I don't know."

"May I keep this?"

"Sure."

"Any more details you can share about him?"

"Why are you interested in this guy? Do you think he is connected to her death?"

"I don't have solid facts at this point, ma'am. I need to follow every rabbit trail I come across."

"That makes sense, I guess."

"Yes, ma'am. If you think of any new details that strike you as odd about this guy or any of her other clients, let me know."

She frowned. "Sure."

He thanked her again for her time and promised to be in touch. As soon as he slid behind the wheel of his SUV and turned on the engine, he dialed Corwin's number.

The phone rang several times and then a male voice-mail message said: *"You've reached Howard Corwin of Corwin Enterprises. I'm traveling this week so leave a message, and I'll get back to you."*

Bragg hung up and stared at the card. Anyone could make a card. But fooling a seasoned real estate agent like Sara Wentworth would take more than a bogus number. He flipped on his computer and searched Corwin Enterprises. A second or two later he had a Baltimore number that did not match the number on the card. Stood to reason Corwin's direct line wouldn't match the Web site number. Still, he dialed the Web site number.

As the phone rang, he pulled off his hat and tossed it on the passenger seat. On the second ring a receptionist answered the phone. "Corwin Enterprises."

Bragg introduced himself and explained he needed to speak to Corwin. She put him on hold and ten seconds later, he heard, "This is Howard Corwin."

"Lieutenant Bragg, Texas Rangers in Austin, Texas, sir. I'd like to ask you about your recent meeting with Sara Wentworth."

Silence crackled over the line. "I don't know a Sara Wentworth."

Bragg glanced at the card in his hand. "Sara

Wentworth is a real estate agent here in Austin. According to her office manager you met with Sara two days ago in Austin about restaurant property."

"Ranger Bragg, I've not been to Austin in fifteen years. And two days ago I was working in my office here in Baltimore. A hundred people can verify that. I'm not sure why Ms. Wentworth is claiming we met."

"I've a copy of your business card that her office manager gave me. Got your name on it." He repeated the phone number.

"Not my number, Ranger. Whoever this woman met with, it was not me."

Bragg flicked the edge of the card with his index finger. The guy sounded genuinely surprised, though Bragg would do a full background check, and he would verify his alibi.

"So why do you think the office manager at an Austin real estate firm had your card?"

"You might have a card that looks like mine, but I wasn't in Austin. Like I said, I was in the Baltimore office holding a planning meeting. It lasted from eight in the morning to at least seven in the evening. What does Ms. Wentworth want? Is she making some kind of claim against me?"

Bragg tucked the card in his pocket. "Ms. Wentworth is dead, Mr. Corwin. We found her body yesterday. She'd been locked in a freezer and she died of exposure."

A long pause followed. “I give out my card all the time, Ranger Bragg. I’m in the restaurant development business and that’s the nature of the beast. Anyone could have copied it.”

He sat back, his eyes narrowing as he stared at the cityscape. “I’m going to need the names of the people you were in that meeting with.”

“I will help you in any way. Whatever you need. But like I said, I’ve never laid eyes on Sara Wentworth.”

Bragg scrawled the names of several key individuals in Corwin’s meeting, thanked the man, and hung up. Whatever doubts he’d had about Sara’s death had now been satisfied. She’d been murdered.

This would be Greer’s last night volunteering at the Crisis Center for at least six weeks. Soon the harvest would bring long hours in the fields cutting the grapes from the vines and preparing them for transport. She tried to work the phones once during harvest season. It had been nine years ago, and she’d been so exhausted when she’d sat at the phones, she’d fallen asleep.

Therefore, she’d understood even crazed workaholics had limits. Even they needed to throttle back and accept some things had to be let go.

She shifted the gears of her truck and pulled on to Rural Route 71. Thirty more minutes and she’d be in Austin sitting in her gray cubicle with a fresh cup of coffee in her hand.

The cooling breeze blew in her cracked window and teased the loose strands of hair framing her face. As much as she wanted to relax, her fingers gripped the wheel tighter and she sat a little straighter. Driving at night or close to dusk still made her nervous even after all this time.

Absently, she tugged on her seat belt to ensure it was locked. And though it would be nice to listen to the radio, this late in the day she didn't allow the distraction.

In the distance, headlights appeared. She sat straighter, gripped the wheel even tighter, and watched with a careful eye as the car approached. The car drew closer and closer. And only when it passed her by did she release the breath she held.

A half hour later, Greer arrived at the Crisis Center minutes before eight. She'd been volunteering at the Crisis Center for ten years and though there were times when she toyed with letting it go, she never could because once in a while she got someone on the phone who truly needed a kind ear to help them through a dark moment.

"Hey, Danni," Greer said.

Danni had dark short hair and favored black and silver jewelry. She was barely twenty but had been working the night-shift desk at the center for six months. During the day the kid went to school at UT majoring in art. She also picked up a waitress shift and sometimes worked for a local photographer.

Beaded bracelets jangled when Danni raised her hand in greeting. "Greer. Have a phone with your name on it."

"Have there been a lot of calls?" This time of year the lines were generally quiet. The holidays, chock-full of family gatherings, celebrations, and events intended to be happy, often triggered a crisis.

"The early shifts handled calls from lonely people who needed someone to talk to."

Greer dropped her backpack to the floor and took the seat across from Danni. "Good. I could use a slow night. No crisis."

Danni leaned back in her chair and folded her arms. "You're coming into grape time, aren't you?"

"I was testing them today as a matter of fact. Just about sweet enough. We're about two weeks out from harvest time."

"You should have taken a pass on your shift tonight. I would have covered for you."

"I thought about it a couple of times. But it's good for me to get off the property and connect with people. I spend too much time with the grapes."

Danni laughed. "As long as they don't talk to you."

"That's a bad thing?" Greer teased, grinning.

"Well," she said, pretending to think, "I guess it depends on what the grapes are saying."

Greer shook her head. "If any grape talks to me, no matter how sweet the words, I'm in trouble."

Danni laughed. Her console phone rang and she leaned forward in her chair. "When the grapes talk it is not a good day."

"Exactly."

Danni reached for the phone receiver as Greer moved to her simple gray cubicle. "I'll be at my station.

"By the way, you're still welcome to work the harvest. You'd mentioned making a little extra money and we are a little shorthanded this season.

"I'm in. Always looking to make an extra buck."

"I'm training a new farmhand this week, so if you can come out I can double up the training."

"Name the day."

"I'll text you tomorrow."

Greer's station was stocked with one phone that could accommodate up to six lines. She spoke to one crisis client at a time but there'd been times when she'd believed her caller was in real trouble, had to make an excuse, put the caller on hold, and called 911 for a trace. Emergency personnel were dispatched to the caller's location. Most nights weren't that dramatic. She usually extended a sympathetic ear. Many of her callers weren't in real trouble as much as they were lonely.

She set her backpack on the desk. She always brought work from the office, knowing some nights no one called. During those times she balanced accounts, outlined harvest schedules, or updated personnel files. The vineyard could be jealous and required she fill every pocket of spare time.

She rarely questioned her long hours, which initially had been her salvation. But tonight when she looked at her backpack crammed full of ledgers, resentment flared. She had the life she wanted. Loved her vineyard. Was excited about the winery. And yet she heard the faintest whispers of loneliness.

Most nights she was too exhausted to notice that she climbed into bed alone. Most nights all she wanted to do was sleep and not dream. But most nights weren't all nights.

Her mind turned to Bragg and again she wondered what it would be like to touch him, to kiss him. With him in her bed, the nights would never be boring. And she doubted she'd get much sleep. Color warmed her cheeks as she thought about his naked body pressed against hers.

When she realized that Danni hadn't sent the call her way, she reached in her backpack and pulled out a stack of technical articles on winemaking that she'd need to read. She wasn't sure how long she sat in the silence combing through the articles. Her aunt had always joked Greer filled every second of every day, and Greer had always countered that time was the ultimate resource. It wasn't limitless. Once it was gone, game over.

When her phone rang, she pulled off her reading glasses, cleared her throat, and on the third ring picked up the phone. "Crisis Center, this is Greer."

They had a script to follow and protocols to adhere to in all situations. She wasn't a licensed counselor and if the caller sounded to be in real trouble, she signaled Danni to contact the doctor on call.

"Greer, is that you?" The woman's voice was soft, insistent.

Her fingers tightened around the phone. Occasionally a caller would ask for her by name but not often and it always unhinged her a little. "Yes, this is Greer."

"Good. Good. I was hoping you'd answer the phone tonight. You've not been at the call center for days."

She sat straighter. She always kept a clear line between her personal life and the work she did here. "Who am I talking to?"

A hesitation. "You don't recognize my voice?"

"I'm sorry, I don't."

A heavy silence drifted through the line.

Greer shifted in her seat. "Who is this?"

"You should know." Her voice had an eerily smooth quality.

She began to doodle squares on her pad. "I'm sorry. It's late. Tell me."

"I'm not going to tell you," she teased. "You have to guess."

She rubbed her forehead with her fingertips. "I'm here to talk if you need help, but I'm not here to play games. Do you want to talk to me about something?"

"I want to talk about someone who takes their own life. Do you think suicide is a sin?"

For a moment the room stilled. She spoke carefully. "I think it's sad. It's a terrible shame when a person is so lost they see no way out."

"But is it a sin?" The last word came out in a hiss.

She tucked a stray curl behind her ear and considered signaling Danni. "That's not for me to say. I know other people more qualified than me to talk to about this."

"I think you are qualified."

"I'm not."

"Didn't you try and kill yourself? Didn't you try to take the easy way out, Elizabeth?"

Elizabeth. She gripped the phone. Her blood pressure plummeted and she grabbed ahold of the desk to steady herself. She'd changed her name from Elizabeth to Greer to get away from her past mistakes. No one in her current life knew about the past but when she'd held that party on Wednesday night she'd opened a portal to the past.

"Who is this?"

"It doesn't matter. What matters is I know there was a time you wanted to die more than live."

She shook her head trying to push back the terror rising in her chest.

A moment's hesitation followed and then, "I think it's okay to end the pain when it's too much."

Greer had had all kinds of calls. Desperate people. Angry people and yes, some creeps like this one. But this person had her radar standing on end. She rose and snapped her fingers to get Danni's attention.

The girl saw Greer pointing to her phone and recognized it was a signal to call the police.

Danni nodded and turned to her phone to dial. Seconds later she was talking quietly to the police.

"Greer?" the caller said.

"Yes?"

"Did I lose you for a minute?"

"I'm sorry. I was thinking about what you said."

"That suicide is a relief."

"Right," she lied.

"You agree?"

She kept her gaze on Danni as if it were a lifeline. "When suicide is an option in someone's mind they're in a desperate place. It makes me sad for them and I want to help them get past the pain."

"Is that possible or are you making that person suffer needlessly?" Urgency lurked behind her words.

"The pain is not forever."

"Has yours gone away?"

Anxiety banded around her chest. "I'm here to talk about you."

"I'm fine. It's you that I worry about."

"Why do you worry about me?"

No answer.

Danni held up a handwritten sign: COPS TRACING THE CALL.

Greer held her thumb up. "Who is this?"

"You should know me."

"I'm sorry. I should remember, but I don't."

Danni held up another sign: TWO MORE MINUTES AND THEY'LL HAVE IT.

"Are you in pain?" Greer didn't want an opinion but wanted to keep the caller on the line. Most people liked to talk about themselves, especially when they thought they had a captive audience.

"No. I'm like you. I help those that are hurting," she said. "Some people aren't meant to live on this planet. It's better they move on."

"At least give me your first name."

More silence and then, "Looks like our time is up."

"What do you mean?" Greer said. Less than two minutes. Two lousy minutes. "You haven't told me your name."

"Think hard enough, and you'll figure it out." A pause. "You should have dug the razor deeper when you sliced your wrists. You didn't try hard enough to die."

"Tell me your name!"

She chuckled. "You can fool yourself, but you can't fool me."

The line went dead, and for several seconds Greer sat there, her heart pumping in her chest.

"Hey, are you okay?" The sound of Danni's voice behind her made her jump.

She slammed the phone into the cradle and moved away from the cubicle as if it were a pit of snakes. "That caller gave me the creeps."

Danni frowned as she moved toward Greer. "Hung up too quickly. The cops couldn't trace it."

Greer shook her head, trying to ward off a bone-deep chill. "I think she knew we were tracing her."

"How?"

She fussed with the bracelets on her wrist. "I don't know, but she said our time was up."

Danni cocked her head, studying Greer closely. "What else did she say?"

Some people aren't meant to live on this planet. "She kept asking me if suicide was a sin."

Danni planted her hands on her narrow hips.

"Judging by the color of your face I'd say she said more than that."

"It doesn't matter. We both know strange calls come into this place often enough. We are a hotline, and she was jerking my chain."

"You're shaken."

She folded her arms over her chest. "I'm fine."

Some people aren't meant to live on this planet.

Chapter Sixteen

Saturday, June 7, 10 P.M.

Bragg stepped inside his front door and immediately spotted Mitch asleep on the couch. And cradled in his arms was the ugliest damn puppy he'd ever seen. So ugly, he paused to stare. Mitch didn't stir, but the pup opened his eyes, no, eye, and glared at him as if he were the intruder. The pup growled. Bragg smiled.

Before he could approach, his phone rang so he stepped outside to take the call. "Bragg."

"Ranger Bragg this is Austin dispatch. We just received a nine-one-one call from the Crisis Center."

Austin was a big small town and if you had connections word traveled fast. He quickly learned the crisis center had received a threatening call. Normally, he'd not have been alerted, but dispatch indicated the volunteer involved had been Greer Templeton. Days ago, he'd flagged her name, making it clear that if her name came up, he wanted to know about it.

"Thanks."

He rang off and checked his watch. Ten minutes after ten. If he hustled, he'd catch Greer before she'd left for the night.

When he pulled up in front of the center, Greer stood by the glass front door with a young girl who looked to be about twenty. Greer walked the girl to her car, wished her a good night, and then headed for her own truck.

"Greer," he said.

She turned, her expression wide-eyed. He stepped out of the shadows.

He saw her clutching her fingers at her side and realized she held a can of Mace. Dread seemed to seep from her body. She'd struck him as many things, but never jumpy. The caller had done this to her. A primal urge rose up in him, and if he could hunt down the caller right now, he'd tear him limb from limb.

When her gaze met his, the stress eased from her face. He wasn't sure why that mattered, but it did.

The reverse lights on the dark-haired kid's car lit up, and she backed up her car. She rolled down her window and glared at Bragg.

She was a slip of a girl, but her eyes burned with

ferocity. She held up her phone. "Greer, who is this guy? I have the cops on speed dial."

Greer shook her head, the ghost of a smile on her lips. "Thanks, Danni, but he *is* the cops. His name is Ranger Bragg."

"Ranger Bragg." Danni eyeballed him a moment longer. "And you know him, Greer?"

"I do."

Bragg held Danni's gaze as Greer approached him. "We met a few days ago."

Danni's gaze didn't flicker from his. "Name some of the Rangers that work in the Austin office."

Greer clutched her backpack with her hand. "It's okay, Danni."

Danni didn't budge.

Bragg arched a brow, not sure if he should be annoyed or impressed. "This is a quiz?"

"Yeah, asshole, it's a quiz. Give up some names or tell it to the cops."

"Danni," Greer warned.

He rested his hand on his hip. He admired Danni's spunk. "Santos, Winchester, Beck."

"Beck." The Ranger's name eased most of the suspicion in her face. "I know him."

"Were you at his wedding?" Bragg tossed in the detail knowing not many outside the Ranger circles would know about the marriage.

That mention deflated the last of her trepidation. "No. I had to go back East and visit my mother. I would rather have been at the wedding. Beck's wife, Lara, is my favorite teacher."

Bragg arched a brow. "Does that mean you're convinced I'm not here to bother Greer?"

She didn't answer right away. "Yeah."

Aware Greer watched him closely, he kept the menace and growl from his voice. "Good. Now scram so I can talk to her."

Danni's eyes narrowed. "This about the call and the trace?"

"It is."

"So, you'll figure out who rattled her?"

"I will." And he meant it. The urge to put hands on the guy remained strong.

"Fine. See you next week, Greer. Looking forward to working the harvest."

"Thanks, Danni, for everything. You're a rock."

She grinned. "I know."

Both watched the kid drive off.

When her taillights vanished around a corner, Greer eyed Bragg. "How did you know about the call?"

He met her gaze, noting the dark circles under her eyes. She worked hard, maybe too hard. Technically, her life outside his case was none of his business. But he'd never wasted much time on technicalities. "Word gets around."

"Not that fast."

"It does when I tell everyone with a pulse that I want to hear about it if your name comes up."

She arched a brow as annoyance snapped. "Really?"

He didn't mind the annoyance and preferred it to the fear that had flashed when he'd first called out her name. With no hint of apology, he nodded. "Until my case is solved and my nephew is off your property I'm keeping an eye on you."

Her fingers clutched the strap of her backpack. "I'm not sure how I feel about it."

Ignoring her statement, he said, "There's a coffee shop a couple of blocks away. Let's grab a cup."

She combed long fingers through her hair. Bracelets rattled. "I have an early call at the vineyard."

He wasn't going to let her go that easily. "Me, too. But a half hour won't make a difference either way. I'll follow you." Saying *please* didn't come easily to him. He wanted to find out about the caller and to spend time with her. "Please."

Finally, she nodded. "See you there in a few."

In his SUV, he followed her the two blocks and when she climbed out of her truck, he was there. Inside he ordered a house coffee, black, and she ordered a latte. With soy. He reached for his wallet.

"I got this," she said.

He shook his head. "No, I do."

"I can pay."

"Not while I'm breathing." He tossed a twenty-dollar bill on the counter and a scrawny teen with spiked hair scooped it up.

When they were settled in a booth he gave her a moment to sip her coffee and savor it. In the café's brighter light those circles under her eyes looked darker and her hair a little messier as if she'd run her hands through it. She wore the silver bracelets like always. Even at the fancy party the other night she'd worn the bracelets.

"Tell me about the call."

She stiffened. "Creepy. We tape all our calls."

"I'll be sure to listen to it. But I want to hear it from you."

She shook her head as she traced the rim of her coffee cup with her fingertip. "I've heard it all. Sad people. Angry people. Despondent. Desperate. But this gal. She said my name as if we'd met."

"A woman?"

"Yeah. She had a strange voice. Almost child-like."

"Did you recognize the voice?"

"No."

"Did you use your name when you answered the phone?"

"Yes. I always do. It makes it more personal."

"Greer is an unusual name."

"Kind of why I used it. It was different from Elizabeth."

"Is it a family name?"

"No." She sipped her coffee. "My mom loved

old movies. Greer Garson was one of her favorites. Jeffrey's middle name was Robert for Robert Taylor."

He sipped his coffee. Right before dispatch had called tonight he'd been fighting fatigue. Now he was wide awake. Not because of the coffee but because of Greer. She injected energy into him. "So what did the caller say?"

"She talked about sin."

As she gave him the rundown, anger and fear banded in his body. He really did want to take this person apart. "What did she mean by 'you and the others'?"

"I don't know. But she must know about me and my past."

"Your past is not hard to dig up. A Google search tossed out a good bit of it when I searched."

She frowned as if the idea unsettled her. "At first I thought it was someone's idea of a sick joke." She ran her finger under the bracelets. He caught the faintest glimpse of those thin white scars. "But she was serious. She believes everything she said."

"Did she mention Rory or Sara?"

"No."

"Anyone else from Shady Grove?"

"No."

Her hands and the silver bracelets encircling her wrists drew his gaze. The urge to lay his hand over hers intensified as the seconds ticked by. "What do the bracelets mean? You never take them off."

The question caught her off guard. She glanced at them and realized she'd been touching them. Straightening, she shrugged. "They're just bracelets."

"You always wear them. Always. And when you're tense you touch them. They're important to you. There are three of them."

She stared at them, her gaze pensive. "You are a Ranger, what do you think?"

He sat back in his booth and stared at the challenge in her gaze. "In the accident three people died. Your brother, his girlfriend, and Elizabeth."

She nodded slowly. "Bingo."

"But you didn't die."

"The person I was did perish. I could never have slipped back into Elizabeth's life after the accident."

"It's been twelve years."

"And time changes nothing. Jeff and Sydney are still dead. I never want to forget what happened."

"No sane person forgets that kind of an accident, Greer. No one. You don't need bracelets to remember."

"I'm afraid I will." She whispered the words as if it were a dark secret. "I'm afraid one day I won't think about Jeff or Sydney and it will be as if they never lived. I can't let that happen."

"When did you start wearing the bracelets?"

"My aunt Lydia gave them to me when I told her I was afraid of forgetting. She pulled the three bracelets out of her jewelry box and clasped them around my wrist."

"Did you wear a bracelet at Shady Grove?"

Her brow furrowed. "Yeah. Red rope bracelets. I made them for everyone. I called us the red team. I left mine behind."

Both his victims had worn red rope bracelets. His gut knotted.

"Why do you ask?"

"No reason." He managed a smile. For now, he'd keep the detail close. "Do you always wear those bracelets?"

She hesitated as if the words bore too heavily. "On the anniversary of the accident, I go to church and have them blessed by the priest. I pray for the dead. I want them to know I still care. Still remember."

So much life bubbled inside of Greer. He saw it every time he looked at her. She had much to offer, but the past hung around her neck like an anchor. "Anybody go with you?"

"No."

"Your mother?"

She sighed. "Mom tries. She does. But losing Jeff just about killed her. He was all she could ever have dreamed of in a son. No mother should have to bury a child."

"I've read the accident reports, Greer. You were fifteen and no one should have let you drive home that night. No one."

"I thought I could handle it."

"You were a kid. It wasn't your call."

"I didn't want to disappoint Jeffrey."

"He shouldn't have put you in that position."

"You make it sound like it was his fault. I'm the one that swerved off the road."

He nodded. "It was partly his fault. He was twenty-one and had a blood alcohol three times the legal limit. His girlfriend was equally drunk."

She shook her head. "I really don't want to sit here and malign them."

"I'm not asking you to. But let me be clear. That accident wasn't all your fault." He thought about her claims about the second driver, claims the officer at the scene had dismissed. "What can you tell me about the other driver?"

Her gaze sharpened. "No one has ever asked me about him. They think I made him up."

Desperation radiated from her. Whatever the cops believed, she believed there'd been a second driver. "I'm asking."

She fingered the bracelets and pursed her lips. "We were driving home. Everything was fine. I was sober. And then the headlights on the road. I didn't think about it at first. And then he switched into my lane. I thought he'd move, but he kept coming. I hit the horn. And he kept coming. At the last second before we were to cross a narrow bridge I panicked and swerved. I hit the tree. My air bags deployed, but Jeff and Sydney were thrown clear."

Her hands trembled now and the urge to touch her intensified. "Anything else you can tell me about the second car?"

"Until last night, no."

"What happened last night?"

"I dreamed about the accident. I dreamed the other driver came up to my car and touched my hair. Told me I'd saved his life." She shook her head. "I guess the stress of Rory and Sara is pulling all kinds of weird stuff out of my brain."

"Or a memory."

"The police never found traces of a second car."

"By the time you were conscious and mentioned the second car it had rained heavily. If there'd been traces, they were washed away."

A half smile tugged the edge of her mouth. "It sounds like you believe me."

"I do."

Her gaze sharpened. "Really? Why? Everyone else thought I made the second driver up."

"Summing people up is what I do for a living. I believe you."

Her gaze softened and held his for a long moment. "Thanks."

She'd trusted him. Now he'd trust her.

"I believe Sara was murdered."

Her face paled. "What?"

"We found her car miles away from where we found her body, and she didn't strike me as the kind of gal who walked that kind of distance especially in heels. There is no record she called a cab or a friend to drive her to the second location."

A wrinkle furrowed the soft skin between her eyes. "Sara was murdered."

"Yeah."

"So she couldn't have killed Rory?"

"I don't know how the two figure together. But I've two people who both stayed at Shady Grove and both are dead from apparent suicide." He tapped the edge of his cup with his index finger trying to gauge how much he should tell her. Like a fisherman tosses a baited line in the water, he opted to give her a detail. "I went to Shady Grove the day before yesterday to get the list of kids who were there the same time you were."

She shook her head. "And I'll bet you didn't get much."

"Not yet. But I will."

"Use your biggest legal guns on them, Ranger. Their clients paid for super-secrecy, and they expect their secrets to stay buried forever."

"I'll get the answers I need." He frowned. "Has anyone else bothered you lately?"

She sighed. "Rick Dowd. Sydney's brother."

"When?" he growled.

"At the feed store the other day. He's hurting. I know that. But he was rude."

"I'll talk to him."

She met his gaze. "No, don't. Like I said, he still grieves for his sister, and seeing me was a surprise."

"Was it a surprise?"

"It was for me."

"And you're sure it was for him?"

A wrinkle furrowed her brow. "I assumed so."

"Okay."

"Okay, you'll let this drop and leave him be."

"I'm not making any promises on that score." She stared at him as if searching. "What do you want to say?"

"I'm not sure I should. You might go raging out of here."

He raised a brow. "I don't rage. Too much."

His honesty made her smile. She studied him as if she too were doing a little fishing. "I spoke to a woman today who was with me at Shady Grove."

"I thought you didn't know any real names." He fought a surge of frustration.

"I saw her a couple of years ago at a wine festival. She told me the name of her dress shop. I tracked her that way."

When they'd met and discussed Sara, why hadn't she told him about this person? But he didn't press, sensing the brittleness of Greer's trust.

Carefully she picked up her cup and took a sip. "I visited her yesterday after I talked to you about Sara. I wanted to make sure she was okay." She tossed him a tentative if not guilty smile. "I told her I wouldn't tell anyone about her."

"Why?"

"She has a new life. She doesn't want to remember the past. When she approached me two years ago, I wasn't happy to see her. And I don't think she'd have talked to me if she weren't a little drunk."

Secrets simmered in this elite group of the privileged. And if he pushed as much as his gut demanded, she'd scramble back into her ivory tower never to be seen again. And so he did what he didn't do well. He waited.

She shoved out a breath. "I asked her about Sara. Asked if she'd seen her recently. She hadn't. Nor had she seen Rory. And like I suspected she didn't want to talk."

"What's her name?"

Her brow furrowed as she studied his face. She wanted to trust him. Wanted to, but wasn't ready to make the leap. "I told her I wouldn't reveal her past."

Greer needed to learn he was a man she could trust. Just like she enticed those nags to trust her, he needed to persuade her. "I can't protect her if I don't know her name."

"She'll be upset."

His muscles tightened and pinched with impatience but he kept his voice steady. "Greer, I can't help her or you if you don't put faith in me."

She fiddled with her bracelets.

"Greer. Tell me."

Her gaze locked on his, she nodded as if deciding to leap. "Jennifer Bell. She owns a dress shop in Austin called Elegance."

Satisfaction having nothing to do with the job burned through him. He'd extended a hand to her and she'd taken it. "I will talk to her."

Her cheeks flushed as if she'd betrayed a dark secret. "She won't talk to you."

"Why do you say that? I can be subtle when I put my mind to it."

His rare attempt at humor passed her by. "Because she's afraid her past will be exposed. A lot of the kids at Shady Grove came from families who value status above all else. My parents were like that."

"And yet you're talking to me."

"I left that world behind. For me it was about survival."

"She might not be as attached to that world as you think."

"She is."

"I need to talk to her, Greer. That's not negotiable."

Frustration churned in her gaze. "I told you she didn't keep up with the other two."

"I'll ask my own questions during an investigation."

"Jennifer and I were friends at camp. If she'd planned to talk to anyone, it would have been me."

"I can be persuasive."

A frown furrowed her brow. "She'll know I sent you."

"If she's smart, it won't be a big leap for her." He leaned forward a fraction, wanting to ease the anxiety rippling through her. "She doesn't need to know you sent me."

"It's not that. I'm not afraid of what she'll say. I feel like I'm betraying her. But I'm afraid if I stay silent, she could be hurt."

"You were right to tell me."

"Easy for you to say."

"Why did she end up at Shady Grove?"

She shook her head. "No. That's for her to tell you, not me."

"How did she try to kill herself?"

"Ask her."

Bragg admired Greer's loyalty. When Greer pledged her fidelity he knew it was rare. He wanted her full trust. He wanted her on his side. He wanted her. "Fair enough."

Bragg rarely offered information during an interview. He took. Didn't give. But he sensed if he offered her a measure of trust he'd reap more than he gave.

"Red rope bracelets were found at both Rory and Sara's crime scenes."

"What?"

"They were made of a standard crafting yarn. Three strands, braided tightly together, and tied in a knot."

She swallowed. "Sounds like what we had at Shady Grove."

"Who else knew about the bracelets? Was it a tradition at the camp?"

"No. It was just our pod. My idea. They symbolized our friendship. How would anyone know?"

"That's what I need to find out."

"Do you think I could have caused this?"

"No." He injected harsh determination into the word. "This is not your fault."

"Okay."

"Don't allow this killer to add to your burden."

She tried a smile, but it failed. "Carrying burdens seems to be my thing."

Worry flattened her mouth into a thin line, and he wanted to ease it. "I saw that damn ugly dog sleeping with Mitch on the couch at home tonight."

"That would be Jasper. He's smart."

He didn't miss her defensive tone. She was also a champion of lost dogs. "Well, at least the Good Lord didn't shortchange that dog totally. Where the hell did you find him?"

"Feed-and-seed store. No one wanted him."

But you took him. "He's lucky you happened along."

"I think we'll find we're the lucky ones."

"Maybe."

A silence settled between them and then finally she sipped her coffee and pushed it away. "The vineyard is calling. There's much to be done."

As she rose so did he. "I'll walk you to your truck."

"Thanks."

Her easy acceptance spoke to how much the caller had rattled her. He followed her outside the coffee shop, holding the door for her. She moved quickly but her short strides couldn't have kept pace with his long legs if he'd walked his normal pace. He slowed his stride and found he liked having her beside him. Liked the way the top of her head barely reached his shoulders. Liked the perkiness radiating from her. Liked the curve of her body and the way her hips swayed as she walked.

At her truck she opened the door and slid behind the wheel. She started the engine and rolled down the window. "Go easy on Jennifer. She talks tough but she's not."

"You're always taking care of everyone. Who looks out for you?"

"I do." She shifted into reverse. "Have a good night, Ranger Bragg."

"Be careful."

She smiled. "Always."

He watched her drive away and with each rotation of her tires, a bone-deep resolve took root. "Going forward, Greer Templeton, I'll be looking out for you."

Jackson watched Greer drive away in her truck, wanting to follow, but not daring because the Ranger stood there for a long moment staring after her truck.

"Calling her tonight wasn't smart," he said.

"An indulgence, I'll agree. But I wanted to talk to her. Wanted to connect. You care so much about her. Curiosity got the better of me."

"You should have stayed out of it."

She laughed. "That's not my style."

"It's not Greer's time yet."

"I know. But that doesn't mean I can't play a little. Want to know what she said?"

He hesitated. He liked watching her and learning new bits of information about her. "Sure."

"I scared her. She was rattled when I hung up, but she's smart. She had the call traced."

"And that's what brought the Ranger." He hadn't been happy with the Ranger. Hadn't liked the way he'd looked at Greer, as if he'd staked a claim. The Ranger was a miscalculation. An unforeseen complication that had to be managed.

But where there was a will, there was a way.

He thought about the Ranger's raw desire for Greer. The Ranger could want Greer. He could care for her. Desire her.

But in the end the Ranger would not win the fair Greer. He would.

He would grant her dying wish.

And there was nothing the Ranger could do to stop him.

Chapter Seventeen

Sunday, June 8, 8 A.M.

Bragg stared at the mangy puppy who ate his food as if he were half starved. The pup had risen early and, to Mitch's credit, he'd gotten up with the dog and taken him for a walk. Bragg, who'd always been a light sleeper, had gotten up and offered to make coffee and feed the pup while Mitch took his shower. The plan was for Mitch and Jasper to drive out to the vineyard today. With harvest coming, Greer needed all hands on deck. For the next couple of days Mitch and Jasper would bunk at the vineyard with the other workers in the barracks. Mitch didn't mind a bit.

Bragg cracked a half dozen eggs in a bowl and scrambled them with a fork. When he was alone he didn't bother with cooking but since Mitch's return he'd made the effort. At first, Mitch had refused to eat and a lot of eggs and toast had ended in the trash bin. Since Greer, his appetite had returned with a vengeance.

Since Greer.

He let the image of Greer Templeton fill his mind.

When he dropped four strips of bacon in another skillet the pup sniffed, glanced at his food and then back up at Bragg. The dog barked, but kept a watchful eye on the food he already had in his bowl.

"That's smart. A bird in the hand is worth two in the bush." He cut off a small piece of bacon and handed it to the dog who greedily accepted it.

Mitch lumbered down the hallway, his hair wet from the shower and slicked back. He wore jeans, a Bonneville T-shirt, and boots. He carried his rucksack packed full with his belongings.

He sat at the table, and Bragg set a plate loaded with eggs, bacon, and bread in front of him. Jasper hustled over to sit by Mitch's feet. "Have a busy day?"

"Yeah. Got the horses and Greer's going to explain about the harvest. Everyone at the vineyard helps with the harvest. She's even got some girl, Danni, coming in to help."

"The girl from the Crisis Center?"

"I guess."

Bragg pushed back a budding sense of hope. He

didn't want to hope too much. "You've jumped into this with both feet."

He stabbed a mountain of eggs. "Didn't mean to. The place just kind of sucked me in before I realized it."

It wasn't the place. It was Greer. "Have you seen where you'll be living?"

"It's a barracks. Several guys bunk there. A lot like basic but nicer." He took several big bites.

"How's Greer as a boss?" The woman stirred up so many questions it was hard to choose which to ask first.

"She's okay."

He heard the growl under the last word. "Meaning, what?"

He shrugged. "She can be a pain."

Bragg held back a smile. He had no doubt. "How so?"

After a moment he huffed out a breath. "She's making me talk to Dr. Stewart."

He'd not seen that coming. "Why?"

"I don't know. I'm doing everything she asked me."

"Then why's she pushing?"

Mitch shrugged his shoulders. "I don't know. She's yammering about the wisdom of a professional."

Holding his breath, he didn't dare remind Mitch they'd had this same conversation, and that Mitch had turned angry and resentful. They'd had one hell of a fight, but nothing had been resolved. "You gonna do it?"

He loaded his fork with eggs. "She's sending me into town anyway for supplies on Wednesday and said I could take an extra hour or two and see the doc."

Getting the boy to open up was like pulling teeth. "So that's a yes?"

A pause. "Yeah."

Greer had given his nephew a job, a purpose, and now she had him visiting Dr. Stewart. She was mending the scars left by the war. She'd done more for his boy in a week than he'd been able to do in months.

Gratitude rubbed against a dark restlessness he couldn't pin down. Physically, he was attracted to Greer. He respected her. He imagined a trust forming between them.

Bragg wanted to be at the vineyard today, working with Mitch and watching Greer. He wanted to be in the hot sun working side by side with her, watching how she handled herself with Mitch and her other employees. He wanted to see how she managed problems. And how she filled out her jeans and T-shirts, both of which he thought about a lot.

He wondered if she dated or if she slept alone. The idea of her in bed with another man had jealousy gnawing at his gut like it never had before.

Greer took up more and more of his thoughts. He could pretend she was a fleeting fancy, but he'd be wrong.

Bragg pulled up in front of Jennifer Bell's dress shop and grabbed his hat. It was a frilly kind of place not meant for men. A place he'd have avoided if not for work. When he had an overnight date, some would leave behind frilly feminine doodads, sometimes a scent of perfume lingered as a reminder of their evening. He'd rarely noticed let alone cared. And it had been years since a woman had bothered to leave behind reminders. He thought about Greer's scent lingering on his pillow. He'd not be quick to dismiss any mementos if she left any behind.

Bells jingled over his head as he walked into the shop. A couple of women, glitzy and polished, lifted their gazes from the clothing racks to toss him a speculative glance. Their perfectly styled hair and ritzy outfits had him hankering for the lady who favored jeans, T-shirts, and dusty boots.

Irritated that his thoughts wouldn't stay away from Greer, he moved with purpose to the front register where a tall brunette studied him with resentment. "Ranger Tec Bragg. I'm here for Jennifer Bell."

The two customers on the floor stared with obvious curiosity, which unsettled the woman more. "I'm Jennifer Bell. Why don't we go back in my office?"

Turning, she pushed through the curtains, nodding as she vanished into the back.

He followed knowing if she were a man he'd not tolerate her walking away like that.

She faced him, manicured, long fingers resting on trim hips. "Greer sent you, didn't she?"

Her tone had his hackles rising and his loyalty demanding he rise to Greer's defense. "No one sends me anywhere."

Silver earrings jangled as she shook her head from side to side. "You wouldn't know about me if not for Greer."

If he'd not been studying her closely, he'd have missed the flash of pain in her gaze. "Why do you say that?"

Disdain flattened her lips and covered the momentary flash of hurt. "Because my family paid well to ensure the past stayed in the past."

"And what past might that be?"

With a flick of her wrist she attempted to dismiss him. "Don't play stupid with me. She told you everything."

Other than telling him the two women had met at Shady Grove, Greer had not told him anything about Jennifer's past. But he'd baited hooks before with skimpier morsels. "I know about Shady Grove."

Her face flushed and for a moment she closed

her eyes before she met his gaze again. "I can't believe she told you. You know, I actually felt sorry for her once." She shook her head. "I knew nothing good would come of it when she showed up. What did she tell you?"

He resisted the urge to defend Greer's loyalty to Jennifer. "I got a real good idea of the whole picture."

Painted red lips pursed. "She is such a bitch. Such a bitch. Fucking past. I've paid for it enough."

Bragg's hackles rose higher. A second or two longer and he'd speak his mind. "Tell me about her."

She reached behind her and picked up a pack of cigarettes and a lighter. With a steady hand she lit the tip. After a couple of puffs, she said, "She really sent you?"

"No one sends me."

"But you are here." She shook her head, her disgust clear. "She always came off as caring and sweet at camp. I had sympathy for her. Thought I could trust her. Thought if I told her she'd understand. Now I realize trust is for fools."

The woman's words mirrored his brand of cynicism. Jennifer judged Greer unfairly and he'd been guilty of the same. "She told you about Rory and Sara."

He wasn't here to answer questions but to ask them. "When was the last time you saw Sara or Rory?"

"Rory. That was years ago. At least ten years. His mother was still alive so his family hadn't cut him off. It was the Western Country Club, and he was drunk. In fact, I think he tried to hit me up for money." She shook her head. "Jerk."

"And Sara?"

"A couple of years. We saw each other around town and were polite but we didn't really speak."

He dangled another bit of bait into the waters. "Greer told me everyone at the camp tried to commit suicide."

Green eyes narrowed. "I guess she also told you I popped a handful of pills."

He let the silence goad her.

"Why couldn't she let the past stay buried? We've all gotten on with our lives. No good could come of going back and dredging up what couldn't be changed. There's no changing past mistakes."

He remained silent, watching.

"You know I saw the picture of her in the paper six months ago. She'd just joined the board of a crisis center. I remember thinking, 'Can't you stay hidden?' She couldn't let her past stay past; she had to drag all that shit up to help others."

Greer acknowledged that she'd never forget her mistakes, but she was moving forward, whereas Jennifer hadn't let go. "She's done some good work."

"This may be wrong of me, but I don't care.

She's stirring up the past and it will come to no good. No good. There's nothing any one of us can do to change the past. Nothing. All we can do is try to live our lives, which is what I'm trying to do."

"Why do you want to keep it buried? Everyone makes mistakes."

Her face paled a fraction as if a fear chased up her spine. "There are some mistakes one can't recover from. Those mistakes have to be buried and forgotten."

"Like your suicide attempt?"

She swallowed as if forcing back bile and fear. "Christ, what do you think my boyfriend would say if he knew? Do you think I'd still have a business? No, that kind of past chases people away. It keeps you in the 'freak' category forever." Her voice dropped to a pained whisper.

"You seen anyone else from your pod at Shady Grove?" With luck she'd toss him a name, and he'd have another piece of the puzzle.

"I saw Sam a few months ago."

"Was that his real name?"

Her gaze sharpened. "No."

"Do you know what it was?"

A half smile tweaked the edge of her mouth. "He was wearing a name tag that read 'Michael Sycamore.' "

A solid, real name. "Did you talk?"

"No. He saw me. I saw him. And with one

glance we both agreed not to speak to the other. Nothing personal. Just keep your distance." She arched a brow. "Greer didn't tell you about him?"

"No. She didn't know his real name."

"Or if she had she'd have told you. Figures." She sighed.

"See who he worked for?"

"No."

"Anything else you can tell me about him?"

"No. And he won't welcome a visit from you, either. I could tell he didn't want to talk about the camp. He was with a woman. Pretty. Blond and wearing a big engagement ring." She shrugged. "I notice details like that."

"Why was Michael at the camp?"

"Greer didn't tell you? She's in a talkative mood these days."

"I'm asking you."

She studied him a long moment. "He threatened to shoot himself. He was caught stealing from his parents. And not just nickels and dimes. He stole nice pieces from the house and was selling them."

"Why'd he need the money?"

"That's the thing, he didn't need the money. He just liked stealing. His father found out and threatened to cut him off, and he freaked out. He took one of his father's pistols and pressed it to his head. His father tackled him and sent him to Shady Grove."

"Where is he now?"

"Houston, I think." She folded her arms over her chest. "That's all I know. So would you and your little snitch leave me alone?" She pointed her finger at him. "I don't want my name in the press."

His patience now paper-thin, he bared his teeth in an unfriendly smile. "I don't take orders from you."

She arched a brow, leveling what she must have thought was a withering gaze. He suppressed a laugh. He'd handled far worse than this woman could ever dish out.

A faint flush colored her face and when she raised her cigarette to her mouth, her hand trembled slightly. She held his gaze a beat longer and then dropped it. "Just leave me alone."

"Don't think this is finished, Ms. Bell. I'll do whatever I have to do to solve this case."

She stubbed out her cigarette into a crystal ashtray. "Be careful of Greer, Ranger Bragg. She'll get into your head. Like she wormed in Rory's. Like she got into Sara's and mine. And once she sinks her claws into you and you think you can trust her, you're done."

Bragg glared at Jennifer, surprised her words hit the mark. Greer had gotten into his head.

Michael stared at the letter from his attorney, anger boiling so hot in him that he thought his head would explode. He'd reread the letter several times and each time the outcome was as grim as the last. He was being sued. For money they said he'd stolen.

Crushing the paper in his hands, he rose and moved to a simple wooden kitchen table where a half-empty bottle of scotch stood. He grabbed a chipped mug from a rustic kitchen cabinet and filled it to the brim with scotch. It might be morning but he didn't care. Maybe getting piss drunk would dull the outrage thumping in his chest.

He took a long, even drink. The liquid slid down his throat, burning a little as it passed. Moving to the window, he stared out into the rolling hills. He'd not been to the family cabin in a decade and the place had fallen into disrepair since his father's illness. In truth, he really didn't like the place. But it was his only sanctuary now.

Turning, he picked the balled letter off the floor and read it again.

> Dear Mr. Sycamore: This letter is to inform you that Jay & Brighten Accounting firm will be filing suit against you in one week if the two million dollars in question are not returned. Though your termination cannot be revoked, restoration of funds will avoid the suit and legal action.

He'd worked for that company for eight years. He'd brought in more business than many of the partners. He was a goddamned rising star. And because some asshole couldn't add numbers, he was being accused of theft.

He hadn't stolen a dime. Not a red cent. And he'd fight these charges as long as he had breath in his body.

Pressing the cup to his throbbing temple he closed his eyes. He'd been fired. Was being sued. And his fiancée had returned the ring. Even his old man wasn't speaking to him.

Fuck.

Life was crushing him to death.

He couldn't go on like this.

But he would. He would find a way.

Bragg left Jennifer's annoyed. He wasn't sure if he was irritated because she'd been difficult or her warning about Greer had struck a nerve. Like it or not, Greer had struck a nerve. Not good.

As he pushed through the doors of Ranger headquarters and made his way to his office, he put a call in to Winchester. The call landed in voice mail, so he left a message requesting he find Michael Sycamore. As he gave what details he had on the man, he tossed his hat aside and then ended the call. He shrugged off his coat before sitting behind his desk and opening Greer's accident file Deputy Eric Howell had given him.

Bragg opened the file and studied the photos of the mangled car. He cringed and wondered how Greer could have survived the accident.

This accident didn't relate to the cases on his desk. It was over a dozen years old. And yet it had been the catalyst for the events that drove Greer to Shady Grove and for someone to kill two people in Greer's pod.

David Edwards had been clear he didn't like Greer's association with his brother. But it was Sydney Dowd's brother, Rick, who'd confronted her. Rude and pushy didn't necessarily make him a killer, but he was the lone person now linking the present to the past. And the man had hassled Greer, which in his book was reason enough to pay the man a visit.

It didn't take much checking to discover Dowd now worked as a vet and ran a large animal clinic ten miles outside of Austin. Dowd's practice was successful and enjoyed a solid reputation. His clinic cared for many of the area's most elite thoroughbreds.

Bragg drove west until concrete transformed to rolling green hills. He followed directions through a couple of small towns until he found the white building and barn at the edge of town.

The freshly painted building had a bright bold welcoming sign. He parked in the small gravel parking lot and moved down the sidewalk to the main door. Inside he found a receptionist, a young girl about fifteen years old. Dark hair swept up into a thick ponytail accentuated wide brown eyes and high cheekbones.

She grinned up at him. “How may I help you?”

He softened his expression, which on a good day could pass for a scowl. “I’m looking for Dr. Dowd.”

Bright eyes flickered with recognition. “That’s my dad. You have an animal that needs tending?”

“No, ma’am. I’m with the Rangers and have a couple of questions.”

“Is it a question I might be able to answer? I’ve been working here since May.”

“I appreciate the offer, ma’am.” He touched the brim of his hat. “But your dad is the fellow I need to see.”

“Dad’s in the barn out back. He’s the only one out there now so he won’t be hard to find. I’d go with you but I’m answering phones now.” On cue, the phone rang.

“I should be able to find it if you point me to the right path.”

“Sure.” The young girl directed him to a barn where he’d find Dowd in a back stall examining a black gelding. She then picked up the phone. “Dowd Animal Clinic.”

As Bragg left the clinic and walked toward the barn, he thought about Greer’s caller last night. A woman. Sounded young. Could Dowd have put his daughter up to the call?

Frowning, he found Rick Dowd in the barn exactly where his daughter had described. The vet had light hair that brushed the top of his collar and his skin was fair, leaving Bragg to assume the little girl up front favored her mother. Dowd wore dark glasses and a jean jacket smeared with mud.

Waiting until the vet stepped away from the animal, Bragg said, "Dr. Dowd?"

Dowd grabbed a rag from his back pocket and wiped his hands. His expression was mild, his smile genuine when he met Bragg's gaze. "Yes, sir. What can I do for you?"

Bragg waited until the man had exited the stall and closed the gate behind him. "Name's Ranger Tec Bragg. I'm with the Texas Rangers."

Dowd nodded as he wiped his hand on a rag. "I saw the star right away. What can I do for you?"

"I wanted to ask you questions about Elizabeth Greer Templeton."

The doctor's expression hardened. "Did she send you to talk to me? Be like her to stir up trouble."

Whatever goodwill Bragg had mustered vanished. His gaze sharpened. His stance tensed. "She mentioned you'd had words at the feed store the other day. I thought I'd ask you about it."

Shaking his head, Dowd shoved the rag back in his pocket. "I probably shouldn't have said anything to her. Christ, it's been twelve years. But seeing her took me by surprise. I guess because she looked so good. Pretty and happy. Suddenly it didn't seem right she'd be moving around, laughing and smiling, and my sister was dead and buried in the ground for more than a dozen years."

"I've read a good bit about the accident. According to the medical examiner your sister had well over the legal limit of alcohol in her system."

Dowd shook his head. "She might have had a beer or two at the party, but the fact remains she did not get behind the wheel of the car."

"She'd been drunk enough to let a fifteen-year-old drive."

His face crumbled with the kind of blame rising from too many nights of second-guessing and *what ifs*. "I told her not to drink that night."

"But she did."

"She wasn't driving," he insisted.

"No, sir, but her judgment was impaired."

"Where the hell is this going?"

"I did a little digging. Your sister worked for you here at the clinic?"

"That's right. I'm eight years older than Sydney and with Mom and Dad's help I had set up this place. Sydney knew I couldn't afford an assistant so she volunteered to help out." He hesitated, as if emotion clogged his throat. "I always looked out for Sydney. She followed me everywhere, always chewing on my ass." The words were spoken with tenderness, not malice. "That summer she was working here, mucking stalls and helping me with the animals."

"She'd been a student at the University of Texas."

"That's right. Biology. Honor roll. She'd talked about going to vet school and joining me in my practice." As he recounted the facts of his sister's life, his jaw set as if the telling stoked the embers of his anger.

"And she dated Jeff Templeton?"

"That's right. For about six months. Our family didn't have the kind of money his family did. They ran in the highest circles. We warned her his kind used girls like her, but she always defended him. She said he loved her."

"How'd they meet?"

"At UT. She'd taken courses at UT the spring of her senior year of high school. She was pretty smart. He was a junior."

"You were vocal after the accident. You pressed for the lawsuit against the Templetons."

His jaw hardened. "Not right she'd just get away with it. Her bullshit story about another driver was an insult. I wanted her to feel my loss."

"She lost her brother."

He shook his head as if he didn't want to hear. "She was reckless. I've seen how it goes with the rich. I've worked with enough of them. Money can buy you out of all kinds of trouble."

Bragg rested his hand on his hip. "You think money bought Greer out of trouble?"

"I think she'd been drinking. I think she shouldn't have been behind the wheel, and I think she made up the second driver to cover her tracks. And her family backed her up."

His index finger tapped against his belt. "Did you know she'd stayed in Austin after the accident?"

"I know after she tried to kill herself she vanished. I asked around but wherever she went no one was talking. Eventually, I had to give it up and move on with my life."

"And you ran into her by accident at the feed store?"

He shook his head, astonishment evident. "Yeah. Like seeing a ghost from the past."

"And you confronted her."

"She'd been laughing. And it made me mad. I can promise you if my sister had been driving that car twelve years ago and she'd killed Elizabeth and her brother she'd have done jail time."

"Greer was fifteen and sober."

"Sober. Right. Families like the Templetons can make donations to the sheriff's re-election campaign and ugly facts like a drunk daughter vanish." His fingers curled into fists before relaxing a fraction.

"She was about the age of your daughter at the time of the accident."

Dowd paled. "Don't compare Jenna to Greer. My girl is a hard worker. Makes good grades and is a straight shooter. She doesn't run around with rich country club kids. I won't allow it."

"You know about Greer's time at Shady Grove?"

"No. Why would I? I do know it's a place for rich kids who can't cut it."

"You ever know anyone who stayed at Shady Grove?"

"Like I said many of my clients are rich. If they or their kids spent time at the place, I didn't know about it. I keep it polite with that kind because they're my bread and butter, but I don't mix with them."

"Greer received a call the other night at the Crisis Center. The caller was female. She said some mighty nasty things to Greer."

"So?"

"She said the caller sounded young."

"What does that have to do with me?"

"Your daughter is young. Would you have put her up to the call?"

The color drained from his face. "How dare you drag my daughter into this. She was just a baby when Sydney died."

"She loves you very much. Maybe you put her up to the call."

"No. Never."

Bragg looked around the barn, absorbing details. "I'm going to have to ask you to stay away from Greer Templeton."

"Why, Ranger? I was mad and I told her so. Last I checked it's a free country."

He bared white teeth into a smile that was not a smile. "Yes, sir, it is. But I'm offering you a friendly warning where it comes to Ms. Templeton. Leave her be."

"What's she to you? She your girlfriend?"

He had no idea what Greer was to him, other than a name in an investigation or a mentor to his nephew. He'd known her all of five days, but it was enough to care. To protect. But Dowd didn't need a speech on the matter. He took a step toward Dowd. "I don't need to explain myself to you, Dr. Dowd."

Dowd took a step back but mutiny burned in his gaze.

A blistering headache pounded behind Jennifer's eyes as she moved across the parking lot toward her car. She clicked the entry and moved behind the wheel, savoring the heat of the seats. She'd been cold all day, unable to shake the chill slithering into her bones the moment she'd stepped into the shop today. The shop had felt off, wrong. She'd searched for signs of a break-in or trouble, but when everything checked out she'd attributed her unease to Greer's visit.

Greer had stirred the cauldron of her emotions. She'd rattled her. Made her edgy. And then that damn Ranger had arrived. He'd reminded her of an ancient barbarian. No conscience. No concern. Even the thought of the man made her stomach churn.

The afternoon in the shop had been crazy busy and she'd set a record in sales. Any other day and she'd have been brimming with satisfaction, but today panic burrowed as if the foundation under her feet crumbled.

Needing to connect to the present, she dialed her fiancé. He picked up on the third ring. "Hey, babe," she said.

"You headed home?" His soft smooth voice soothed her. Unlike Bragg, Adam was a sweet, kind man.

She wasn't sure how she'd gotten that lucky, but she'd landed a great guy. She'd do anything not to lose him. "Yes. We were late closing. Couldn't get rid of some customers. One didn't buy a single item, but the other bought a nice Vera Wang. The sales justified the extra half hour."

"Good job."

She traced the steering wheel with a manicured finger. The day's stress ebbed from her muscles. "So what are you doing?"

"Hanging out by the pool waiting for you, babe. Hurry home. We can go skinny-dipping."

She laughed, reaching for her water bottle. "Sounds fun. See you in a few."

She drank deeply from the bottle, savoring the cold water. It refreshed her. Fuck Greer and all the bullshit from the past. She was in a good place now, and if someone really did figure out the truth, what could be proved? Nothing.

She yawned as she backed out of her spot and headed down Congress Avenue. She was glad Adam's house was a couple of miles from her store. She was more tired than she'd thought. At a second stoplight she closed her eyes determined to rest them for only a minute. The honking of a horn behind her startled her awake and had her shaking her head. What was wrong with her? She'd not experienced this kind of bone-weary fatigue since . . . since the night she'd taken that bottle of her mother's pills.

Fear rosc up from a hidden part in her, and she gripped her steering wheel. She'd not touched a drug in twelve years. Not even an aspirin. And she'd not had a drink of alcohol in over a year. But she felt drugged. Panic growing, she pulled her car over to the side of the road and reached for her cell phone. Her vision blurred as she stared at the numbers that now danced and spun. Just like before, she panicked after taking the pills and dialed 911.

She hit the nine but an extreme heaviness had her head tipping back against the headrest. *Wake up!* She fumbled her thumb from the nine to the one and managed to hit it once. She hit the second one but fatigue pried her fingers open and the cell dropped from her hands before she could hit SEND.

• • •

Greer dreamed of the accident again. Lights, a horrendous crash, and screaming.

She sat up in bed, and shoved a trembling hand through her hair. Her heart raced and her mouth had grown as dry as cotton. A glance at the clock told her it was minutes after three.

Rising, she moved into the kitchen, took a glass from the cabinet, and filled it with water. She drank heavily, savoring the water as if she'd not had any in days.

Finally, when she didn't feel extremely parched she turned and leaned against the sink, cradling the glass close to her chest. The thought of returning to bed left a chill in her bones. She didn't want to risk reliving the accident again. There was work, always work, but she was weary of staring at numbers and worrying over the ripeness of her vineyard.

Restless, she set down the glass. If Lydia had been alive, she'd have risen by now, made them both tea, and together they'd sit at the kitchen table and discuss everything and nothing. Now without Lydia, she was adrift.

Her mind went to Bragg. Perhaps if it had been the clear light of day she'd have pushed thoughts of him away, but here alone in the dark she welcomed his warm embrace, if merely in her imagination.

After moments passed, she felt foolish standing

here alone thinking of a man out of her reach. She pushed away from the counter, set down the glass, and returned to her room. With a wary glance toward her unmade bed, she went to her closet and turned on the light inside. Her gaze roamed over her collection of shirts and jeans up to boxes that were stacked high on the top shelf. She reached for the lowest box but at first her fingers only grazed the dusty cardboard. Finally, she grabbed a chrome chair from the kitchen and placed it in front of the closet.

On the chair she had a better view of the boxes that stored what little she'd kept from her old life. When she'd left Shady Grove she'd had a suitcase full of clothes, but over the next month her mother had sent more and more of her belongings. Holding bits of her life before the accident had been too painful to bear, but she also couldn't let go of her *before* life either. To do that would erase Jeff. That's why she'd stored each of the boxes in the closet.

She scanned the boxes and found the one she wanted in the middle on the far left. Leaning forward she tugged carefully at the box until it slid out.

Greer climbed off the chair and sat on the edge of her bed. She removed the box top and stared at the collection of trinkets. They'd been what she'd brought with her from Shady Grove. On the bottom she found what she'd been searching for—

an image. The picture Bragg had of Rory and her had been taken from this picture, which also featured Sam, Jennifer, and Sara. She studied the picture of the five smiling faces. Such bruised gazes in such young faces.

She remembered that night. It was their last together, and she'd been despondent. She'd threatened not to come to the final roundup at the campfire. Instead, she'd stayed in her room, nursing bitterness over Rory's leaving.

It had been another kid, Jack, a quiet shy boy with stringy blond hair and thick glasses, who'd come to find her. He rarely spoke to her or anyone but that night he'd coaxed her out of her room, waving his camera and telling her she had to be in the picture. The others said the picture wouldn't be complete without her. And so she'd pushed aside her anger and gone to the fire. Rory had tossed his arm around her, as if nothing were wrong, and kissed her on the lips. Then all of them had grinned at the camera. Jack had snapped the picture.

She traced Rory's beautiful face. She'd read in the paper that his funeral was Monday afternoon. She wasn't welcome but she'd be going. It seemed fitting.

Her gaze moved from face to face in the image. Two of the five were now dead. What had they done to warrant death? As she fingered the edge of the fading image she knew she had to give this to Bragg.

• • •

When Jennifer woke to the sharp scent of ammonia, a bright light shone in her eyes. Her brain, drowsy and sluggish, struggled to focus. She pushed through the confused thoughts, trying to remember what had happened. If she didn't know better, she'd say she'd taken too many sleeping pills.

Ammonia cut through her airways.

She coughed as she sat straighter and realized her wrists were handcuffed to a bed.

"What is this?" Her voice sounded garbled and muffled like a drunk's.

"It's your chance." The man's voice came from beyond the light.

More sharp smells of ammonia and she coughed and shook her head no. "Get that away from me."

He chuckled. "As soon as I know you're awake."

"I'm awake. I'm awake." Fear hadn't penetrated the thick grogginess.

"Good."

She moistened dry lips. The last she remembered, she was in her car struggling to stay awake. She'd had a sip of water and wondered why she'd felt so drugged. "What's wrong with me? I feel drugged. But," she said, moistening dry lips, "that can't be right. I haven't had a drink in a year."

"You've got to be careful about what you eat and drink."

"I am."

"Not careful enough."

As her head began to clear, she looked into the face of the man speaking. His expression wasn't menacing and his demeanor relaxed. He dressed well. Smiled.

She tried to sit up but her head spun. A glance around told her she was lying on a bed. She looked around the room. Simply furnished, there was a television, a desk and chair, and the two windows had been covered with black plastic and duct tape. "Where am I?"

"Somewhere safe."

Fear flickered as did annoyance. "What does 'somewhere safe' mean?"

"It's a place where we won't be bothered. Where we can talk."

"I don't want to talk." Again, she tried to sit up but found she was almost completely immobile. She jerked her hands. The cuffs rattled but didn't budge. "What the hell?"

"I'm giving you an opportunity."

"What are you talking about?" The sharpened edges of her voice belied his soft tones.

He turned away from her and sighed. "A chance to purge. To release the burden you've been carrying for twelve years."

Twelve years. A cold chill oozed through her body freezing away any traces of annoyance. Some secrets, no matter how painful, had to stay buried. Now more than ever. “I don’t know what you’re talking about.”

He faced her, his smile sad and almost soothing. “You know exactly what I’m talking about, Jennifer.” An edge had crept into his voice. “You need to release the secret.”

“I don’t have a secret.”

“Yes, you do. And before this night is over, Jennifer, your soul will be cleansed just as you’d dreamed of it being for years.”

Chapter Eighteen

Monday, June 9, 7 A.M.

The day’s heat had already kicked in when Bragg arrived at the murder scene a half hour after receiving the call from Winchester. Jennifer Bell had been found in her car, unconscious. The paramedics had removed her from the car, opened her airway, and begun CPR, but despite a frantic dash to the hospital, the doctors had pronounced her dead fifteen minutes ago.

Lights flashing, the area around the car had been roped off, but a growing number of curiosity seekers now stared at the technicians as they photographed Jennifer Bell’s car.

The area was on a residential side street near the entrance to Northwest Park. It was going to be a pretty day with milder temperatures and soon this area would be teeming with folks out to enjoy a Monday morning jog.

Bragg settled his hat on his head as he moved toward the crime-scene tape billowing in a soft breeze. He was clean shaven, his hair still wet from the shower. "What do we have?"

Winchester tore his gaze from the empty car. "She somehow managed a call to paramedics an hour and a half ago. She wasn't able to speak, but they traced the GPS on her phone."

He pulled plastic gloves from his pocket and put them on. "Did she say anything else to the nine-one-one operator?"

"She didn't say a word. The operator asked her a bunch of questions but she didn't answer."

He glanced past Winchester to the car. The door was open and the ground around it littered with the paramedic's discarded wrappers. "Are we sure she placed the call?"

Winchester shrugged. "All I can say for sure is the call was placed from her phone in this location."

Frustration snaked up his back and curled around his shoulders. His first thought was for Greer. He reached for his cell and dialed. The phone rang twice before she said, "Greer Templeton."

"Greer. Tec Bragg."

A heavy silence followed. "What can I do for you?"

He turned from Winchester and the other cops and stared off toward the wooded park. "Where are you now?"

"At Bonneville. I'm getting into my truck and headed into the fields with Mitch as soon as he waters the horses."

Relief corralled his anxiety. She was on her property. Safe. And Mitch was with her. "Do you have time to meet later today?"

She dropped her voice. "What's this about?"

Around him cop-car lights flashed. Media gathered. "Not over the phone."

A heavy hesitation sizzled over the line. "Sure. I'll be on the property until two."

"Where are you going at two?"

"Austin. Is there a problem?"

He didn't want to tell her about Jennifer like this. "Just need a few details clarified."

"Sure."

He rubbed the back of his neck. "Why are you coming into the city?"

She paused. "I'm going to Rory's funeral. It's today."

He frowned, his mind targeting all that could go wrong at the funeral. "Is that such a good idea?"

"Doubtful. But I'm going."

"Greer, think about this. David Edwards is only going to cause you trouble."

"I'm just going to pay my respects. I'll keep my distance."

He considered all the logical reasons she shouldn't go and sensed he could lay them all out and she'd still do as she pleased. He checked his watch. "The funeral is at three?"

"Yes. The Catholic church in West Lake Hills."

He catalogued the information. "I'll meet you there."

"You don't have to."

"It's as good a place as any. We need to talk."

"Okay."

"Stay close to Mitch. He can look out for you."

"You're making me nervous."

"Don't mean to." It took effort to soften his voice.

"Okay. See you then."

He closed the phone and stuck it back in his belt cradle.

Winchester studied him. "What was that about?"

"Checking in with Greer."

A small smile tweaked the edge of Winchester's lips. "You wanted to make sure she was okay?"

No sense denying it. "Yes."

Winchester studied him closely. "That's not like you. In fact, I don't remember you ever taking such a personal interest in a person associated with a case."

He shrugged. "I am now."

"Why? And don't give me a story about it being about the case. I sang that song enough when Jo was in danger last year."

Bragg squared his shoulders. "It's about the case."

"It's about her." Winchester shook his head. "Don't bullshit me or yourself."

Bragg shifted his stance. "What is this, like our special girl-sharing time?"

Winchester laughed. "You care about the woman."

Bragg considered a rebuttal and then squashed it. The truth wasn't as hard to swallow as he'd thought. He cared about Greer. "I hardly know the woman."

Winchester chuckled. "Doesn't take a lot of facts or time to form an attraction. She's a good-looking woman and looks like she could go up against you and not break a sweat."

"She's a tough gal."

"Men like us need strong, independent women. Not easy being with a Ranger. Shit, danger aside, we work ungodly hours. Jo gets that. And Greer would, too."

"Last I checked you had her figured for a suspect."

Winchester shrugged. "I might be amending my opinion."

"Why?"

"For one the analysis on the tire tracks at Rory's crime scene came back. They don't match any of Greer's vehicles. And I got the analysis surveillance tapes from area hardware stores about an hour ago. We targeted stores selling generators. All were men."

"Any positive ID?"

"No. But none were Greer."

He didn't need confirmation on Greer's innocence, but having evidence would help her avoid any undue scrutiny from the law later.

Bragg rested his hands on his hips as he surveyed the crowd. His feelings for Greer ran deeper than attraction. But the last damn thing he was going to do was discuss this with Winchester or anyone other than Greer.

Being with a Ranger. Yeah, he liked the sound of that.

"Has Jennifer Bell's next of kin been notified?" Bragg said.

Winchester wrestled a grin from his face. "Her boyfriend is calling her parents who are in Europe right now." He reached in his pocket and pulled out a small notebook. He fished through several pages. "His name is Adam Owens. He'd been contacted and he's on his way to the hospital."

"Good. I want to talk to him."

"I'll pull Jennifer's phone records. Maybe the killer called her before she died. And I'll get the uniforms going from door to door. They can hunt down security cameras and possible witnesses. Maybe somebody or a camera caught something."

"Any word on Michael Sycamore?"

"Not yet. His secretary in Houston says he's on vacation and won't return for another week."

"Does she know where he went?"

"No, but she's trying to track him."

"We need to find that guy as soon as possible."

"Think he's behind this?"

"If he's not, he's in danger."

"So is Greer."

"I know."

Bragg drove to the hospital emergency room. The hum of machines mingled with the chatter of doctors, nurses, patients, and family. He went straight to the information desk and after showing his badge was directed to the curtained cubicle where the doctors had worked on Jennifer.

"Her boyfriend is in with her now," the nurse said. "He asked the doctor for a moment."

"Thanks."

Bragg found Jennifer's cubicle, arriving as Adam Owens stepped out from behind curtain dividers. His dark hair was slicked back as if he'd just gotten out of a shower, and he wore madras shorts, a white shirt, and deck shoes. The faint scent of aftershave drifted around him.

Adam glanced up at Bragg, red-rimmed eyes taking in the Ranger star, white hat, and gun. "You're here for Jennifer?"

Bragg nodded. "Mr. Owens, I'm very sorry for your loss."

He pressed the heel of his hand to his temple as

if it pounded. "We were talking on the phone last night after she closed the shop. She was supposed to come by the house, and we were going to have dinner. She sounded excited and happy. I was going to grill steaks for us. And then she texted me and told me she wasn't feeling well. Said she'd call in the morning. I texted her back and told her I loved her. She sent back a heart." He shook his head. "I can't believe she'd overdose. That does not make sense."

What made sense was that she'd been murdered. Three people now who'd lived together in the same pod at Shady Grove were dead. All that remained were Greer and Michael. "She gave you no indication there was a problem?"

"No. She was in a great mood." He glanced back at the curtained walls that separated him from Jennifer's body. "She was running late but it was because it had been a busy day at the store. Sales had been exceptional."

Bragg frowned. "Did she say anything about those customers? Any one of them strike her as odd or out to make trouble?"

"No. Not a word. She was really happy. We were supposed to get married in the spring. She went to New York for her wedding-dress fitting last week. Both her parents came. She's an only child and the sun rises and sets on her."

Bragg searched for words to heal, but couldn't find the right ones. Best he could do for this man was find Jennifer's killer. "I'd like to have a look around her shop."

Owens dug in his pocket and pulled out a set of keys. His hands trembled as he tried to find the right one.

Bragg took pity on him, remembering how rattled he'd been when his sister had died. He took the keys. "Show me."

Owens shoved out a sigh and handed Bragg the ring. "Third on the right. It's gold."

Bragg found the thick brass key. "Can I take this off the ring?"

Owens threaded long, lean fingers through his hair. "Sure. You can have the ring."

"No, sir, you're going to need your keys when you get home. Did you drive yourself here?"

"Yes."

Bragg held on to the ring of keys. "Is there someone you can call to drive you home?"

Owens stared at the floor as if the enormity of the moment hit him like a truckload of bricks. "What?"

Bragg softened the edges of his voice. "Someone you can call to drive you home?"

Adam shook his head. "I just can't believe she's dead. She appears to be sleeping. She's so beautiful. It makes no sense."

Bragg pulled his cell phone and dialed DPS and ordered a patrol car. "Sir, I'm going to have an officer drive you home. I don't want you driving."

Adam shook his head. "I can drive."

"No, sir." Instead of handing the keys back to Owens he flagged a nurse and gave them to her with instructions to hold them until an officer arrived. He also told her to find the hospital chaplain.

A half hour later he opened the front door of Jennifer's shop. He flipped on the lights. An eerie silence greeted him, making him feel as if the shop had died with its owner. Looking at the attention to detail in the displays and window dressings and the way the counter had been left clean and ready for business on Monday, he could tell she'd clearly loved and took pride in this store.

He went back to her office and turned on more lights. He checked receipts for the day neatly organized in a pile in the center of her desk. He noted five purchases. All over three thousand dollars. All cash. It was as if a parade of patrons had flocked to her door. Her most successful day had been her last.

It didn't take much effort for Bragg to locate the church holding Rory's funeral. It was in West Lake Hills, nestled in a small residential neighborhood. He glanced at his watch. Ten minutes before three. After parking, he scanned the area and spotted Greer's truck parked under a tree. To his surprise she was still in the truck.

Out of his SUV, he moved closer and saw she'd brushed out her hair, letting it flow over her shoulders. She wore a black dress, no jewelry except for the bracelets. In the big truck's cab she looked small and vulnerable—both descriptions would no doubt make her angry.

When she saw him approaching, her frown deepened. She slid out of the truck. "Why did you want to meet me at the funeral?"

The sun beat on his back but the warmth building in him had to do with her. "I'm here for you."

"Why? I can handle this."

A slight breeze teased the hair framing her face. The urge to touch her was strong, undeniable.

When he didn't answer, she glanced toward the church's large wooden doors. "I should be going inside. The service starts soon."

"Why haven't you gone inside yet?"

Her brow furrowed. "I've been sitting here for the last fifteen minutes hoping to gather my courage. But now I really must leave."

Without thought, he took ahold of her arm. The touch of her skin electrified, felt better than he imagined.

She glanced at his hand and when she raised her gaze back to his, her cheeks were flushed. She made no move to pull away.

"I wanted to give you the news in person." He paused. "Jennifer Bell is dead." He studied her face, watching it transform from curiosity to shock to horror. The urge to comfort was so strong, but he shoved it aside.

She cleared her throat. "What happened?"

He wanted to tell her. "Tell me about Jennifer. Why was she at Shady Grove?" This close his height could intimidate, but she didn't shy away.

She lifted a chin. "She never wanted anyone to know."

He hesitated, feeling the weight of the words he needed to speak. "She's dead."

A sigh shuddered from her.

His fingers squeezed her arm gently, urgently. "Greer. Tell me."

"She came to the camp about a week after I did." Questions demanded answers but he held them at bay, giving her a moment to explain. "At first, she wouldn't tell us what she'd done. It had to be bad to land at Shady Grove." A silence settled between them as if she had stumbled into the past.

"Greer. What did she do?"

"She took an overdose of her mother's pain-killers. Her mother found her barely in time. Her stomach was pumped, and she was sent to Shady Grove."

"Why did she try to kill herself?"

"She and her brother were at the family lake house. She said she dove into the lake and then dared her brother to do the same. He didn't want to, and she called him a coward. He got mad and dove. When he hit the water he struck a log and broke his neck. He died days later. She blamed herself."

He thought about what Adam Owens had told him about Jennifer being an only child. Was she the only remaining child or had she lied to the group at camp? Lies seemed more common than not at that place. "Rory had been heard saying he wanted to see you again. Your picture was nailed to the tree where he was hung and his body was on your property. Sara wanted her mother's forgiveness for an abortion. There was a tape of her mother's voice playing over and over in the freezer. And we found a baby doll in her trash can. Jennifer was found dead of an overdose. This killer is re-creating past failures, granting last wishes, and then killing suicide survivors. What did Jennifer want?"

"I don't know. I guess she wanted to wish away her brother's accident." Tears pooled in her eyes.

"Her fiancé said she was an only child."

"That doesn't make sense. I remember her telling me about her brother. It was a bond we shared." Greer swiped away a tear, shaking her head. "Jennifer was a complicated girl. I always suspected there was so much she wasn't saying. Sara picked up on it in camp. She pressed Jennifer one night to be truthful, but instead of talking, Jennifer left the circle."

"She left her shop late yesterday afternoon.

First, she spoke to her fiancé, Adam Owens, and then she said she was on her way home. Minutes later, she texted Owens and said she was sick. Twelve hours later she's dead. Where was she? What happened?"

"I don't know."

"Whoever killed those three has to be connected to Shady Grove. Someone who knew you and the others and who also knew intimate details of those kids' lives is killing them one by one."

Her hands shook. "Why?"

He shook his head. "That's a question you can answer better than me."

"How would I know?"

"You lived inside that camp. You knew the players better than I did. I'm pushing hard now for a search warrant for the medical records, but I need your help."

She pulled out of his grip and reached inside her truck and from her purse removed a picture. She handed it to him. "I found this in a closet last night. I'd planned to give it to you."

He instantly recognized Greer leaning into Rory, a handsome boy with an electric smile. Next to Rory stood Sara and beside her Jennifer, a haunted pain lingering behind her smiling eyes. Next to her stood a tall lean boy with dark hair. He had a goofy, over-the-top grin that suggested he overcompensated for hidden fears.

"That is Sam," she said, following his gaze.

"His real name is Michael Sycamore. He lives in Houston and no one has seen him for a week."

"I've not seen him since camp."

"There's been no one around you that you've seen, say at the party, that could have been him?"

"No."

"What about the caller at the Crisis Center. You said it sounded like a woman, but could it have been him pretending?"

She frowned. "No. I mean at the time I thought I was speaking to a woman but now I don't know."

"Tell me about the night this photo was taken."

"It was the last night we were all together. I didn't want to go at first. I hate good-byes, and I didn't want to see Rory go. But I went and we sat around that night clinging to each other because we knew our time together was ending. Rory was being sent home the next day, and we knew Sara, Jennifer, and Sam, I mean Michael, would follow soon." She traced Jennifer's face, closed her eyes, and then as if a memory drifted from the shadows said, "That last night we all shared our dying wish."

"What were they?"

"Rory said he'd die happy if I were the last person he saw. Sara wanted her mother to love her."

"Did Jennifer say she wanted her brother back?" Bragg asked.

She closed her eyes and then when she opened

them he saw surprise. "No, she said she wanted forgiveness."

"Are you sure?"

She nodded. "Yes. I'd almost forgotten."

"Whom did she want forgiveness from?"

"She never said. I'd assumed her family. Mine hadn't forgiven me."

"But you didn't ask for forgiveness. You wanted your brother back."

She swallowed. "All that mattered to me was that Jeff wasn't dead."

"Think back to the conversations you had with Jennifer. What did she say?"

Frowning, she shook her head. "That last day we were all together I knew she wanted to talk to me, but we were all filled with emotion, just like any other teenagers. She struggled. But she never told me what was bothering her, and I never pressed."

"What did Michael want?"

"For his father to pay attention to him. That's why he stole from him in the first place."

"This all started at Shady Grove."

"It wasn't a bad place. The doctors there were kind and loving, and it did a lot of kids good. I don't understand why anyone would want to find us."

He took her elbow in hand. A possessive move but he couldn't resist not touching her any longer. "Be careful, Greer."

Bright blue eyes sparked with a tiny hint of humor. “Sounds like you care about me.”

He studied her. “Maybe I do.”

For a moment she was silent as she stared into his gaze for signs of deception. “How do you know I’m not the killer?”

He brushed a strand of hair back away from her eyes. “I’m going on the assumption that you’re not. Plus, Winchester found evidence that cleared you.”

“The truck tires.”

“Yes.”

“Why do you care about me?”

“Maybe because of Mitch. Maybe I just like you.”

She shook her head. “Don’t put your trust in me, Ranger. I’m not so sure I deserve it.”

He saw the hurt in her eyes and it troubled him. “Why do you say that? You’ll never forget the accident but Jeff wouldn’t want you living like this, would he?”

“No.”

Seconds later a hearse pulled up in front of the church. The doors to the church opened, a priest dressed in brightly colored vestments materialized, and organ music drifted out into the street.

Behind the hearse was a long black stretch limo. It stopped and out stepped David Edwards, dressed in a crisp black suit, and a tall blonde wearing sunglasses. He pressed his hand into the blonde's back.

Greer's body tensed and she drew closer to Bragg.

Greer wasn't sure exactly when she'd decided to go to Rory's funeral. There was no moment. No knowing. She'd just woken up this morning realizing it was something she had to do. She owed Rory a good-bye.

But now as she stared at David Edwards's stiff-back posture, panic reared and clawed at her gut. As much as she wanted to slip back into her truck, hide, and let the moment pass, she held her ground.

"You all right?" Bragg said.

She felt the color drain from her face. "I'm not great at funerals. I've only been to my aunt's."

"What about your father's?"

"I wasn't invited. And you know I missed Jeff's because I was in the hospital."

She watched as a handful of pallbearers moved behind the hearse and opened the door. She recognized Rory's brother, tall and broad-shouldered.

Other cars arrived. A handful of mourners trailed into the church. Pallbearers supplied by the funeral home removed a polished walnut casket and each grabbed a brass handle and lifted the weight to climb the stairs. Organ music grew louder. Edwards followed his brother's casket into the church.

Bragg rested his hand on her shoulder and she jumped. "I'm right here."

"I'm not backing down."

As if understanding her need to do this, he reached past her, pulled her keys from the ignition, and closed her truck door. "We'll go in together."

Unable to speak, she nodded.

He took her elbow in hand and guided her into the sanctuary and to a pew in the back. He removed his Stetson and reached for a hymnal. She accepted it, grateful for the task of finding the song. Finally she found the page and held it up for the two of them.

The room was not full. Little more than a dozen people, clearly acquaintances of David's, hovered in the first pews. Rory's brother sat on the right with the lovely blond woman at his side. The other pallbearers stood to the left, and they all wore tags bearing their names above RYDER FUNERAL HOME.

Her hands trembled until Bragg's hand came up under hers to steady it. Neither sang. She stared at the casket, sorry for the boy she'd once known. He'd been so beautiful physically that he drew women who wanted him and even men who wished they were him. But he had chosen her above all the others. And for a short time she'd felt loved and whole.

Only later did she realize under the beauty there'd been weakness.

The song ended and a white-haired priest dressed in ornate vestments stood in front of the casket. He spoke of Rory as a young man, full of hopes and dreams. Of too many wrong paths taken. The priest's prayer spoke of Rory finding a place of peace and happiness.

More prayers followed and the priest offered the final blessing. Greer grew rigid as the pallbearers took the handles of the casket and lifted it.

She replaced the book in the seat pocket and glanced toward the door, wanting to make a quick escape before she was noticed.

"Steady," Bragg said.

"I should go."

"See it through. You'll be better for it."

"David doesn't want me here."

"You've every right."

Bragg was not her friend. He was a cop. But he'd shown up to personally tell her about Jennifer and to support her. She couldn't deny her attraction for him grew by the moment. She leaned into him, hoping to draw a little of his strength.

At first he didn't move. He stood steady, afraid if he moved she'd pull away. When the casket passed, her grip tightened. When David spotted her, his gaze turning predatory, Bragg tightened his hold on Greer and tugged her a step closer as a signal to both David and Greer she was under his protection.

David Edwards glared and didn't say a word, but his gaze bore the promise of paybacks to Greer for trespassing. The remaining mourners left the church, leaving Bragg and Greer alone.

The strain abated from her body and she realized he held her hand. Gently, she pulled away. "David is not pleased."

Bragg grunted. "He'll survive."

She lingered, clearly hoping the funeral party would clear away before she had to leave. He seemed content to stand there alone with her. "Shame Rory had so few friends in the end."

"Will you go to Sara's funeral?"

"Her family hasn't announced when it will be. But yes, I'll go. I owe her that. And I'll go to Jennifer's."

"What do you owe them?"

"A proper good-bye."

He took her elbow and guided her out of the church. Harsh sunlight assailed them as they moved to the top of the church steps. He scanned the area, searching.

"Who are you looking for?" she said.

"The killer."

"He would come here?"

"It's been known to happen."

"Why?"

"Part of reliving the kill. The thrill of knowing he's upended so many lives. To gloat. A lot of sick twisted reasons."

"I never thought about that."

"I want you to be thinking about it all the time now. Be very careful."

"I will."

He walked her across the street to her truck and waited as she climbed in and fired up the engine. She rolled down the window. "Thanks for the moral support."

"Sure. What are you going to do today?"

"Work, what else? I'll be consumed for days with that." She sighed. "The vineyards to the rescue again."

"How so?"

"Like I said before, the land doesn't care about any troubles. It expects me, needs me. And right now I'm glad to be needed."

Loneliness rose up from her as if it were part of her scent. He wanted to take her hand again. Tell her this storm would pass. "How many acres will you be harvesting?"

"We'll start with the back one hundred and work our way forward."

"Good luck. Be careful and call me if anything isn't right."

She shifted into first gear. "Thanks again, Ranger Bragg."

He touched the brim of his hat. "Ma'am."

From her rearview mirror, she watched him, standing on the sidewalk staring after her.

Chapter Nineteen

Monday, June 9, 5 P.M.

The autopsy of Jennifer Bell revealed no signs of any major trauma. No scratches, no nicks. The medical examiner had run extensive tox screens, but Bragg was betting blood work would come back positive for barbiturates, Jennifer's drug of choice the first time. The water she'd been drinking had also been tested. Forensics had pulled fingerprints from the bottle but all had belonged to Jennifer. They'd removed all the water bottles from the refrigerator and were also testing those for barbiturates.

Bragg moved into his office and flipped on the lights. The killer was re-creating suicide attempts and granting last wishes. Greer's wish had been to see her brother again. The dead did not come back to life and the only way to grant her wish . . . he refused to consider that option.

He rubbed the tightness in the back of his neck and then shuffled through the phone messages on his desk. An unforgiving restlessness stalked him. The walls of his office had shrunk, and he'd get no work done tonight.

Bragg grabbed his keys and hat and left the office. He told himself he had no good reason to drive out to Bonneville vineyards. Mitch was doing fine. Greer would be exhausted from a day at the funeral and in the fields. But the longer he reasoned with himself the more determined he was to make the drive.

And so he drove the thirty miles of Texas back roads. The dust kicked up and the city faded from sight. The closer he got to the vineyard and Greer the more his nerves eased.

He pulled up to the main building. It was just after six and Greer was crossing the front yard to her home. When she heard the crunch of gravel she turned. Her head tilted in shock, and she moved toward him, her frown deepening with each step. “Ranger, what are you doing out here this late? Everything all right?”

“Came out to check on you.”

A smile teased the edge of her lips. “I’m doing fine. But thanks for asking.”

He’d made it this far and wouldn’t leave. “Ready for harvest?”

She nodded, her body relaxing. “Better than expected. Mitch has a knack for this kind of work.”

“That so?”

“He might end up a winemaker after all.”

Bragg laughed. “Never say never.”

She nodded toward the big house. “I’m about to have a glass of wine. Care to join me? I’ve beer in the fridge.”

"Sounds good."

He followed her up the hill to the main house. From the front porch there was a view of the vineyards below and above to the house where Louis lived. Refusing to think about him, he let the land's calm energy draw him away from worry for just a little while.

The screen door squeaked and he turned to find her holding it open. He entered the ranch house, removing his hat as he stepped into the foyer.

The cabin was rustic, furnished with old-fashioned furniture arranged around a large stone fireplace hearth. He smiled at the well-used hearth. She'd found a use for what had seemed useless to him. He could imagine Greer curled up on the sofa, a glass of wine in her hand and a fire crackling in the hearth.

On the mantel stood a collection of framed photographs. Most were of a smiling Greer standing with an older woman. Vines always surrounded the two either here or on a European hillside. The aunt's grin was broad and her arm was slung recklessly around Greer's shoulders. Though her hair was graying and her face lined, her gaze sparked much like Greer's.

"You look like her."

"That's what my mom always said."

In another image a younger Greer had swept thick hair into a ponytail. Despite her youth, her gaze reflected a world-weary wisdom. "When was it taken?"

"Ten years ago. That's the first vineyard I planted."

There was a tenderness in her voice as if she spoke of a child. "How long did it take to harvest the grapes from that vine?"

"Three years."

He studied more pictures, intensely interested in details other than the accident. "Looks like you and your aunt traveled."

She chuckled. "We had a thing for vineyards."

He settled on a picture of a much younger Greer and a tall young man, or rather, boy. The kid had a big beefy arm thrown around her shoulders. Her broad grin reflected pride and youthful joy. No sadness or loss lingered behind those blue eyes.

"That's Jeff," she said. "It was my fifteenth birthday."

Bragg reached for the picture and then hesitated. "May I?"

"Sure."

He took the picture and studied it. The boy didn't resemble Greer, but there was a familiarity that the two shared. Perhaps it was the tilt of their heads or the smiles. He also looked like Mitch, which took him back a little.

"You see the resemblance to Mitch as well," she said.

Bragg nodded. "Yeah. Buzz Jeff's hair and they could pass as brothers."

"I saw the resemblance the first time I saw Mitch in the bar." Her voice was whisper soft. "Threw me off for a second but in the end I'm sure that's what drew me."

To see Jeff again. Her dying wish. He tried to shut off his cop brain as he replaced the picture on the mantel. "I'm glad you did choose him."

She moved into the kitchen, reached in the fridge, and pulled out a beer. "I want to thank you for today."

He turned from the images and laid his hat on a table. "For?"

"Coming to the funeral." She twisted off the beer top and handed it to him. "You didn't have to, and I appreciate it."

He accepted it, and took a long pull, and liking the flavor, studied the label. "Lydia and your mother weren't close."

"Yes. Mom said often enough when I was growing up that I was like Lydia." She shrugged. "Those comments were usually made in frustration so I don't think it was meant as a compliment."

She retreated to the kitchen and poured a red into a sparkling glass. "They had a terrible falling out. Love triangle involving my father."

"And she came to get you after Shady Grove."

"Yeah, amazing."

He took a pull on the beer and was pleasantly

surprised again by the taste. "I've never seen this brand before."

"Very small brewer. He doesn't have many retail outlets." She swirled her glass, took a moment to study the way it caught the light, and then took a sip. She savored the flavor.

"That made with your grapes?"

She smiled and studied the way the light hit the glass. "Mine mixed with other varietals."

"And next year you make your own."

Ambition gleamed in her eyes. "I will. With luck we'll have enough grapes to at least start out with five hundred cases."

"I've no doubt you'll get it done."

She nodded, no hint of apology in her demeanor. "I will. Bonneville will make a mark in the world."

They retreated to the couch in front of the fireplace. She curled up like a cat and faced him. She hesitated as if, like him, small talk was a skill yet to be mastered. "Is there any more news on Jennifer's case?"

He didn't like the shift from personal to professional but accepted it. "Not yet. We're running down every lead we have right now."

"And Michael?"

"We haven't found him yet."

She sipped, arched a brow. "I'm guessing then you came out here about Mitch."

He wanted to see her, know she was okay. "You said Mitch was doing well."

She sipped her wine. “He is. He works with the horses, and he was in the fields today. Worked harder than anyone.”

“Where is he now?”

“With another kid I hired. Danni Sinclair.”

“Your pint-size defender at the center?”

She laughed. “Yes. She invited him out for a movie.”

“And he said yes?”

“He was taken aback but he managed to say yes.”

“Good thing she did the asking. Not sure if he’d have gotten around to it. This a date?”

“I’m not sure if either would cop to that but they were laughing when they climbed into his truck.”

Bragg shook his head. “I owe you my thanks, Greer. Two months ago I feared that boy would never smile again.”

“He’ll never forget what happened. But he’s learning to live a little more each day.”

He sipped his beer and before he thought he said, “What do you do for fun?”

She arched a brow, amused by the question. “Me? I work. That’s what’s fun for me.”

“You volunteer, you run the vineyard, take in stray dogs and horses and ailing ex-marines. What do you do for yourself?”

“I don’t know.” She shrugged. “I don’t think about it.”

“You deserve to live a little, too.”

Her gaze darkened and he had the sense she did not agree. “That so?”

He shook his head. “You do your best to keep everyone else going, but you don’t do for yourself.”

She sipped her wine. “I don’t need much.”

Her skin glowed in the evening light. “Why do you deny yourself?”

“Like I said I don’t need much.”

He swirled the beer in the bottle. “You deserve happiness like the rest.”

She stiffened and stared into her glass.

He watched her brow knot. “You don’t believe that.”

Smiling, she shook her head. “I feel like I’m having a session with Dr. Stewart. He has a knack for zeroing in on sensitive spots.”

“And what do you do when he does?”

“I dodge and weave.” Her eyes danced with humor. “Spin denials.”

“Like now.”

“Exactly.”

“Why?” The man, not the Ranger, wanted the answer.

She was silent for a long moment. “It’s a little hard to embrace happiness.”

“It’s been twelve years since the accident.”

“And my brother and Sydney are still dead.”

“So you stay in limbo until the end of your days.”

“I don’t know. Maybe.”

“It’s a waste.”

“It’s my life to waste, Ranger Bragg.”

“Tec. My friends call me Tec.”

“I’ll stick to the formal, if you don’t mind.”

“Why?”

She straightened. “Better we each stay on our own side of the fence.”

He’d put her nerves on end. But those nerves weren’t jumping with fear but something else. “You pulled my boy over to your side. Makes it a bit more personal to me.”

She glanced toward the mantel, the army of photos facing them. “He won’t be here forever. One day he’ll get his legs under him, and he’ll move on. That’s the way it should be. And then you’ll return to the life you had before Mitch.”

When he looked back at his old life he saw loneliness.

“I’m in a good place,” she said. “I work hard and I manage to sleep hard these days. I can go months at a time without crying, and I’m hoping the recent nightmares are a passing thing.” She sipped her wine. “All this introspection since Rory’s death has brought a lot to the surface and I don’t like it.”

“Anything new?”

“No. Same old, same old.”

An image of Greer, a blond girl standing on the far side of the country club all those years ago, popped into his head. “Did you run into anyone from Shady Grove at the country club? Ever. A lot of the kids came from wealthy families. Stood to reason you’d cross paths. What club was it?”

“Western Country Club.”

“Jennifer was a member there?”

She frowned. “I didn’t know that, but there were hundreds if not thousands of members. And back then I was all about riding my horses. I showed up at the club when commanded.”

“Do you still ride?”

“Not since the accident.”

“You should pick it up again. Though I’d stay away from Beauty.”

She laughed. “Duly noted.”

A strand of hair dropped in front of her eyes and he resisted the urge to brush it aside. Instead he set his beer on an end table, freeing up his hands.

He took her hand in his, smoothing his fingers over the calluses on her palm. The calluses extended to her heart but under the toughness was tenderness. “A lifetime for one moment. Doesn’t seem right.”

She met his gaze. “One devastating moment changed too many lives.”

He sat still for a long time, simply holding her hand. Her scent rose up to tease his nose. His gaze dropped to the swell of her breasts and then up to her eyes. She was staring at him. But there was no sadness in her gaze now. Only need.

And then slowly he rose pulling her with him. If she resisted, he'd let go. But she moved willingly, stopping mere inches from him. She wasn't tall. The top of her head barely reached his shoulder but he sensed if he held her she'd feel right.

He drew circles on her palm with his thumb and then bent his head toward her lips. She moistened her lips, glanced up at him, and then, rising on tiptoes, closed the distance. Her lips were soft, sweet, but he sensed in her a deep vibrating energy that likely had been building for years.

He leaned into the kiss and she absorbed him as if half starved. He threaded his fingers through her hair, closing his fist around the softness as he pressed his other hand to her hip.

Greer's senses burned toward overload. Every muscle in her pulsed, and desire built in her body. She'd dated a few times in technical school, but the unshakeable guilt she carried over her brother's death had driven her away each time.

Now, the guilt buzzed around her head, but she shooed it away. She had the rest of her life for regrets and guilt, and right now she enjoyed this incredible sensation that was sweeter, more intoxicating, than any wine she'd ever tasted.

A deep seductive growl rumbled in Bragg as his hand cupped her breast. Slowly he backed her up toward the couch and he eased her down, covering her body with his. Hard sinew and muscle covered her.

His hand slid over her belly and to the snap of her jeans. "Greer?"

The unspoken question hung in the air. He was giving her a choice. He would stop now. How many times had she kept herself in reserve, away from the world as if encased in a layer of ice? She wanted to melt the ice, to feel a connection—a connection to Bragg.

"I want this," she breathed.

He ground a kiss into her and cupped her breast with his hand. Sensations shot through her body, as if it had come alive, awakening from a deep sleep.

Her hands skimmed over his shoulders and down his back. Muscles rippled under the surface of his shirt. Restrained power radiated.

Seconds and then minutes passed as feelings swirled around her. She kissed him, clutching his shirt before reaching for his belt buckle. He stopped her hand, unfastened his belt buckle, and set his belt and gun on the floor. She unzipped his pants and reached inside the fabric to hold him. He sucked in a breath and a growl rumbled in his chest. "You're going to break me, woman."

"In a good way."

"A very good way."

He pulled her hand away from him and tugged down her pants, which slid away. He smiled at the delicate white panties and kissed her stomach and the tender skin above the lacy waistband.

Impatience seemed to drive him as he rose, tugged off his boots, and removed his pants. "Later it will be slower."

"Later. Fast now," she said.

He tugged down her panties and laid over her, his erection pressing against her. Instinctively she parted her legs for him.

He studied her face as he slowly positioned himself. Another hesitation. And another chance to back out. She kissed him and whispered, "Yes."

He kissed her again, hard on the lips, and then pushed inside of her.

She sucked in a breath as she lay savoring the feel of him inside her. Slowly he began to move back and forth. The sensations grew and for a quick moment all the darkness and sadness skittered away leaving her with only light, hope, and the building pressure of desire.

When he ground into her, every nerve in her body exploded. She tipped over the edge and plunged through layers of isolation. It was mere seconds before the storm passed, but she was left sweaty and breathless underneath him.

He collapsed against her and burrowed his face into the hollow of her neck. His heart beat strong and steady, thumping through his shirt and against her bare chest.

“You all right?” He rose up on an elbow and smoothed wisps of hair from her eyes.

She moistened her lips, wishing this moment could be bottled and saved forever. “I’m good.”

“Just good?” he teased with a crooked smile.

Laughter rumbled in her chest. “Okay, great. It was great.”

He kissed her on the lips. “That’s more like it.”

She’d had moments of feeling good, almost human, over the last decade. When the vineyard was ripe and full and the farmhands began to pluck the grapes from the vines. When she and her aunt had completed the big room that would house the winery next year. Yes, there’d been happiness, but she’d not allowed herself to bask or enjoy.

Now, however, she clung to the pure joy making her heart beat fast. She should shove away the peace and happiness, but she just couldn’t.

“I can feel your body tensing,” he said. He stared at her with his signature intensity warming her soul. She sensed he wanted to peel back the layers and read her mind.

“I’m not used to feeling good.”

He smoothed his hand over her forehead as if he didn’t tire of touching her. “It’s time to let yourself out of prison.”

“But . . .”

“But nothing, Greer. You’ll honor your brother more if you live your life.”

Tightness banded around her chest as unspoken

words begged to be voiced. "I want to be happy."

A gentle smile tugged the edge of his lips. "That's a good thing."

"Is it?"

"Yeah. Not a thing wrong with it, darlin'." He kissed her on the lips as his hand cupped her breast. "Not a bit wrong."

She relaxed into the kiss and let the pleasure pulse in her like a heartbeat. She wrapped her arms around his neck and tightened her hold, kissing him with all the pent-up emotion and denied desire she'd stored.

Another growl rumbled in his chest as he opened the front of her bra and kissed her breast. She accepted him willingly.

Winchester's search for Michael Sycamore proved to be frustrating. Sycamore's secretary had had no luck finding him, and a GPS search of his cell had come up empty. It took a handful of calls before he was on the phone with Donald Shepard, the managing partner of Michael's firm.

Winchester learned Sycamore had made a name for himself in a prestigious accounting firm and at thirty was already on partner track. Men like that did not just vanish. They stayed in touch with their companies.

Winchester paced his office. "Mr. Shepard, I'm Brody Winchester with the Texas Rangers."

"Yes, sir, what can I do for you? I hear you been

raising holy hell with my staff." The drawl was deep and long and very Texas.

"I'm calling about Michael Sycamore. I've spoken to his secretary but she tells me she can't find him. Just don't sound right to me you'd lose a potential partner so easily."

A heavy pause. "I don't discuss my employees."

"Let me remind you I'm working three murder cases right now and if I find out you're holding back, I'm not going to be happy."

More silence. "What do you need to know about him?" Hesitation in the man's voice hinted at a bigger issue.

"How about you tell me where I can find him."

"I don't know where he is."

"He works for you."

Still another hesitation. "Not as of two weeks ago."

"Why's that?"

More silence and then a sigh. "I fired him."

"Why?"

"He embezzled from several clients. Once I found out I let him go. He denied it of course, but I had the evidence."

"Evidence?"

"Financial statements that showed the paper trail leading to him."

Michael's first suicide attempt had been triggered when he'd been caught stealing. And now he'd been caught again.

Winchester rubbed the back of his neck with his hand. "Has anyone seen him since he's been fired?"

"Not that I am aware of. I've had to do some fancy talking to keep this information quiet. It would ruin my company if it was discovered."

"When was the last time you saw Michael?"

"The day I kicked him out." Anger threaded through the statement.

"He's not answering his cell."

"Likely hiding with his tail tucked between his knees like an old hound dog."

"I need to find him."

"Has he stolen from someone else?"

"My call isn't regarding a theft. People he once knew have been murdered and I need to talk to him."

He sighed heavily. "Hold a moment and let me buzz my secretary. That woman is the pulse of the company."

"Sure."

The man put him on hold and Winchester paced. Michael could be his killer but he'd bet money the man was dead.

A second later the man came back on the line. "Ranger?"

"I'm here."

"Michael has a cabin about seventy miles north of Austin."

Winchester moved to his desk and jotted down

the address. That would put him in easy striking distance of the murder victims. "And no one has seen him in two weeks?"

"Not according to Marge, my secretary."

"If anyone hears from him, I need to know about it."

"Will do."

He checked his watch. If he hurried, he could be at the cabin in an hour.

Bragg hated leaving Greer. She'd felt warm and soft in his arms and he could have stayed in bed with her for days. But he couldn't stay locked away from the world and neither could she. They both had work. Minutes later, he dressed. As he stood at the door holding her hand, he gave her a list of warnings and cautions, reminding her to keep her cell phone close.

She smiled up at him, her gaze warm and inviting. When he added emphasis to his warning, she'd pretended to listen and then smiled. He'd given up and kissed her one last time before he left her standing on the front porch of her house.

The call from Shady Grove came fifteen minutes after Bragg left Greer. He drove out to the facility annoyed that it had taken days to get the list of campers.

He pulled into the tree-lined drive and parked by the entrance, took the front steps two at a time, and rang the bell. This time laughter didn't drift from the woods. A solemn quiet had settled on the place.

The slim woman, who'd greeted him before, opened the door. She eyed him and stepped aside. "Ranger Bragg. Dr. Leland is waiting for you in his office."

"Ma'am." He followed her down the long hallway, his boots clicking against the wood floor. He found Dr. Leland sitting behind his desk, frowning, tapping his index finger on a slim manila file.

"I'm not happy about this," the doctor said.

"I don't care," Bragg said, moving toward the desk.

The doctor glared up at him and then lifted the file, extending his arm barely so that Bragg had to reach out and take the file. He opened it and scanned the names. Quickly he saw Rory, Jennifer, Elizabeth, Sara, and Michael, the one person in the pod yet to be found. He flipped to the boy's profile and studied Michael's sullen headshot. He scanned Michael's bio, which confirmed much of what Greer had told him. He'd been seventeen when he'd entered the camp and been assigned to Greer's pod. Michael had landed in Shady Grove because he'd tried to shoot himself.

"I'm counting on your discretion," Dr. Leland said.

"I'll do what I can." If he could, he'd keep this

quiet for Greer but he didn't give a damn about this place or the doctor's good name.

As he studied the picture of the young camp kids he thought about the unseen participant. The photographer. "Who would have taken this picture?"

Dr. Leland shook his head. "I have no idea."

He dialed Greer's number and was frustrated when it went to an answering machine. She was busy. But she needed to answer her phone. He listened to her succinct message and was about to ask his question when he heard a click and a breathless, "Bragg."

He turned away from the doctor. "You sound out of breath. You all right?"

"Yes, it's fine. I'm a little crazed right now."

He imagined her in her vineyard sweatshirt, snug jeans, and boots. She'd be covered in dust and sweat by now but still the thought of her made him hard. "Greer, who took the picture of you and the other kids at Shady Grove?"

A pause. "I think his name was Jack."

"Jack."

"Yeah. Jack. He was there before me but I didn't have any details about him. He kept to himself."

"Okay. Thanks. I'll call soon."

"Be careful." The simply spoken words caught him off guard. He couldn't remember anyone saying those words to him.

"Will do." He hung up and faced the doctor.

"I'm looking for the kid that took this picture. His name might have been Jack."

The doctor hesitated.

"The more you work with me, the more I'll work to keep this out of the media. Jack would have been here a dozen years ago."

The doctor nodded and turned to his computer, plugging in the dates and the name. He hit SEARCH and waited for several seconds before he shrugged. "We had a Jackson Trenton here that summer. He went by the name Jack Jenkins. According to his records he tried to kill himself after his sister died."

"When did he leave the camp?"

"Late August that same year."

"Do you have any other information on him? Forwarding address? Family address?"

"I have his father's address." The doctor hesitated. "I'm going to have to contact the family for permission. I cannot just release information. You specified the people in Ms. Templeton's pod."

"I need anyone here that summer."

"I'm addressing the names in your search warrant. Jackson's name was not listed."

Bragg clenched and released his jaw. "I'll have a warrant in twenty-four hours."

"If it gets out our former residents were murdered, we'll be ruined."

"That's out of my control."

The doctor stood, his fists clenched at his side.

"It is within your control. You can keep this quiet."

"I'm not one of your fancy rich clients who values privacy at all costs. I'll shout all the details of the case from the rooftop if it means I can solve this case."

"You'll ruin us."

"I don't care."

Bragg left the doctor angry and sullen. In his SUV he called Winchester. "Are you headed north to find Michael?"

"I'm on the road and about fifteen minutes away."

"He's the only kid in the pod unaccounted for. I also found out the kid who took the picture's name was Jackson Trenton. I'm calling the magistrate now for a search warrant. Call me when you have details."

"Will do." He rang off.

When he hung up he called Mitch. "Bragg."

"Where are you?"

"The vineyard." In the background he could hear the puppy barking. "What's up?"

"I need for you to keep an eye on Greer."

The sound of the dog barking faded as if Mitch moved away from him so he could hear better. "Is there some kind of trouble?"

He cut in and out of traffic. "I think there might be. I've a bad feeling we're running out of time."

"Do you have details?" Mitch's clipped tone

told Bragg his nephew's marine training had kicked into gear.

"There is someone out there who is targeting people from Greer's past. I think she might be next. Keep a close eye on her. Someone comes around that doesn't smell right, I want to know about it."

"Consider it done."

"Thanks. I know I can count on you."

"Who are you thinking about?" she said.

"You."

Jackson drove down the dusty road away from the mountain cabin. His gaze on the road, his hands tightened on the wheel. Blood was splattered on his shirt and hands, but he'd not stopped to wipe it off. He had a schedule to keep.

"Why?" It always pleased her when she was in his thoughts.

"You were shouting in my ear when I raised the gun. I couldn't hear myself think. You need to know when to shut up."

"I only tell you what you need to hear. And you need to hurry up. I'd bet money the cops see the pattern and are on their way up here."

He pressed his foot into the accelerator. "I can't think when you're shouting in my ear. He nearly got the gun from me."

"But he didn't. You shot him right in the face."

"It won't look like a suicide."

"Deal with it."

Jackson, angry and resentful, grew silent and sullen. For many miles he didn't say a word, focusing only on putting distance between the cabin and his truck.

He was running again. Always running. Since that day. And she had been chasing him since.

"What are you thinking?" she said, breaking the silence.

"That day."

"By the pool?"

He spotted a produce delivery truck headed in the opposite direction on the road. He eased up on the gas and relaxed his grip on the wheel. "I remember."

That sunny afternoon he'd found her by the pool sunning. He'd had no intention of hurting her. He'd only wanted to talk . . . to tell her his deepest thoughts. She'd sat up bleary-eyed and confused as he'd sat on the edge of her chaise. At first he couldn't find the words. Fear came naturally to him, and he was now afraid. But he'd been tired of hiding his feelings and so he'd told her.

Instead of acceptance, her narrowing gaze possessed a dark loathing. She'd called him a pig and told him to leave her alone.

At first the rejection had left him frozen with pain and unable to move, but as she kept calling him names, hurt had turned to anger and then rage.

He didn't remember what happened next. The events were blurred by adrenaline. When his mind cleared he realized he'd dragged her to the pool and had held her face under the water until she'd drowned.

"Ah, the dark and dangerous moment?" she cooed. "You're thinking about it again."

"Yes."

"And you wonder yet again how you could have killed me—someone you loved so much."

"Yes." Panic washed over him as he remembered how cold and still her body had felt in his arms.

Slowly the shock had ebbed and he thought in terms of his own survival. What if someone had heard her rant? His heart thrumming in his chest, he'd quickly released her body and climbed out of the pool. He'd gone to his room, stripped, and toweled off. Dressing, he took his wet clothes and tossed them in the laundry hamper.

He slid behind the wheel of his car and drove. It was all he could think to do. Later he'd try to recall what had led to his rage, but he couldn't. As hard as he tried to imagine the moment he'd snapped, he couldn't summon it.

When he'd arrived home, he'd wanted to retreat to his room and hide under the quilts on his bed. But his father had been waiting for him, his face white and angry. Behind him his younger sister had stood teary-eyed and quaking. As he studied his little sister's face, he'd had the idea she somehow knew what he'd done to their other sister. But with his father standing there staring at him, he feigned shock when he heard of Meg's death.

For an instant, Jackson thought he could convince the old man of his innocence. He had always been good at pretending and making people believe. Then he noticed the videotapes from the security cameras. His father had seen. He knew.

He had been terrified.

"Dad was so mad at you," she said, pleased. "And the more you denied it, the madder he got."

As his little sister had stared at him from behind their father, the old man had backhanded him across the face, splitting his lip in two.

The moment Jackson had stopped talking to his father, Meg had begun talking to him. She'd spoken only in whispers at first and for many years he'd been able to ignore her. But in recent years, her voice had grown louder and louder. There were days when he thought her talking would drive him insane.

The old man's edict had been clear and strangely unavoidable. Jackson would go to the Shady Grove treatment facility for therapy until the old man decided he should be released. They'd concocted a story so no one knew the truth . . . that Jackson had murdered his sister during an attempted rape.

Jackson had refused. He declared that he wasn't sick or broken like the poor losers dumped at Shady Grove. He had no desire to die or hurt himself. Sure he'd lost his temper and Meg had paid a price, but he was fine. It wouldn't happen again. He promised. He swore.

However, his father had moved with lightning speed, wrapping long smooth fingers around his neck and pinning him to the wall. In a quiet whisper the old man told him that there'd be no public accusations or trial. He would lock Jackson, his only son, in the basement of the house, where he'd stay for the rest of his life. Go to Shady Grove and get help or go to hell.

Jackson choked, struggling to draw in air, staring into old eyes filled with sadistic satisfaction. Unable to draw in a breath, he'd simply nodded. He'd agreed to a stay at Shady Grove and to get better.

The coming weeks and months had been a string of endless boring days. He met with a counselor, talked about his feelings, and learned what he needed to say to gain freedom. He'd not changed but had been biding his time.

And then he had seen Elizabeth for the first time at camp. He'd known in that instant he'd found a kindred spirit.

Though she was broken and damaged he learned quickly she was a healer and a caregiver. The other broken birds at the camp flocked to her and fluttered around her hoping she would say the right word to erase their pain.

He'd kept his distance but he too hadn't been immune to Elizabeth. He'd stayed on the fringe, but he always made a point to linger close. The others had little time for him. Wrapped up in their own sorrows, they ignored him. But not Elizabeth. She'd brought him into the circle.

That last night at the campfire he'd known he was half in love with her. He'd taken the group picture not so he could remember the others, but so he could remember her. The next day the others began to leave. After they'd left Elizabeth had drawn back into herself. She didn't have a smile or a kind word for him. She'd gotten lost again. And then she'd left. And he was alone and left to languish in the camp intended to make him better.

"I rotted in that camp for a year."

"But you're a clever boy. You finally won Father over." No missing the anger rumbling under her laugh. "But your sweet Elizabeth was gone. And you never could find her."

He hated the sound of her voice. "My suffering gives you pleasure."

"Poor, poor baby boy."

He had had no choice but to go on with his life. He'd gotten an education, married, divorced, and lived like any other man. And then eight months ago he'd seen Greer Templeton on television. His Elizabeth.

In that moment he'd known what it would take to make her truly happy: re-create the old group and ensure none of them ever abandoned her again.

The others were dead.

They'd been granted their dying wish.

Now it was time for Greer.

Chapter Twenty

Monday, June 9, 9 P.M.

The drive up Route 12 took Winchester deep into the Hill Country and it was pitch black dark when he arrived. Despite the late hour, heat rose up off the stone driveway.

Sycamore's cabin was a modest one-story ranch with a wide wraparound porch stocked with a couple of rockers. Chipped white paint on the house suggested the home had weathered too many summers without attention. Not surprising. From what he'd heard about Michael, the guy had traveled a lot for business and now only retreated up here when he needed a few days off. It had been five years since Michael had been here last.

Winchester got out of the car and, jangling his keys in his hand, surveyed the property. A black Range Rover was parked by the weathered ranch house. No flowers or knickknacks to show a woman's touch, this place was plain and simple, a suitable getaway for a man. Thirty, engaged, and by all accounts a success until he'd been caught embezzling.

Winchester walked around the house. The grass had browned and dried up in the heat making it more like the bristles of a brush. A rusted weather vane squeaked in a gentle hot wind.

According to Greer, Michael had threatened to shoot himself with his daddy's shotgun when he was eighteen. His mother had persuaded him to give her the weapon and when he'd complied, the parents had shipped the troubled boy to Shady Grove. There the family had learned he had been crumbling under the weight of his father's need for perfection in his only son. By all accounts Shady Grove had helped the boy grow into a successful man.

Winchester's boots thudded against the porch steps as he moved toward the front door. Hand on his gun, he stood to the side of the door, poised to knock. Before he could rap his knuckles against the door, he saw that it was ajar.

Winchester drew his gun and stepped to the side as he pounded a fist on the doorjamb. "Michael Sycamore! Texas Rangers." No answer. "Mr. Sycamore, are you in the house?"

When he received no answer he pushed on the door with his boot. The rusted hinges squeaked and groaned, as it swung open.

Winchester spotted Michael Sycamore immediately.

He sat on the center couch. A shotgun lay on the floor at his feet. And his face had been obliterated by a shotgun blast.

The blood staining Sycamore's chest and splattering the wall behind him was fresh. He'd been shot within the last hour.

Winchester backed out of the house and reached for his phone. Two rings and he heard Bragg's curt reply. "This is Winchester. I found what's left of Sycamore."

While his conversation with Winchester still replayed in his head, Bragg pulled up into the Central Austin neighborhood just before eleven. The Hyde Park area was exclusive, home to many professors and professionals who preferred the character of the older, smaller homes built in the 1920s and '30s. Moonlight glowed over shade trees drooping over sidewalks and yards with picket fences. Lights glowed in the windows.

It had taken Bragg less than an hour to get the search warrant for the Shady Grove records. The rich liked to keep their secrets but they even turned on their own when three Texans from well-connected families had been murdered within the week.

According to the records, the boy had been sent to Shady Grove because he'd taken an overdose after his older sister had drowned in the family pool. Jackson had been devastated by the loss. More phone calls revealed that Jackson's parents were dead but his surviving younger sister lived in Hyde Park.

Kate Trenton's house wasn't large but very nice. Made of brick, it had a shade tree in the yard and a planter on the front porch filled with bright yellow flowers. The house would have been inviting if all the shades had not been drawn closed.

Bragg rang the bell and stood inches to the left of the door as he waited. Finally, footsteps sounded inside the house and he saw the flutter of curtains in the window by the door.

Locks clicked open and the door cracked open a fraction. A tall woman in her mid-twenties stared up at him with bright blue eyes, which set off pallid skin.

Bragg touched the brim of his Stetson. "Ms. Kate Trenton?"

Her gaze narrowed. "That's right."

"Ma'am, we are trying to find your brother, Jackson Trenton."

Her body tensed and she drew into herself. "I haven't seen him in a year."

"When was that?"

Her fingers curled into fists. "He came to our father's funeral last year, but I've not seen him since."

Bragg tried to restrain his impatience. "Ma'am, may I come in? I'd like to ask you a few questions about your brother."

She hesitated. "Why?"

"Ma'am, I don't think you want us to have this discussion outside."

She closed the door and he heard the scrape of the chain leaving the lock. She opened the door wide. Dressed in jeans, a red short-sleeved shirt, and tennis shoes, she hesitated and then invited him into the house.

Bragg stepped inside to a central living room with polished wood floors. It was furnished with neat crisp European furniture and Oriental rugs. Light from a crystal chandelier glistened on a round glass coffee table.

Bragg removed his hat. "Ma'am, I need to cut to the chase, if that's all right."

Kate smoothed her hands over her jeans. "Sure."

"Your father sent your older brother Jackson to Shady Grove Estates twelve years ago." Not a question, but a statement.

Her lips flattened and her skin paled all the more. "That's right."

"According to your brother's records, he tried to take an overdose."

She raised her chin but didn't answer. Her gaze darted away before returning to him.

"Your brother lived at the facility for a year."

Again she held back.

"Ma'am, I need answers, pronto. Why are you hesitating?"

"I'm not hesitating."

Bragg struggled to keep his patience in check. "Ma'am, I need for you to be honest with me. I need to find your brother."

"Why are you asking?"

"We are investigating several murders."

For a long moment she didn't speak, as if the burden of an old secret weighed on her. "Who was killed?"

"Former residents of Shady Grove."

Her hands trembled. He'd hit a bull's-eye.

"Ma'am, I can tell by the look on your face something is wrong. Tell me about Jackson."

"Like I said, I haven't seen him since our father's funeral."

Bragg didn't speak but waited, sensing her story bubbled under the surface.

When she didn't speak, he said gently, "Ms. Trenton, you need to tell me. Why was Jackson at Shady Grove? His file said he tried to overdose after your older sister's accidental drowning."

A bitter smile twisted the edge of her mouth. "He didn't overdose." For a long moment she didn't speak. "He drowned our sister."

"What?"

"I was twelve. He was twenty and Meg was twenty-one. Dad and I came home and discovered

Meg floating in the pool. Jackson was nowhere to be found. Dad pulled the security footage of the pool area. And he saw what Jackson had done." The words rushed out as if she'd released infection from an unhealed wound.

He ground his teeth. "Jackson drowned your sister."

She nodded, tears welling in her eyes. "There was no audio so we don't know what had been said but we watched as Jackson approached our sister and then she shook her head and shouted. He got angry and dragged her to the pool." She closed her eyes. "He held her under the water until she stopped moving. And then he ran. Dad followed his wet footprints to his room and then to the garage. His car was gone. Jackson came home several hours later. Dad had cleaned up the footprints and called the police. He told them she'd killed herself."

"And he moved Jackson to Shady Grove."

"Dad thought if he kept Jackson medicated he could control him. And he did. For a time. And then Jackson convinced him he was desperately sorry over Meg's death. Dad wanted to believe him. Finally the old man relented, and he let Jackson go."

Bragg drew in a deep breath, trying to control the anger rolling through his veins like liquid fire. "Has Jackson contacted you at all?"

She swallowed. "He's afraid of me. I have the

security video from the night Meg died. If anything happens to me, it goes to the police. Dad set it up that way years ago."

"Do you have a recent picture of your brother?"

"No. But when I saw him at the funeral I was shocked. He's changed a lot. His hair is short and dark and he doesn't wear his glasses anymore."

Digging up a grave in a cemetery was no easy task. It required permission of the family, viable reasons, court orders, and of course a crew of workers. But Jackson had none of those. No one would give him permission to dig up a grave and day workers were a suspicious lot and fearful of cemeteries at night.

So Jackson had abandoned the idea of digging up the grave. The tall granite headstone was a powerful image and would suffice. He picked up the wilting white roses, sniffed them, and then tossed them into the shadows.

"What time is it?" she said.

He checked his watch. "Time to go."

"This is the last one. You can't screw this up."

Irritated, he shut his eyes and clung to his temper. "Shut up! I'm sick of hearing you talk, Meg."

She laughed. "That's too bad. Because you're stuck with me until the day you die."

"Bitch."

"Murderer."

The time had come. Time to act.

As he turned, he tipped his head to the headstone: JEFFREY ROBERT TEMPLETON.

Chapter Twenty-One

Monday, June 9, 10:45 P.M.

A rustle outside her window had Greer rising from her desk. At the window she pushed back the curtains and stared into the night. A light by the barn caught her attention. Mitch had already bunked for the night, and José would be fast asleep. So who was outside?

She tugged on her boots, laced them up, and, grabbing a flashlight, headed outside into the day's lingering heat. Her flashlight cut through the darkness as dust and gravel crunched under her boots as she moved toward the barn.

"Mitch?" she asked.

The black mare brayed and snorted. Nothing unusual but the brown horse now swished her tail with worry. That wasn't right.

With Bragg's warnings to be careful, fear rose up Greer's back as she approached the corral toward the horses. Both were agitated.

It wasn't like her to get spooked. She'd been running this place for years and was accustomed to chasing off wild animals, even vagrants.

She paused as the rush of footsteps barreled toward her. As she turned, a sharp sting bit against her neck. Electricity shot through her limbs, and she crumbled to her knees. Strong hands grabbed her arms and kept her from falling face-first into the ground.

Mitch had heard the car when it had arrived on the property. Since he'd served in the Middle East, it didn't take more than a shift in the wind or the rustle of branches to wake him. He still slept in basketball shorts, T-shirt and boots by his bed. Mortar fire in Central Texas wasn't likely. Logic told him that. But a gut trained to be ready for IEDs, sniper shots, and explosions didn't care about logic. So he was always ready for trouble. Just in case.

When he heard the car door close he sat up alert and wide awake. Jasper perked up his ears as Mitch slipped his feet into his boots, pulled the laces tight, yanked on his shirt, and grabbed his cell phone, wishing it were his service revolver.

Shoving a hand through short hair, he left the dog in his room and headed outside in time to see Greer drop to her knees and a man haul her up. His arm banded around her waist, and if he'd not been supporting her she'd have fallen.

Fuck. His heart pounded as he gripped the

phone, wishing he could chamber a round. "Hey, what the hell?"

The hooded man turned and in the dusky moonlight glared at Mitch. "Fuck. What are you doing here?"

He didn't answer. No hint of worry or fear, just a grim determination that reminded Mitch of an insurgent who'd blown himself up. Determined fanaticism.

In the next seconds, Mitch barely shook off his shock as the other's hands twitched and reached for the .45 tucked in his waist. Training had Mitch diving to the ground as the man fired.

But Mitch wasn't fast enough. As he hit the ground the bullet cut through his side. Pain burned through his body.

Greer's muffled anguished cry nearly broke his heart but also told him she was alive.

Anger and frustration blocked all the fear. Ignoring the pain, he rose up on his knees as the man dumped Greer in the truck's front cab. Still gripping his cell, Mitch staggered to his feet.

"We can't leave him." Greer's voice slurred the words.

The truck started, turned, and headed toward him. He stood his ground, one hand pressed to his side and the other gripping his cell. Mitch waited, knowing he'd have just one shot. The truck picked up speed. Seconds before it hit him, he tossed his cell into the trunk bed as he jumped to the right.

The cell clunked against the bed as he hit the ground. Pain burned through his gut. He'd accomplished the task but had he failed Greer?

He tried to push up and get back to his feet but the pain burned at each twitch of a muscle. He rolled on his side and pulled his hand from the wound. Blood turned black by the moonlight glistened on his hand. Tears stung his eyes.

Mitch wouldn't survive losing someone else he cared about.

As soon as Bragg left Kate Trenton's house he'd called Greer and when she didn't answer, he'd called Mitch. Two no-answers had added up to trouble. He'd not hesitated to call the Rangers and the local sheriff. He wanted every officer within fifty miles of Bonneville.

As he barreled down the dark highway, he called Winchester and gave him a brief description of the situation. Winchester was an hour away, still at the Sycamore crime scene.

When he arrived he saw the flash of lights from a dozen police cars and two paramedic trucks. His heart sank and for an instant he imagined the ground shifted under his feet as his world crumbled.

He rushed toward the stretcher as the paramedics were loading it on the truck. Mitch's colorless face stared back.

"Mitch."

The boy's eyes snapped open and he grabbed his uncle by the forearm with surprising strength. "Bragg, I tried to save her but I couldn't."

"Greer?"

Mitch winced as he tried to sit up. "There was a man. He took her. Shot me."

Bragg's heart twisted for the boy before him and for Greer who'd been taken. He wanted to stay with Mitch but had to trust him to the paramedics. His gaze nailed the paramedic. "How is he?"

The paramedic checked the IV running into Mitch's arm. "He's sustained a gunshot. We won't know until we get him to the hospital."

Bragg was an expert at pushing back emotion and dealing with the worst kind of situations. Now, however, he struggled to keep focus. He took Mitch's hand and squeezed it hoping he could convey in deed what words could not. He loved this kid like a son and would do whatever it took to save him. "Okay."

He released Mitch's hand and latched onto his own fears with an iron grip. Mitch winced as the paramedics raised the gurney. "I threw my cell phone in the bed of his truck."

The first flicker of hope cut through the mire. "And if I know you, it's fully charged."

"They left here an hour ago. There's plenty of battery life so you can ping right in on that asshole."

"Good job."

Mitch winced. "I had the chance to save Greer and I blew it."

"She'd have been completely lost without you, and at the end of this day when I find her alive it will be because of you."

Mitch swallowed back emotions and nodded.

Bragg leaned close, his gaze pinning the boy. "And your buddies, you didn't let them down. They know that. Greer knows it. I know that. Now you need to believe it."

Mitch nodded.

Bragg patted Mitch on the shoulder. "Mitch, can you describe the man that took Greer?"

Mitch's eyes darkened. "I can do better. I can give you the motherfucker's name."

Greer awoke in stages, her mind a muddy, water-logged mess. She was vaguely aware of cool grass and a warm breeze blowing over her. She was outside and for a half second wondered if she were camping.

And then her senses cleared enough and she immediately remembered the sting of her attacker's stun gun and of her legs crumbling. He'd pressed a rag to her face when she'd started to rouse and the foul chemical had knocked her out cold.

Now, she sat up, ready to fight. Her head spun. Her stomach churned, and she thought she'd throw up. She turned to her side, prepared to retch.

But after a few deep breaths, her stomach held steady. A small victory in a war she suspected was long from over.

She glanced up expecting to find someone looming over her. To her surprise she was alone under a sky filled with too many stars to count. She moved to stand but found her legs wobbly and unsure. Drawing in a breath, she tried again but her body would not cooperate.

What was wrong with her?

She studied the stand of woods in front of her and realized they were familiar. The woods at Pinewood Cemetery. She glanced back around her and found herself nose to nose with a head-stone.

JEFFREY ROBERT TEMPLETON.

Jeff's headstone.

Panic rose up in her, choking her throat and she scrambled away from the slab of granite, now afraid to be close to it. Her legs and arms would not function, and she found herself crawling away from the marker, more desperate with each inch. This had once been a place of comfort, solace, and guilt, and now it terrified her because she remembered the dying wish she'd confessed to the group all those years ago . . . to be with her brother.

Her heart thundered in her throat as she struggled to crawl. Panic clawed and sliced at her. She'd loved Jeff. In life she'd followed him like a silly puppy. And she'd carry her brother's death with her for the rest of her life.

But she did not want to join him in death. She wanted to live.

"Where are you going?"

She glanced up. To her shock she recognized the face. Only instead of kindness simmering behind the eyes, she found crazed longing. "Dr. Stewart?"

"Greer." A smile tipped the edge of his lips. "I guess you figured out by now why you're here."

"I don't understand, Dr. Stewart. Why are you doing this?"

"I'm hurt you haven't figured it out."

"Figured what out?" She'd beg if she had to. "Please, I don't want to die." She tried to sit up but her head spun.

He knelt just a couple of feet from her and studied her face. "We've known each other a long time, Greer. You just don't remember."

Her mind blurred, she searched his face. Eye color, hair color, weight, and the way he held himself didn't produce any matches. But there was an intensity emanating she'd not seen in him before. That intensity triggered memories. The first conclusion to spring to mind didn't make sense but despite logic she couldn't help but whisper, "Jack?"

A grin tugged at the edge of his lips. "I knew you wouldn't forget me."

But she had forgotten him until just a day ago. If

not for the deaths of the others she'd likely have never thought about him again. At the camp they'd barely spoken. He'd been a passing acquaintance. Clearly, his attachment to her was much stronger. "No. I didn't forget."

"I've thought about this moment a lot over the years. Dreamed about it. I know life has been a struggle for you. I know it's been hard."

"Dr. Stewart, I don't want to die. I'm not that girl anymore."

"But you must. I just killed Mitch, a boy who reminds you of Jeff. You must be feeling the sharp knife of loss."

"Mitch." She could barely speak his name. "He can't be dead."

"He is," Dr. Stewart whispered. "Dead like Jeff."

Tears clogged her throat and spilled over her cheeks. Oh, God. What would Bragg do?

"Our core selves do not change, Greer, or should I say Elizabeth. You confessed your deepest desires that night at camp. And when you spoke I knew we were connected."

Dear God, he'd held on to an image for over a dozen years of a girl who no longer existed. "I've changed. My life has changed. I don't want to die."

"I've seen you come here often. I've listened as you talked to your brother."

Her mouth felt dry and her breathing grew

labored. Whatever was in her system was burrowing in and pulling her closer to unconsciousness. “I don’t want to join Jeff.”

“That’s not true.” His voice was soft and soothing. “That was your dying wish.”

Before she could respond, he straightened for a moment and glanced behind him. Eyes narrowing, he shook his head. “Shut up, Meg. Shut up.”

Greer searched the darkness but saw no one. “Who is Meg?”

“No one.”

He grimaced and turned again. This time he seemed to wave someone away. “Shut up.”

“I don’t see anyone.”

“How could you not see her laughing face? She’s mocking us both right now.”

Dr. Stewart was hallucinating. If only her brain wasn’t cripplingly drugged she could argue. “Dr. Stewart, let me go.”

Hands fisted at his side, he turned from his invisible tormentor. “Not until I give you your dying wish.”

“What are you talking about?”

He smiled, dragged a shaking hand through his hair, and calmed. “You don’t remember what you said that night?”

She moistened her lips. “My mind is getting foggy, Dr. Stewart.”

He smoothed his hand over her hair. Gentle. “I know. I know. I won’t make you work for this.”

He hesitated and then said in a low voice, "You said you could die happy if you knew for certain there'd been a second driver on that lonely road. You wanted to know the accident that killed Jeff and Sydney wasn't your fault."

A jolt of energy shot through her system, cutting through the haze. "What are you talking about?"

"My dear Elizabeth, you were right all those years ago. There had been a second driver on the road. A drunk driver who had caused you to drive off the road."

"I don't understand. The police said there was no other driver."

"They found no skid marks. The driver intended to crash into you. That driver wanted to crash head on into your car and to die. But you veered. You saved yourself and you saved her. Unfortunately, Jeff and Sydney paid the price for her selfishness."

She studied his face, blinked to clear her fading vision. "Who?"

A satisfied smile eased from him. "Jennifer."

"What?"

"Jennifer Bell."

"She never said a word."

"Not to you, but she caused your accident. She killed Jeff and Sydney. She kept the secret close but all these years that secret has eaten into her soul far deeper than the demons that had originally sent her out on that road long, long ago."

"I don't believe it. She had a brother. He dove into a lake."

"A lie." He pulled a tape recorder from his pocket. "Listen."

Jennifer's slurred drugged voice said, "I wanted to die. The fight with my boyfriend had been awful. So I got behind the wheel of the car . . . and when I saw the headlights I thought if I could crash into that car my life would end, and I wouldn't have to be perfect anymore."

A heavy silence and then Dr. Stewart's gentle voice: "And what happened, Jennifer? It's okay. You can tell me."

"I don't want to die."

"Tell me. Tell me."

"The other car swerved. It missed me and I drove past. I drove for at least a mile before I decided to turn around and go back." She sighed. "I saw what I had done. Two people were dead. And the other girl, I recognized her. I'd seen her at the club. She was in so much pain."

"You didn't try to help that girl."

She whimpered. "No."

"And then you took the overdose and ended up at Shady Grove."

"Yes."

"Why didn't you tell Elizabeth?"

She began to weep. "I wanted to tell her and I almost did. And then I left the camp and life went on. I thought what was done was done."

"Do you want to say you're sorry to Elizabeth now that you're dying?"

"I don't want to die!"

"Are you sorry?"

"Yes."

The tape clicked off.

Tears dampened Greer's face as she mourned not only for Jeff and Sydney but also for Jennifer. Greer understood carrying a burden so heavy your knees threatened to buckle.

"So you see," Dr. Stewart said, "the accident wasn't your fault."

Greer wasn't sure if she'd ever truly believe that. She shouldn't have been driving that night. She'd been too young and too inexperienced. Would an experienced driver have avoided Jennifer? She'd never know.

Though she struggled to keep alert, the drugs took a stronger hold. Though her mind rapidly fogged, one thought was razor sharp.

She wanted to live.

"You must hate her," Dr. Stewart said.

"No," Greer said. "I don't. I want to move on with my life."

He smoothed soft fingertips over her hair. "You can't move on. You're trapped in the past. You have been since the accident."

She had been trapped. But she wasn't like that anymore. Somewhere along the way that first forced step toward the vineyard had been her journey to freedom. And now she had the beginnings of something with Bragg. A future to anticipate.

Her tongue felt thick in a cottoned mouth. “My head is spinning.”

He picked up her wrist and traced the faint scar. “Yes, it must be spinning hard. Soon, you’ll fall asleep, and as you do I’ll cut into this tender flesh as you did once. That’s what you wanted all those years ago . . . to just slip away. Now you can.”

She clung to consciousness. That last time she’d cut her own wrist it had been seconds before the drugs had pulled her into unconsciousness. She’d not cared as her life had seeped from her body.

Now, an unwelcome specter of death frightened her. She blinked hard and thought about Bragg and Mitch. Would they know this man had killed her or would they believe she’d taken her life? And dear God, her mother. What would she say when her body was found on Jeff’s grave? She’d be devastated.

Anger rose in Greer and cut through some of the fog. “I’m not going to die. I am not.”

His smile was gentle. “Of course you are, but don’t worry, I’m going to be right behind you. When you’re gone, I’ll find the courage to finally take the leap and follow you. We will all be together forever. Happy. Complete, just like at Shady Grove.”

"Why do you want to die? You have so much."

His dull gaze reflected sadness. "Not really. The only person I ever really cared about was Meg and then you. I stayed here for you, but Meg keeps telling me I can't stay here anymore. She is tired of waiting."

"What?" She struggled to sit up and when she couldn't she focused on stringing her thoughts together.

"My sister. She is with me always. She won't leave me alone." His voice grew agitated and he cursed.

The connections between her thoughts frayed more and more with each passing second. She wanted to understand him. Wanted to ask questions but she couldn't summon her voice.

He rubbed his hand over her head. "That last night at camp you said we'd all be friends together and we all made a pact. We all promised we'd be friends. And then everyone left one by one. I thought you'd stay but you left and simply vanished." He shook his head. "I didn't think you'd leave me."

"We barely spoke at camp." She tried to pull her wrist away from his grasp but he held her steady. She barely had the energy to lift her head.

"But when we did, it was special. I recognized the connection and so did you." He traced the old scar. "You wanted to die. Pills and a razor. Yes, you wanted it."

She shook her head and managed to ball her fingers into a fist.

And then the glint of a razor in the moonlight. "No."

"Yes."

The slice was quick and clean and over in an instant. Warmth spread over her cold skin. She opened her eyes. Blood trailed from her wrist.

Greer shook her head. "No, I don't want to die."

The ping on Mitch's cell phone led Bragg to the cemetery. He glanced at the digital map on the laptop in his car and traced the road ahead up a small hill. Jeffrey Templeton's grave was at the top of that hill.

He cut the lights of his SUV and scanned the hill ahead. Red running lights burned in the distance. For a split second Bragg was faced with a decision. Gun the engine and risk Stewart's being alerted and killing Greer or cutting the engine and running the rest on foot hoping for the element of surprise.

Greer's life rested on a split second.

He gunned the engine, his tires eating up the distance in seconds. As he crested the hill he saw Jack . . . Dr. Stewart . . . leaning over Greer. Blood from her wrist glistened under the glare of his headlights.

Stewart rose and reached his hand around to his waistband. Bragg didn't hesitate. He drew his weapon and fired three times, hitting Stewart squarely in the chest. The doctor stumbled back, but then lunged at Bragg. Many thought a bullet could bring a man right down, but shock and adrenaline could keep him moving for several more deadly seconds. Bragg fired again, hitting Stewart who this time fell beside Greer.

Stewart gasped. His breath gurgled in his chest and he reached for Greer's hand and whispered, "We made it, Meg. You, me, and Greer. We'll be on the other side soon." He closed his eyes and his breathing stopped.

Bragg holstered his gun and ran to Stewart, handcuffing the man's hands behind his back and rolling him away from Greer.

As he pulled a bandana from his back pocket to wrap around her wrist, sirens wailed in the distance. He tightened the knot and tightly gripped the makeshift bandage, hoping the extra pressure would stem the flow of blood.

He held Greer close against him. Pale in the moonlight, her face possessed a deadly stillness. "Greer! Baby. Wake up!"

She didn't move or speak.

"Greer! Open your eyes! Open them, goddamn it!"

Her eyes fluttered open and then focused on him. A smile flickered at the edges of her mouth. "Bragg."

"It's going to be all right, honey. Help is on the

way." As he spoke the sirens grew louder and louder until finally the flash of red lights radiated around them.

"I didn't do this. I didn't . . ."

He cradled her close, keeping a tight hold on her wrist. "I know. I know."

"Mitch?"

"He's okay. At the hospital."

"Thank God."

Tears choked his throat. He'd grown accustomed to a solitary life, making peace with the fact he was destined to be alone. Now the idea of living without Greer made him angry and fearful.

She was his life, and he would be damned if he'd lose her.

Epilogue

Eight months later

When the transfer to El Paso had crossed Bragg's desk, the decision to retire had come more easily than he ever could have imagined. He'd loved being a Ranger. He had been with DPS ten years. But that part of his life was over.

As he drove up the drive, the star pinned to his chest for the last time, a sense of peace washed over him as he stared at the rolling landscape. He turned off the rural route into the entrance of Bonneville Vineyards. He was home.

The winter had been mild and the vines were strong and promised a good harvest come summer. Greer checked her vines daily and though they'd not seen each other in a week, he talked to her daily. He was anxious to hold her.

He parked in front of the winery, now abuzz with activity. Construction of the winery, was complete and the fermenters and tanks had arrived last week. Out of the SUV, he savored the cool temperatures of early spring.

The sound of a barking dog greeted him and Jasper, still the ugliest dog he'd ever seen, came bounding around the corner. At nine months he'd grown to his full size, which wasn't saying much. He couldn't tip the scales at twenty pounds, but he barked as if he were massive. When he spotted Bragg he wagged his tail and ran up to him.

Bragg knelt down and scratched the dog between the ears. "How are you, boy? Keeping everyone safe?"

The dog barked and licked and ran around in circles.

Greer appeared at the winery's main door. She'd bound her dark hair in a braid. Jeans and a white blouse hugged her figure and already he imagined peeling both off.

She smiled when she saw him and crossed to

give him a kiss. She felt warm and soft in his arms and he hardened at her touch. "I was beginning to think you got lost."

"Had some final paperwork to fill out. Never thought retiring would be quite that much work."

Her brow knitted. "Are you sure about this, Bragg? We could manage the distance to El Paso. It wouldn't be easy but we would manage."

"Afraid it's too far for me. And it's time I didn't spend so much time on the road but here with you and Mitch."

She studied his face as if searching for signs of doubt. There were none. She smiled. "Well, it will be nice having you around the old homestead."

He wrapped his arm around her shoulders and tucked her against him. He'd damn near lost her, and he wasn't going to take any moment for granted.

When the ambulance had arrived she'd been in bad shape. The drugs Jackson had pumped into her system had suppressed her breathing and slowed her heart. That slow-beating heart, docs figured, is what saved her. She'd not bled out as fast as Jackson had anticipated, creating barely enough time to stop the bleeding and clean the drugs from her system.

Mitch had also survived his wounds. After his recovery he'd asked to return to Bonneville. Greer had gladly agreed, and he now worked with José managing the fields. He also talked about studying viticulture at UT.

Unraveling the tangle of Jackson Trenton's life had taken time, but Bragg and Winchester had unraveled each knot. Jackson's father had been hiding his son's violent behavior for years until finally it had exploded in fury and Meg Trenton had been murdered.

Jackson's father, worried about scandal, had lied to the doctors at Shady Grove, saying his son needed time to recover from his sister's death. Jackson had stayed at Shady Grove a year.

At the camp, Jackson had become obsessed with Elizabeth. When the other kids had left, he'd witnessed Elizabeth's sense of loss. That image had remained with him all these years.

When Jackson had finally broken free of Shady Grove, his hope was to find Elizabeth. But she had vanished, and his father had kept a careful, watchful eye on his son. On Jackson's release, he'd changed his name and gone to medical school, proving to be a brilliant and talented student. Ironically, he'd gained prominence as a gifted psychiatrist who'd helped countless people. When his father had died last year, Dr. Stewart, no longer under his father's scrutiny, had stopped taking his meds. And then he'd seen Greer on television and his old desires had roared to life. As a medical professional, he'd found a way to consult with Shady Grove and gain access to old records, containing real names.

Months ago, his attack on Greer had left her bleeding badly, forcing the medical professionals to cut off her bracelets, so they could stop the hemorrhaging. When she'd awoken, she found Bragg sitting at her side holding the cut silver rings, his chin covered in thick dark stubble and his eyes heavy with fatigue and worry.

Her mother had also come to the hospital and sat at her side until she'd woken up. The two had hugged, cried together, and were trying to mend fences. The progress was slow and uneven but they were trying.

Bragg had stayed at Greer's side through her recovery, and three days later when she'd been released he'd driven her home.

When her bandages had come off and the stitches were removed, Greer asked for her bracelets, saying she didn't want to forget the past. It had been her mother who'd taken the bracelets and had them refashioned into one that now included gems for Rory, Sara, Jennifer, and Michael. Greer never took off the bracelet, but she also no longer dwelled on the past as often.

Now as Bragg held Greer close, he savored the warmth of her body. He rested his chin on her head. Words that had never come easily to him slid over his lips. "I love you."

She hugged him closer. "I love you."

He grunted and hugged her tighter. “Still want me underfoot?”

Greer leaned back, studied his serious face, and grinned. “You sure you’ll be elected sheriff?”

He winked and kissed her on the lips. “Lady, with you at my side, I’m sure of everything.”

Center Point Large Print
600 Brooks Road / PO Box 1
Thorndike ME 04986-0001 USA

(207) 568-3717

US & Canada:
1 800 929-9108
www.centerpointlargeprint.com